I0745403

Hawktales
Stories from Northnest and Beyond

Katherine A Smith

Tales in the Northnest Saga

Available from author Katherine A Smith

The Northnest Saga

Hawkwind's Tale
The Fledging of Hawkwings
Hearthsraven

Hawktales

The Dragonic Voyages

Dragons to Loose
Dragonic Freedom
Dragonic Pride
Dragons to Keep

Children's Books

Otter Twin Magic
Otter Sea Magic

Hawktales
Stories from Northnest and Beyond

Katherine A Smith

Tales in the Northnest Saga

Kasmith

Art & Books

Kasmith Art and Books

Fort Bragg, CA

To that tall, good-looking dancer
from The Marsh in San Francisco,
who came all the way from Chile.
My memories of you have been with
me all this time, and will remain so.

I'm talking about a Cocoi Heron, of course.
They're common to South America and...
What did you think I meant?

Tales

** to avoid spoilers, recommended reading order is after reading "Hearthsraven."*

Northnest Timeline

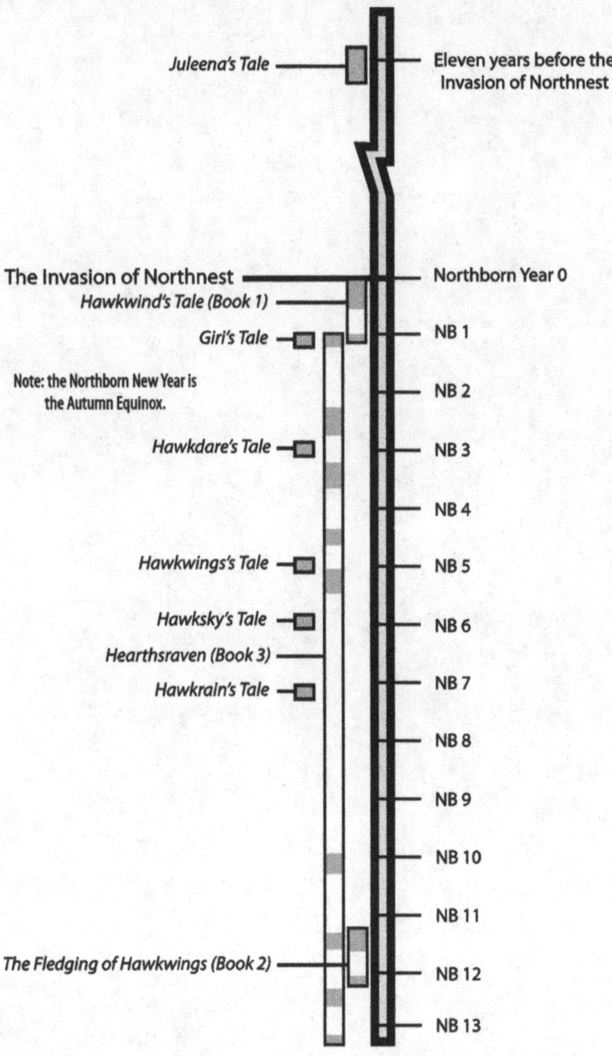

Hawkdare's Tale

The following events take place three years after the invasion of Northnest when Hawkwind escaped with the four children.

Rikah sat back with a thump on the grassy border around his field. He wiped the sweat off his face with his sleeve and surveyed his hard work.

"Is it done?" Kassandra asked in her fawn-like voice, from where she was perched on a fence post, keeping watch.

"Yeah," Rikah grunted. "I think so."

The eight-year old girl jumped down from the post and paced around the tilled area with her hands clasped behind her back, eyes narrowed critically. Rikah had spent a month clearing this little patch of meadow of big rocks and bushes. He'd gotten the help of a few idle young griffins to make and install the fence and drag off the heaviest rocks. Ripping up the grasses and forbs and tossing out the remaining rocks he'd done by himself, with Kassandra's occasional help, and it had taken him another month.

"We can plant things now?" Kassandra queried.

"Yeah," he repeated.

"What are you going to plant?"

Rikah rubbed his shaggy bangs off his forehead. "I don't know. I'll have to ask Thorndawn."

Rikah and Kassandra, with two other children, Jessika and Karolan, lived with the griffins of South-scree Aerie. The griffins ate almost exclusively meat, but the children wanted more than that; they craved a more varied diet and became fussy and sickly when they didn't get it. They gathered from the forest sometimes, but Rikah had come to the conclusion that what they

1

needed was a field where they could grow their own plants.

The only griffin to do any farming was a female called Thorndawn, and she had agreed to advise Rikah in his efforts. Her field was not far from his, close enough that if he shouted for help, she could come running—be it help with the farming or help fending off an animal from the forest that liked the looks of a stringy little boy for supper.

All four children had spent the first five or six years of their lives in a human settlement: Northnest, so Rikah knew well enough what farming looked like in general, but his father had been a blacksmith, and traded his work for most of the family's food. His mother had kept a small garden and some chickens, in addition to helping his father and doing all the other household chores and taking care of the children, but Rikah had been more directed towards learning his father's trade—when he wasn't playing or learning letters and numbers at the nearest children's hall. Rikah had had an older sister who'd been learning how to tend the garden, but she wasn't around to ask anymore. The rainbow drakes that attacked Northnest had killed her and— Rikah assumed—his parents and grandmother.

Now, Rikah had cleared some land, built a fence, and prepared the soil as Thorndawn had instructed and as well as he could guess how. Once the soil was ready, he knew what had to happen next. He needed to grow things in it, but he didn't have any seeds. He looked hopefully at Kassandra.

"Do you know how to get seeds?"

She shook her head, making her long black hair wave and hide her face. "My dad was a castle guard, remember? He didn't farm."

Rikah remembered. They didn't talk about their human families much. It was all so long ago, to them, even though they'd only been living with the griffins for about three years. Their memories of their time in Northnest had faded to lavender-tinted impressions, soft-edged and fuzzy and obscured by the pain of the attack.

"I guess I'll have to ask Thorndawn for more help. I'm not

sure how she grows her stuff."

"Karo might know," Kassandra whispered.

"He might, if he'll tell us," Rikah grumbled.

"He's learning important stuff," the girl objected under her breath.

"Stupid magic," Rikah huffed back, finding a pebble in his tilled dirt and chucking it over the fence to where it bounced off a tree.

"Magic isn't stupid," she went on, even quieter.

This time Rikah didn't say anything, if he had even heard. Instead, he got to his feet and tried to brush dirt off his clothes. Jessika had spent a long time making his clothes for him. He couldn't help getting them dirty sometimes, but he did want to keep them looking nice.

"Let's go back, maybe Mother will have some ideas," he said.

Kassandra looked away, out at the trees. "I want to walk. I'll come back later."

"You shouldn't be out here alone. Mother said so."

"Why not? You're out here alone a lot."

"Thorndawn isn't far away, most of the time when I come out here. I tell Mother where I'll be and I come back before dark, and I have a fence and a staff to keep me safe."

"I'll be safe," she murmured. "I'm not alone out here."

Her dreamy eyes continued staring off into the trees.

"Fine," Rikah shrugged, picking up his sack of wooden tools. "I don't care what you do."

"Yes, you do," Kassandra whispered without looking at him.

He bit back the urge to tell her to shut up; saying such a thing wouldn't be nice of him.

"I'm going to go," he said instead. "Be safe, and see you when you get home."

"Bye," she breathed.

Rikah didn't look back as he headed up the worn trail between the trees, stepping over exposed roots and jutting rocks. A walk of just a couple minutes brought him to Thorndawn's fields. The mature female griffin was unharnessing herself from her plow, and raised a wing in greeting. Thorndawn was big and rangy, with larger leg muscles than most griffins because of all the ground-bound farming she did. In color she was mostly a plain sort of tawny yellow, but her feathers were banded and tipped with rich brown and the same color gave her striking stripes on her face and crown.

"It's done," Rikah told her eagerly. "I think I'm ready to plant."

"Congratulations," she grinned at him, "as am I. What are you going to plant?"

He squirmed. "I don't know. What do you plant?"

"Lots of sniffwort, for starters. Everyone needs that to prevent feather mites. Then there are a few things I plant and tend for the herbalists and healers, for them to use in their salves and potions. Besides that, a whole field and a half of grasses and cottons used for rope and sacking. We don't grow much of our own textiles; other Aeries specialize in that and we trade for them."

"So you don't grow food," Rikah confirmed.

"That's right."

"So you don't have any food plant seeds you could give me?"

Thorndawn's feathers flattened in discomfort. "I'm afraid not. What kind of food plants do you want?"

"I guess, vegetables?"

Thorndawn's blank look removed any hope Rikah had remaining that she might be able to help him.

"I'll have to get the seeds somewhere else," he nodded stalwartly.

"Where? I don't think any Aerie grows food plants," Thorndawn said tentatively.

"I'll figure it out," he declared. "Good luck with your planting."

"If there's anything else I can do?"

"I'll let you know," he assured her with a grin. "I appreciate you keeping an ear open while I'm down here, just in case anything crawls out of the forest and tries to eat me."

"Of course, glad to," she bobbed her head back at him.

Satisfied he'd cheered her back up, Rikah resumed his trek up the path. It was a twenty-minute fast walk, although it had taken him much longer when he'd first started making it, and it gave him a little time to think. There seemed only one solution: he would have to go to a human village and get some seeds or seedlings. He wouldn't be able to do something like that alone. He didn't even know where the nearest human village was, and he knew enough to know that certain plants grew in certain places and not others. His farm was high on a mountain; he'd need plants that would grow there, so he'd need to visit a village of similar location, he supposed. Were there any human villages this high in the mountains?

He scaled the last section of the path with steady, strong legs that no longer trembled under the strain of steep, rocky trails in high altitudes. Tenacious trees gave way to rocks and shrubs and lichens and Rikah all but trotted through the griffin city of South-scree on his way back to the set of stone buildings and caves that served the Hawk Line, where he lived.

The buildings were crammed together in the slightly flattened V formed by two peaks of a great mountain, sharing walls and roofs and floors, stacking up along the slopes, and hosted a great variety of lichens in multiple colors that made the buildings look like they'd been splatter painted. There were balconies on most rooms for the flying griffins to use as entrances, but also sets of stairs that led up to heavy wooden doors. The main door to the Hawk Line home was currently thrown open to the brisk mountain breezes. It was spring, but snow had not long ago deserted the craggy mountain peaks and the wind didn't seem to have gotten the message yet that it was supposed to turn warm.

Rikah skipped up the stairs and through the door and ran right into a griffin, bouncing off her furry chest, and staggering her not a step.

"Dare, you're back."

Rikah looked up into the visage of the griffin he had come to call Mother, although her first name had been Hawkwind. She'd called him by his Line name, Dare, short for Hawkdare, as only a fellow member of the same Line would.

"How goes the farming?" she asked him, bending her head down to nibble his hair, as if preening feathers, in greeting.

"I need seeds, Mother," he said right out.

"Seeds?"

"For the field, and Thorndawn doesn't have any for food plants that we can eat. I have to go to a human village and get some."

By subtle shifting of the feathers on her face, Hawkwind frowned, not in censure but in distress. It seemed to Rikah that she didn't like being reminded of human society or even that he and the other children were human. It wasn't like she could miss it, that they had human shaped bodies instead of griffin shaped ones, but somehow they were accepted as griffins, even though they didn't have the right shape. She called them by their griffin names, and never spoke of their human heritage if she could avoid it: as if ignoring it would make it not have happened.

She, too, had lived in a human settlement once, although it had been shared with griffins. That castle, the capital of Northnest, had been conquered by an invading army. Hawkwind and the four human children were the only survivors they knew of. It seemed Hawkwind didn't like to think about it. Rikah supposed the memories hurt her too much. Her whole family had died there, like his.

"I don't know," Hawkwind murmured. "Can you gather seeds from the forest plants, and just grow more of those?"

Rikah bit his lip. "Uh, I didn't think of that. Do you know how to do that?"

Her frown turned to deeper dismay. "I, I'm afraid I don't, but you gather them frequently, Dare. Haven't you noticed seeds?"

"Sort of," he shrugged, thinking hard. "I suppose I could try that, but there might not be seeds until things are mature, in the fall, and it would be a lot easier to get a bunch from someone, all ready to go. I could grow a lot that way. We need food other than meat, especially in winter, when we can't go searching for stuff from the forest. If I can grow enough things we can store—"

"I know, Dare, I know," Hawkwind placated. "That's why I let you start the farming in the first place, but going to a human village to get seeds is too dangerous."

"It's been three years."

"That doesn't mean anything. I promised Thornmother I wouldn't bring any human attention onto the Aerie. I must keep my promise. You'll have to find another way, Dare. Try gathering seeds from the forest plants. Maybe it will take longer, but you can do it, I'm sure. Now come inside for some food. Where's Sky?"

He shrugged again, kicking at the worn stone step before him. "She ran off into the forest again. I told her not to."

"I guess the forest is safe for her, what with everything," Hawkwind subsided with a distracted tail shake, turning to lead the way deeper into the complex of rooms.

She'd been referring to Kassandra's unique situation: her strange relationship with the unicorn herds. Rikah didn't understand it either. Probably only Kassandra, Line name of Hawksky, did.

Rikah paced Hawkwind. "How are you doing?" he asked eagerly.

"Not yet, but soon," she answered.

Hawkwind was due to deliver another chick any day. It would be her third chick, her second pregnancy, the first having been twins she'd produced about a year and a half ago.

"Why were you up anyway?" Rikah asked with a frown.

She chuckled at him. "I appreciate your concern. This isn't like when I had Night and Day. A single chick is much easier on me. Swift thought a little walking would be good, might get things moving. I don't think it worked."

They passed empty rooms, most of them closed up. The complex of buildings for the Hawk Line was nearly empty because it housed only five griffins at the moment. Hawkwind had founded the Line in South-scree upon the birth of her twins, which had been conceived at approximately the same time she'd adopted two other Linemembers: Hawkswift and her daughter Hawkjoy, both of whom had been rescued from captivity in Snow-in-lee. Now the three females, with the male-chick Hawknight and the female-chick Hawkday, were the only members of the Hawk Line, but there would soon be a sixth.

"Perhaps tomorrow you can gather some seeds in the forest," Hawkwind mused. "Wings is still off training somewhere or other, and I haven't seen Rain all day. Joy has gone hunting with Stargold and Rockgentle. I'll be with Swift, and Starbright is here, too, if you need me."

"Where are Day and Night?"

"Thornsoft is watching them. Go say hello if you like."

Rikah stood on his tiptoes and got his arms around Hawkwind's neck for a hug. She patted his back, talons carefully sheathed.

"By morning, I expect we'll have a third little chick to keep track of," she smiled, anxiety and apprehension fluttering at the corners of her eyes.

"Good luck," Rikah said, not being sure how to wish her a happy birthing.

"Thank you. Between your good wishes and the care of Swift and Starbright, all will be well. I'd best get back to them."

Rikah watched Hawkwind walk slowly away. He knew where she was going: back to the cave-room deep down where she'd birthed the twins a year and a half ago. There she would be beyond seeing and hearing anything happening in the upper rooms. Her slim, folded tail vanished around a corner and she was out of sight.

Rikah kept his quick steps from making too much noise, but hurried as fast as he could towards his room. Hawkwind would be out of the way now at least until morning, but that was no reason to dawdle. The sun would be down in a few hours and most griffins did not like to fly at night. He grabbed a canvas sack and loaded it with an extra set of clothes, a knife, a comb, his teeth scrubber and powder, and a blanket. Then he ran to the storeroom and filched a pack of jerky and a waterskin.

As he was running for the exit he almost collided with Jessika, in practically the same spot he'd bumped into Hawkwind not ten minutes ago. Her skin was glistening and her hair was limp with sweat. She looked like she'd just gotten done with her fighting practice.

"You have a rucksack; where are you going?" she demanded without even a greeting.

"I'm going to get seeds. I'll be back. Don't worry about me," he whispered quickly.

"Where are you going to get seeds?" she reiterated.

"I don't know, but it'll be alright," he insisted, edging past her. "You can tell Mother where I went," he called as he started trotting away.

"She's going to be angry," Jessika hissed after him, but Rikah didn't stop.

He ran through the Aerie, taking the twisting stonework paths and stairs to a different Line's home. Griffins he passed gave him little whistles of greeting and he gave his own whistles back, although he couldn't make his sound like theirs. The South-scree griffins were used to the four humans among them now, although at first it had been awkward. Now, they treated the girls and boys much as they would any fledglings: with patient indulgence.

The Line houses had no guards, because the different Lines got along well and everyone was free to come and go wherever they liked. Everyone had friends in different Lines, and no one questioned why a Hawkchild might be visiting the Thorn house. Rikah asked the first Thorn griffin he met where to find Thornwing, and within another few minutes was interrupting the rust, brown, and black griffin in the midst of his dust bathing.

All Line houses had their own dust pit. Griffins bathed in water, too, but not as often as the humans did. Thornwing greeted Rikah with a more enthusiastic whistle than the other griffins had used, and stepped out of the cloud of dust to a platform at the side of the room, where he sat down to preen and beckoned the boy over.

"Thornwing, I need your help," Rikah said at once.

"Of course, little Hawk."

Thornwing was a mature male, still in his prime, and a particular friend of the new Hawk Line. Hawkwind had been a part of the group that two years ago had saved Thornwing from imprisonment in Snow-in-lee. Since then, he had been a steady ally.

"But what is this about?" Thornwing rumbled around the feathers in his bill as he was working on preening his primaries. "You seem geared for travelling, and travelling in a hurry, I sense. The Hawkmother knows you are here?"

Rikah winced. "I need seeds for my garden. I need you to take me to a human village where I can get some."

Thornwing released his wing and arched his neck, examining Rikah with one bright eye.

"You have the Hawkmother's permission to ask my help to take you to a human village?"

Rikah winced again and his stomach clenched. "Well, no, but it's the only way."

"You think so? The Hawkmother gave you no other suggestion?"

The raptorial gaze of a griffin was no easy thing to bear, and Rikah folded under it. "She said to get the seeds from plants in the forest, but Thornwing, that's impossible. I don't know how. It'll take forever. We can't just keep eating meat. It doesn't make us feel good. Karo was sick last winter, and we all felt bad, and I think it's because we only had meat. She should understand," he declared. "She lived with humans in Northnest. Why won't she understand?"

Thornwing gently took Rikah's shoulder, and Rikah realized after his impassioned declaration that his chest was heaving and his cheeks were wet.

"All she cares about is having more chicks," he blurted. "What about us?"

Thornwing purred from somewhere deep behind his keel and patted Rikah. "Well, Mothers do get fixated on their purpose: sustaining the Line's population as the only breeding female. She does still care about you, Hawkdare."

"Do you know where there's a human village, one in the mountains, that you could take me to?"

The griffin rippled his feathers with uneasiness. "Both Thornmother and Hawkmother have forbidden trips to human villages. You know that."

"They don't have to know. It will be a quick trip. No one will see us."

"You intend to steal the seeds you need? How will you even know which seeds to take, if you cannot recognize the seeds you need?"

Rikah bit his lip. Thornwing was poking holes in his entire plan. "I don't know," he blustered. "I'll figure it out."

"Little Hawk, I want to help you. Surely, you must know that I do." He swung his head side to side. "But I cannot disobey not only my own matriarch, but yours as well."

"You ran off with Thornfire to Snow-in-lee all those times," Rikah argued.

"I had never been forbidden to go. Thornmother had expressed her concern, but never ordered that the trips cease."

"But," Rikah whimpered, "I thought, if anyone would do it, you would. Who else can I ask?"

"You shouldn't ask anyone," Thornwing told him, firmly without being fierce. "You should stay here."

"No, I have to fix this. It's a problem," Rikah started shouting.

Thornwing set a hand on his head. "Not so loudly, please. When Hawkmother has had her chick and is recovered, I will help you talk to her about it."

Rikah stepped out from under Thornwing's hand, batting it away. "You care more about her, too. No one cares about me and the others."

"Hawkdare, you know that's not true."

"Is this one your chick, too?" Rikah demanded.

"Excuse me?" Thornwing's feathers quivered and almost rose.

"Day looks just like you. I know you're her dad. I know how that works, with males and females and stuff."

Thornwing looked around nervously at the other griffins using the dust bath, and encircled Rikah with his wings and ducked his head under their cover. "Hawkdare, we don't talk about those things."

"But you are, aren't you?"

"I don't know. I wasn't the only one."

"Yeah, Night looks like Thornsoft, I know, he's his dad, too—"

"Please, Hawkdare, keep your voice down."

Rikah tried to push Thornwing's wings away, but he might as well have been pushing on the stone walls. "So are you this chick's dad, too? Is that why you care more about Mother than helping me?"

"I am not this chick's sire," Thornwing emphasized as quietly as he could.

"Yeah? How do you know?"

"I know. I know more about how 'this stuff' works than you do. Hawkmother did not choose me this time, and I don't know which male she did choose. The matriarchs chose males from different Lines to diversify the blood of the Hawk Line. That's what Linemothers do, no matter how they may feel personally or who they like to spend time with socially."

Rikah finally managed to push through Thornwing's feathers and escape his grasp. The griffin reflexively preened smooth a secondary he'd rumpled.

"I thought you'd help me. We're sick and you don't care," Rikah threw at him.

"I do care," the griffin told him. "I'm asking you to wait a few days, and I'll go with you to talk to Hawkmother. Until then, I'll help you gather plants from the forest."

"That's no good," he refused. "They aren't mature; there are no seeds in them. Thorndawn is planting now. I need seeds now, saved from last year's plants, and I don't have any."

The boy turned sharply and began to stride away.

"Hawkdare, where are you going?" Thornwing called after him.

"I don't know," Rikah shouted back.

"Just don't leave the South-scree territory," Thornwing commanded.

The boy didn't turn around again.

Rikah walked to the edge of the Aerie and didn't know where to go. With the intricately stacked stone buildings at his back, he stood, sack over his shoulder, and stared out at the descending mountains and hills. Northnest was out there somewhere: his original home. He didn't remember much of it anymore, and wouldn't have known how to make his way back to it even if he'd wanted to go there. Besides, the griffins were right, it was dangerous.

The last time Hawkmother had taken him and the others to a village, the enemy's drakes had attacked them, and some of them had been seriously injured. The drakes had all been killed and they had escaped, but the griffins involved—Mother, Swift, and Joy—still carried the scars of it, and Jessika could have died. Exactly who the enemy was they didn't know, but that didn't really matter. Rikah had had no way to find out who the enemy was, and he couldn't go back to any territory formerly held by Northnest.

"Hey, you, there."

Rikah looked around at the call. A rather young griffin had come up to him. By the voice, he guessed a female. She was counter-shaded black and white except for white wing bars and a totally white head. Her eyes were red like a goshawk. She was unusually lean, with a blunter head than he normally saw among the South-scree griffins, and much longer and pointier wings.

"I heard you say you want to go to a human village," she went on. "I'm Thornspike. I'll take you if you want."

Rikah rocked back on his heels a little. He thought he might have seen Thornspike around, but he'd never spoken to her before. "Why do you want to take me?"

She rolled her shoulders. "Because Wing won't. He should, but he won't."

"I guess he has his reasons," Rikah grunted.

"And I don't like it, how things are around here. It's not fair."

Rikah eyed her. "You'll get in trouble."

"Good," she bit off.

She was angry with someone; he could see that. Well, he wasn't that much of a stranger to anger either—or at least frustration. Still, a worm of uneasiness stirred in him.

"No one else will take you," she said, maybe noticing his reluctance. "They're all too obedient." She all but sneered the last word.

"Do you know where a human village is?"

"I do," she boasted. "See these wings? They're extra fast. I got them from my sire, but I'm not supposed to know that. The previous Thornmother purposely travelled to In-the-wind to get them for me. There's a Line of griffins there that look like this. She had to arrange a trade, you see. They wanted mage powers in their Line, so she made Thornfire go, too, to mate with their Line Mother, and she mated with a male from the Line that had the conformation she wanted. Now I'm supposed to be Thornmother here in a few years, to get this conformation into the Thorn Line, so they tell me, like they can just order me around, like they've got it all figured out."

"Ah," Rikah murmured with understanding.

"I can fly fast, really fast. I travel farther in a day than the others. I've been far enough away to see human villages from above. I'll take you to one. What kind do you want?"

"Um," Rikah hesitated.

"Well?" she prodded, flipping her wings. "Come on. It's getting late."

"I guess," he began.

"Get on. You'd better hold on really tight. I go fast."

Like a tadpole in a drying puddle, Rikah's belly squirmed and flopped. Going to a village had sounded perfect when he'd thought it would be Thornwing who'd take him. Going with a griffin he'd never met before felt reckless. Thornwing was reckless, he knew that, but this was a different kind of reckless. This was a recklessness that even Thornwing wouldn't have condoned, and Hawkmother would be furious. Jessika would probably shout at him. Kassandra might cry. Karo only, would probably be totally disinterested.

Actually, thinking of Karo, of his blankly unconcerned eyes that would return without distress to his magic studies, made Rikah more determined to go. It washed out his prevarication like a flood of water pushing through logs in a river, bursting and rushing away. Karo, the one who had been sickest over the winter, wouldn't care if Rikah had done something risky, but he would still eat the plants Rikah would grow and harvest and store for him.

"Let's go," Rikah nearly snarled, fists clenching.

"Great, get on," Thornspike repeated. "Where to?"

The griffin knelt and Rikah pulled himself up onto her using the straps of her harness, one like all griffins wore most of the time. "I need a village high in the mountains where they have fields full of crops."

"Got it. I know exactly where, but it will be after dark when we get there. Can you stay awake to hold on?"

"I will," he told her, winding loose straps on the harness around his fists.

"All right. Here we go."

Thornspike took several running strides down the path that led from South-scree. She veered off it to run off a sharper drop-off to one side, launching herself into the air and snapping out her wings. She had to flap at first, and Rikah held on gamely against the jerky motion and swirling air. Then she was airborne and slicing through the wind, taking flaps at regular intervals.

"I fly differently from the others," she shouted through the ripping atmosphere.

Indeed she did. The wind seared past much more quickly than Rikah was used to, and it burned him with cold. He wished he'd put on several extra layers of clothing, but it had been a long time since he'd flown, and he hadn't expected it to be quite so fast or so cold. He rotated his hands so his fingers were against the fur-feathers of Thornspike's back, and put his face into her neck feathers. Whatever was in contact with her stayed warm; his pack kept one part of his back warm; the rest of him felt like his skin was turning to brittle ice. There was no fear of him falling asleep with this level of discomfort. Rikah closed his eyes and bore it.

He didn't open his eyes again until he felt the cold begin to relent. Thornspike's wings were open and steady now, not flapping, but they were still jetting rapidly through the sky and Rikah thought she must have begun the descent. He peeked out at a black landscape where only the tips of trees were silvered and the mountainsides lay slate grey under a lighter sky lit by a partial moon.

"There are some lights down there. I think that's the village. It's where it should be, if I remember right," Thornspike called over the rushing wind.

Rikah nodded against her and wondered if his cold-bitten skin would ever be the same. Thornspike landed on a slightly level portion of mountainside and together the two looked down at the little valley among the peaks. Rikah could indeed see a few glimmering lights.

"What do you do now?" Thornspike murmured.

"I guess I go down there and look for seeds."

"You're going to steal them?"

"I wish I could pay for them," he admitted, "but I only need a little. My field isn't huge. It only has to feed four children, and in the fall I can try to get seeds out of the plants for next year."

"Should I wait for you?"

"I don't know."

"I should walk you through the forest, to the edge of the

village. There could be predators, but they'll think twice before attacking a griffin. When we get there, you can tell me what I should do."

"All right."

"You can stay on me, if you like."

Rikah agreed. As long as he was against Thornspike, he had a source of warmth. Walking alone, he would have frozen. The griffin picked her way carefully down the hillside and into the trees, where the temperature was slightly higher, but still not warm. They encountered nothing dangerous and arrived at the edge of the village fields, a split-rail fence blocking their path.

"Now what?" Thornspike asked in a bare whisper.

"I guess I go look for seeds in the outbuildings."

"Should I stay here?"

"Um." He didn't know.

"I'll stay here and wait. If dawn comes and you're not back, I'll go up to near where we landed and wait. In the daytime you can probably go safely through the forest to meet me."

"All right," he agreed.

In his chest, his heart pounded like a waterfall. He slid down off Thornspike's back and was immediately colder. He took off his pack, fished out his blanket, and wrapped it around himself before putting his pack back on, using its straps to hold the blanket in place. It helped a little, but his fingers and toes and nose and ears still prickled with cold-pain.

As silently as he could on numb feet, he began creeping along the fence, under the cover of the trees. When he reached the closest he could get to what appeared to be an outbuilding—probably storage for both seeds and mature crops—he wiggled through the gap between the fence rails and stepped onto the fresh fields. He would leave footprints, but had no choice. Tiptoeing, Rikah made his way to the building. The walls were solid and felt like wood on the outside, but he sensed a deeper sturdiness, and wondered what else they were made of. Somewhere would be a door; he edged around the perimeter, searching.

There, he felt the seam with his hand trailing lightly over the wood siding. He located the latch: a rough length of rope that wrapped around two handles, one on the door and one on the frame, which held the door shut. In the dark, he felt for a knot or loose end. Out in the darkness, he thought he heard something, like a few quick springy steps over the ground. More quickly now, he fumbled with the rope until he got enough slack to start working the part wrapped around the door handle loose.

Almost there, and the noise was coming closer out in the dark. It sort of sounded like Thornspike had decided to come trotting across the field to help or something. Rikah freed the door handle and pulled at the door. Stubborn hinges groaned. Behind him, something was running, skidding to a stop. Then he heard a growl that turned into a snarling bark: a dog.

Fear hit him like a hot poker and Rikah squeezed through the door that he'd only managed to open a crack, knocking his head on the doorframe and banging his knee. The dog lunged. He felt it impact his side and clamp its jaws onto the blanket he'd wrapped around himself, missing getting any skin. Snarling and yowling through a mouthful of blanket it set its feet and shook its head. Rikah cried out in fear before he could stop himself.

From the corner of his ear he heard a commotion: people scolding and shouting and the banging open of a door. The dog released its fruitless hold on the blanket and lunged again, this time catching Rikah's thigh and biting into flesh. Rikah screamed and tried to pull away. He had the leverage of both arms and a leg inside the storage building and he pushed, fear giving him strength. He pulled himself in and tried to shut the door, smacking the dog's head between door and doorframe. The beast yelped and let go, so Rikah could pull his leg in and shut the door. Rikah leaned against the door in panic, his bitten leg shaking and hot.

With the door shut, the room was totally dark and he couldn't see if there were windows he could try to escape through. Would Thornspike come rescue him? Through the seam between door and frame he saw a flicker of light and heard a half dozen voices.

"Down, Mack, down."

"What have you got in there, boy?"

"Good boy, good boy."

The dog started barking again, and then a second set of barks joined it. One set of barking began to move away at a quick speed.

"What's going on here? Trouble?" someone with a big gruff voice asked.

"Mack, boy, come back. Come here."

"There's something out in the trees," someone shouted.

"Mack is after it. Let Digger go."

The second set of barking ran off, too.

"Get the pikes, just in case."

"No, no, no," Rikah whined under his breath. "Thornspike, run away."

"Let's see what's in here. Good, get that pitchfork ready."

Rikah pressed his hands against the door, body angled and feet pushing hard against the flagstone floor, but his injured leg had started to ache and spark with pain, and even had he been unhurt it would have been no use. One boy was no match for a trio of grown men pulling from the other side. He couldn't hold the door and it was flung open. Rikah had to let it go, and tumbled to the side against some scratchy sacks of something or other. Lantern light shone in and a sharp pitchfork was suddenly before Rikah's eyes. He squinted against the bright light.

"It's a boy."

"What are you doing in my store shed?"

"Pa, did Mack bite him? Are you alright, there?"

"A thief in the night is what he is."

"What did the dogs get?"

"Dunno, looks like it got away."

"They all right?"

"Seems so."

"Well, get you up, boy. What have you got to say for yourself?"

"Pa, good sirs, you're scaring him half to death," that was

a lean young man, maybe only a few years older than Rikah himself.

The dogs had returned and started barking and snarling behind the legs of the men.

"Hold the dogs," someone shouted, and they were taken away.

"Dunno what you thought you were doing here," said the man who had spoken of the storage shed as his.

"He's not a village boy," one man with a lantern and an extravagant grey mustache and chops remarked.

"Where'd you come from?" another asked.

At last the pitchfork was stowed away somewhere, and Rikah got cautiously to his feet, trembling from head to foot, almost falling when it hurt to put weight on his bitten leg.

"The nearest village is three days by horse," grey-mustache said.

"Pa, Mack got his leg, look."

"That's what a thief gets," someone else called from the back.

"Enough of that, the boy's hurt and nothing's been taken," the shed-owner scolded.

Rikah looked down at himself. He didn't think the flesh had been torn open, just bitten into. His pant leg hadn't been ripped, but was now starting to turn red with seeping blood.

"Let's get you inside. We'll see to your leg and hear your story, and then we'll decide if you should be thrown out for the ice-lions or locked up in the hall or just let be. Are you going to let us help without fighting?" the shed-owner asked.

Rikah, transfixed by the reddening fabric of his pants, just nodded. Someone grabbed his arm and then hoisted him up. He was being carried by human arms. Adults looked so big. He'd forgotten. Even Jessika wasn't as tall as one of them. They were going up a few steps; a door was pushed open.

"What was it, Michale?" a woman's voice asked.

"A strange boy in the shed," the man carrying Rikah answered. "Mack got his leg."

"Put him on the table. Brutus, go fetch Maryann," the woman ordered.

Rikah felt himself set on a hard surface. He looked up at a bare ceiling. Lights were lit. The woman, who was wearing a thick old robe over a nightgown, was putting a kettle on an iron rack inside a fireplace, which was recessed into the floor down a few steps. The man, having set Rikah down, was bringing in a few fire logs. As the man revitalized the fire, the woman came over.

Her eyes looked firmly into Rikah's. "I'm Nola. Our dog, Mack, bit you in the leg. We're going to make sure it mends right."

Rikah managed to nod back, mind overwhelmed like a kitten in a flooded river. The woman stripped his trousers from him and used them to cover up the uninjured parts of his lower body, preserving dignity.

"It's not that bad," she told him. "Mack just bit down and shook a bit, but didn't tear anything, and you're not bleeding so badly we need to worry about that. As long as we keep infection away, you'll heal up fine. Our town healer, Maryann, will be here to help in a few minutes. I sent my boy, Brutus, to get her."

The woman looked up at the sound of small feet.

"Back to bed, Bonny."

"What's happened, Mama?" a young, female voice asked.

A smaller copy of the woman appeared by Rikah and he was very glad the mother had been sure to cover him up.

"This boy was in our store shed," the woman answered with a reluctant sigh. "Mack got a bite of him. Don't worry about it. Back to bed."

"I can help."

The girl looked like she was about the same age as Rikah and Jessika, around eight or maybe nine. Her hair was blonde and long and straight, and her eyes a grey-blue. She had abundant freckles. Her eyes looked down at Rikah with a firmness that matched her mother's.

"What's your name?" the girl asked.

Rikah stared back, but didn't answer. He was afraid of these people.

The door opened and a tall stately woman with weathered brown skin and graying brown hair up in a bun came in with the boy Brutus, who'd been sent off.

"Dog bite, Brutus said?" the woman stated at once.

Rikah glanced briefly at the tall woman as she set a bag on the table and began taking little jars and sacks out of it, but then returned his gaze to the freckle-faced girl. There was activity around his bitten thigh, and some of it hurt, but he let it all float over him without resisting, like a stone in a river. At some point he fell asleep, still looking at the girl's grey-blue eyes.

Morning light and the sound of chickens awakened Rikah. He was in a bed, a real bed, as he'd not slept in since Northnest, with a mattress and sheets and blankets and pillows. It was all the quality of a farmer's life—cotton and worsted and wool, no silks or satins—but it brought heavy clouds of memories swinging down like axes. The smell of corn cakes and sausages filled Rikah's mouth and he sat up.

The room felt so normal, so right, and yet Thornspike would be waiting for him, probably wondering what had happened.

"You're awake. Ma, the boy is up."

It was the tall lean Brutus that had noticed. Seeing him in the daylight, Rikah decided he must be in his teens, with the height of a man but not yet the bulk. His flyaway blonde hair looked like a clump of straw on his head, but his eyes were bright as new coins and his smile friendly. He, too, sported a mess of freckles to match his sister's.

"Well then, how are you this morning?" the mother, name of Nola, Rikah remembered, asked as she clomped across the big main room to the cubby where the bed stood, the boards creaking under her feet.

Rikah swallowed against the rock of nervousness in his throat. "Fine, thank you ma'am," he whispered, turning back the covers once he was sure he was dressed underneath. "I'm sorry for the trouble, and thank you for mending me. I wish there were a way to repay you."

Her brows were furrowed a little, and Rikah hoped she wasn't going to be angry.

"I really need to be on my way," he said as strongly as he dared, swinging his legs out of the bed.

"On your way? Where to?" Brutus asked.

At the same time, Nola said, "I don't think that's likely to happen."

Rikah pushed himself to his feet, and immediately half collapsed against the bed. His bitten thigh sent spiky messages that it refused to support his weight. Nola tsked and Brutus stepped forward to help Rikah sit back on the edge of the bed. Rikah felt his thigh. It was swollen and tender even to a light touch through a thick bandage.

"No walking for you, my boy, for at least a couple days," Nola said.

"No, I have to go," Rikah objected. "I can't repay you with anything, and I'm really sorry about that, but if someone could just cut me a crutch from a tree branch, I'll take myself out of your way."

"I can't let a youngster like you just hobble off into the forest," Nola declared, "even if you did try to steal from us."

"Mom's right," Brutus nodded, as sagely as though he were decades older. "There are dangerous critters out there that would hunt down even a healthy grown man if he were alone and unarmed."

Rikah bit his lip. "I have somewhere to be," he squirmed.

Both his captor-saviors paused to eye him.

"You have family, friends waiting for you?" the mother asked, planting her hands on her hips. "You were trying to break into our storehouse last night. You were going to steal supplies for your friends?"

"No," Rikah moaned, "or, well, yes, but not because I wanted to steal."

Wooden steps creaked under sturdy boots, and the man

Rikah remembered from last night stepped into the house.

"How's the patient?" he asked with a grin that had seen its share of sorrow.

"Talking, but not walking, much as it seems he wishes he were," Nola answered, leaning back against the kitchen table and folding her arms. "We were just getting to discussing what he was doing in our storage shed last night."

"Indeed, young man," the father nodded, folding his arms in unconscious imitation of his wife. Rikah remembered his name was Michale. "You're not a village boy, yet you're out here all alone, three days ride from the next village, and with hardly any supplies. Do you want to tell us what your story is?"

Rikah shook his head, biting his lower lip.

"Says he wants to leave," the mother said, "asked for someone to cut him a crutch."

Michale frowned. "Here now, if there's a crew of strangers out in the woods, we need to know about it. You have friends out there? You couldn't possibly have gotten out here alone unless you dropped from the sky."

Rikah gulped. The man clearly wasn't serious, but Rikah actually had dropped from the sky, in a way.

"The dogs went off chasing something or someone last night, remember Pa?" Brutus contributed.

Rikah's heart was starting to speed up. He was caught without a good story. He couldn't tell them the truth—the griffins were supposed to be secret—but he couldn't think of a good lie either, and wouldn't have wanted to tell it even if he could have. He'd always known lying was wrong.

"Why would they send an incompetent thief to steal from us?" Nola asked softly.

The two adults looked at each other, and something passed between them that Rikah couldn't interpret. The father looked back at Rikah, apparently chewing the inside of his cheek in agitation.

"You'll stay here until you're well, at least," Michale said. "I'll speak with the mayor about this."

He turned smartly, gave another meaning-laden nod to his wife, and strode out the door.

"Now listen here, you're not to try to go crawling out into those woods," Nola ordered. "There is more than one ice-lion that frequents these parts, and worse things than that besides. You may have tried to steal from us, but that's not enough of a reason to throw a little boy out to his death. Bonny," she called.

A moment later the girl Rikah had seen the previous night came running to the kitchen. Her blonde hair was bundled back in a braid now and her face and hands were dirty.

"Are you finished gathering the veggies?" Nola asked.

"Yes, Mother," the girl whispered.

"Get them washed and soaking, then you'll be carding wool today. I want you in here watching this boy."

For just a moment the girl's face fell with disappointment, but then she gave an obedient "yes, Mother," and ran off again.

"My Bonny will keep an eye on you, and you'll be thrashed within an inch of your life if you lay a finger on her."

Rikah felt himself swell with indignation. "I wouldn't," he declared. "I've never hurt anyone." He supposed jabbing a stick into the eye of a drake in self-defense didn't count.

"Well, that's good to know," Nola said roughly, and Rikah couldn't tell if she was serious or sarcastic.

Bonny came back with a sack over one shoulder and a pail of water in her opposite hand. Nola exited without another word. Brutus paused in the doorway.

"Bonny, I'll be splitting wood by the shed. Shout if you need me."

"I'll be fine," the girl replied coolly. "I'll just kick him in his hurt leg if he does anything bad."

Brutus went out, and Rikah sat in silence as the girl began trimming several leafy vegetables, putting the greens aside and dropping the bulbous yellow roots formerly attached to them into a pot she had filled with water.

"What are those?" Rikah asked as she was finishing.

She eyed him. "Tell me your name and I'll tell you theirs."

"Rikah," he admitted, not even thinking to lie.

"They're butter turnips," she said.

"You grow them?"

"Yes. I just harvested them a few minutes ago. Where are you from?"

"Huh?"

The girl turned to face him, hands fisted on her hips, "a question for a question."

Rikah swallowed, thinking fast. "I'm from another part of the mountain," he answered.

"That's not really an answer," she argued.

"It's true."

"You have a village?"

Rikah squirmed. "Yeah, sort of."

"What's it called?"

"I can't tell you."

She looked affronted. Silently she fetched a big sack and a wooden box. She pulled a bench over near the door where there was plenty of light and opened the box and removed two items that looked something like square, multi-pronged combs. From the sack she pulled a handful of wool, which she pressed down onto one of the strange combs.

"What are you doing?" Rikah asked.

"I'm carding wool, just like my mother told me to," she replied stiffly.

"You raise sheep?"

"We don't. My father's a farmer. We trade for the wool." The girl looked up from her work and raised her eyebrows at the table. "I think my mother left that plate of food for you," she said.

There was indeed a plate with a couple corn cakes and sausages sitting on the table. His stomach rumbled; he hadn't eaten since the middle of the previous day, and he hadn't had sausages or corn cakes for about three years. Rikah pushed himself up again, keeping his weight totally on his uninjured leg. Arms windmilling wildly for balance, he hopped himself over to the table, pulled out a stool, sat, and pulled the plate to him.

He ignored the curiously watching girl, and fought to keep some semblance of manners as his hunger demanded he cram the food in as fast as his hands could shovel. Jessika had always hissed at him and the others about manners. The griffins had their own sort of manners, but they didn't generally extend to dining. They didn't cook or cut up their food before eating. Although Hawkmother had been the recipient of some human-made dishes when she'd lived in Northnest, griffins couldn't taste sweet or spicy, so culinary efforts generally fell on deaf ears, so to speak.

For Rikah, however, the part meat part vegetable sausages seasoned with herbs and the corn cakes augmented with honey and milk lit up long unused taste buds and sent vibrations of delight through his whole body. His hand holding a part of a corn cake trembled so that he almost dropped it, and a groan of bliss escaped him.

"Are you all right?" the girl asked with what seemed genuine concern.

Rikah looked over at her, almost crying while a wide grin of joy threatened to leap off his face at the same time. "This is so good," he managed.

"They're just sausages and corn cakes," she frowned.

"You have these every day?" he panted between bites — bites that he tried to make as small as possible, to savor the meal.

"No, only on some days. Usually we have some kind of porridge, sometimes with fruit or nuts in it."

Rikah groaned again, his eyes almost rolling up into his head as he squeezed them shut at the thought.

"What is wrong with you?" Bonny demanded.

"I haven't had porridge in three years," he told her.

She stared at him, carding apparently forgotten. "What do you eat?"

Rikah hesitated, wondering if it would reveal too much. "Mostly meat," he confessed finally, "from the forest."

"Is that healthy?"

"No, not really. At least, I don't think so, but it doesn't hurt the—" Rikah clamped his mouth shut.

"Hurt what?"

"Nothing," he denied.

Bonny narrowed her eyes at him and went briskly back to her carding. Rikah let her and went quite happily back to his eating, trying to savor every scrap. When he'd finished, he licked the plate and then hopped over to the sink, intending to clean his plate, but the sink set-up this house had was different from his vague memories of the house where he'd lived in Northnest, and he wasn't sure what to do.

"Oh, I'll do it, just leave it there," Bonny said from behind him.

"I'm sorry," Rikah apologized. "Can I wash my hands? I don't want to get grease on anything."

"Open the cupboard under the tub there. The catch barrel is in it, and you can use that, and the towel right there."

She pointed and Rikah figured it out, although crouching down was difficult with his hurt leg. Once cleaner, he managed to push a stool closer to where Bonny was sitting, and sat down facing her, to watch what she was doing. She gave him only a token glare.

"Hey, I think I've seen those before," he announced after a few moments. "My dad used to make them, I think. He was a blacksmith."

"The blacksmith here makes them, too," she answered civilly enough. "I'm not very good at carding yet. It takes me a long time. I just started learning last year, when Mother decided I was old enough not to shred my fingers on the spikes, but sometimes I still do."

She went on with what seemed to Rikah to be careful, practiced movements, preparing the bunched up wool for spinning. Her movements were rhythmic and even hypnotic, so that he went quiet, watching her hands and lost in a level of musing less than conscious thought. When she started humming a song, it nearly put him to sleep.

Rikah only jerked out of his reverie when the mother, father, and son came trooping back into the house for the midday meal. Even then, everything around him seemed hazy.

"Are you well, boy?" Nola asked sharply, feeling his forehead. "You haven't a fever." A sharp glance from her went flying at her daughter like a dagger, and the girl shrank before it.

"I was just humming a little," Bonny whispered. "I thought it would relax him."

"Lunchtime," Nola snapped.

They all gathered around the table for slices of raw butter turnip dusted with dried herbs and salt. Rikah had never tasted them before, and they had a complex play of sweet, rich, and bitter flavors that intrigued the tongue. They crunched between his teeth, releasing cold hydrating moisture. His body sang to receive them while the family talked quietly of the chores that had been done and needed doing, the status of the crops in the ground and the crops yet to be sown. He tried to spare some attention from the rejoicing of his tongue to listen for advice on farming.

As the meal was drawing to a close, Rikah caught at Nola's sleeve, who had been sitting closest to him, and implored both her and her husband with his eyes and words.

"Please sir, ma'am, let me do something, too. You heal my wounds and house and feed me. Let me pay you back with my hands."

"I'd say that's fair," the father said at once. "What can you do?"

"I'm learning to farm, but I also can cook, a little, and butcher meat, and sharpen knives, and do crude sewing, but not clothes, though I can clean them."

The whole family appeared to digest that.

"You intend to keep yourself a mystery as to where you come from, but you know how to do all that, do you?" Michale remarked.

Rikah bit his lip. He wanted to tell these people, but he couldn't. He wanted their help, and wanted to help them, but he also had to leave, had to get back to South-scree. What would

Hawkmother do when she got the truth out of Thornspike?

"I don't like the thought of giving the boy knives just yet," Nola opined.

"His name is Rikah," Bonny spoke up.

"Is it?" Michale smiled. "Well, there's always work to be done here, even for one who can't walk about. I'll find you some, Rikah."

Rikah spent the rest of the day sanding, polishing, oiling, or otherwise cleaning any item that was brought to him. He sat just outside the door, in the chilly spring sunlight. Periodically, he looked up, towards the forest or the sky, but he saw no sign of Thornspike or any other griffin. When dusk came and the family went inside for dinner, he looked back over his shoulder anxiously. Would Thornspike even be there anymore if he went out to the meeting spot? Surely she would have gone home by now. Would she come back? Would he ever go back to South-scree?

The family spoke again of what had been accomplished during the day and what yet needed doing. Once all the reporting and planning was done, they ate in silence. Bonny was staring dreamily at her empty plate, and after a few minutes started humming.

"Bonny," her mother scolded immediately.

The girl whipped her head around, and Rikah caught a brief glance of her face, starting to snarl with an expression he would have never thought he'd see on such a thoughtful, clever girl.

"Bonny," Nola repeated, but in a different tone, as if trying to rouse the girl from sleep.

Suddenly, Brutus got up and started collecting the dirty dishes. Michale scraped together the scraps of remaining food and carried them out for some purpose—to give to the dogs or pigs or the compost heap, Rikah supposed. Nola quickly grabbed Bonny's upper arm and pulled her daughter away to a side room. Rikah almost jumped out of his seat when he heard a shriek of anger from the girl, but then Nola shut the door and there was sudden quiet.

Brutus had his back to Rikah, starting to wash the dishes. Rikah had just managed to hitch a hesitant question into his throat when the front door opened again and Michale came clomping back inside. Maryann the healer was with him.

"—a look at her. It's been a stressful day," he was saying.

"I can only imagine: what with a new face around the place." Maryann smiled at Rikah. "Nice to see you more conscious than last night, Rikah, is it?"

"It is, ma'am," Rikah stuttered.

"I'm going to take a look at your leg, see how you're healing up, in just one minute."

Without another word of explanation, the woman let herself into the room Bonny and Nola had gone into and shut the door firmly. Rikah's question caught in his throat like a bit of deer gristle, and he swallowed it instead of choking it out. It seemed the safer course. Maryann wasn't long in the room. She came out with a calm smile that she cast around the room like flower petals.

"Let's see that leg now," she urged.

She swept up Rikah in her arms before he knew what she was doing and deposited him on the bed he'd slept in. She helped him wiggle out of his trousers and she changed the dressing on his wound.

"It looks good, very good," she told him. "Still swollen, but no signs of infection."

"It hurts," he complained.

"That it will," she nodded.

"How long before I can walk again?"

"Stay off it another two days, I'd say, and then see how it feels."

Brutus stuck his head into the sleeping cubby. "Here's a nightshirt, Rikah. It's one of my outgrown ones. Hope you don't mind."

"Thank you, Brutus," Rikah said, taking the long white garment.

He went away again, and Rikah looked back at Maryann.

She was putting her little bags and jars back into her satchel. His question bubbled back up into his throat.

"Ma'am?" he whispered.

"Rikah," she replied levelly.

"Is Bonny alright?"

Maryann looked him straight in the face, a little quirked smile on her mouth. "Right as rain. Don't you worry. She's just tired from the day."

Rikah stared back. He wasn't sure if he believed her or not. They watched each other: the boy with a frown and the woman with a smile as gentle as buttercups.

"What's wrong with her?" Rikah demanded under his breath.

"Do you want to tell me where you come from and why you're here?" the healer countered.

Trading questions and answers: was that all the people here did? "No. I can't."

Her eyes held simple sincerity against his stubbornness. "Tell me that, and I'll see if Bonny's family wants to tell you of their deepest suffering."

Maryann stood up and marched back into the main room, leaving Rikah feeling somehow horribly ashamed. He didn't listen as she said farewells to the father, son, and mother who emerged from the side room. The closing of the front door proclaimed the healer's departure, and the three family members sat together at the table a while longer, speaking in quiet voices. Rikah changed into Brutus's outgrown nightshirt, lay down, pulling the covers over him, and closed his eyes. Uneasy thoughts followed him down into the world of dreams.

The next day was much the same. Somehow, they never ran out of things for Rikah to clean or sand or polish, and he soon realized that they were having other families bring objects over, to take advantage of someone who couldn't do more mobile work, freeing up other people in the village. Bonny didn't watch over him this day; she followed her mother around like a shadow, doing whatever she was told to do, and Rikah saw her only part of the time.

From his perch, he watched Brutus and Michale preparing the tilled land and seeding it during the morning. At one point in the day, another man brought over a cart full of manure, pulled by a hardy-looking donkey. The man stayed and helped the two men spread the manure on one section of the fields. Even Bonny and Nola went over to help. That took them most of the rest of the afternoon, and other villagers came over at dusk to retrieve the objects Rikah had worked on for them. Most of them thanked him with a nod or a smile.

Brutus helped Rikah into the house and this evening the meal was conducted without any anomalies from Bonny's quarter, although Rikah was still thinking on her behavior. Everyone smelled faintly of manure, even after a quick scrub, but it couldn't overwhelm the strong scents of stewed greens and chopped root vegetables.

"Never seen a young one devour veggies like you do," Nola commented. "I couldn't get Brutus to eat ice-chard until he was twelve."

"I still hate it," the teenager grinned, conveying a spoonful of the objectionables to his mouth.

"I haven't had them in a long time," Rikah explained eagerly.

"Bonny mentioned something about that," Michale mused idly.

A prickle of caution went through him; he'd gotten too relaxed again. Being with these people was new but enjoyable. He still had to go back to South-scree—didn't he? He certainly couldn't tell them about it. He wondered what Hawkmother and Jessika and Kassandra were thinking or planning. Hawkmother must have had her chick by now. Was it a boy or a girl? Rikah wondered. Then he gulped. Would he ever meet it?

Would he ever see Hawkmother and Jessika and Kassandra and Thornwing and Swift and Joy and little Day and Night and Thornsoft and the others again? Would he ever go home?

Suddenly his throat clenched and he realized he was about

to cry. The budding of manly pride sent sharp alerts — he mustn't cry. His leg still hurt too much for him to walk on it; he even needed help going to the privy. He couldn't get away from the table. He was about to cry right here in front of everyone.

"Brutus, take the scraps to the compost, if you will," Michale requested.

"Yes, sir," the boy answered, getting up, even though there were hardly any scraps to be spoken of.

"Bonny, the dishes," Nola urged.

"Yes, ma'am," the girl nodded.

In the distraction of people moving around, Rikah rubbed his arm swiftly across his eyes and bent down to examine the last bits of food on his plate. Hurriedly, he shoveled them down before Bonny took his plate.

"Lad, come take a walk with me," Michale announced, sweeping Rikah up into his arms.

Rikah had no chance to resist, and the father walked them out the front door right behind Brutus carrying the pail of scraps. Mack ran up, tail wagging, showing not an ounce of animosity for Rikah. The man of the house ate up the ground with long legged steps as he strode out towards the fields.

The pair stopped and Michale looked up at the sky dusted with stars.

"Rikah," he said, "you seem to me to be a good lad. I can't imagine you being the baby thief of a band of outlaws, or if you are then more the fool me for being taken in by your splendid acting."

He paused and Rikah didn't know what to say.

"What should I do with you? The town council agreed to leave you to my discretion since it was my shed you broke into. I see no need to punish you. That bite to your leg seems punishment enough, and you've done honest work for me."

"Thank you, sir," Rikah mumbled.

"So will you tell me what you'd like done with you?"

Rikah's tongue stuck to the roof of his mouth. He still didn't know what to say.

"I'll tell you that you're free to stay with us, until your leg heals and you want to go, or longer, if you want." This last was said with a degree of hesitancy, but not—Rikah sensed—because the man didn't want to offer; he wasn't sure if Rikah would be interested in such an offer.

"If you're not sure, that's alright. I can tell there are some big secrets and maybe some big things that are worrying you. You tell me if you want to, but if it's something that could endanger my family, I ask that you share it with me now. I've had sorrow fall upon my house, and I would protect my wife and children from more."

Rikah took a moment to wonder if Hawkmother or another griffin would think of attacking the village. That didn't make sense. The griffins of South-scree wanted to remain hidden, unknown to humans, and didn't enjoy senseless bloodshed. He thought they might try to pass him a message, or even sneak him away without being seen, but they wouldn't attack.

"I don't think there's any danger, sir," Rikah said finally.

"You're sure?"

"I," he hesitated, "I do have some friends that are missing me, but they won't attack," he confessed.

"You want to go back to them?"

"I," his throat choked again. Did he? He was living with people, with his own kind, in a house. Even though there would be plenty of hard work, it would still be easier than living in South-scree. He thought of his fields, yet to be planted and tended and harvested, of the challenges of living in a home made for griffins, so high in the mountains, where the snows fell deeper than Hawkmother's wingspan.

And then he thought of the play of light over Thornwing's feathers, of the deep liquid shining of the gold in Hawkmother's eyes, of the joyful shrieks and chortles of Day and Night, of the warm and pulsing thrumming of Thornsoft when he cuddled and preened the sleepy chicks. Jessika's snappy passion, Kassandra's dreamy not-quite-there gaze, and even Karolan's brusque determination were his treasured companions, that he knew like his own hands. How could he leave them?

"I don't know," he blurted.

"Do they know where you are?"

"Yes, but they probably don't know all the details."

"Do you want to send them a message, or meet with them somehow?"

"They won't come where anyone can see them."

"Ah, I see."

"I don't even know if they're out there."

For a few more minutes they stood in silence watching the dark forest and the lighter sky with its brighter stars. A partial moon began rising.

"You let us know then, what you want. The spring festival is in a few days, and your leg will probably be healed by then. You should at least stay for that. It will be a joyous celebration."

Still carrying Rikah in arms that never seemed to tire, Michale turned and carried him back to the house.

The next day Rikah took his first wobbly steps since the dog bite. Brutus stayed right by his side, in case he started to fall. It didn't relieve him of his duties of sitting and cleaning things, but it did encourage him that he would be able to walk and even run again soon.

He now started to see the first signs of preparation for the spring festival. Michale and Brutus, with some help from the women of the family, finished with the fields in the morning. After that, Nola began unpacking the family's finest garments from an old cedar chest. Bonny helped her air them on the clothesline when they weren't taking their turn getting ironed. The men began an intensive cleaning of the small cart the family owned and prepared to give it a fresh coat of whitewash.

At one point in the afternoon, Nola came to Rikah with a bundle of clothes.

"My man Michale says you'll be staying for the spring festival. Is that right?" she asked.

"Yes, ma'am," Rikah nodded, not sure what else to say, "I

suppose I will be."

"There's these festival clothes, if you'd like to wear them. I think they'll be about your size. If you'll come try them on, I can see if they need to be tailored a bit."

"Yes, ma'am." Rikah stood up, using a hand on the wall of the house to help balance, and followed her inside.

Bonny was there, standing up on a stool in an inside-out pink dress that was obviously a few sizes too large for her.

"Bonny outgrew her last festival dress beyond my ability to modify it," Nola explained. "This one was her grandmother's. I'll just pin it to see if I can take it in while you try on these."

Rikah took the bundle she offered and stepped into the cubby where he'd been sleeping. He put on the trousers, shirt, and jacket. They were certainly finer than anything he'd worn in a great while, in patterns of green and white, with darker green and brown embroidery of leaves on the jacket. When he hobbled back out to the kitchen, Nola looked on him with a sigh of satisfaction.

"It fits you like it was made for you," she said huskily.

Bonny was staring at him accusatorily, as though he'd done something wrong.

"I'm almost finished here. I'll pin the pant legs up a bit. How are the sleeves?"

Rikah stretched his arms out. "Pretty good."

Bonny pulled the dress off over her head and stood there unashamedly in her shift once her mother finished pinning.

"Was this your brother's?" Rikah asked tentatively, trying to understand her heavy glare.

Behind him, Nola made a stifled movement. Bonny snatched up her plain, everyday dress from the table and flung a vicious "yes" at Rikah before stomping out the front door.

"Bonny," her mother scolded.

"I'm sorry," Rikah tried, looking up at Nola for some kind of help or understanding.

"Don't worry about it," Nola said firmly, with a multi-flavored smile.

Rikah nodded his acceptance but couldn't put Bonny's strange behavior out of his head that easily. As Nola pinned the trouser legs up a few inches, he wondered, too, about Nola's quick, suppressing smile. It wasn't like she was lying to him, but he had the feeling she wasn't telling him everything either. Once he'd changed back into his now usual clothes and left the fancy ones with Nola for hemming, he went back to his stool to resume his chores, and worried the kinked little oddities over in his mind, getting nowhere, but it gave his head something to do while his hands worked.

The next morning there was a feather on the doorstep. Brutus came in holding it up after finishing his dawn chores.

"Would you look at this," he exclaimed, drawing everyone's attention away from their porridge breakfasts. "Ever seen a feather this big?"

Rikah choked. Nola pounded his back until he was able to swallow and gasp out, "sorry, big chunk of walnut."

The rest of the family passed the feather around, marveling at its size. When it got to Rikah, he held it in his hand, knowing exactly what it was. By the color, it was one of Thornwing's coverts: a dull, washed out rust with blurry white banding characteristic of his underwing. It wasn't even that big, only about the size of Nola's hand, but that was bigger than anything a regular bird would produce.

Rikah passed the feather to Bonny without comment. She took it eagerly and stroked her cheeks with it. "It's so soft," she crooned.

"Did you get that walnut down alright?" Michale asked. "You look pale, Rikah."

He nodded vigorously. "Yeah, it just scared me a little when I choked."

"Have some water."

"Right." Rikah drank obediently.

The griffins were looking for him, and now knew where he was. That feather was undoubtedly a message. He should ask

Michale for some seeds and walk off into the forest with them where the griffins could pick him up; he just didn't know how to pay for them.

"The festival is tomorrow, so final preparations, everyone," Nola said.

"Will there be contests at the festival?" Rikah blurted with a sudden idea.

"Yes, a few," she answered.

"And prizes?"

"For some things."

Rikah fisted his hands. That was it. He'd have to win some contests and give the prizes to Michale in return for the seeds.

"What kind of contests?"

The day of the festival dawned crisp and clear. Nola had finished altering all their clothing. The cart was bright with whitewash and bedecked with flowers picked by Bonny and strung by her, Brutus, and Rikah. The breakfast that morning was another fancy one, including sausages, pancakes, and more slices of butter turnip. After a cold wash presided over by Nola to ensure that the backs of ears and knees were properly scrubbed, everyone put on their festival best and loaded the cart. Nola took with her some bundles of dyed wool that she'd spun into yarn. Brutus had a basket of small wood carvings he'd made of birds and beasts.

"Festivals are a time to trade and sell more frivolous, less practical little things we make in our free time," Nola explained, holding up her sack, "like my pink and purple yarn. I use different types of plants to dye it."

"And during the winter, when we can't do much outside, I carve animals," Brutus said. "I'm not very good at it yet, but you can sort of tell what they are now, and I don't cut myself much anymore."

Nola's briefly rolled eyes suggested that Brutus had presented her with more than a few bloody nicks and cuts for bandaging. Rikah, however, found the little carved animal charming.

He wondered if he could ever carve something so clever.

"Mostly we exchange our goods with friends," Nola went on, "and if we feel indebted to anyone for things they've done for us recently, we give them more than a fair trade."

Rikah nodded and looked at his empty hands. "I wish I had something. I owe everyone for helping me."

Michale reached over and ruffled his hair as he passed. "Don't worry, Rikah. You've been helping out a lot around the house. I think you've paid us back."

The cart took them down to the village's town square, where Rikah hadn't been yet. Other families were pulling up, too, some with their own carts, and some coming on foot. The carts were arranged in a circle around a central well. The village people fluttered and chattered like colorful birds in their cheerful festival clothing. Rikah sat in the cart and watched, not wanting to hobble about on his injured leg in such a crowd.

Brutus had run off right away, and Rikah spotted him across the square in a huddle of other boys his age. Each boy was showing off some bit of craft or art or handing out fruit or little sacks of something or other. Michale and Nola were walking around together, more sedately, arms linked and greeting neighbors, embracing and shaking hands, showing off their yarn and looking over the goods of others. Every now and then Rikah saw goods exchanged.

Bonny however, hadn't wandered off, and was just standing by the side of the cart. Rikah was wondering if he should say something to her when the healer-woman, Maryann, came striding over. The woman was smiling widely, and had a blue woven shawl wrapped around her shoulders.

"Bonny, Rikah, how are you enjoying the festival?"

"It's my first one, ma'am," Rikah said.

"I can tell by how wide your eyes are," the healer grinned. "How's your leg?"

"I can walk on it again, but it does still hurt a bit."

"Glad to hear it's mending. Bonny, not going to find some other young ladies to run around with?"

Rikah winced, thinking that Bonny probably did not want her self-chosen solitude pointed out as unusual. There were in fact three girls that looked about Bonny's age sitting on a low wall near the well. Every now and then one of the girls would look over Bonny's way with curious or even sad glances.

"I think Millie, Catie, and Lana are missing you," Maryann went on. "It's not often you all get to see each other."

One of the girls tentatively raised a hand in Bonny's direction and waved, but Bonny only gave a half-hearted wave of her fingers back, and didn't return the smiles.

"Don't be so nervous," Maryann chastised the girl with a nudge that was probably meant to be encouraging. "Well, enjoy yourselves. The Spring Festival only comes once a year."

The healer strode off, and hard on her departure came a stocky boy with a belligerent expression that said clearly that anything from puppies to angry bulls would be kicked out of his way. The boy marched up to the wagon and glared up at Rikah.

"You must be the thief," he announced. "You shouldn't be hanging around Bonny's family."

Rikah took a step back in surprise, trod on a fallen daffodil and winced at the crunch. "I'm not a thief," he denied.

The boy's eyes narrowed. "Whoever you are, you aren't needed here. You should go away."

Without another word he reached out and took Bonny's arm with a gentleness that was at stark contrast to his declamations at Rikah. He murmured something to her, and she didn't resist as he walked off with her. Rikah opened his mouth, about to object, but then his courage quailed and he went to sit on the floor of the wagon instead, legs dangling off the end. The twittering and fluttering of the crowd continued around him, like a flock of colorful chickens going after scattered seed. He picked up the daffodil he'd crushed and twirled it sadly in his fingers until the broken petals fell off.

At some unspoken signal, the gathering of people began to fragment and shift. Most of the people returned to their wagons, fetching baskets and baskets and bundles, and began carrying them towards wooden tables that a few sturdy men and women were lugging into the square and setting up around the well. Rikah stayed out of the way until the families started spreading out food from the baskets for easy access; then he went and helped Nola and Brutus. Bonny hadn't reappeared.

"Now we all eat food?" he checked with Nola.

"This is the first round of food, the snacks," she answered with a grin.

"All this is for snacking?"

No family had brought copious amounts, but each one was unloading at least one basket. There were baked breads and rolls studded with dried fruit or nuts or herbs, pressed bars of grains and nuts or seeds held together with sticky mashed dates or figs, salads of greens and other early vegetables, squares of dried and salted meats like pork or even some fish, and other preparations of things Rikah couldn't recognize but figured must be dried fruit or vegetable based. Most of the food was things a person could easily pick up and walk off with without needing a dish or utensil.

"After the games and before the dancing, the mayor will start serving the pig," Brutus explained. "Every year for the spring festival the mayor's family cooks up their biggest pig in a pit in the ground. Then everybody gets a piece for dinner."

"I've never heard of that. Is it good?" Rikah asked.

"It's a rare treat," Nola said. "Some people in the village raise animals, but it's harder than farming, because you have to grow or buy the food for the animals, and it takes more food to raise the animals than you get from eating them. Most everyone likes a little meat now and then, though, so people who can afford it make the effort to do it, and the whole village appreciates it."

Rikah made a grunt of acknowledgement, but he was thinking about the griffins, who ate virtually nothing but meat. They didn't have to raise their animals; they let the forests do it for them, but they were painstakingly careful about how many animals they killed, and how big their population was. They even had a quota of how many baby griffins they'd make each year, based on how well the prey population was doing.

"Why don't you just hunt for meat?" he wondered aloud, "instead of raising it?"

Brutus and Nola glanced at each other. "The forest is dangerous," Nola said. "Sometimes a party of hunters will go out there, but they don't go far, and they have to be cautious. People from our village have died out there."

"You wanted to compete in some of the games, right Rikah?" Brutus piped up, changing the subject in an abrupt manner that did not escape Rikah as anything other than deliberate. "Grab some food if you want, and I'll take you to the field."

Rikah went along. Winning some prizes was the most important thing; that would allow him to barter for seeds from Michale, he hoped.

"Looks like they're setting up for a three-legged race," Brutus commented as they approached. "I'd do it with you, but we're such different sizes it would make it too hard. If you can't find a partner your size, I'll be happy to try, though."

Boys and girls were running about, finding partners. Rikah started to join them, but had to stop as his leg twinged with pain. He bit his lip. Well, he'd just have to push through the pain. Gritting his teeth, Rikah waded into the confusion, forcing himself to shout and push like the others until he'd found a skinny, freckled boy close to his height who was pouting over two of his friends pairing up with each other instead of him. Partner secured, he lined up with everyone else. Bits of rope were handed out and the finish line was drawn.

"Let's run as hard as we can," he encouraged his partner.

"Yeah," the freckled boy agreed with a scowl. "I've got to beat Kevrin and Sam."

A tall bearded man shouted out and the race was on. Rikah pushed himself as hard as he could, and his partner huffed and strained right alongside him, determined to do better than the friends who'd chosen each other over him. Rikah's leg hurt fiercely by the end, but they came third. The prize for third was lengths of pretty red ribbon. Rikah wasn't sure how valuable it would be for trading for seeds, but he rolled his carefully and tucked it in a pocket.

"Thanks," his partner told him. "You did good."

"You, too," Rikah replied.

"Barrel-balancing is next if you want to do that, too."

Rikah let him lead the way to a flat section of road where four barrels were lined up, with a few more standing on their flat ends at the side of the road. He listened to the instructions from the man leading the contest and quickly gathered that the contestants would complete in groups of four, each one attempting to balance on the barrel and roll it down the road to the finish line. The winners from each group would compete against each other until the fastest person was the overall victor. Contestants were not allowed to hit or push their neighbors off their barrels.

"But everyone tries to do it anyway," Rikah's three-legged-race partner whispered. "If you get caught, you're out. Getting knocked off a barrel can get you hurt."

Rikah nodded, and went to join the group of boys jostling for position behind the starting line. A pair of men arranged them into rows of four each, saw that at the end were two boys and made the last two rows of three each instead. Rikah was in the third row, with his three-legged race partner and two more boys. It was all ages, and some of the boys were much taller than he was, and some shorter.

The pair or organizing men trotted down to the finish line and the leading man directed the first line of boys to be ready to mount their barrels. Rikah restrained himself from fidgeting with nerves. He'd never done something like this and had no idea how good his balance would be on a barrel. He tried to see around the boys in front of him to watch the technique of the first racers. At a cry from the leading man, the four boys got on their barrels, some struggling more than others, and began to roll their barrels down the road, with them balanced on top.

"It's alright if you fall off," Rikah's new friend said, also watching anxiously. "You just can't roll the barrel along while you're not on it."

Rikah saw evidence of this for himself. Sometimes the boys did fall off, but men and women and older children not competing lined the road, and would catch runaway barrels and bring them back to where their riders had lost control, and make them continue from there. There was one boy particularly skilled, and he easily won the race.

"His ma is a brewer," Rikah's companion confided. "I think he gets to practice a lot on their empty barrels, but what do the rest of us have? We have rain barrels, full of rain, never a chance to practice. He'll probably win, but there's still the second and third place."

The second row of boys got ready to begin, and Rikah felt his nerves prickle more viciously. He needed to do well, to win something—though he was sure there were more contests if he lost this one. He glanced around. The barrel rolling contest had gotten a big audience. Michale and Nola were both watching, with Brutus beside them. They were among those lining the road. Down past the finish line, Rikah thought he saw Bonny with the stocky boy who had taken her from the wagon.

Rikah didn't want to show poorly in front of any of them, but especially not that boy with Bonny. Still, his leg was aching, and the more he did with it, the worse it would get, he expected. He had no idea how it would like being told to help him balance on a rolling barrel. Back behind Bonny and her boy, Maryann stood with her arms folded, a look of disapproval on her face for the whole event. Rikah supposed if there were injuries, she would be the one having to treat them.

The second row of boys began their race. These were all older boys, and fairly well matched, but by the end one boy had pulled away, and won by a few barrel lengths. Now the third row, Rikah's row, stepped up as the barrels were rolled back to them. The crowd was having a good time, and Rikah even heard Brutus shout out wishing him luck. It didn't help calm his pounding heart or jittery muscles.

"Ready, gentlemen?" the leading man directed, and Rikah and the others nodded at him.

"Set, then."

With the other three boys of his group, Rikah lifted a foot up onto his barrel and grabbed the edges.

"Off you go," he cried.

Rikah pulled himself up and almost immediately fell off. The barrel crunched against the grit of the road, shifted, but didn't start rolling by itself. Rikah pushed with his feet, leaning his body. Beside him, the other boys were doing the same thing, getting their barrels to start moving. One got his to roll out a few feet, picking up speed, and then lost his footing and had to manage a mostly in control dismount. Someone caught his barrel and brought it back to him.

Rikah got his rocking a little, and then started it moving. The planks of the barrel were dusty from the road, and not completely smooth, but he found it hard to keep traction with his shoes. Everyone had their barrels moving now. Rikah found himself concentrating hard, not even paying attention to if he was in the lead, at the back, or in the middle. All he could think was to roll the barrel forward and not fall off.

As expected, his bitten thigh did not like this at all, and ached continually. Sweat ran into his eyes and he blinked it away. Still, his barrel was moving, rolling, and he was getting the hang of it. It was moving faster now without getting away from him. His confidence rose. He could do this. A smile stretched his face. He was going faster, and faster.

Then a cheer went up.

Rikah looked up. Had he reached the finish line? Had he won?

No. Someone else had gotten there before him. In fact, all three of the other boys were ahead of him. His concentration broken, his thigh sparking with pain, his feet fumbled on the quick-moving barrel. It rolled out from under him and he fell back, striking one buttock against the barrel as it trundled away, and then he hit the hard road.

The air knocked out of him, Rikah struggled not to cry. He pushed himself up with his hands, bowing his head so his shaggy hair would hide his face and a few traitorous tears. Michale was there beside him then, asking if he was alright. His palms were scraped from where he'd caught himself, and his right butt cheek hurt, but he hadn't hit his head.

Then Maryann the healer knelt down in front of him.

"I told them we shouldn't do this game anymore," she was fuming. "Someone always gets hurt. And what were you thinking competing in this one? You should barely be walking, much less—"

Rikah surged and stumbled to his feet. "I'm fine," he declared. "I'm fine."

Through his bangs, he caught sight of Bonny and her boy. Bonny looked concerned, but the boy beside her was grinning in a pleased way. Rikah clenched his bruised hands and glared.

"You should sit down," Maryann was saying. "No more running about."

Rikah ignored her. He took unsteady steps towards Bonny and the smug boy, but Bonny's concern flashed into fear then, and she tugged on her companion, saying something Rikah couldn't hear, pulling him away from the crowd. The boy went, and Rikah followed, limping only a little. He thought Michale and Brutus were calling him, but he ignored them both, following instead wherever Bonny was leading.

"That was a good try," he heard his three-legged race partner say as he passed the finish line. "Barrel rolling is really hard. I didn't win, either. Don't feel bad."

Rikah ignored him, too, and pushed through the gathered people, who parted a little, maybe feeling sorry for him. Bonny and her boy had left the road, but no one was looking in their direction. Here at the edge of town, there were no fields lining the road, only a few yards from which the trees and undergrowth had been removed. Rikah hesitated for a partial second, and then went on.

Bonny was leading them into the forest.

***

There was a trail, but it wasn't wide or smooth. Still, it was more than a deer trail, suggesting to Rikah that the villagers did pass this way from time to time—or something did. There was no hint of danger, however. The chatter of the festival-goers vanished as Rikah entered the forest, but birds were flitting about in the canopy and undergrowth, chortling and chirping. It was spring, after all, and apparently these birds weren't going to suspend their territory-claiming and mate-seeking just because of a few human children passing by.

"Bonny," he heard the boy ahead of him saying, "we're not supposed to go to the waterfall alone."

Rikah couldn't hear if Bonny replied, but he thought he heard humming, or wordless singing even, soft and slow. The boy did not object again, and Rikah followed with single-minded intensity. He didn't know why Bonny was leading them into the forest, but he would find out. He needed to follow her like he needed to breathe, and his leg no longer hurt him.

The trail curved a little and began climbing, not unbearably steep, but definitely uphill. Rikah labored on gamely. The village was now several minutes of hiking behind him, and ahead of him he kept Bonny and the other boy in view, but didn't try to catch up, not yet. Over the constant humming he began to hear another whisper, and as he hiked on, he soon knew what it must be: the waterfall.

The land rose sharply ahead and to the right, and Bonny was leading the boy over the shoulder of it. Rikah saw a hint of mist in the air, catching the light. The whispering was growing to a growling, and he could hardly hear the singing anymore, but he followed anyway. Bonny and the boy had disappeared over the rise, and now Rikah approached it, too, seeing more and more mist the closer he came, as he followed the curve of the trail.

Then the waterfall came into view.

It stretched up and up, to the top of the rising cliff, and plunged down in a wide sheet to a frothing pool below. How tall it was, Rikah could only guess. Twenty of his own height perhaps? Thirty? He'd seen waterfalls before, but none this tall. He felt miniscule beside it. From the trail he stood one, he thought he was two-thirds up the height of the falls. Bonny and the boy were climbing down the much steeper trail below, to the pool at the foot of the falls.

There were a few branches piled up, crossing the start of the trail like a barrier fence, but Bonny and the boy had clearly climbed over them. Beyond them, the trail was rocky and damp, with many switchbacks, festooned with mosses, ferns and other vibrant green flora. On another day, Rikah might have considered the trail too dangerous, especially with his hurt leg, but today, with that hint of song still in his ears, he knew he had to go where Bonny went, and he began his descent.

With feet and hands on the slippery rocks, Rikah made his way down. Something in him was urging him to hurry, but he didn't want to slip and fall, either. His bitten thigh was also starting to twitch and shudder beyond his control. It still didn't hurt, but if he made it take too much weight, or stretched it too far, it would shake uncontrollably until he adjusted his position.

Stealing a glance below, he saw Bonny and the other boy had reached the bottom and were walking along a gravel shore: just a crescent of beach where the turbulent pool began to calm and order itself into a departing brook. He was almost there, too. It seemed like Bonny or the boy might have navigated the trail very slowly, so Rikah had caught up some. He could hear the singing again, only it was louder, and he thought there was another voice now, maybe even two more.

With a little hop that almost made his leg collapse, Rikah jumped down the last bit of rocky trail to land on the gravel beach. Bonny was at the edge of the water, just a few yards away. She had squatted down, and didn't seem to mind that the skirt of her dress was getting wet where it trailed into the water. She had a hand extended, almost touching the water. The boy she'd brought along stood behind and a little to one side of her, back a couple paces.

He looked tense, like he was preparing to leap to safety, and yet he stayed, watching Bonny as if unable to look away. Rikah found himself stepping up beside the boy, all enmity forgotten, also watching Bonny. There were ripples in the pool, more than what the waterfall was making. The singing went on, over, or below, or with the rushing of the falls. Rikah wasn't even sure he was hearing the singing with his ears. It was inside his head, and he wasn't sure if it had used his ears to get there or not.

"Bonny," the other boy said, but the word was faint.

"He's here," the girl said dreamily. "You see, he's here. It's alright."

"Your dress is getting wet," the boy went on hesitantly.

Without looking, almost as though she didn't know she was doing it, Bonny gathered up the skirt of her dress in one hand, the other still reaching for the water. She drew the fabric to her knees, and there on her calf, emerging above the top of her sock, was a healed but still red bite scar.

"Benny," the girl cried out, "Benny, come on. It's safe. I'm here."

That dragged Rikah's gaze back to the water, to the ripples, which had increased in frequency. Something rounded and pale was surfacing in their midst. Distantly, Rikah felt a chill of fear, but still that singing went on, and he found he couldn't step away, even as that pale shape broke the surface, gliding smoothly, slowly.

"Benny," Bonny greeted, laughing even, as a child's head surfaced, with waterlogged blonde hair, and white skin faintly tinted with blue.

The eyes were too big, and all dark, with no distinction between iris, pupil, or sclera. The cheeks were hollow, the lips thin and cornflower blue. Tendons stood out in the wasted neck as the childlike creature emerged further, focused on Bonny, coming to her joyous cries. The girl held out her arms, dropping her skirt again, hiding the scar.

"No!" a woman's voice shouted out. "It's not Benny, Bonny."

A hint of the song's spell cracked, and Rikah looked up to

the trail, where Maryann the healer was hurrying down, as fast as she could go without falling, but she was still near the top. The child from the pool was only a few feet away from Bonny. It reached out an emaciated arm, but couldn't seem to crawl any closer, leaving it submerged from the waist down.

"Bonny," it said, voice like a gurgle of water. "I want to go home. Carry me home."

Water trickled from its open mouth. Its teeth were blackened and its tongue darkest indigo. He thought he saw, beyond the teeth and tongue, something glistening in the throat—something writhing, with claws, or fangs. Rikah still couldn't seem to move, but within he recoiled in aversion.

"Come help me," Bonny pleaded, not turning from the thing in the water, but Rikah felt the request hit him like a hook, and he took a step closer.

Beside him, the other boy matched him. He didn't want to go closer. He wanted to run away, and yet he took another step. He managed to look over at Maryann, who was still doing her best to get down the trail, slipping and sliding and sending down cascades of rocks and gravel, but she was only halfway down. She wouldn't get to them before they got to the edge of the water.

"Hurry," the creature urged.

Bonny stepped deeper into the water and gripped the creature's wasted wrist with both hands. Now Rikah and the other boy had reached the edge of the water, too.

"Help him," Bonny insisted. "Help him. He's my brother. He needs to go home. Take his arm. Pull him out."

The other boy was closer, and reached out, hands shaking. The pale blue creature, so like a thin and starving child, gaped its mouth wide. Skinny fingers weakly clutched and stretched. Its arms trembled. The boy took hold of its free wrist, and he and Bonny began to pull, but Rikah looked past its bedraggled hair, past its bony shoulders and back, and down towards its rump.

He felt himself start to shiver, and stared, transfixed.

It had no legs.

Where a child would have had legs there was just nothing. There were hips and buttocks, but the legs were gone. Instead, entering the base of the body like a hand up a puppet was a round attenuated shape, like a smooth branch or small log, only it flexed like a snake's body, and the far end vanished into the deep darkness of the pool below the waterfall.

"Bonny!" Maryann demanded. "Stevry! Rikah!"

He could hear her running feet on the gravel, but he still stared, unable to look away from the thing that wore a child's corpse and used it to lure others in. For that was the only thing it could be, and though Bonny and the other boy, Stevry, were barely into the water, and Rikah still on the shore, it took its chance.

Two limbs lashed out of the pool, long and skinny and festooned with flexible gripping fingers. They lashed around Bonny and Stevry's arms and jerked them forward, towards deeper water, but Maryann reached them in time. She swept the two children up, one in each arm, and set her feet, water sloshing up her shins. The creature still had them, and still pulled, but Maryann pulled back.

"Bonny, Stevry, Rikah," the child lure gurgled, now slumped down so its face was almost in the water. "Help me."

Rikah shook all over, still unable to move. Bonny screamed and struggled against Maryann's grip, but Stevry had started fighting the monster's coiling fingers.

"Rikah," Maryann summoned, voice shaking and cracking. "Rikah, take my knife, at my belt. Cut it. Cut them loose."

He managed to turn his gaze to her, where she stood in the thrashing water, playing a deadly tug-of-war with the two children as the ropes. Her feet were dug in, her back arched, arms squeezing Bonny and Stevry hard around their middles. Bonny and Stevry both had their arms stretched out tight as the creature pulled. Both were screaming now.

"Rikah," Maryann commanded shrilly. "You have to do it. I can't let go."

He stumbled, his hurt leg weakening below him, and caught himself with his hands on the gravel. Then he shoved himself back up, and went into the water beside the healer. The gripping limbs, jointless, like eels, were starting to twist up, and something bigger was emerging from the depths.

Rikah fumbled at Maryann's belt and got her simple utility knife from the sheath. He almost dropped it, and then took it one hand, and then added his second hand. He lifted it up above his head, point down, and jabbed it into the nearest tentacle, the one holding Stevry.

The point barely went in, and he drew back and stabbed harder, and again, and again, using the full stroke of his body. Blue blood leaked from the little wounds. At last, perhaps the fifth or sixth stab, the knife bit deeply, and the writhing limb loosened. Stevry pulled hard, and yanked his arms out of its grip. Maryann twisted and flung Stevry away, back up the gravel beach. The boy landed hard, but without complaint.

"Go Stevry, go," she shouted. "Run to the village for help."

The boy scrabbled on the rocky shore for a moment, getting his feet under him, and then pelted for the trail up the cliff side. Meanwhile, Maryann had gotten both arms around Bonny now.

"Get it, Rikah," she ordered.

He stabbed with the knife again, and again, gasping after his breath and heart pounding, until, quite suddenly, the monster let go. Maryann fell backwards into the shallow water, Bonny still screaming in her arms, and then rolled herself over, trying to get back to her feet. The child's corpse sank back into the water, fine blonde hair floating down last.

The water calmed, and Rikah caught his breath.

Then the wounded tentacle came lashing out of the water and hit the knife out of Rikah's hand. The other tentacle came darting for his face—

And a griffin slammed into him, knocking his breath from him and tearing him away from the water monster. Furry arms pinned him tightly to massive pectoral muscles, and the griffin backwinged, sticking out its hind legs, and skidded to a halt at the far side of the little beach. Behind him, over the thundering of blood in his ears, Rikah heard the water erupt.

"I gotcha, stay with me," a young female voice said above his head.

Rikah opened his eyes and saw white fur. He identified Thornspike. She folded her wings and he was able to see past her. Hawkswift and Thornwing were fighting the monster in the waterfall pool. Swift had gotten a hold on one tentacle and was in the shallows, pulling the beast out of the depths with tenacious strength. Thornwing was perched on its back, biting and clawing at everything he could get traction on.

It was not a big beast, no bigger than the griffin on its back, and shaped like nothing more than an oblong with limbs and tentacles of various length around its edges. The back side might have had some fins, but Rikah couldn't see that end very well. There did appear to be a trio of black eyes at the end pointed towards the shore, with several shorter, slender feelers beside and below them. The two tentacles it had attacked with seemed to be the biggest ones. Swift had one clamped in her bill, keeping on the tension, and it seemed that Thornwing had already clawed up the other to the point that it could no longer move.

Rikah looked aside, to where Maryann had Bonny clutched to her chest, the girl's face hidden. The healer was watching, wide-eyed. She seemed to sense Rikah looking, and darted her gaze over to him. Worried she might think the griffins were enemies, too, he gave Thornspike's shoulder a friendly pat.

Over in the pool, the battle was subsiding. Rikah looked back and saw that Thornwing had managed to sever most of the end where the eyes and lots of tentacles were. It looked like he'd dyed his feet and face blue, from the creature's blood. The monster was twitching, but gradually going limp. After a few more moments, Thornwing made a graceful leap to shore, and Swift released the senseless tentacle. The male griffin found a cleaner section of water and began rinsing his claws and bill.

Thornspike stepped out of the way, and Rikah found himself face to beak with Hawkswift.

His insides seemed to shrink. Hawkswift was the oldest member of the Hawk Line, though technically not old enough to be counted an Elder yet. Nevertheless, she was steady and wise and firm, but also compassionate, just like an Elder should be, and the expression in her eyes and feathers showed the most extreme disapproval Rikah had ever seen on her.

Hawkswift couldn't speak aloud, but she could communicate using gestures, and did so now. "Hawkdare," she signed.

And in her eyes was the inescapable weight of her disappointment, fear, and love.

"I'm sorry," Rikah rasped, shaking with cold and leftover adrenaline.

"Thornspike, the Hawk Line is indebted to you for your assistance," she said, turning her head with great mobility to nod at the younger female griffin, and gesturing her words. "Might I ask you to take to the air again? I will join you shortly."

Most of South-scree had learned the hand language that Hawkswift and several other voiceless griffins used, so Thornspike nodded and made no other reply except to comply, struggling into the humid air with heavy wing beats. Then the big female's regard returned to Rikah and he flinched.

She lifted both hands to speak, gesturing rapidly. "Dare, you ran away without telling anyone where you were going, on the eve of the Hawkmother's birth, so that we would all be distracted and she could not follow you. You got yourself injured trying to steal from a human village, and now you were nearly killed."

"I'm sorry," he whimpered again, tears starting in his eyes.

"Now we have been forced to show ourselves to humans, when we have been expressly forbidden from allowing any human knowledge of our presence."

"I'm sorry, Swift, I'm sorry," Rikah sobbed.

"Will you be returning to South-scree?" Hawkswift asked abruptly.

Rikah lifted his wet face, scrubbing at his cheeks with his even wetter sleeves. "Yes, yes, of course," he answered immediately, automatically.

"Shall I take you now?"

"Uh, oh, please Swift, I have to get seeds. I came to get seeds," he explained through his sobs.

"Then get them. Tomorrow we will pick you up."

"Yes, Swift. I'll meet you where Thornspike said to go. I promise."

The griffin slowly looked over at the woman huddled with the girl child in her lap. Bonny was crying steadily, seeing nothing. Maryann's eyes were scared but hopeful. Hawkswift seemed to sigh. She turned her head to where Thornwing looked to have finally washed most of the blue blood out of his fur and feathers. He was a bit bedraggled. He stared back at Hawkswift for a moment, exchanged a few quick gestures, and then looked to Maryann.

"We don't kill humans," he said aloud to the woman. "You'll forget you saw us?"

"Yes," Maryann whispered.

Thornwing looked over at the dead monster. "I don't know how you'll explain the wounds."

"Don't worry about it," the healer replied. "The village will just be glad it is dead. If you can push it back into the water, I can see to it that no one looks too closely. This is a cursed place already. No one wants to linger here. But, if you could leave the child's body, his parents might want to give it a proper burial. There was nothing to bury before, when he was taken."

Thornwing did as requested. The limb that had acted as puppeteer for the boy's corpse now slid smoothly out of the grisly remains. It was multi-branched, with lots of fine tendrils, and what looked like a biting mouth at the most terminal end. Thornwing pushed the monster's body back into the water, where it sank except for a few mangled tentacles that floated to the surface. The little boy's body remained on the shore, but now the eyes were shut, the skeletal limbs relaxed. It was no longer so fearsome. Now it just seemed sad.

"I will fly you to the top of the trail," Hawkswift told Rikah by hand.

Thornwing launched up into the air with a burst of wing beats and vanished above the trees. Obediently, Rikah climbed onto Hawkswift's back and gripped her harness, but his hands were still shaking. Hawkswift seemed to realize by his trembling that he had no hope of holding on, and instead urged him back down. She sat back on her hind legs and balanced there, so she could take him in her arms. Now he clung to her, crying into her wet fur, as the griffin awkwardly extended her wings, and managed a takeoff.

Hawkswift landed with Rikah at the top, just behind the fence of branches, and set him on his feet. He looked up at her, still crying a little, and tried to thank her, to apologize again, but they both heard voices down the trail.

"You'd better go," he choked out.

Behind the cover of the trees, Hawkswift leapt into the gorge created by the waterfall, and flew off. Just as she was flapping out of sight, the human rescue party from the village ran up to Rikah with cries of alarm. Rikah, too hurt and cold and tired to do anymore, fell into the arms of the first person to grab him, and stopped trying to keep track of anything more.

Rikah woke up in an attic, and for a brief second felt a piercing pang of homesickness—not for the Aerie, but for his home in Northnest, where he'd spent the first few years of his life with his human family. His little bedroom had been tucked into the attic. The ceiling he looked up at now bore a striking resemblance, but of course, he was not back home.

Memories came to him to fill in what had happened. He'd followed Bonny down to the waterfall. There, some kind of creature—with Bonny's bewitched help—had lured them into the water. Maryann the healer, and then the griffins, had arrived in time to save Bonny, Stevry, and Rikah from getting pulled in. Rikah could only assume the monster would have eaten them, or maybe used one of their corpses as a new puppet.

Rikah looked around and saw that there were three more beds crammed into the attic. Two looked to be occupied by

Bonny and Stevry. Both children seemed to be in restful sleep. Rikah sat up and felt himself over. His bitten leg still hurt, but had been re-bandaged. He was clean and dressed in a long sleeping shift. Aside from a few aches, he seemed to be well, and swung his legs out of the bed.

Outside the window at the end of the attic, the sky was reddening towards sunset. Rikah slid his feet into the slippers that waited by the bed. They were too big, but he wore them anyway, and went to the steep stairs that led down to what he assumed was the healer's house. As he'd guessed, once he was halfway down, he was able to see Maryann in her kitchen blending herbs into a paste. She looked up as he came into view, and offered a tentative smile.

"Rikah, how are you feeling?" she asked.

"A little sore," he admitted.

"Come sit, if you like."

She pulled a chair out at her table and then fetched a cup and poured tea.

"You must have heard Nola and Michale leaving a moment ago," Maryann said. "They were checking on Bonny, but she's still in a deep sleep. So is Stevry. I'm surprised you're up."

"I'm alright," Rikah whispered, taking the tea.

"It's hot," she cautioned. "I have some cookies here."

"Miss Maryann," he began, before he could lose his nerve, "I should probably explain."

She looked a little surprised at his forthrightness, but calmly took a seat at the table with him. "It might be good if you did," she agreed.

"You have to keep it a secret."

Maryann folded her hands before her on the tabletop. "Is it something that could endanger the village?"

"No," he assured her. "I don't think so. In fact, it's probably better if the village doesn't know anything."

"Really?" she murmured. "Alright, go ahead and tell me, and as long as it isn't anything that could cause us trouble, I won't tell anyone."

"Alright," Rikah agreed, and took a careful sip of tea as a way to get a moment to think. "I live with griffins," he began, "me and three other children."

Maryann nodded politely, though he could see questions gathering in her eyes.

"We came from Northnest. When it was attacked, one of the Feathyrs got us out and found where wild griffins were living, and now we all live there."

"There are no other people? No adults?" Maryann asked.

"The griffins are people," Rikah retorted, a bit sharply. "They are smart as anyone."

Maryann gave another polite nod. "I heard that one speak."

"They take care of us, as a family."

"I see. Then why did you come to the village?"

"The griffins mostly just hunt meat. That's all they need, but the other kids and I, we need fruits and vegetables."

"I agree," she said. "A healthy diet has variety."

"So I'm trying to start farming, just enough to grow some food for us, but I don't have any seeds."

"Ah." Maryann seemed to have put the pieces together. "That's why you were in Michale's storage shed. You were going to steal seeds."

"Yes," Rikah admitted, feeling ashamed.

Maryann took a cookie and broke off a bit, looking thoughtful. "I told you that if you told me where you had come from, you might learn about the great sorrow in Bonny's family."

He nodded and took another careful sip of tea. It was sort of flowery, and not bitter.

"You have upheld your side of the bargain, and seen their sorrow for yourself now, so I might as well tell you. That creature in the waterfall pool attacked Bonny and Benny a few months ago. They were twins, if you hadn't guessed, and into all kinds of mischief, most of it innocent. It was the first warm spring day of the year, and I think they must have been sick of being stuck inside. They went down to the waterfall.

"There's a lot of superstition about the place being full of bad luck, even though it is so beautiful. People have accidents there, make stupid decisions and get themselves hurt, but I had never heard of anything like a monster in the pool. Anyway, Bonny came running back to the village hoarse from screaming, with bloody bites on her legs, quite out of her mind with terror and grief. She said Benny had been sucked into the pool.

"Of course, a group of men went right down to investigate, but they didn't find anything, not even Benny's body, and hardly any sign of a struggle. I was trying to treat Bonny, but she was frantic, and eventually I had to give her a drink to make her sleepy. The bites healed, but they never found Benny."

Maryann glanced up at Rikah. "You heard Bonny humming, and singing, didn't you?"

"Yes," he admitted.

"Bonny started doing that after Benny was taken. She also wanted to go back to the waterfall, but no one would let her. One time she almost charmed Brutus into going there with her, but Nola caught them. The singing didn't seem to affect adults like it did children."

"It's magic?" Rikah asked.

"I'm not sure. I think it might have something to do with the bites Bonny got off that creature. She was also very close with Benny. I'm sure Benny was dead, that the monster killed him, but the monster also was singing, wasn't it?"

Rikah nodded, feeling a chill, and took another swallow of hot tea to combat it.

"Maybe," Maryann said slowly, "that bond between Benny and Bonny might have carried the monster's influence to Bonny. We might never know. I hope now, with Benny properly put to rest, and the monster dead, that Bonny won't do that singing anymore."

"Bonny's really nice," Rikah muttered. "I hope she'll be alright now."

"I hope so, too." Maryann gave him a little smile. "I think she will be. Thank you for helping me save her and Stevry. You were very brave, Rikah."

He bowed his face towards his tea cup, and felt the steam make his cheeks warm and a little damp.

"You're welcome," he whispered.

"I think Michale and Nola will give you some seeds if you ask politely, and tell them it's for growing your own garden."

He looked back up hopefully. "You think so?"

Her little smile grew. "I think so."

Maryann gave Rikah and the other children an evening meal, but they slept there in the attic that night. Brutus came over and slept in the fourth bed, in case any of the children woke in the middle of the night. Rikah did have a nightmare, but when he woke, Brutus was already awake, sitting up with a candle lit, cuddling Bonny, who was sobbing quietly against his chest.

Rikah and Brutus glanced briefly at each other, but Rikah gave him a nod and lay back down. He watched the brother and sister until Bonny's crying subsided, and then was able to fall asleep again himself, and sleep until morning.

The next day, Stevry's parents came to fetch him, and Nola showed up for Brutus, Bonny, and Rikah. Stevry avoided looking at Rikah, but his parents thanked him profusely for his role in helping to save their son. It made Rikah blush and he muttered disclaimers in the direction of his shoes.

He walked back with Nola and her children to her house, where a big breakfast was waiting. Bonny was very quiet and wouldn't look at him, but no one pressured her to behave otherwise. She went and fetched a worn doll as soon as she was excused from the table, and sat hugging it on a bench outside the front door. Nola took some sewing and went to sit beside her.

"Brutus," Michale said, "will you see to the dishes?"

"Yes, Father," he said formally.

"Young Rikah, will you take a short walk with me?"

Rikah twitched, dropping his fork, but nodded obediently. Taking a walk seemed to be how Michale discussed important things. They got up and went out, passing the women on the bench. Rikah followed as Michale began a slow walk around the border of his fields.

"Maryann told me how you helped save Bonny and Stevry," the man said.

"Yes, sir," Rikah confirmed. "She told me what to do, and I did it."

"You must have stabbed that monster quite viciously."

"I did my best, sir," Rikah mumbled.

"Bonny might not be here, were it not for you."

Rikah didn't know how to respond, and just gave a guilty glance up at Michale.

"I'm glad she's alright," he said eventually.

"You know that body that was down there, that the monster had, it was my son, Benny. He was Bonny's twin."

"Maryann told me, sir."

"Oh," Michale grunted. "Did she tell you how he came to be down there?"

"Just the basics, sir," Rikah said quickly.

"I suppose the basics are enough, so I'll accept the basics that thanks to you and Maryann that monster is dead or gone, and I can put my son to rest, and my daughter is free of whatever hold that thing had on her."

Michale stopped walking, and Rikah stopped beside him.

"What were you trying to steal from my shed, young Rikah?"

He winced. "Seeds, sir."

"Seeds?" Michale seemed surprised.

"Where I live," Rikah began to explain, "the people I live with, they only hunt for meat, but me, the other kids and I, I mean, we need to have some vegetables and fruit. I prepared some ground for planting, but I haven't got any seeds. I didn't think to save some from last year when we gathered plants in the forest."

Michale stared down at him for a long moment, and then set a hand lightly on his shoulder.

"When Benny would have been ready to plant his first fields, I would have given him the starter seeds," the man said finally.

"I think you've earned what Benny would have gotten. I'll give you the seeds you need, Rikah, from one farmer to another."

He felt his throat choke up, and desperately fought not to cry, but when he spoke, his voice came out shuddering and broken. "T-th-thank you, s-s-sir."

Michale knelt and put an arm around Rikah's shoulders, and Rikah cried against his chest, like Bonny had cried on Brutus last night.

That afternoon, Rikah hiked to the clearing Thornspike had spoken of before. He still limped a little, but the pain was mostly gone. Over his back he had slung a small sack, full of a dozen other smaller sacks of different types of seeds. Michale had explained when and how to plant each of them, and how to care for them. He'd even taken a piece of palimpsest from the family's meager store, and written some tiny, cramped notes beside a drawing of each type of seed and what the seedling would look like when it sprouted.

He'd also told Rikah that he could come back anytime for more seeds or advice. Once Rikah had explained the size of his little field and the temperatures of spring, summer, and fall, Michale had adjusted which seeds and how many he'd given. It was not nearly as much as he would have actually given Benny, had Benny lived to start a farm of his own, but Rikah's needs were more modest than that.

Hawkswift was already waiting when Rikah reached the clearing. Her posture and the lay of her feathers revealed that she was relieved to see him, but hadn't yet forgiven him fully for running away on Thornspike. Still, she preened his hair and nibbled his ear in greeting, and helped him securely fasten the sack of seeds to her harness.

He was able to hold on this time, and she flew him safely back to South-scree. The whole time he worried about what he would say to Hawkmother. He had his precious seeds and the knowledge to plant them, but if it hadn't been for Thornspike and Thornwing and Hawkswift, the waterfall monster probably would have eaten him. It wasn't the first time he'd had a close brush with death, but he had to admit that his reckless behavior made this time a lot more his fault than the previous times.

After Hawkswift landed and he stored his seeds safely in his bedroom, he walked with her to the nursery. There, Rainsoft was entertaining Day and Night by letting them pounce on him, and Hawkmother was curled up in a fluffy ball amidst a deep nest of leather and fur covered cushions and pillows.

Hawkswift stopped several yards away, letting Rikah make his final approach alone. Hawkmother seemed to be sleeping, and Rikah hesitated a few feet away, but then she lifted her head to regard him.

"Hawkmother," he whispered, before she could speak. "I shouldn't have run off. I'm sorry. I got upset and frustrated and jealous, and it put me in danger and another human saw griffins, but she says she won't tell anyone. I did get some seeds, so now I can plant, but I realize I just should have waited for help. I'm really sorry."

The Hawkmother's crest fluffed up a little, and the feathers below her eyes lifted, like the cheeks of a human do when smiling.

"I'm so glad you're safe," she said.

Rikah let go a breath, and felt the easing of his tension.

"Come here," the griffin invited. She lifted a wing, revealing a fluffy ball of grey tucked against her hot apteria. "Meet your new sister. This is Hawkdawn."

The End

Hawkwings's Tale

These events take place five years after the invasion of Northnest when Hawkwind escaped with the four children.

"Good, excellent, faster now," Thornwing urged.

"Do you know what you're doing?" Hawkwind muttered to him.

"Not at all," he grinned back.

Jessika swung the heavy staff at the hanging bag, miscalculated, hit her fingers where she held the staff, and dropped it with an exclamation of frustration. She whirled on the grinning Thornwing.

"I can't go any faster," she shouted. "It's too heavy."

She kicked at the fallen staff, missed, and almost overbalanced. Thornwing tilted his head.

"You're too weak," he explained.

Jessika snarled and grabbed her hair in both hands. "I hate you," she declared.

"Hawkwings," Hawkwind scolded. "You do not."

Thornwing nudged the big female. "I know she doesn't. Watching humans grow is amusing. Griffin chicks go through similar stages."

Jessika seethed. "It's not a stage," she argued.

"Heard it before," Thornwing smirked. "Not impressed."

"You could be a bit nicer," Thornsoft gestured from where he was playing with Dawn, Hawkwind's newest chick. From her coloration, Jessika was pretty sure Thornsoft must be the sire, but the color of a chick's fluffy baby down could be deceiving, and there were more male grey griffins in South-scree than just Thornsoft. But still, Jessika was pretty sure.

"That would only encourage her," Thornwing said back.

"Isn't encouraging good?" Thornsoft asked by hand. Thornsoft couldn't speak aloud, and used a sort of sign language combined with posture and feather-talk instead.

Thornwing shook his head, human-like. "I'm talking about a different kind of encouraging."

"I'm done with this," Jessika declared, storming from the room.

"If you can't fight, how will you take back your kingdom?" Thornwing called after her.

Jessika didn't pause to reply. She headed down to the bathing chamber. She was awful at beating the hanging bag with a staff—she knew it—but the exercise still got her sweaty. Four years had passed since Hawkwind had been accepted at South-scree. Jessika and the other children were growing out of childhood. In a few more years maybe they could try to retake Northnest.

Jessika knew she had to learn to fight. The griffins had very few metal items, since they didn't mine and only a couple griffins in all the Aeries had any skill with metalworking, so learning to use a sword just wasn't possible. She'd been presented with a stick: a long, heavy stick. Hawkwind had seen human soldiers training with staves back at Northnest, so it was the best she could offer her adoptive daughter. Jessika's skinny arms just couldn't handle it.

Jessika stripped off in the bathing room. It looked like the glow stones hanging from the ceiling had just been renewed, so the room was nearly as bright as day. She started to put her sweaty clothes in a pile—and then stopped as something dark caught her eye. She fished the garment out and held it up: blood.

What was blood doing there?

Jessika checked again a few hours later. There was more blood. She fetched a clean bandage and hid in her room, her stomach in knots. Why was she bleeding? She hadn't gotten hurt. Soon, her belly was hurting even more than could be blamed on nerves. A couple hours later, the blood was soaking through the bandage.

"Wings?" Rikah called from outside her hanging leather door. "Want to go gather peas with me?"

"No, go away," she retorted.

"Oh, right, sorry." He left.

Jessika covered her mouth with her hands. What if the bleeding didn't stop? Her belly clenched and twisted and she transferred her arms to wrap around her middle. Tears leaked from her eyes and she started to tremble. She didn't know what to do.

"Jessika?" called another voice. She recognized Hawkwind. "May I come in?"

"I want to be alone," she said.

"Thornwing didn't want to hurt you. He was just being his cheeky self. You know that right?"

The male griffin's silly, provoking comments were the farthest thing from her mind. "Yes, I know. It's fine," she agreed.

"Are you still upset with him?"

"No, it's alright."

"Will you come out?" Hawkwind prodded.

Her throat choked up. "I want to be alone."

"What's wrong?"

"Nothing."

"Are you sick? Did you hurt yourself in practice?"

"No, I'm fine."

"Jessika," she said after a moment. "I'm coming in."

"No," she cried out, but the griffin was already pushing aside the drape and stepping through the doorway.

Hawkwind paused at the sight of her. "You are hurt, or ill. What happened?"

Jessika bit her lip, face burning with shame. Her pride resisted, but a deeper part of her knew she had to have help, and after only a few moments the sobbing began. Hawkwind went to her at once, encircling her in her wings, and in halting, broken words, Jessika whispered what was going on.

"I have never heard of this illness," Hawkwind said.

Jessika clung to her, weeping muffled against her furry chest. "Am I going to die?"

"No," the griffin assured her. "You're going to come with me. Can you hold on for a flight? We're going back to that village Rikah found, to talk to that woman."

They fetched a fresh bandage. Hawkwind told Hawkswift only that they were going out and not to expect them back until tomorrow. The older female looked surprised, but didn't say anything to challenge the Linemother. Jessika bundled up for the chilly flight, and Hawkwind carried her into the afternoon sky.

They flew into the night. The cold, the pain in her belly, and Jessika's anxiety kept her wide awake. Hawkwind's eyes weren't the best for night flying, but Hawkswift had taken her to scout the village before, after Rikah's little adventure with it, so she knew where to go. Once the moon was up and high, she eventually located it. Jessika was shivering almost hard enough to fall off by the time Hawkwind began circling down over the houses.

The midwife and healer Maryann had a cottage away from the best fields, since she was often paid in food for her work and didn't need to grow more than a small garden—mostly of medicinal herbs—for herself. The villagers kept dogs that would alert at strange sounds and smells, but Hawkwind arrowed straight down towards the cottage anyway. She flared her wings and landed on the path up to it.

"Get off now," the griffin urged. "Can you walk?"

Jessika slid down off her back, her cold, cramping legs buckling below her. Hawkwind helped her stand.

"Knock and go inside," the griffin told her. "The woman is a healer. She'll heal you. I'll come back and check on you just before dawn."

Jessika staggered, and looked back over her shoulder. Hawkwind nodded encouragement, and then leapt back up into the air. Jessika shivered in the wash of wind from her wings. She didn't think waking people up in the middle of the night was a good way to get their help, but Maryann was a healer, who was probably used to working all hours and getting disturbed for emergencies. The griffin healers were like that, though they didn't know much about healing Hawkwind's adopted human children.

Jessika looked to the house. She hadn't noticed before, but a candle was burning in the window. Heartened, Jessika approached and stepped up to knock—the door opened before she could.

"Well, hello," a tall older woman greeted her. She seemed to be dressed for day work, in a sturdy dress and apron, her hair under a cap, not like she'd been sleeping.

"Are you Maryann?" Jessika asked softly.

"That is I. Come in."

It was less an invitation than an order, and Jessika obeyed.

"Have a seat." The woman gestured at a stool by a large, rectangular table that dominated the room. "Cinnamon cookie?"

Jessika sat and stared at the lumpy round of confection Maryann placed in her palm. She took a timid bite as the woman shut the door and went to put a kettle over the low glowing fire. Then tears flooded her eyes again and she could barely swallow for the sobbing.

"There's blood, and my tummy hurts," she choked out.

Maryann provided a plate for the remains of the cookie, and held Jessika's quaking shoulders with firm hands.

"You're not from the village." It wasn't an accusation, just an observation.

Jessika shook her head. "I live with the griffins."

"I see. I suppose you're one of Rikah's siblings, then. What's your name?"

"Hawkwings," she said, holding back her human name from long habit—she was a princess of Northnest, and kept her identity secret both for her safety and the safety of other humans.

"How old are you?"

"Eleven, I think."

"Yes. Listen to me, Hawkwings. What's happening is normal."

That shocked her out of her crying and she looked up with wide eyes. "Normal?" she echoed, aghast.

Maryann smiled a little in sympathy. "It happens to all human females. I suppose it doesn't happen to griffin females?"

Jessika shook her head with confusion.

"If there were an older female living with you, she could have told you." Maryann pulled up another stool and sat. "You're not hurt or sick or dying. Since you didn't know about it, it makes sense that it's scary."

"This happens all the time?" Jessika breathed.

"No, not all the time: once a month. Let me explain, although some of it is still a mystery, even to a healer like me." She smiled a little with her shrug, and Jessika felt herself begin to descend from her panic, just a bit.

"It happens to you, too?" she asked.

Maryann nodded firmly. "It happens to me, too. This bleeding is a sign of your body maturing to your adult form. Once it starts happening, it means you could start having babies."

Jessika drew back in horror.

"You know how babies happen?" Maryann checked critically.

"Yes," Jessika replied. "It takes a male and a female, um."

"Having sex, right," Maryann filled in without a blush. "It's a completely normal process that most animals, and even plants, participate in. Your griffins make babies, right?"

"Only some of them: awakened females," Jessika answered. "Does this mean I'm awakened?" she gasped. "Does that make me the new Linemother? No, it couldn't," she answered her own question. "I couldn't make griffin chicks with—" She blushed so hotly it felt like her face was on fire.

"Well, if you had sex now with a human male, you could get pregnant," Maryann concluded. "Well, not right-now-right-now. Often, sex during the bleeding time won't result in pregnancy, but there are exceptions. Sex when you're not bleeding is more likely to get you pregnant. Have you been having sex?"

"No," Jessika blurted. "No, of course not."

Maryann gave only bland, calm reactions. That at least seemed to slow Jessika's ascent towards hysteria. "That's fine. If you don't want to, you shouldn't, but you live with that boy who came here a couple years back, Rikah?"

"Yes," she admitted.

"He'll be maturing soon, too. If you start having sex with him, you'll probably make a baby. Do you understand?"

Jessika could barely stay on her stool. "I'm not going to have—" she stuttered and choked. "I, no, not with Rikah," she declared, as though declaring she was not going to eat raw frogs.

Maryann nodded and said mildly, "You say that now, but you might change your mind as you both get older and more interested, or you might get interested in someone else."

"I won't," she insisted.

"Well, maybe you won't," Maryann allowed. "Some people never marry or have offspring, and that's their choice, and yours. I just want you to understand that sex leads to babies, now that you're old enough and maturing."

"Alright, fine," Jessika subsided through clenched jaws.

Maryann nodded and went to fetch the hissing kettle. Jessika nibbled at the rest of the cookie. It was quite good. She never had anything like cookies living with the griffins. Maryann came back with two steaming mugs and a jar of something. From the jar she sprinkled pinches of herbs into both cups.

"As for dealing with the bleeding," she went on softly. "That's something every woman has to face. Some women feel proud of their maturity and don't find it that much of a bother. Others are scared or upset, and even angry about it. It's possible you'll feel all those different emotions from time to time. Other than the blood, do you have any other symptoms?"

"My tummy hurts," Jessika confessed.

"That's something many women experience. Others have headaches or backaches, and moodiness. Drink this, it will help."

Jessika took the mug and Maryann stood again.

"There are other remedies. I'll give you some and write down the recipes for you. You can read?"

"Yes," Jessika retorted a trifle defensively. "Both griffin and Northnest writing."

"That's one more than I can," Maryann smiled, probably trying to soothe her.

"What do I do about the blood? How do I make it stop?"

"It should stop by itself after a few days, maybe as many as seven."

"Seven?" Jessika gaped, horrified.

"If it doesn't stop, come back and see me again. In fact, you can come see me whenever you want. Here, I'll also show you some different techniques to handle it."

Maryann was fetching books and paper and some other mysterious items and arranging them on the table. Jessika stared, trying to take in everything and wrap her brain around it.

"This is going to happen all my life?" Jessika asked weakly.

"No," Maryann said calmly. "It will stop, if you live long enough to become old. It also won't happen while you're pregnant or nursing a baby, probably."

Jessika wrinkled her nose. Maryann noticed and smiled.

"I'm glad you don't want babies right now," the healer said. "I think you're too young for it. Some women get married as soon as they start bleeding, and then you can imagine that the first baby comes soon after. Some young mothers get through having babies just fine, but others have trouble. Having seen a lot of births, I think women should wait until they're at least fifteen years of age to start. By that time they've gotten most of their full height and size."

"Griffins usually don't start having chicks until that age, too," Jessika offered.

"Oh?" Maryann said politely. "Do griffins marry?"

"No. They mate with whoever they want, when the females are in heat, but only one female in each Line is in heat at once. It's sort of complicated."

Maryann sat back down with her and began writing out of a book onto a spare piece of paper: tiny but legible writing, so she could fit a lot onto the one piece.

"Do you think you'll live with the griffins forever?" Maryann asked.

"I don't know," Jessika confessed, "but I don't think so, maybe though, if nothing else works out."

"You could come here to live," the healer said. "The village made the same offer to Rikah. He turned it down."

Jessika looked around the room. "You're not married."

"No, I'm not."

"And you don't have kids?"

Maryann gave her another little smile. "I don't."

"Why not?"

"All the children of the village are like my children. I'm there as they all come into the world. I've been there as some of them leave the world, too. Ever since I watched my father at this same work, I knew I would do as he did. He taught me all he knew. Who else would continue to take care of the people of this village when he was gone?"

"What about your mother?" Jessika asked after another sip of tea.

Maryann regarded her own mug silently for a moment. "My father delivered many babies with great success for both mother and child, but when it came time for his wife to bear the child he'd made with her, all his skills could not keep her in this world. The birth was too difficult. He saved me. He lost her."

"Oh," Jessika murmured after a few moments. "I didn't know. I'm sorry."

"It's alright. I never knew her, but he told me many stories about her."

"Are you afraid you might die, too, if you try to have a baby?"

"Of course," Maryann confirmed. "Any woman with sense would be afraid, but that's not why I chose not to."

Jessika nodded with understanding. "So who will take care

of your village when you're gone?"

Maryann nodded as she wrote a few more lines. "I need to choose an apprentice. I've been waiting for the right one to appear." Now she looked up, meeting Jessika's gaze across the table. "Would you like to stay here with me, and learn to be a healer and midwife?"

Jessika's eyes flew open. She became intensely conscious of the golden wings she knew—even though she could not see them—were tattooed on her back. She felt also a tug towards this woman: a human, someone who understood these things that were happening to her, who could relate as no griffin ever could, who could take care of her as no griffin ever could, who could teach her all the things she needed to know, and share with her all the extra things she needed to do and make to survive as a human.

It would be easy—well, not easy, but so much easier than how she lived now. She could live in a house, not a cave. She could use a kitchen to make human food, like cookies. Here in the village, there would be cloth and tools that would help her make the clothing and shoes she needed—or maybe she could even trade or buy them from an expert. Instead of learning to fight with a huge heavy stick she hated, she could learn to heal and help.

But there were golden wings tattooed on her back. Jessika shook her head.

"I can't."

"I see. If you ever change your mind—"

"No," she interrupted. "I'm sorry, I mean, it's not that I wouldn't if I could, but, I have a different destiny."

Maryann eyed her. "You choose your own destiny."

"You didn't. You were born to it, and you embraced it. I was born to mine, too. Of course, I didn't know about this bleeding thing. It's going to make things harder."

"I'll show you all the options and tricks I know. Has the tea made your tummy feel better?"

Jessika blinked with surprise. "Yeah, I do feel better."

"Good. That's one remedy that will help you then. You can also put the herbs on your food, or roll them into a tight little ball, coat it with honey, and swallow it. Look, I've written down the recipe. Do you know these herbs?"

Jessika looked and shook her head.

"I'll draw pictures of the plants, so you can harvest them, and give you a little supply of dried ones for now. You can come back and get more later, if you need to."

"You're very good at drawing," Jessika observed, as Maryann dipped her quill and went to work copying from her book.

"Thank you, Hawkwings. We all have our skills, and I've done this a lot. Normally, the women of the village can come to me here, for any remedies they need, but you live farther away, and though I'd always be happy to see you, I don't suppose you can easily come every month."

Jessika shook her head, finished her cookie, and drank the last of the tea while Maryann filled a couple more pages with writing and sketches. She went on to explain how to contain the bleeding, and handed over some supplies.

"Now, there is one more thing I want to talk about," Maryann said softly. "I've gone and scared you about dying while having babies and getting pregnant too young and all that, but let me ask you: do your griffin friends have sex for fun?"

"Urk, uh," Jessika's face heated in a blush again.

Each Line had a series of rooms for its matriarch. Some of course were for sleeping or relaxing or socializing, but there was always one room with a sliding door that opened onto a wide porch—so males could come and go. The rest of the Line avoided that room. It was private, just for the matriarch and her favorite males from other Lines.

Jessika swallowed roughly. "Yeah, sometimes."

Maryann smiled. "So do humans." She pushed another piece of paper at Jessika. "This is a recipe in case you someday want to have sex for fun, without having babies. You must drink this tea every day, except when bleeding. And," she grabbed Jessika's hand with both of hers, "it is possible for it to fail, rarely, but it happens. Keep that in mind. Whenever you have sex, even if it's just for fun, it could result in a baby."

Jessika swallowed. "Alright."

"Some people also say, that avoiding sex for the week after you stop bleeding, can avoid pregnancy, but that doesn't always work, either." She let go of Jessika's hand, and Jessika put the paper with the others. Maryann sat back and propped her head on her fist.

"Sex and love can be complicated," the healer said softly. "Sometimes, no matter what advice you get, even when you try to make the best choices, you make mistakes. Sometimes those mistakes have life changing consequences. Other times you just get emotionally hurt. I say 'just' but emotional hurt is not inconsequential, either."

Jessika shrugged, "I'm not going to be—"

"Hush and listen," Maryann instructed firmly. "It is possible to find someone to love deeply: who loves you back. More likely you'll encounter more imperfect matches. If you just want to have sex for fun, make sure the other person knows that, and feels the same, or you might hurt him, or her. It can go the other way, too. A person you like might just want sex for fun, but you want more. People aren't always honest. People aren't even always honest with themselves, much less with others."

Maryann sat back a little, and cradled her mug of tea in her hands. Her expression clouded over a little.

"Relationships that seem good can fall apart. People can get hurt. Some people are even abusive to the ones they're with. I am of the opinion that you should never want to hurt someone you love, and if someone hurts you, they don't love you, and you shouldn't tolerate it. It's also possible someone might try to force you to have sex, or coerce or pressure you into it."

The healer took a swallow of cooling tea. "I don't think you should have sex with someone unless you want it with every fiber of your being. If you feel uneasy or aren't sure," she speared Jessika with a look, "don't do it just because they want you to."

Jessika gave a weak nod.

"Of course our bodies inspire us to do foolish things," the healer went on, looking off into a corner of the room. "It's possible for your body to want it when your heart and mind don't. Most people make mistakes. Everyone gets hurt eventually, in some way. You'll learn from it. Take life as it comes, and accept your mistakes. You mustn't judge yourself for them. They're just things that happened. Learn from them; that's really the most you can hope for."

Jessika couldn't really grasp what she was talking about, but she nodded again anyway. Maryann leaned forward again.

"And one last thing," she said. "The first time you have sex will be exciting and maybe a little scary, and might not feel really good, so don't get your hopes up for ultimate bliss right away, alright?"

"Alright," Jessika grunted begrudgingly.

"Some people also try to frighten their daughters into not having sex by telling them that it's going to hurt. Have you heard that?"

Jessika shook her head.

"Well, they're partly right, maybe. It could hurt for some women, since there's a membrane—do you know what that is?"

Jessika nodded. Griffins ate their food raw. She'd seen a lot of anatomy.

"There's a membrane in you that's been helping to protect your developing insides. Once you're grown up, you don't need it anymore, and the first time you have sex it could make it uncomfortable, it could even hurt. Do you understand?"

Her eyes had widened. "I, uh, think so."

"Now, if you're happy about it, and excited to be with your chosen partner, then it will hardly be a big deal. Those girls who hear horror stories from their mothers and grandmothers? They're all scared of it. There's even a chance they end up getting married to someone they aren't really in love with. For them, they're frightened, they don't like the man, and have been told it's going to hurt." Maryann spread her hands. "Well, of course it hurts, in that situation."

Jessika was staring at the table, unsure what to think or say.

"If you've worked yourself up into all this fear of pain, there's no way you're going to be able to enjoy the good parts." Maryann shrugged. "So I say, pick someone you really want, acknowledge that the first time will be an awkward, new experience, and that there could be a bit of a sting, but let me also assure you that it can be extremely enjoyable, so look forward to that part. Most good things in life come with a bit of pain in one form or another."

She shrugged again. "And you know, the awkwardness you feel, your partner will probably be feeling it, too. Men have to figure out sex also. Some of them may strut around like roosters, but it's just bravado. It can be scary for them, too."

Maryann went silent, and Jessika continued examining the wood grain of the table.

"My words are just bouncing off, aren't they?" she remarked. "That's usually how it is."

"No, I'm listening," Jessika whispered.

"I can imagine all this is a big shock, especially considering you've grown up among griffins, and had no warning."

"Yes," she agreed. "I guess I hadn't really been thinking ahead to how adults make babies and that someday I could be involved in that. Some of it's really unfair, isn't it?"

"It can feel that way. The monthly cycle is a big price for women who never have babies."

"There's nothing to make it stop?"

Maryann gave her a sympathetic look. "I'm afraid not. You have no choice but to deal with it. It's rough sometimes, but getting angry doesn't improve the situation. You can, of course, get angry, if you want to, if it makes you feel better."

Jessika took a deep breath and let out a sigh. "I'll have to tell all this to my little sister, Hawksky."

"She's younger than you?"

"A little."

"Bring her here if you want, and I can tell her."

"Maybe that's best."

They sat in silence for a few minutes. Maryann refilled their mugs.

"Do you have any other questions?"

"There's too much in my head to be able to think of them," Jessika confessed.

"Come back any time and ask. Your griffin family is loving, I'm sure, but there must be a lot they don't know about being human. How did you get here, by the way?"

"A griffin dropped me off. She'll come back and get me just before dawn."

Maryann got up and cleared away the cookie plate and empty mugs. "I'll make up a bed for you in front of the fire, where you can sleep until she comes for you. I was just finishing up some remedies. I'm afraid that my hours are rather irregular."

"The light won't bother me," Jessika assured her.

Jessika awoke when she heard the sound of wings and a heavy thump. The night was still dark outside the windows, but Jessika got up and opened the front door to go see if it was Hawkwind. She hadn't been sleeping very well anyway. Maryann looked curiously through the door behind her. Hawkwind had landed, panting, dropping a dead and bled deer right before Maryann's front porch.

"I hate night hunting," the griffin grumbled. "Took me forever to catch it."

Jessika stepped onto the porch, and Maryann followed, staring wide-eyed at the deer.

"This is Hawkwind," Jessika introduced. "She's like my mother now. I think she brought the deer to thank you for all your help," she told Maryann.

The healer squeezed her shoulders. "You're very welcome."

Hawkwind pointed at the deer with a wing tip. "You know what to do with that?" she asked.

Maryann nodded. "It will be handled. Thank you."

Hawkwind's posture and feather-speak was still wary. "Did you cure my chick?"

"I'll explain it all," Jessika interjected. "I'm going to be fine."

"Yes," Maryann whispered, "you are."

Jessika turned impulsively and gave the healer a quick hug. Then she leapt over the deer and ran to Hawkwind. Her sack of new supplies securely around her shoulders, she pulled herself up onto the griffin's back.

"Have a safe flight," Maryann said.

Jessika waved, and then Hawkwind launched up into the first hints of dawn, wide wings carrying them back home.

The End

Hawksky's Tale

These events take place six years after the invasion of Northnest when Hawkwind escaped with the four children.

Kassandra Hawksky would have gone barefoot if she could have; she hated shoes, and all clothing, really. Unfortunately, both the rocky mountainside and the forest floor were too hazardous for unshod human feet. She ran from the high paths around South-scree almost nonstop down into the tree line, and skidded down the side of the steep ravine towards the snow melt-fed pool at its bottom, with her feet safely protected by a few layers of thick rawhide strapped to her soles.

Another spring had come to the mountain. All around, the delicate little alpine wildflowers were spreading their petals to the weak spring sunlight. Kassandra was ten years old, and knew better than to jump into that icy pool in the cleft of the ravine. In the peak of summer the weather would be warm enough—even up on the mountaintop—for swimming, but her fragile human body would have a hard time recovering after a dip in that water now. She still wore her heavy winter clothing, and the snow was barely off the ground.

She managed to halt her momentum and not go plunging into the pool. Her heart was pounding; a run like that after a season of inactivity deep under the rocks and snows of the Hawk Line burrows had left her weaker than usual. She stopped to crouch by the pool, tipping her face down over it to see her reflection breaking up and reforming over and over as more snow melt joined the pool from a dozen rivulets feeding it and sending ripples across the surface.

For a few minutes she sat there, panting and feeling the

cold radiating off the water while the sun just barely warmed her back. It didn't take long; as she'd hoped, as she'd expected, another reflection soon joined hers. Face near to bursting from the smile that bloomed across it, she lunged upward, throwing skinny white arms around the neck of the unicorn that had come to join her. For his part, the unicorn had lowered its head, but turned it, so that Kassandra's enthusiasm would not lead her to accidentally impaling herself on his horn.

"I'm so glad to see you," she babbled, "happy spring."

The unicorn made a pleased sound in his throat, though he sounded nothing like a horse. Kassandra's father had been a soldier in the Northnest castle, and she'd spent her first few young years there, too; she'd seen and heard a good number of horses, but the unicorns sounded nothing like them for the most part.

"I'm pleased to see you, too, little Sky," the unicorn replied.

He never moved his mouth, but Kassandra heard his words nonetheless. It had been like that ever since she'd first met him, six years ago when Hawkwind had been escaping the destruction of Northnest. When rainbow drakes had found them and attacked, Hawkwind had done her best to defend them, but it was this unicorn that had sprinted into the fray and ensured their victory. He'd been wounded. Kassandra still didn't quite know what he'd done or why, but he'd struck her in the forehead with the tip of his horn.

She pressed her face against his neck, breathing in his warm, slightly floral forest scent—nothing like how a horse smelled. The spot on her forehead where he'd struck her tingled like when her feet tingled if she sat the wrong way on the floor for too long, and she rubbed it against the unicorn's coarse winter coat, not that it made the tingling stop.

After he'd struck her forehead, after the fight with the drakes, she remembered she'd gotten really tired and had fallen asleep. She'd had nice dreams, such nice dreams that she'd never forgotten the way they'd made her feel. There had been such warmth and lightness. The hunger pains and sleep fatigue had faded out of her body and she'd seemed to float for a while.

In her mind she'd seen flowers and water and dark starry skies.

"What winter news have you to bring me?" the unicorn asked.

"Hawkmother had her next chick, a boy this time. She's calling it Hawkdusk. And Hawkwings matured."

"The Northnest princess, Jessika?" the unicorn clarified.

"Yeah."

"She's left her childhood?"

"Yeah. Now she's going to bleed every month, and have belly pain and headaches and stuff. It's sort of like when Linemothers have a monthly heat, but not exactly the same: messier and more painful."

The unicorn nodded his head a little. "Right. Not exactly the same. She is eleven years old?"

"Yeah."

"And you are ten."

"Yeah. Maryann the healer says it will happen to me, too, soon."

Kassandra kept her face against the unicorn's neck and hugged him a bit tighter.

"I don't want it to happen to me."

He went still, stiller than usual—which was already very still—and said nothing. Slowly, Kassandra drew away. The unicorn had his head slightly turned, eyes closed. He looked good, like he always did, even with his winter coat starting to get patchy. In winter his deepwater blue coat grew out into winter sky blue, and the rusty edging got sort of pink. His hock hair and chin hair got thicker, too, nearly hiding his smoky hooves in the case of the former. The blotches and speckles of mist gray and moon glow white on his coat were obscured and mostly hidden, although his steel and silver mane and tail remained largely unchanged, as did his long and loosely spiraling horn of ice smoke.

Kassandra put her little palms on his cheeks. "Glacier?" she whispered.

She almost never used his name, as it made him quiver, as it did now, but it got him to open his long lashed eyelids and turn his night-pool deep eyes onto her.

"Little Sky," he breathed into her mind, "if you mature as Hawkwings did, we unicorns will become uncomfortable around you."

"I won't see you anymore?" she blurted.

"You may see some sign of us," he murmured, "but you will move on into full humanness. You will take possession of your womanly power of creation, whether you use it or not. That is something we have difficulty being in close proximity to."

"No," she refused, wrapping his neck again with her arms, "maybe it won't happen to me. That's right, it'll never happen to me. Maryann says it's for making babies, and I don't care about making babies. It's stupid. Lots of female griffins never awaken; I won't either."

He sighed. "Yes, you will. It's not something you can stop. It's not your choice. You don't want it. Yet still, it will come."

The unicorn pulled away and then danced himself in sideways, curving his body towards her.

"Let's ride," he invited.

Unicorns did not have facial expressions similar to humans. They couldn't really frown or smile the same way, but they did move their face muscles, and the angle of their large deer-like ears expressed even more. Kassandra knew enough to interpret his face, ears, tone of mental voice, and body language as a cheerful smile—and a desire to move away from the conversation topic.

She went along with it, grabbing a handful of silvery mane, and hoisting herself up with a vigorous hop of her legs. Glacier wasn't as tall as many horses she'd seen, although another unicorn she'd met had been as large as the draft horses that had brought the massive carts of food and supplies into the castle. He was, however, agile and speedy enough that he made deer look lame. Kassandra wrapped his mane around both hands, lowered her chest flat to his back, and tucked her legs around his barrel, with her feet gripping under his belly. From there she had a view with her head against his withers, as he took off into the spring forest.

Giggles burst forth from Kassandra as Glacier leapt and danced through the trees, never showing any sign of fatigue. It was better than flying, she thought. As she rode, she glimpsed other unicorns joining them. Mostly, it was the red and gold females that seemed to live in the same area of the forest as Glacier. She knew their names because she saw and talked to them quite a bit. The fiery red one with black points was Volcano, and the gold one dusted with white and umber was Witch Hazel.

Kassandra tired first, long before Glacier was done running, and she simply closed her eyes and rode, her body perfectly in tune with his, feeling every stride and twitch and relaxation of muscle. His breath and heartbeat kept time with the thundering of his hooves, making a rhythm that lulled her half to sleep, and she felt again that warmth and lightness, and dreamed of water and flowers and starry skies.

She hardly noticed it when she slipped from his back and into the softest embrace of meadow grasses she could imagine. They somehow seemed to catch her and lower her slowly, so she didn't smack into the ground. Scents of spring flowers surrounded her. Birds sang uproariously, vying for territories and mates with their songs.

When Kassandra opened her eyes sometime later, Glacier, Volcano, and Witch Hazel were all gathered in the little meadow cropping the grass, which never seemed to get shorter. Even as she watched, areas they'd eaten over grew before her eyes to regain the lushness they'd had only minutes ago. How that could happen, she never knew. Certainly normal grass didn't do that. She sat up, feeling more than herself, as she did after every time she rode Glacier.

"Awake again?" he smiled with his ears and eyes.

"Yes," she said aloud.

Then she jumped to her feet, ready to repay the favor of the ride. She started with Glacier, sinking her fingers into his itchy winter coat and scratching, scratching, and scratching. Shed unicorn fur floated into the light, refracting rainbows along the hair shafts as she'd never seen griffin fur do. He rumbled and sighed—actually much like a horse this time—as she sought out all the little spots that she knew he couldn't scratch well himself. Of course, unicorns could and did get together to help scratch each other, but they seemed much pleased by human fingers.

When she was done with Glacier, she found Witch Hazel had moved closer. The golden unicorn stretched out her neck, nudging Kassandra's hand. The girl smiled and went to work on her dingy winter coat, too. On Witch Hazel it dulled her usually brilliant gold to a muddy yellow. Witch Hazel also smelled slightly different than Glacier, more like wind and sunlight. Volcano was the most distant of the three, but she too came over for winter coat scratches, and when Kassandra was done with the three of them, her fingers were aching and her clothing was coated with shed fur.

All during the scratching session she'd been noting the three unicorns tilting their ears at one another. She knew what it meant.

"So what were you all talking about?" she asked, trying vainly to brush the fur off her clothes.

Ears swiveled like daisies in a stiff breeze, all around the meadow. Abruptly, Volcano and Witch Hazel leapt away, vanishing into the shrubbery. Kassandra was too used to it to be insulted.

"We were talking about you," Glacier admitted.

"Talking about me taking up my womanly power and how you're all going to avoid me?" she replied, knowing her voice sounded bitter.

"We don't want to avoid you. We like you."

She sensed him hesitating. "But?"

Glacier walked over to a patch of chill spring sunlight and folded himself down into it. "Will you sit with me?"

Kassandra walked over, still trying to dust off the fur with her palms. She sat facing him, instead of how she usually sat leaning against his shoulder. He just looked at her for a while.

"Kassandra," he began softly in her mind, "surely you have wondered what it meant when I marked you, five years ago."

With exacting precision, he tipped his horn forward and touched the tip to the flower mark on her forehead. It sent a sharp shock through her, and she leaned away, rubbing her head.

"You've been here with us almost every day when you weren't snowbound in the griffin burrows," he went on. "You have seen more of us than any unmarked human, but soon the time will come for you to make a choice."

"What do you mean?"

"Before you take up your womanly power, as you put it, you can choose to stay with us. I gave you that choice when I took from you what I needed to survive the poison of the drake's evil." He switched his tail over the grass. "I could not leave such a debt unbalanced. I chose to get involved. I chose to step in and save you and your companions. I was hurt. That rainbow drake carried a great evil within it—put there by a vile magician. It entered my body, past my skin and my defenses. I would have died from it. You saved me. You didn't know what you were doing, but you came and touched me, and I felt your life, and I took a piece of it to heal."

Kassandra sat, hands clasped in her lap. "So that's what happened."

"I could not take, and not give something back," he went on. "All I could give was an offer of a choice. I marked you so other unicorns would know, and protect you."

Kassandra frowned, trying to figure it all out. "You took some of my life? So that means I'll die early? Sooner than I would have?"

He shook his head humanlike. "What I took grows back. I cannot directly alter your fate. Your presence then gave me a choice. Thus, I gave you a choice in return."

Her hands were clasped together so tightly they hurt. "What's the choice?"

"So that you understand, I must tell you a little about unicorns," he said. "We are immortal. We do not die from old age or illness, though we can be killed. As we do not die, we must be made. We cannot breed ourselves naturally, as other animals do. All the copulation in the world will not make a baby unicorn, unless we have a donor."

"A donor?" she echoed.

"It requires an offering, a gift, a promise and a sacrifice, a willing one, only and ever. Little Sky, close your eyes."

She found she'd gotten chill bumps. "What?"

"I'm not going to hurt you. Close your eyes and allow yourself to recapture what you feel when we're running through the forest. I want to show you something."

Trembling a little, she obeyed, and felt Glacier's warm, oddly alive-feeling horn slide gently against her right temple, near her hairline.

His voice seemed to resonate in her head more than usual. "When you are ready, when you have that feeling, open your eyes."

It took her a few minutes to still the nervous pounding of her heart, but at last that sense of flowers and stars permeated her thoughts, and when she opened her eyes, her heart nearly stopped.

Kassandra threw herself backwards with a shriek of surprise, and the vision vanished. Glacier sat before her looking as not-quite-horse-like as he always did, but for just a moment, when she'd opened her eyes she'd seen something else.

There had been a boy not much older than she, with sandy red hair and freckles, dressed in rough farm clothes, lying on his belly, smiling, and holding her hand, forehead with a little pink five petalled flower shape on it, not much more than a few inches away from hers. His eyes had been blue.

She put her hands to her mouth, shaking.

"That was me, a long time ago," Glacier said gently.

Kassandra surged up to her feet, pacing blindly around the clearing. She touched the shape on her forehead.

"I was marked," he went on. "I made my choice."

"You, they, you can turn me into a unicorn?" she blurted.

He shook his mane. "Not exactly. There are a couple stages to the process. I can explain it to you, at least some of it, if you'd like to hear."

Kassandra took deep breaths like she knew people were supposed to do when they were upset, to help calm down, and sat again facing Glacier.

"All right then. Tell me."

"No power I know of can transform your human shape into that of a four legged creature like a unicorn. You cannot be turned into a unicorn in this life. You can, however, be prepared and promised, so that when you die, your soul is already set in its path, to have you born a unicorn foal a year later. This cannot happen if you mature into an adult human female."

"Does that mean I have to die soon?" she whispered back.

"No, not at all. Instead, you become a nymph for the rest of your human-like years. Whenever you do happen to die, you begin your immortal life as a unicorn."

"How do I become a nymph? What is that?"

"You bathe in a certain pool, with two unicorns in attendance. Nymphs are creatures of nature, of the forest, of the wild. You would retain all your memories, knowledge, and abilities. Your mind would remain completely you, but your body would be somewhat changed, and you would never mature into an adult human."

Kassandra found herself shivering again. Glacier threw his head up a little, tossing his mane.

"Little Sky, you must ask yourself what you want in your life. Do you want a human mate and children? If you do, this path is not for you. Also, after becoming a nymph, you won't be quite like your human companions in the griffin city anymore. There's no reason you couldn't still live with them and do everything with them that you do now, except that you will be a little different, and if that bothers them or you, then it won't be the same."

"I don't do much with them even now. I only see them in

the morning and evening, and sometimes not even then, if I stay overnight in the forest with you." She looked at her fingers and arms. "I'd still have my hands and everything?"

"Yes."

"How would I be different? Other than not having the monthly bleeding thing and not being able to have babies?"

Glacier didn't look directly at her. "You won't feel the cold as much, and won't need to eat as much. You'll be quicker, more agile, have better vision and hearing, be sleepier in the winter, and crave the sun. You'll have," he paused as if to search for a word, "an affinity with plants and animals."

"Are there any nymphs I could meet? To see what they're like and hear their stories?"

"No, but every unicorn was once a nymph. I enjoyed it."

"How did you choose?"

"I went out in a blizzard to find a lost sheep. I got lost myself, and found not the sheep, but a unicorn foal, also lost. I carried it to a sheltered place. Its parents were grateful, but I was near death from freezing. They gave me the choice to save my life. I agreed. They took me to the pool directly, and I changed to a nymph. It was the only thing that saved my life. Then I had many years, a full life, as a nymph."

"How did you die in the end?" Kassandra asked breathlessly.

Glacier was silent for a few minutes, and Kassandra let him take him time. "Nymphs don't really show age. They don't get wrinkled and grey like humans do. They start to get slow and quiet. They pick a place they like and stay there. Eventually, they grow down into the soil and up towards the sun. Then after a while, their mother comes to visit them, and the soul departs, moving from the tree into the mother unicorn."

"You turned into a tree?"

He pointed with his chin. "That one."

Kassandra looked. A massive oak tree stood to one side of the clearing. She got up, went to it, touched its bark lightly, and then leaned against it. It felt like a good tree.

"You don't need to decide today, little Sky," Glacier said.

"But soon."

"Yes, this summer probably. I doubt you will remain a girl another winter." He stood up to shake his coat. "If you decide to do it, there is something else you must do first. You will need to choose your parents. Both must be present when you bathe in the pool."

"I get to choose?"

"You do." He slowly stretched each leg, carefully not looking at her, although she was watching him. "Although I marked you, you do not necessarily have to choose me as your sire, but I would be honored if you did. I have never sired a foal."

Pressure welled up in Kassandra's chest and she ran to him, throwing her arms around his neck again. "Of course," she exclaimed, "of course I'd choose you."

He bowed his head over her, hugging her with his chin against her back. "Little Sky, you must take some time to consider before you decide if you want to become a nymph and promise your soul to the clan."

"Oh," Kassandra hiccuped. "Right. I guess, I just jumped ahead to thinking I'd do it."

"Go back to South-scree, see your friends. Think about it for a while."

To confirm, she asked. "If I don't do it, I just go on being human?"

"The mark on your forehead will fade to the faintest freckle, and we unicorns will melt back into the forest. From then on, if you see us, it will be only by accident. You will mature and be able to fall in love, have children of your own, and die as all mortal things do, in your time."

Kassandra drew slowly away. "I understand. Please take me back to South-scree. I'll do as you suggest, and think about it."

She mounted up and he took her, more slowly this time, back through the forest. She dismounted where he'd met her that morning and she began walking away, back up the ravine, her only farewell a little pat on his shoulder. She passed Rikah's field where he was at work cleaning up detritus now that the snow was off, doing the earliest preparations for planting. He waved. He'd gotten pretty good at farming, but it would still be easier for him to supply them all with vegetables if she were eating less.

She saw the griffins flying about in the chilly air before she reached the edge of the settlement. Chicks born during the winter were getting their first glimpses of the sky before being bundled back inside where it was warm. Dozens of young griffins were out on balconies and rooftops vigorously preening. Their feathers shone scarlet, onyx, steel, silver, umber, gold, and snowy white, fresh from their winter molts. Older griffins, feathers fluffed up, attempted sunbathing in the still frigid air. Kassandra knew some of them by name and a few greeted her with waves and calls.

Karolan would be off somewhere with Thornfire, probably. He was the other human child of South-scree that she saw least frequently. Jessika would probably be in the practice hall or with Hawkmother and the chicks. Kassandra trotted into the Hawk Line burrows and sought out the nursery.

It was a few halls and turns and a long ramp down, through some canvas and leather and tanned fur doorways, ever darker, ever deeper, and ever slightly warmer until Kassandra turned into the nursery. It was a large room with some narrow air shafts up, lit mainly by stones in the walls that Starbright or Thornfire, and some day Karolan, had used magic on to make them glow.

Hawkday and Hawknight, the oldest chicks, were playing some kind of game that could probably best be named "pounce on my sibling's butt." They didn't have tail feathers yet; all of their body parts that would have feathers in another year or so still only had downy feather fluff in shades of brown, gray, and rust. The third chick, Hawkdawn, was curled up with the newest chick, Hawkdusk, and Hawkmother in a pile of pillows. Hawkdusk was still quite tiny, and his eyes were still sealed shut. He made almost constant soft chirping sounds, and Hawkmother was rumbling back to him, reassuring him of her presence. Hawkdawn had her eyes fixed on him, as if fascinated.

"Sky," Hawkmother greeted with a smile.

Kassandra walked over to the trio and knelt on a pillow. She'd already met Dusk, although she couldn't imagine that he had any real idea of who or what she was. She'd never say it aloud, but the chick looked decidedly unappealing to her. She expected human babies would give her roughly the same reaction.

"Swift and Joy are bringing back some food," Hawkmother said.

"I saw Dare looking over his field. He'll be planting food soon, too," Kassandra contributed, just to be polite.

"And what have you been doing?"

The question was friendly, completely without malice, but Kassandra found it hard to reply.

"I was in the forest," she said. "I saw many signs of spring."

Hawkmother nodded. "It's my favorite time of the year."

Kassandra stood. "I think I'll get myself something to eat."

"Are you feeling all right?"

"I'm fine. I'll see you later."

Kassandra left the nursery, went to the larder, and got some dried meat to chew on. She didn't like meat much, but it was all there was now, all the stores of dried peas and potatoes having been used up. Meat in hand, she let herself wander out into the streets of South-scree. The griffin city did have streets, although some of them were still covered in a little melting snow where shadows fell, but the streets were not often straight or regular, as the city had been built rather randomly over time, without much direction from the central governing body. Plus, griffins could always fly, hopping over buildings as needed, so efficient streets hadn't been a high priority.

Kassandra simply wandered, looking around. There was nothing in particular she liked about the city. Griffins didn't care much for appearances so there was no attempt for architectural greatness, and little grew up this high except for lichens so there were no gardens. The lichens did color much of the stone in patches of reds, oranges, yellows, and whites, and there were a few features like signs made out of wood, but mostly the city was uninteresting. The forest fascinated Kassandra far more than this mountaintop town ever could.

"Hawksky," called a cheery but rough old voice.

Kassandra looked around to spot a griffin approaching. It was Thornfire, an elder and mage of the Thorn Line. He'd been one of the first griffins to extend a friendly hand to Hawkwind and the four human children when they'd arrived in South-scree. He was still helpful to them, and was training Karolan in magic.

"Thornfire, good afternoon," Kassandra said.

"And to you," he replied, still cheerful. "You look pensive today. Might I walk a bit with you?"

"Certainly, you may," Kassandra replied politely.

They continued down the path she'd been walking.

"What troubles you on this fine spring day?" Thornfire asked lightly.

"My future," she said simply.

"Ah. We all can become troubled about our future. Yours indeed may be different than most. There is little precedent for humans growing up with griffins. Might I venture that you need not spend too much effort on gnawing over it for at least a few more years yet?"

"No, I need to think about it now," she said, "but thank you for your reassurance."

"Hawksky, even adults with far more years of life behind them than you have are often at a loss as to how their lives should be spent. I feel that way, and I have already lived probably more than half of my allotted years."

Kassandra nibbled her lower lip. "So what do you do when you have a chance to make a huge choice that will completely change your life, and you have to decide quickly?"

Thornfire eyed her with a slightly more serious gaze. "You turn to your trusted loved ones, like you parents or siblings or elders, and ask their advice, and then you spend what time you have to try to make the best decision you can, all the while understanding that it may not be possible to make a decision you will not regret in some way, when you get older and wiser."

"Yes," she said slowly, "I suppose that sounds right."

Then she stopped and gently grabbed two handfuls of Thornfire's thick winter fur. He stopped walking compliantly.

Kassandra struggled to put her thoughts into words. "But what if you know what you want to choose already, but choosing it means such a huge change, that other people might not like, and that will mean nothing will ever be the same again."

He looked seriously down at her, and then pulled her aside, off the path so others could use it. Thornfire sat down in front of her and put his wings loosely around her back.

"Hawksky, Kassandra," he murmured slowly, "in all things, you must follow what is in your heart, not what anyone else wants, but what you want, unless your actions would hurt someone you have responsibility for. You are a child, and no one depends on you for protection or food or shelter, so your life is entirely your own."

She absorbed that for a few moments, but didn't speak, sensing that he wasn't done.

"I don't know what huge change, or choice, you are talking about, since you haven't confided to me the details, and I'm not going to ask you for them. My only concern is that you take care of yourself. Don't put yourself in a place where you surrender your safety to someone you don't trust completely, and if you need anything, anything at all, you can ask me and I will help you. Is that all right?"

Kassandra nodded, doing her best to smile. "Yes, Thornfire, yes. Thank you."

He set a hand on her head. "You're getting tall," he grinned. "Everyone who knows you wants you to be happy, and this place is not the best for humans. If you have a chance at something different, something better, something that makes your soul sing, then perhaps you should take that chance. In times when I cannot decide which course of action to take, because neither is perfect, and I may have regrets no matter what I choose, I try to choose that which I feel I am destined to do. However, sometimes that is not the easiest choice, and it can lead me to places I did not expect. Do you understand?"

"Yes, yes, thank you," she said again.

Kassandra lunged in and hugged him, rubbing her face into his neck fur and feathers.

"Have I given you some assistance with your thinking?" he asked.

"I think so," she declared.

He bowed his head a little. "I am glad to be of service."

Kassandra pulled away and reached out to smooth the feathers she'd rumpled. "How is Rain these days? I almost never see him."

"Hawkrain does well in his studies, although his attitude is improving less quickly," Thornfire said. "He is stubborn and overeager and impatient, much like many young mages. Magic requires discipline, and all mages must learn it. He will learn, too, in time."

"Because he has such a good teacher," Kassandra winked.

"Flatterer," Thornfire teased. "You have learned that from my brother."

"I think I'll go back to the Line now," she said. "Thank you for the chat."

"Any time. Fair winds to you, Hawksky."

Kassandra turned and started to run off. She waved over her shoulder. "Goodbye."

Glacier's flank provided a warm, slightly moving pillow as Kassandra lay in the little meadow under the oak tree Glacier had once been and watched the leaves flickering among the branches. The leaves were bright green and new in the spring sunlight. She felt she could watch them forever and never be bored. Over the past week she'd thought and thought and reexamined her mind and heart multiple times a day, but her longing never changed.

"Glacier," she whispered, "I've decided."

His body shifted as he lifted his head and curved it around. His silver mane brushed Kassandra's cheek as he angled an eye down at her.

"You've decided?" he echoed.

She reached up and twined her fingers through his mane. "I want to stay with you, here, in the forest. I want to become a nymph and someday join your clan, and I want you to be my sire."

"Are you certain?" he asked slowly.

She nodded, once. "I am certain."

A breeze played through the meadow, stirring leaves and grass and Glacier's mane. It felt like the forest had just witnessed and approved her decision.

"Then we must begin preparations," Glacier said. "You'll need to choose your mother. The chance to mother a foal is something that comes along so rarely, most of the mares here will be interested, and I am not unpopular."

"How many mares are in the clan?"

"Oh, a dozen or so, but it's important you feel a genuine connection to the mare you choose, so don't choose hastily. There will also only be a few times the ceremony can be done. A new moon is required, and it must be at night. As close to midsummer's day as possible would be best, although my ceremony was during the winter, but it was close to midwinter's day. Those two days are the most powerful, and the closer you are to one of them, the stronger your magic will be."

"Magic?" Kassandra's eyes popped wide.

He bobbed his head. "Of course. Unicorns are magic, though it is not magic like the mages have. Nymphs have some magical qualities about them, too."

She sat up and folded her hands. "So, as for choosing my mother, can it be Witch Hazel?"

Glacier chuckled both in her head and aloud. "Oh, no, I'm afraid not. She is my big sister."

"What? You never told me that." Kassandra felt slightly offended.

His eyes seemed to twinkle. "She's the one I saved from the blizzard when I was a human boy. Her dam and sire are my dam and sire, too, for they're the ones who took me to the pool."

"Oh, I see."

His amusement faded a little. "I can tell already that Volcano would not be your choice."

"She's nice but," Kassandra trailed off.

"You two have never developed a particularly affectionate bond. That's all right. You can't force something like that."

"I don't know the other mares of the clan very well."

"You shall meet them all. You'll have a couple months to pick."

Kassandra had never seen so much of the forest. Glacier took her long distances to visit unicorn mares of every age and coloration. There was Willow, the pure white unicorn who had particular ideas about what being a unicorn really meant. Kassie found her to be a bit too snooty. The gloriously orange and indigo Sunset was joyous and careless—so careless that Kassie feared entrusting her future helpless newborn foal self to her. Whisper was a shy, gentle mare, light blue in color and of a truly sweet nature, except that she didn't seem to have any enthusiasm for the idea of being Kassie's future mother, although she said she'd do it if they couldn't find anyone else.

There were others, a dozen others, and at last when Glacier had taken Kassandra to meet them all and the pair returned to Glacier's meadow to watch the leaves dancing in the wind, Kassie stared at the sky and felt a little concerned.

"I suppose Whisper would be acceptable," she said to Glacier. "The most acceptable, I mean, out of all of them. At least she seemed responsible and kind. You're excited about having me as your foal, even if my mother wouldn't be. That would be enough, I guess."

Glacier rumbled uneasily. "I didn't see a true match for you with any of them. Even those that were interested didn't seem to fit your personality. I confess I'd thought this would be easier.

It is your choice, but I'm not sure I liked any of them for your mother, although they are all lovely and unique." He sniffed and shook his head until his ears flapped. "Perhaps my standards are too high. I just want the perfect mother for you."

"There's no one else?"

"Not in this clan. We could look outside the clan, but it would mean venturing farther away. It is done sometimes, when options are limited."

Kassandra stroked his mane and pondered the mares she'd met again. As friends, she would have liked any of them. As her future mother, she had a different set of criteria.

At last Glacier said, "There is one other."

"Oh, who?"

"She is not an active part of the clan. She keeps to herself. I have not visited her in some time. Many years ago, she was splendid. Since then she has ventured far afield and her journeys have changed her. We would need to see how she is now."

Kassandra sat up excitedly. "Let's go see her. What's her name?"

"Violet. She is far older than I am; she might not consider me a worthy mate. She was also rather disturbed the last time I saw her. Don't get your hopes up. Let's save the visit for tomorrow."

Kassandra tried to squash down her excitement. "All right. I can wait until tomorrow."

"It is still a few weeks until the new moon nearest to midsummer. We can still go visit another clan if Violet is not the right choice."

The next day, Glacier took Kassandra in a direction away from the glades where the clan unicorns lived. They crossed into a rocky area where only twisting, hardy pines grew. The footing was difficult even for a unicorn, but Glacier made it through without injury. At the edge of the rocky area they came to a patch of thick leafed thorny plants. Glacier stopped before them.

"I believe this is Violet's demesne."

"What's a demesne?"

"In the case of unicorns, it's something like our home territory, but it is more than that. We can affect it, consciously or unconsciously. If we want we can purposefully cause certain plants to grow there, or try to attract certain animals. Our thoughts and feelings can also affect our immediate surroundings. If we are happy, sad, angry: any strong internal sensations might manifest themselves in the world around us."

He nodded towards the wall of thorny, spiny plants. "If this is Violet's demesne, it does not bode well."

"What happened to her?" Kassandra asked softly.

"None of us know all the details. She was happy for some time, the old ones say, until she decided to travel and see other parts of the world. She took a short trip, and came back pensive and discontented. Then she took a long trip, and no one saw her for many years. When she came back, she was ill and distraught. She couldn't bear to be around other unicorns anymore. She came here. In time, this grew up around her."

Glacier's head swayed. "I had hoped she might have started to recover. I only met her a few times before she began her travels. I must admit to you, Sky, that I was smitten. I was easily impressed in those days to begin with, but Violet had some quality to her that strongly appealed to me, something of unbridled joy and thoughtless enthusiasm. She lived and breathed in the moment, following with such agility the music of the world, the steps of the life-dance. I met her again after she came back, when this started growing, and saw that her fire had been snuffed out."

Kassandra petted his neck. "Let's go in. Let's see her. Whether she should be my mother or not, maybe we can help her. Has anyone tried to help her?"

"Many tried to help her. She refused to be helped. You'll see."

Glacier touched his horn only lightly to the first vicious frond blocking their path, and it withered before their eyes, dripping into black goop. They continued slowly into the knot of plants, stepping over or around what they could, and melting anything unavoidable with a brush of Glacier's horn. The plants were tall, dark green and veined with purple and red. They could have been lovely if they hadn't been twisted into hulking shapes, and so thickly studded with thorns and prickles. The leaves and stalks closed over them and shut out the sky, so they moved through murky twilight.

Soon, Kassandra noted a change in the vegetation. The big leafed plants with the potential for loveliness gave way to heavy, winding briars with more thorn than leaf. They didn't stretch up so high, however, so a little more light leaked down to the ground, which was bare except for patches of moss and occasional tenacious forbs—and here and there a thin, climbing pale green vine which limped and stretched its way up among the needled giants, with soft little leaves and tiny lavender flowers. It reached weakly towards the sun.

Then the briars revealed a clear spot, and at the back of it, lying on naked rock, was a unicorn. Kassandra slid down from Glacier's back and put her fingers to her mouth. She took two unsteady steps and then knelt down. She didn't know whether to cry or shout in anger.

"Can you help her?" she begged. "Glacier, can you get her out of there?"

The unicorn had a coat the color of stormy skies, and an indigo and black mane and tail, but she was so filthy the colors could hardly be seen. Dirt, grime, and sludge caked her fur and hair, and mixed liberally with the clotted blood from open wounds all over her body. Some wounds looked like burns, others like rips and slashes from claws. All of them were festering. Interspersed with the open wounds were bruises and contusions in the multi-colors of purple, blue, yellow, and green.

Wrapped around her were those briars that had become more common the closer Glacier and Kassandra had come to the center of the demesne. They were a brown so dark as to be black, with sharp straight spines as long as Kassandra's palm and as thick at the base as her thumb. The briars were entwined around the unicorn's body, with the spines sunk into her flesh more than half their length. Where they pierced her, the skin was swollen and crusted with blood and pus.

More phlegm and seepage coated her mouth, nose, eyes, and was caked around her tail and back legs. She lay in a pool of it. As Kassandra watched, her chest heaved to take a breath, and then went still for several of the girl's own breaths, before taking another one. The unicorn moaned a little on each exhalation and seemed totally unaware that she had visitors.

"I can do nothing, little Sky," Glacier said softly. "We are at the center of Violet's demesne. All you see here she has wrought herself. She is far older than I am, and her magic is stronger. To try to change her demesne here at its core is far beyond me."

Kassandra lifted her palms. "Then, can I touch her and help her?"

"You can touch her, if she'll allow it, but you don't have the power to change her demesne either. Anything you do she will restore immediately, because all this you see isn't real. It didn't grow by itself. That path I managed to make to get us to the center will have been repaired already. What we are seeing is an external manifestation of what she is feeling and thinking."

"But she looks sick."

"She is sick, but not physically. She is wounded, but not to her body. Those briars are wrapped around her because her mind has put them there. She only looks like this because of what she's making with her magic."

"So she's doing this on purpose?" Kassandra asked, wide-eyed.

Glacier touched her gently with his nose. "Not on purpose, but yes, she's making it this way. In a way, she has trapped herself her, and doesn't know how to escape."

"Why is she doing it? How do we get her to stop?"

"I'm not sure. Others of the clan have tried to help her, but nothing has made a difference."

"How does she eat and drink? Can we at least bring her some food?"

Glacier shook his mane. "Unicorns don't have to eat or drink.

We won't starve to death; we'll just get very hungry, forever."

Kassandra stared a while longer. "Can I at least go talk to her?"

Glacier nodded his heavy head. "I'd rather hoped you would, but you have to accept that she might not even acknowledge your presence. It could be that what is left of her consciousness is too deep for anyone to reach."

Kassandra shook her head and stroked his mane. "No, did you see among the big thorny plants, there were these little ones, with purple flowers?" Kassandra sought around until she saw one of them, struggling to grow up vainly among a patch of briars. "Here, did you see these?"

Glacier followed her over to look, his ears twitching in surprise.

"See?" Kassandra said. "Part of her is still reaching for the sun. Part of her still wants to make beautiful things. She's just struggling under all these briars, under all this pain."

Without waiting for Glacier's response, she strode over to the motionless Violet and knelt in front of her nose. The unicorn had her neck and head stretched out along the ground: head on its side so only one of her closed eyes was visible. There was a little puddle of congealed pus under her face. Her horn was dark and cold.

"Violet," Kassandra began evenly, "I came to see if you'd like to be my mother. I'm going to be a nymph. Glacier chose me because I helped to save his life, and I've chosen to accept the gift he's offering in return. Glacier said you're wise and strong, and that you were once full of bright joy. He said he was smitten with you, but that now you're in pain, that you're hurt. Will you tell me what happened to you?"

Violet made no response, but Kassandra thought there might have been a slight quiver of her sunken eyelid.

"When I was five years old some magicians and monsters attacked my home," she went on, her voice quavering. "They killed everybody. My mother was already dead, before that. A man from the city hit her when she was coming back from the market and she died. After that, we moved to the castle and my dad became a guard. During the big war my father took me to the safe room in the castle, and then he went back out to fight. I guess he's dead now, too. Hawkwind got me out and now I live in South-scree with the griffins. Now the monsters and magicians live in Northnest. All the griffins that were there are dead, too, I guess, except Hawkwind."

The unicorn's eyelid quivered again. Some clear liquid leaked from it, melting the crusted yellow seepage sealing it shut, and then it opened. It looked at Kassandra and she looked back.

"That's what happened to me. So what happened to you?" Kassandra asked.

For a moment, there was no response, and then Kassandra cried out and clutched her head as a sudden flood of images poured into her mind, replacing the true sight of her eyes, giving her no choice but to see them.

Violet, venturing afield, pristine coat and mane and tail streaming in the wind, met a winged horse—a pegasus, a gentle, sweet pegasus with a dark golden coat and even darker mane and tail. They roamed together for a while. Upon parting, he nuzzled Violet: affectionately.

Confused, Violet wandered back to where she'd started, but could not forget him. She returned to the wilds, but could not find him. She found instead a strange looking creature that Kassandra knew no name for. It looked rather like a large goat, but with thick, black shining fur and dramatically arching horns.

In the visions, Kassandra saw how the creature pranced and charmed and cajoled. At first, Violet tried gently dissuading the goat from its overly friendly advances, but the unicorn, still seeking the pegasus she couldn't find, soon was instead distracted by the company of the goat-beast, and clung to it in her state of loneliness. The goat appeared to have no qualms about taking advantage of that.

Then Violet began breaking from the goat's company, starting to regret when he didn't express the same affection for her that she was developing for him. The goat simply trotted off as though nothing had happened. That gave Kassandra some thoughts to chew over, but there wasn't time. In the visions, Violet had resumed her search, although with somewhat less enthusiasm now.

Violet's visions skipped ahead, implying the passage of time. She journeyed alone now, rejecting any company. Finally, in a summer season, she found him. He looked more beautiful than he had before, fuller of wing, more graceful of leg, stronger of neck and chest. Kassandra felt Violet's elation through the vision. The unicorn ran to him with feet that practically flew over the ground.

And then another pegasus stepped up beside him. It was a female: his mate.

Violet's legs locked into solidity harder than stone. Kassandra whimpered as she felt Violet's emotional pain. Palaces of foolish hope and devotion burned into cinders, leaving a barren, empty plain behind. There had once been a forest of freedom and joy, before Violet's dream palaces had encroached. Now, all was gone; nothing would grow there.

Through the pain, Violet was polite. Her face smiled and her words were friendly even as her city of folly burned. She got a moment alone together with her pegasus, briefly, before departure, before the last structure burned, and she told him of her regard. There was still the chance to stop the fire and rebuild.

His rejection was kind and gentle.

Violet fled, not with fury, but with the simplicity of falling down, of letting go.

She wandered without destination, and in time started to recover, but she'd done damage to herself, and it showed. Deep, bruised sores appeared on her body. Her mane and tail lost their luster. Her horn dimmed.

She met another creature on her now aimless travels, one different from the goat and the pegasus. He was more like a dog, or a cat, with paws instead of hooves, a long tail, and luxurious thick fur, but Kassandra didn't have the knowledge to put a name to what he was. His frisky, sunny company brought some cheer back to Violet. For three seasons they kept company, and at times Violet looked almost healed. This magical creature of the wilds seemed to comfort and care for her, and it was clear he had captured her mending heart.

Yet, at other times she was gripped by deep sorrow and pain that shook her, and she could do nothing but endure them until they faded for a while. Her companion could not heal her of such episodes, and sometimes avoided her when she was in the grasp of them. It seemed that Violet couldn't blame him for that; she couldn't control the bouts of weeping and didn't know where they came from, either.

A day came after several moons together when Violet confessed her love for her companion, although Kassandra sensed that the unicorn wasn't sure of it even as she said it. Maybe the object of her affection sensed the same thing, for he did not reply in kind, but only with polite words of friendship. Still, Violet did not leave him, and Kassandra thought perhaps even one sided love was better than solitude when there were so many wounds to the heart.

She did not get to keep her furry companion, however. He announced he had to go away, not because he disliked Violet, but because his pack needed him elsewhere. To Violet, it was another wound. She asked if she could go with him; he did not seem to care. Violet realized that nothing would be different if she went with him. He still would not return her love.

He left. Violet mourned. Although she knew she could follow him, he had not filled her emptiness, only provided her with a distraction, and in some way she was grateful to be parted from him. Violet turned her hooves towards home. As she walked, she allowed her emptiness to eat away at her. She thought back over all her mistakes, treading them over and over until they wore a path into her psyche. Eventually, she ended up where she was now, too rotten with her own self-loathing to go any farther. Her demesne had grown up around her, and she wallowed in it.

Kassandra blinked a few times as the enforced visions faded and she sat again before the current Violet. Behind her, Glacier shook his head until his ears flapped.

"When she first came here, others of the clan, including myself, came to help her, but she only spoke to us," he said in his usual mental fashion. "Unicorns powerful with age, like Violet, can make others see visions, but the rest of us can only project our voices. I hadn't known so much about her as she showed to us this time. I wonder why she chose now to reveal it."

Kassandra sat quietly, mentally reviewing what she'd seen. Having lived with griffins who were free and open with their selection of lovers and felt no shame in it, she was educated enough about what went on between males and females. She'd learned that griffins usually didn't fall in love with a single partner, the way humans did. Whether it was common in unicorns or not, it appeared that Violet had at least believed she was in love with the pegasus. She didn't seem to have had as much conviction with the furry cat-dog creature, but there had definitely been a particular attachment of some kind. As for the goat-beast, she seemed to have been confused, reaching for something that wasn't there, and gotten more than she'd wanted.

None of them had returned her feelings to the extent that she'd felt for them. It had ended, one way or another, in her losing each of them and being left alone, and surely that had been painful, but Kassandra didn't understand why Violet would feel this much torment that did not heal.

"Telling her to just be tough and get over it, that it wasn't anything to be upset about won't work," Glacier whispered into her mind. "Others have tried that. It only causes her more pain, and she shuts them out. Giving sympathy and trying to cheer her up doesn't work either."

Kassandra furrowed her brow. Perhaps she needed to ask more questions then. Behind her, she felt Glacier walk up and rest his nose gently against her shoulder. Through that contact a soft communication flowed. It wasn't words, yet she got a sense of what he was thinking without having to hear his words, which would have interfered with her own thought process.

"Are you angry at the pegasus for loving someone else?" she said to Violet.

The answer came immediately, and followed a brief mental sob. "No, he found someone he loves who loves him. He's happy. It was my fault, all my own foolish fault. I was stupid. I thought it wouldn't matter that I'm a unicorn. I thought we could get past it. I thought he actually cared about me, but he moved on after we parted."

"Perhaps he thought he'd never see you again?" Kassandra suggested. "Maybe he was sad when you two parted, but he healed and found love again. You were the one that went to seek him out."

"Yes, yes, it's not his fault. I know. I said that." Violet's partly opened eye flew the rest of the way open to glare at Kassandra. "Don't you see? It wasn't his fault. It wasn't any of their faults. I was the one who was stupid. I was the ignorant, naive one, the one who should have known better."

"I wouldn't say the others are totally without blame," Kassandra interrupted. "They should have considered your feelings, that you might be hurt by their actions."

"But I consented to everything, even if I didn't really want to." Her brow furrowed. "I did reject Hirjhan at first, but he," she trailed off and sighed. "They were just being themselves. It's not their responsibility to make sure everyone else doesn't get hurt. It's each person's responsibility to watch out for their own selves, not other's. I don't think they were trying to hurt me. They probably didn't know how much they hurt me."

Kassandra wasn't sure she agreed with that. "Maybe they didn't care if they hurt you as long as they got what they wanted," she guessed, frowning.

"No, they were just ignorant. They didn't know."

"Oh," Kassandra pushed, "just like you said you were ignorant. Well, if they can't be blamed for being ignorant, then how can you blame yourself?"

Violet almost thrashed her body, but the movement failed

halfway there. "I'm a unicorn."

"Unicorns are supposed to know everything then?" Kassandra replied, derisive.

Violet took a brief pause, as though that hadn't occurred to her. "No," she rallied, voice rising with each sentence until she was shouting into Kassandra's mind, "but unicorns are supposed to be wise and pure. I compromised myself. I ruined myself."

The thorny briars tightened around Violet, sinking deeper into her inflamed flesh, and blood oozed from the wounds. Violet groaned.

"I think you only started ruining yourself after you came here and let this grow up around you," Kassandra stated firmly. "You could have been out doing good, helping others, maybe helping someone else keep from making the same choices you did. Instead, you're lying here punishing yourself. Are you getting something useful out of this?"

A tremble ran the length of Violet's body and her gaze shifted off of Kassandra. The girl hoped maybe the unicorn was actually considering what she'd said. The briars loosened their hold slightly. Glacier's thoughts and feelings continued sighing gently into her, and she continued to let them influence her words.

"How does punishing yourself help anybody?" Kassandra pressed. "It won't change the past."

Violet's eye shut again and what were probably tears this time leaked out. "How can I go on living with myself?"

"You've managed it so far." Kassandra folded her arms. "You're still alive."

"I am worthless."

"Well, like this you certainly are. You're not helping anyone. You're not doing anything good like this."

The unicorn looked at the girl again, and Kassandra saw a flicker of vulnerability in her eye. "How do I stop?" she asked in the most breathless whisper.

Glacier nudged her thoughts. Kassandra's expression softened and she leaned forward to put her little hands onto Violet's filthy cheek. "You forgive yourself, at least a little."

Violet moaned, trembled, and the briars dug into her even more deeply. Her voice came out softly. "I saw women, when I was a human, who were merely the objects of others, with no self-respect, no ability to stand up for themselves, who gave in to everything. I was never supposed to be like that. I was supposed to be strong and wise. I was supposed to know better. I was supposed to fall in love with one person, and have a love of respect and kindness and eternal loyalty."

"Well, that's not how it worked out," Kassandra said as gently as she could, "and you can't go back and change it now."

"I'm just like them," Violet whimpered.

"Perhaps," Glacier's voice murmured, "you judged them too harshly."

Violet's trembling vanished. She stared at nothing, and Kassandra somehow sensed a weary relief in her, as though hearing Glacier's words had lifted a burden off of her. Kassandra let it happen, not saying anything. Violet closed her eye, squeezing it shut, and some dry sobs shuddered through her chest. Before Kassandra's eyes, some of the bruises began to lessen. Some of the bloody, crusted wounds began to close. She watched the spines on the nearest plants start to shorten.

Then those delicate green vines with the little lavender flowers began growing across the ground, moving inward from where they'd been struggling among the big thorny plants that circled the clearing. New leaves and flowers budded and matured along their growing lengths with supernatural speed. They slipped right around Glacier's hooves and Kassandra where she sat, and began wreathing Violet's forelegs and neck, twining through her filthy hair, looping her ears and spiraling out along her dark horn. They looked like some kind of decoration, like fine jewelry.

"You see, you have beauty in you," Kassandra whispered. "It never went away, no matter what happened to you."

"These flowers grow from your own demesne," Glacier contributed. "They grow from you. They have been there, fighting to live among all these blackened cacti and briars. They flock to you when you let them."

At his words, the new vines started to wither.

"No, no," Kassandra pled.

"I can't forget," Violet said bleakly.

"It will always be there," Glacier stated. "Always. Of course you can't forget, but that doesn't mean you have to live in those memories. What about right now? What about here? Here is opportunity. Now is your heartbeat and breath."

The vines filled with life again. "I'm wasting myself," Violet murmured.

Glacier and Kassandra both let out tension with a sigh. Glacier nuzzled Kassandra's hair, and then broke the physical connection, so she could no longer detect the flavor of his thoughts.

"This child wants you for her mother," he said. "There is no greater honor than that."

Kassandra hadn't removed her hands from Violet's cheek, and now the vines grew new tendrils that loosely encircled her wrists, brushed lightly against her skin, and then moved to gently push her hands off. She put her hands back in her lap.

"You know what I've done, what's been done to me, what I allowed to happen," Violet said, and Kassandra sensed her words were mostly for Glacier. "Are you sure I am acceptable?"

"Yes," he said, and then there was more, but Kassandra couldn't hear it. She only knew it was there from a slight static in her mind. Violet snorted, as if with weary amusement. Apparently whatever he'd said was intended to be private between the two unicorns. Kassandra didn't want to eavesdrop, so it didn't bother her.

"Away," Violet ordered.

Glacier stepped back and Kassandra got up to her feet to join him, as the vines all over the ground swept themselves expertly to the sides of the clearing so they wouldn't be stepped on. Then Violet heaved her body, starting with her head and neck, just like a cart horse Kassandra had once watched trying to get up. She didn't make it on her first try, and put her head back down with a moan of effort.

"You've weakened from lying here so long," Glacier said. "Try again. Get up and we can go eat, and bathe, and drink."

Violet's forelegs stretched out and she tried again, flailing up with her head and neck to try to get momentum. Her back legs twitched. She struggled for another few moments before having to rest again. Her third try was better, and she managed to roll to her belly, and keep her head and neck lifted off the ground. She got her forelegs out in front of her and bent them to put her hooves flat on the ground. Her legs shook.

"Can you help her?" Kassandra asked Glacier as quietly as she could.

"No," he replied immediately. "She has to do this herself. It's not just about the ability to stand. If she were merely wounded in body, I'd help, but this is about her standing up mentally, too."

Violet was catching her breath. She tested her forelegs, pushing against the ground. And then she lunged. In a massive, barely coordinated heave she got her feet under her and got her legs mostly straight. She stood, head hanging and body shaking, but she was up.

Kassandra clenched down on the ball of cheer and tears in her throat, and clasped her hands against her clavicles. Violet was on her feet. Some of the briars still clung to her hindquarters, but the rest of her wounds had at least closed, although they still looked raw and tender. Her bruises had lessened and much of the crusted scum of pus and blood had vanished.

Violet took a step, and another, limping her way towards Glacier and Kassandra. Kassandra grabbed Glacier's mane and pulled herself onto his back as Violet passed. Where she walked, the thorny demesne melted away. Kassandra looked back and saw that the spot where Violet had lain was still bare and shadowed, but the spiny plants around it were all dying. She wondered if anything would ever grow on that spot again. Still, she knew that nature was resilient. It might take time, but the earth might reclaim the barren spot, even with the shadow of a unicorn's sorrow upon it.

They walked from the demesne, and the darkness withered as they did. Kassandra watched from her perch as the green vines began taking it over, and from between them began to poke other leaves: the spears of crocus, iris, and daffodil. The particularly spiky briars around Violet's haunches, however, did not melt away as the rest of the demesne vanished under a carpet of new green.

Glacier took them downhill—Kassandra doubted that Violet would have had the strength to do any uphill climbing at all. There, they found a pool ringed by trees. In among the trees grew grasses and shrubs, although it was still too early for berries. Violet bent her head to take a timid mouthful of grass. Kassandra slid off Glacier's back and went to dangle her feet in the water, while Glacier nibbled on the foliage, too. She thought the two unicorns might be continuing to talk, excluding her from the conversation. That had never really bothered her; she knew unicorns did it all the time. Any two people might want to have a private conversation.

Kassandra took her time alone to watch the plants and animals around her. Nothing feared unicorns—except maybe rainbow drakes—so the other creatures of the forest continued about their normal activities. The birds especially fascinated Kassandra. They were so like yet unlike the griffins, and several flitted about in the bushes and trees or hopped along the shoreline of the pool.

Then all the birds flew up in surprise as Glacier leapt into the water, sending up a swamping splash. The pool wasn't too deep, only coming up to his chest.

"Everybody in," he wide broadcasted.

The day was warm enough. Kassandra shucked off her clothing and waded into the water until it reached her belly, and then dove in. Violet stood hesitantly on the shore, and Kassandra saw the unicorn glance back at the spiky vines still twined around her body.

"Come on in," Kassandra encouraged.

One foot at a time, Violet carefully placed her front hooves in the water. Most of the sludge on her body had been a part of the magical manifestation of the demesne, but she still hadn't had a bath other than rain for some huge number of years. She walked in until the water reached her knees, and Kassandra swam over to her. Without a word the girl began scrubbing at her legs with her hands and water. Violet's body language said she was instantly taken aback, but Kassandra chose to ignore that, and just kept roughing up the fur with her fingers and watching the dirt be carried away by the water.

"Come on, deeper," Kassandra ordered.

Violet, surprisingly, obeyed, walking in until the water reached her belly, and Kassandra swam all around her, washing her fur. Then, Kassandra got to the briars. She put her hands on Violet's hip.

"Violet, these have to go," she said firmly.

The unicorn looked back at them, eyes lowered.

"Keep the scars if you want," Kassandra suggested, a bit more gently, "but you can't have these anymore. You've had them long enough. Haven't you learned your lesson yet?"

"Yes, I've learned," Violet replied immediately. "You're right. Help me?"

The spines began to shorten. Their tips became blunt and pulled out of Violet's flesh and skin. Kassandra took hold of one of the resulting vines without a flinch and began pulling. As she broke off pieces and dropped them towards the water, they melted into nothingness. After a few minutes, all the briars were gone. Kassandra bathed the little puncture holes they'd left behind with water from the pool. Under her hands, the wounds sealed up.

Kassandra resumed scrubbing, washing away dirt and grime. Violet's mane and tail were tangled. Kassandra painstakingly worked out the knots and combed them with her fingers. She urged Violet into the deepest part of the pool, where the water came halfway up her sides and Kassandra could only touch the bottom with her toes. She pulled on Violet's head and neck, getting her to bend them down so she could wash her face. Violet closed her eyes and let the girl do it.

Lastly, Kassandra reached for Violet's horn. She knew that a unicorn's horn was its most intimate body part. Kassandra trickled water over Violet's, and the unicorn did not object, but her horn stayed dim and rocky. Cautiously, Kassandra put her hand on Violet's forehead, fingers in a V shape, and slid it up until the horn caught against the web between Kassandra's middle and ring fingers.

Violet's eyes opened and she stared at the girl.

"Your horn is still dark," Kassandra whispered.

"That will be as will be," Violet thought-whispered back. "Perhaps someday it will have a reason to be full of light again. Let's not force it."

"All right," Kassandra agreed, and moved her hands away from Violet's head.

The unicorn went on staring at her.

"Thank you for washing me," she said. "I didn't know I was waiting for you."

She cast her gaze over at Glacier, too, who had his head half underwater where he was waving his horn through the water to make waves. He lifted his head up, forelock soaked and dripping water all over his sheepish face. He seemed a little embarrassed to have been caught playing in the water like a foal. A rivulet ran from the brief beard under his chin, and he shook his head to cast off the water.

"I think I'll come back to the clan with you," Violet went on. "Are Shimmer, West, and Thunder still there?"

Glacier seemed to think for a moment. "Shimmer and Thunder are old ones. They have gone to be by themselves somewhere." He glanced at Kassandra. "Old ones often do that. They tire of company and go seek their own forest, make it how they like using the power of their demesne." He looked back at Violet. "I don't remember anyone named West."

Violet nodded. "I wonder where she has gone. She was my

friend. She came several times to try to wake me from my pain. I should try to find her. I must have hurt her by refusing her attempts to help me. Shimmer and Thunder were my dam and sire. Perhaps they went off together to share a forest. I would like to think that, so I think I shall. I suppose the clan must be full of young ones then."

"There are about twenty of us," Glacier said.

"Twenty? So many, and soon to be another." Violet looked at Kassandra as she said that last.

"Not for a while," Kassandra replied. "I mean, I know the nymph ceremony thing has to be soon, but then it will be years, decades, before the next, um, change."

"Yes, the ceremony had better be soon," Violet confirmed. "I can see your mantle of womanhood hovering about you. It will settle on you by the autumn."

Kassandra stifled a gasp and bit her cheeks. She turned to Glacier. "A few weeks," she begged. "You said we have a few weeks until the best new moon near midsummer. Will we make it? Can we do it then?"

He tilted his head, raising an eyebrow as much as his facial muscles would allow. "That depends, on if we have a mother for you."

The three people in the pool looked around covertly at each other. Kassandra clasped her hands. She'd just met Violet that day, and Violet had only a little while ago been in the grips of the deepest sorrow Kassandra had ever witnessed. She tried to think: what did she really want? How did she really feel? Would Violet remain functional and happy all the way until Kassandra was born and independent? How could Kassandra gamble on that when she was so extremely recently recovered?

She looked at the unicorn mare and compared how she felt about her with every other unicorn mare she'd met. Kassandra ran her hands over her face and up into her wet black hair. It was crazy to want Violet out of all of them. And yet, she did. Violet cared deeply — too deeply even. She was gentle, tolerant of Kassandra, and honest with her. She'd shown Kassandra the most vulnerable secrets of her past, the ones that were humiliating and painful, and then she'd let Kassandra help her. That was trust.

Violet was the one she wanted. Kassandra could see her potential, what she could become. With Glacier to help her, Violet would survive and recover. Kassandra believed that.

She walked over to stand in front of Violet and put her hands over the big scar on the unicorn's chest. "Violet, I want you to be my mother. Will you?"

With the physical touch, she thought she could maybe sense a little of Violet's thoughts or feelings, the way it had worked with Glacier, but Kassandra's own were so wild that she couldn't tell if it worked or not.

Violet bent her head down and nudged her nose gently against the flower mark on Kassandra's forehead. "Very well, little one," she murmured, "I will carry you and nurture you, when your time comes."

Kassandra threw her arms around Violet's neck and cried both scared and happy tears into her wet storm cloud fur.

The trio left the next morning. Kassandra didn't go to say goodbye to the griffins or her siblings; she didn't want them to try to stop her. They traveled at the swiftest pace the unicorns could sustain through the day. They slept at night curled together, with the unicorns resting their heads on each other's flanks, and Kassandra in a ball between them. Sometimes she woke in the dawn and saw Glacier and Violet together a ways away, standing and leaning against each other, heads touching, with horns crossed. She always waited until they parted on their own before she got up and disturbed them.

In the sky, the moon shrank towards newness. On the last day, the trio descended into a deep cleft between the mountains as it narrowed to the tiniest sliver. As they walked, they passed stone ruins wreathed with vines and sheltered by ancient trees. Birds watched in silence as they passed. Other animals—deer, squirrels, foxes, and others Kassandra couldn't put name to—

sat in the shadows of the undergrowth, equally as silent as the birds, and bore witness to their passage.

At last, they came upon a plateau of stone encircled by the forest of trees. In the center, rocks jutted up, even forming a few arches, surrounding a still pool of blue water. Kassandra looked into it and couldn't see the bottom. In the midday sun it looked ordinary, unimpressive, and yet the air around it was quiet as if with reverence.

"Tonight," Glacier said.

Kassandra slid down off his back and sat, prepared to wait.

None of them ate. Together they watched the sunset. Kassandra ran her fingers through the unicorns' manes. Stars pricked the night sky until it bled silver. The fully dark disk of the moon rose. The pool of water began to shimmer from below and something moved within it.

Anxiety fluttered in Kassandra's chest. She held tight to Glacier's mane with one hand. He nuzzled her hair.

"Violet and I have both been through this," he mind-murmured to her.

"It is a good night," Violet remarked.

"What do I do?" Kassandra asked.

"Disrobe and enter the water," Glacier told her. "Don't be afraid. We will be waiting when you emerge."

Kassandra shed the clothing Jessika had so kindly made for her. Feet bare on the warm stone, she approached the edge of the pool, ducking under one of the rough arches of stone. There was indeed a glow from somewhere below the gently moving surface. Cautiously, she sat down on the edge, and dipped in her lower legs.

The movement of the water increased, and a dozen or more vines spiraled up from below the surface. They twined around the stone outcroppings and spread rapidly across the ground. In mere minutes, leaves budded and spread open. Larger buds swelled and burst into white flowers that stretched their petals towards the hidden moon. After another few moments, veins of dark purple and black traced themselves delicately along the creases of the large petals.

The barren stone arches and the plateau around them were now coated with greenery grown out of the pool. Kassandra glanced back over her shoulder. Glacier and Violet stood pressed side-by-side, cheek-to-cheek, horns touching at the very tips. Their gazes were lowered as if humbled.

Kassandra put her hands to the edge of the rock and lowered herself into the water. It was cool, but not unpleasant on such a warm night so near to midsummer. She sank into it up to her shoulders, holding to the edge. Looking down, the glimmering glow danced across her skin and a warm feeling welled up. Suddenly, she felt welcomed. The spot on her forehead began to heat, almost to the point of burning.

Feeling a little surge of bravery, she pushed away from the edge, to tread water in the center of the pool. Looking directly up, she could just see the black disk of the new moon, surrounded by its gown of stars. When she looked back over towards the unicorns, however, she was a little disconcerted to see that the vines had grown to cover the arch she'd entered through. She was now enclosed on all sides by stone and greenery, except for straight up, where the moon hung.

She wondered how long she had to stay in the water. She supposed, when the vines retracted and the entryway opened again, she'd be able to exit. This wasn't anything to be afraid of at all. Kassandra spun herself in the water a few times, and then brought up her legs so she floated on her back, eyes on the sky. Eventually, she closed her eyes completely, just enjoying the gentle movement of the water.

It was so peaceful.

Then something grabbed her and yanked her violently under the water.

She didn't have time to get an audible scream out, but she opened her mouth and emptied her lungs in a torrent of bubbles as she was dragged deeper and deeper under the water. The glow surrounded her now, so she saw nothing but the light, and she knew she was about to drown. Any second she'd try to take a breath, draw in water, and die.

The something that had pulled her down was one step ahead of her. What felt like huge ropey vines lashed around her body, stilling her struggles, and one took advantage of her open mouth, diving down her throat. Two little ones plugged her nostrils. Suddenly she could breathe. It wasn't comfortable, but her lungs filled somehow with air. She still couldn't see anything but the glow.

The light expanded, filling her entire awareness, permeating her body until she couldn't feel it anymore. As if from a great distance, she felt pressure, movement within her, and knew that the vines had burrowed under her skin, among her muscles and bones and organs: some as thin as hair, some as thick as fingers. She seemed to float apart from her body, light and freed.

She was in the water, in the vines themselves, and in the rocks. She felt a heartbeat of energy all around her, a force so great it could have crushed her, but instead she floated with it, like blood in a heart. Her mind moved into that pulsing and swelling until she felt more a part of it than she did her own body. In fact that shell of flesh faded behind her, and she no longer cared what was happening to it.

All was power, life, and death, and Kassandra swam in it without fear or regret.

Sometime later she opened her eyes.

She was floating on her back, up at the surface again. She felt her arms and legs and head all intact. She blinked her eyes and swallowed. She moved her fingers and toes. Her toes felt a little stiff. She looked and saw that they were brown, and so were her feet and lower legs, the skin toughened like bark.

Kassandra glided through the water to where she'd entered the pool. Before her eyes the leafy vines began to pull back. The white flowers closed. Below her, the glow faded, and within a minute, all the greenery had retracted back into the pool with splishes and splashes. Glacier and Violet lay cuddled together, heads and necks across each other's backs, patiently waiting.

Kassandra pushed herself up out of the pool. Her body felt lighter, and she realized it was taller and leaner now. Her clothes were still in a pile where she'd dropped them, but she wrinkled her nose at them. She did want to be a little protected and covered though—

The wish seemed to produce them: leaves budded and sprouted from her skin. The sensation was not at all unpleasant, just new. Her curly black hair, unchanged, fell into her face, but another wish made tendrils emerge from her scalp, swirling out to sweep up her mane back and away.

Glacier and Violet looked so weary, and so comfortable, she couldn't bring herself to disturb them. Instead, she climbed up one of the spurs of rock that arched over the pool. Her feet were tough enough now that it wasn't painful in the slightest. There, Kassandra sat and watched the new moon set, experimenting with producing different sorts of leaves and different colors of flowers from her skin.

When dawn came, the unicorns stirred, and looked up to find her shining in the sun. Kassandra leapt down to greet them as they reared and belled with joy. Violet's dull horn blazed like heat lightning at the sight of her, and Kassandra leapt astride her mother's back, to race like the wind into the forest.

The End

Hawkrain's Tale

These events take place about seven years after the invasion of Northnest when Hawkwind escaped with the four children.

Karolan Freyaliv, lately more often called Hawkrain, stared at the stick of wood, teeth bared in a snarl. His hands were fisted on his knees and his shoulders had begun to shake. He pictured the flames in his mind. He pictured them burning the wood: bright, dancing, putting up a little stream of smoke. A headache began between his brows. A growl of frustration escaped him.

"Burn," he hissed. "Burn, rogues take you."

A tiny corner of the stick began to blacken—and the headache snapped out its wings and Karo crumpled.

"Burn," he demanded, voice rising and cracking.

His hold on his magic, already tremulous, dissolved completely and he struck out at the stick with a slash of his hand, sending it flying. It rattled as it bounced off a wall and tumbled across the stone floor. An angry tear slid down his face.

Behind him, he heard a series of quick clacks.

Karo flinched guiltily and rubbed the tear away before turning his head enough to glimpse his master from one eye. His unruly blonde hair fell to cover the other.

"Hawkrain," his master said calmly. "Fetch the stick."

"My head hurts," Karo muttered mutinously.

"Of course it does. You were trying to force your magic."

Karo hunched his head down between his shoulders. The clacking sound came again, and Karo flinched.

"I'm sorry, Master Thornfire," he mumbled.

Something nuzzled and tugged at his shaggy hair. His master was preening him, a gesture of encouragement and comfort,

122

but Karo turned his head away, and heard his master sigh and take a seat with a papery sort of rasping rustle. Again he caught oblique sight of him, of his pale gold and tan feathers and lighter ventral fur—for his master was a griffin.

Thornfire was one of the strongest—if not the strongest—mages in South-scree. He'd recognized the potential for magical talent in Karo not long after meeting him. Now that the boy was leaving boyhood, he could start consciously touching his powers, and Thornfire had started his training. It hadn't been easy. Karo had successfully managed to get shreds of paper to burn, but now he was trying the next step, wood, and it was making him angry. Whenever he got so worked up he started to lash out, his master would rapidly clack his bill in reproof.

Karo was coming to hate the sound.

"Your powers are starting to emerge, young Hawkrain," Thornfire said, "but they aren't fully available to you yet. Forcing them will only hurt you. Perhaps we should stop here for today."

"I can do it," Karo snarled.

Thornfire gently touched his back. "I have no doubt of it. Your powers will be adequate for many things, but they haven't fully developed yet. No more than a chick can fly before its feathers are long enough, there is nothing you can do but wait. I will give you some different exercises tomorrow. Fire is often the easiest, but there are other skills you can work on. For now, you should go rest your head."

His master had been saying similar things a lot, and he was tired of hearing them. Karo shoved to his feet and stormed out, his footsteps heavy but not too stompy—the floor was stone and would hurt his feet if he wasn't careful. He'd discovered that in one of his first tantrums. He was twelve years old now. His powers were starting to emerge, to become accessible to him consciously, or so Thornfire said—but he couldn't do anything. Lighting bits of paper on fire? That was nothing.

He needed to be able to throw bolts of fire and lightning—that would be impressive—or to make stones glow with light and heat—which would at least be useful. Karo stormed out of Thornfire's home and into the street beyond. He almost ran right into a galumphing baby griffin the size of a small pony.

"Night," a voice called. "Watch where you're going."

The little—well, big, he was as big as Karo—ball of downy fluff skidded to a stop. Under the fluff, Karo could see darker points: signs of his first juvenile feathers beginning to grow in. Hawknight was really still a baby though, no more intelligent than any human child of five years.

"Sorry," the ball of fluff said meekly.

His sister, who tended to be more composed, came trotting up beside him. Hawkday had pale, rusty brown down, while her twin brother sported pale grey and brown. She had hard little dark points deep in her fluff, too. In the next few months, the feathers would grow in and they'd lose their baby down forever. Juvenile feathers wouldn't allow them to fly, Hawkwind—their mother—had explained, but they'd start flapping their blunt, feathered wings to build their flight muscles, and taking short leaps and even little glides. Plus, they'd begin to look like real griffins, instead of poofy balls with sharp beaks and claws sticking out.

Two adult male griffins came over to join the babies with considerably more decorum than their charges. One was a bit bigger than the other, because he was older, and had rich brown fur along his underside, with rusty red fur and feathers everywhere else. His longer feathers were banded and tipped with black. His name was Thornwing, and he often assisted the Hawk Line with chick-sitting duties.

The other male was charcoal grey all over except for a paler underside, and was called Thornsoft, though he'd been born Rainsoft and then switched Lines a few years ago, which partly changed his name. If anything, Thornsoft hung around the Hawk Line even more than Thornwing. It hadn't escaped Karo that little Night and Day both bore some resemblance in their coloration to the two males, but griffins weren't supposed to gossip about who their sires were, or speculate about the sires of others.

"Lessons done for today?" asked the rusty red male, the same one who had scolded Hawknight into apology.

Karo made a small effort not to glower, but it was quite a challenge and he largely failed.

"Ah, and I see they go well," Thornwing went on cheerfully.

Karo glared. Thornwing liked to joke, and Karo enjoyed it, except when it was directed at him. He sensed his master come to the doorway behind him. At least his magical senses could do that much for him. His master's powerful aura was like a warm light at his back.

"Hawkrain makes excellent progress," Thornfire said.

And Karo turned and bolted, almost as fast and far more recklessly than Hawknight had just been running. He dashed down stone streets and hopped over rocks, dodging among mostly tolerant griffins, rattled across a wooden bridge over a small chasm, and then finally got up to a full sprint as he reached the edges of town. He didn't stop until he got beyond the border of the Aerie and his feet came down on gravel and dirt paths.

South-scree was a griffin city, called an Aerie, boasting around four hundred individuals. The matriarchs and their advisors were careful to keep the city from growing any larger than that. Griffins were predators and required large quantities of fresh meat. They had to limit their population size, or the wild herds around them would not be able to support them. Since they could fly, a lot of land was included in the area they claimed, but four hundred large predators meant a lot of predation. They monitored the health of the herds they preyed on, and were careful to rotate their hunting grounds yearly.

They also had daily patrols flying over the surrounding mountains, watching for anything dangerous that might be moving in on the territory or outsider griffins who might sneak in to do some poaching. Griffins who refused to live by the rules and regulations of the five allied Aeries were forced to leave. The Aerie griffins called them rogues, and would drive them off or even kill them if they returned to Aerie-held territories.

Karo let himself slow from his sprint into a heavy run, jarring his legs as the path sloped downhill. South-scree was almost on the very top of a mountain, just above the treeline, so every direction out of the Aerie was down except for an unclimbable rocky spire to the northeast. Karo wove between boulders and crags of rock peppered with lichens of every color. Hardy grasses and some other small herbs grew around them, fighting through the gravel. Within another minute of quick walking, the ground cover got thicker with tough, woody shrubs and annual wildflowers coating the slopes.

The first small, twisted trees were ahead. If Karo walked another few minutes, he'd begin to enter real forest, but all the distance he went down, he'd have to climb back up. It was fairly steep, and as his hot feelings cooled a bit and his brain reasserted some control, he decided he wasn't sure how much of a hike he was up for. His legs were getting long with a major growth spurt, and he'd put on several inches in just the past year. That also led to growing pains. He wasn't sure he wanted to put his legs through more just now.

Besides, he'd come plenty far enough to make his moody point. Karo reached the first of the trees taller than he was, and climbed up onto the boulder it grew beside. There in its fractured shade he could sit and sulk to his heart's content, enough out of view that no one was likely to notice him from the Aerie—Or so he thought. A flutter of wings made him turn back to look at the trail behind him. A griffin had landed there.

"Hi Starbright," he said, trying to be polite, but rather wishing he were still alone.

"Are you alright, Rain?" she asked.

He shrugged one shoulder, turning back to looking at the trees downhill. The griffin walked up to his boulder with eerie silence. Griffins were big, some as high as a large horse at the shoulder, but also quite light for their size, and with such agility and poise that they could move as quietly as a cat. This one, Starbright, was also a mage, but she was older than Karo, an actual young adult, and would soon be undertaking her mastery trial that would end her formal apprenticeship.

"I'm fine," Karo grunted.

"Was Master Thornfire being mean to you?"

Thornfire had been Starbright's master, too—still was, in fact. "No," Karo growled, drawing out the word like a baby griffin in a stubborn tug-of-war with a bit of tough leather.

"You're frustrated that learning magic is so slow," Starbright countered, earning her a glare, but the golden griffin just chuckled. "I was frustrated, too. Learning to move all this energy around and do things with it is hard."

"It is," Karo admitted. "Does it ever get easy?"

"No," Starbright said promptly. "You get stronger as you get older. Things that make your head hurt now stop making it hurt, but they're still hard. It's always work to bend the laws of nature."

"I'll never be able to do it," Karo muttered.

"Of course you will, unless you start believing what you just said."

He scuffed a foot against the boulder. "Isn't there," he began, "isn't there some way to make it easier?"

Starbright tilted her head, her crest feathers giving a few light flicks. Griffins didn't have the flexible muscles and flesh on their faces like humans did, and couldn't convey as many expressions that way, but Karo had lived with them long enough to be able to read their body language and the lay of their feathers—along with the angles of their brows, which they could control much like humans. Starbright was expressing polite but somewhat puzzled attention.

"What kind of way?" Starbright asked.

"I remember stories when I was little, before I came here," Karo tried to explain. "Some of them had magic in them. There were magic objects, like wands and balls and—"

"Oh," Starbright nodded briskly. "Yes, some mages do use objects to help focus. I don't know about human mages, of course. I mean griffin mages. I've even seen Master do it, once or twice, when he needed a little extra help on something big."

"Maybe if I had something like that?" Karo suggested.

"Oh," Starbright said, but in a much different tone. Her jaunty crest sank. "Focusing objects are only as good as the mage that uses them. They can't increase your power. Some of them can store power, that's true, but mostly they just help with control. They don't make power for you."

"Control," Karo nodded. "Right. That's what I need. If I could control my powers better, it, I," he trailed off.

Starbright didn't look optimistic. "There are no shortcuts, Rain," she said.

"No, I don't mean a shortcut," he concurred hurriedly. "I mean, like, when you're new at something, sometimes there are extra tools to help you until you become skilled, right?"

The griffin's feathers had slicked down, revealing her discomfort with the topic.

"I just want a helping tool, until I get stronger," Karo insisted. "Do you know of anything like that? What did Master use when he needed that extra help?"

"Well," Starbright said slowly. "When he was helping with some construction, he took a length of rope and wrapped each end around his hands, and then held it taut while he was controlling the—"

"What was the rope made of?" Karo interrupted. "Was it something magical?"

"It was ordinary rope," Starbright answered.

"Are you sure?"

"Look, the rope didn't do anything special," the griffin explained, tone turning a bit sharp. "It was a focus aid. Before and after Master used it, it was just ordinary rope."

Karo heaved a frustrated sigh and turned back to looking off at the forest.

"Hawkrain," Starbright said, more gently. "You will come into your powers. It takes time. You can't force it or trick it or find some way to cheat it."

Karo was hardly listening. He knew there must have been something magical about that rope. What could have made it amplify his master's powers? If Starbright had thought it was ordinary, it couldn't have been obvious. Maybe something magical had been woven into it. Were there magical plants? He'd been reading about herbs used in healing, but the book had implied there was nothing magical about them. What made them useful were their inherent physical and chemical properties.

Not plant fibers then. What else was used in rope? Karo's head snapped up. Hair could be woven into rope, and one of the most magical creatures in the forest had tons of hair, in shining manes and tails. He could even recall the myth about it. Rope woven from unicorn hair could hold the mightiest of beasts, even when chains failed. There must have been unicorn hairs woven into the rope Master Thornfire had used. Starbright just hadn't noticed.

"Rain?"

Starbright had extended a wing up to him on his boulder perch, and was gently touching his back with the wrist.

"It's alright," he told her. "I think I know what to do."

"You do?" she asked, looking none too sure about that. "So you'll continue practicing, and wait for your powers to settle?"

"I'll—" He hesitated. "Yes. Right."

Some of her feathers relaxed, fluffing back out a little. "Oh. Good."

"I'm going to take a walk. It will help me calm down," he said with a confident air.

"Shall I come with you?" Starbright offered.

"I'll be alright. I'll come back before dark, for sure." Karo slid down off the boulder and raised a hand to wave. "Thanks for talking to me," he called.

"Of course," Starbright replied.

He didn't give her the chance to say anymore. Karo resumed his run, trotting down the trail and towards the forest.

Karo rarely saw the unicorns. He saw plenty of other animals all the time: tons of birds, squirrels, rabbits, pikas, and deer—though the deer didn't come very close to the Aerie. If he stayed out until dusk or got up at dawn, he could even spot nocturnal animals like owls, skunks, foxes, raccoons, and badgers. Larger predators avoided the area of the Aerie as well, but he knew there were big cats and wolves and bears that lived elsewhere in the mountains the griffins called home.

The unicorns, however, seemed to be able to choose when they would be seen. Where they hid, how they hid, Karo had no idea. He knew they had secret glades that were special to them, and Karo had stumbled across them a few times, but despite all his efforts to remember the ways to them, they never seemed to appear twice in the same place, even though he knew that shouldn't be possible. With his fledgling magical senses he could tell they were special, but he also knew, instinctively, that their magic and his were not the same.

So how he was supposed to locate the unicorns on command and get a few of their hairs he had no idea. He wandered down into the dense forest, walking the deer trails. Griffins didn't walk long distances, and didn't make trails or roads of their own except within their Aeries. Rikah, Karolan's human Hawkbrother, had made an established trail down to the place where he grew vegetables, but that was to the south of the Aerie. Karo had run off to the west.

After a couple hours of wandering and seeing not the slightest sign of a unicorn, Karo found a fallen log over a trickling stream and sat down to watch the water. Summer was on in full. The days were long, and even at the top of the mountain the air was tolerably warm. The last of the snow was gone, so the streams were shrinking and would vanish entirely just before the autumn rains came. The griffins had deep wells below the Aerie that never ran dry, but they didn't have that much need for water anyway, and could always fly to other water sources if needed.

Karo folded his gangly arms across his tucked up knobby knees, put his chin down on them and heaved a heavy sigh. His tummy was twisting with hunger. He was always hungry these days. No matter how much he ate, he couldn't seem to fill himself up. He felt empty. His stomach was empty. His magic was empty. Even his heart felt empty. Only his head was stuffed with too many worries.

"The water carries the mountain down to the sea."

Karolan startled so violently he almost lost his perch on the log, but it was a voice he knew, and he whipped his head to his right.

There she was.

"I'm sorry. I didn't mean to surprise you," Kassandra said, voice soft like clouds or flowers or willow buds.

Kassandra, his human Hawksister, called Hawksky by the griffins, sat in the same position he was in, though she was a good bit smaller than he was. Her knees were tucked up to her chest just like his, her arms around them, but there her resemblance to him ended.

She looked like a part of the log, a part of the forest. Her feet and lower legs were coated with something that looked like tree bark, but all her toes were visible, so it wasn't like boots. It thinned and turned into her own porcelain-pale human-like skin at about her knees. There was a short expanse of bare thigh, and then clusters of large, tough, red-veined leaves wrapped her hips like a living skirt. Above that, her waist was bare, but her belly-button was gone, and then more leaves, these smaller, paler, and dusted with silver covered her torso, shoulders, and upper arms.

It was only as those leaves became sparser towards her elbows that Karolan could see clearly that they grew right out of her body, attached to her skin. The leaves were her body. They weren't clothes made of leaves. They were part of Kassandra — this strange, new Kassandra. Her slender, white neck and sweet round face were unchanged, though. Her curly black hair was twined through with little vines that grew small white flowers. It could have been just some kind of decoration, except that they were alive. Karo could smell them. They smelled sweet. Even as he looked, a honeybee visited one, busily seeking the nectar and pollen within.

As his shock faded, twin sensations rose inside him. One was nausea. What had happened to Kassandra he had no idea, and she wouldn't talk about it, but it was wrong. This thing she'd become—part plant, part human—was wrong. Despite a sort of alien beauty, it was not her. It was not the quiet, pretty, innocent little girl she'd been, wrapped in her improvised clothing, messy hair falling all over the place.

That little girl's timid smiles had hooked something deep in Karolan, something deeper than his heart, as deep as his soul, he guessed. And that was the other sensation: warm, hungry, thundering need, desire, yearning. He could feel something growing in himself and it was taking over the tender brotherly feelings of his childhood.

It scared him.

"It's alright," he told her, looking down at the stream again. "What was it you said?"

"The water carries the mountain down to the sea."

Karo frowned at the stream. "The mountain isn't going anywhere," he muttered.

"In a million years, the mountain will all be in the sea," Kassandra said.

As an explanation, it illuminated nothing for Karo, and he didn't know how to respond. He wanted to look at Kassie, but he also didn't want to look, so he kept staring at the stream.

"You see," she went on, voice barely loud enough to be heard above the music of the water, "as the water runs, it rubs off a little of the mountain and carries it along. Every year, when the snow melts, it rubs off a little more. One day it will all be rubbed away, and the mountain will be gone."

"Where are the griffins going to live then?" Karo asked, feeling huffy again.

"Someplace else," she said, "if there are still griffins."

"Of course there will be griffins," he grunted.

Her voice stayed quiet, gentle like a light mist of rain. "It will be long after all the griffins we know are gone, after you're gone, too, Rain."

"And you, too, then," he added, irrationally put out.

Her reply was slower in coming this time. "No," she whispered. "I will always be here."

Karolan shoved to his feet. He should have been happy to see Kassie. He loved her, and lately he hardly saw her anymore, but he couldn't stand to be around her; it hurt too much. He turned to begin his walk back towards the Aerie.

Then he jerked to a halt. Somehow, Kassandra was in front of him, standing in a sunbeam as if posing there on purpose. The light lit up her leaves but seemed to make her skin cold like snow in shadow.

"You wanted to see the unicorns," she said in a tone clearly meant to lead him into giving an explanation.

Karolan found his hands in fists and his jaw clenched. "So what," he growled.

"Don't be mean," she whispered. "You want to see them. What for?"

"I," he stuttered. "I'm studying magery. I'm going to be a mage. Thornfire is teaching me."

"That's wonderful, Rain," Kassandra said, with a hint of the timid smiles she used to wear. "You'll be a great mage."

"I'm not a great mage," he burst out. "I'm rubbish."

Her smile faded. "I'm sure that's not true."

"It is," he retorted, voice rising almost to a yell, and then felt ashamed when he saw Kassie flinch. "I need something to help me," he went on, trying to bring his volume down. "When I get older, I'll get all my power, but right now I have hardly anything."

"Sometimes we have to wait," she offered. "Sometimes the time isn't right yet, and all we can do is wait. We can even enjoy the waiting, if we try."

"But I need to be practicing," Karo insisted. "Thornfire is making me practice and I'm no good."

"Practicing is what will make you good," Kassandra pointed out. "You have to be patient, Rain."

"But it's no good if I can't do what he's asking me."

Kassandra stepped to a sapling at the side of the deer trail and slid her slender arms around it, embracing it and tucking her cheek against its young, smooth bark. "What," she asked softly, "does this have to do with unicorns? Their horns are magic, but you know you can't have a horn. It would kill them."

"No, no, no," Karo assured her swiftly. "Nothing like that. I'd never hurt a unicorn."

"They can't teach you, either. Their magic isn't like yours," Kassie said, eyes doe-soft and steady on him.

"I know. I was just hoping for, like, a talisman."

"What's a talisman?"

"It's an object that helps a mage focus their power."

"Like a wand? Like in nursery tales? Or a magic stone?"

Karo nodded. "Yes, something like that."

But Kassie shook her head, rocking it against the sapling's trunk. "Unicorns don't have things like that. They don't need them."

"No, no, of course not," he agreed, stepping closer to her.

Then he stared in fascination as, before his eyes, he watched new leaves budding and unfurling in the canopy of the sapling Kassie was hugging. In just a few seconds, new growth that should have taken a month covered the tree.

"Then why?" she asked, voice a whisper, watching him with big eyes.

He tore his gaze away from the rapidly flourishing branches and back to his Hawksister. "I wanted a few strands of their hair," he confessed.

Kassie straightened, releasing her grip on the sapling, and the new growth slowed. "Unicorn hair?"

"From their manes or tails," Karo clarified. "I thought I could braid it into a bracelet, and it would help me work my magic better."

Kassandra looked dubious. "I don't think it would."

"But it wouldn't hurt to try, right?" he insisted. "And they must occasionally lose strands of hair, just like humans do, right? It wouldn't hurt them to collect the loose strands. You could find some for me."

She was drawing away now, backing a step or two down the trail. "I couldn't," she muttered.

"Oh, why not?" Karo huffed, throwing up his hands. "They're your friends, aren't they?"

"Yes," she allowed, now looking down at the forest floor.

"You can find them. You live with them, don't you? But they hardly ever show themselves to me," he went on. "I've been looking all day and can't find any."

Kassie backed another step away, her fingers clenched on each other before her.

"Please, Sky?" Karo begged.

"I can't," she breathed.

"You could if you wanted to," he argued.

She shook her head.

"I'm your brother," Karo declared. "Doesn't that make me more important than some stupid unicorns?"

Her head snapped up, and her face looked pained. Karo bit his lip, and felt his anger run out of him. Suddenly, he felt ashamed. He'd gotten angry. He'd yelled at his precious Kassie. He walked up to Kassandra, who didn't run away but looked down again.

"I'm sorry," he muttered.

He reached out and touched her forearm. Her skin felt unnaturally cool, but she wasn't shivering.

"It's just, we're family," he fumbled, "and I didn't think it would be a big deal. It's just some hair. It won't hurt them. I don't understand why you can't help me. We're like siblings."

He stared at her, gaze curling around with the highlights on her hair, following the soft edges of her eyebrows and the curve of her cheek. Strange the plant life might be, but under it she was still very pretty. Her black eyelashes were so very long, and her lips were petal pink.

Karolan felt his skin heat, and wondered if she'd feel his hand on her arm getting hotter. He slid his hand down to hers and tried to get her to hold his, but her fingers stayed locked together. He stepped closer, and finally she lifted her face again. Her eyes seemed very big and liquidy, like pools of water at midnight. He thought he might fall into them. They would be cool, and put out the heat of his skin.

"You're like my sister," he managed, almost choking. "You're more than my sister. And they—they're just like colorful horses. They don't talk. They're not human. You should come ba—"

Kassandra jerked away like his hand had only now burned her. She stared at him, into his eyes, and he got the strangest feeling that now he was looking at a wild animal, like a doe frozen with fear, not sure yet which way she was going to leap.

"I'm not human, either," Kassandra gasped out.

Then almost so fast he couldn't follow, she did leap like a deer into the underbrush, and was gone.

Karolan stood, feeling more confused and more upset than he had in a long while. He went to the sapling she'd hugged and leaned against it, but it didn't grow when he touched it, not like it did for her. He clasped his hands around it as if it were something's neck, as if he could strangle it. For a moment, he wanted to chop it down—but the griffins had raised him with deep respect, even reverence, for the growing world. Trees were never cut, not without a serious reason.

He felt himself crying, and wasn't sure why. At the same time, a great frustration, restlessness, had invaded his body. He kicked at the little tree, doing it no damage, paced up and down the trail for several yards, running his hands through his shaggy hair. Kassandra's last words made him the most upset. Not human: how could she not be human? She'd been born human. She'd been just like he and Jessika and Rikah for years. Why had she had to go off into the forest with the unicorns and change into something freakish?

Karo pressed his hands to his forehead and let out a sound—something of a snarl, a howl, a moan, a scream, all mixed together. Some birds fluttered away from the nearest trees. He did it again, a bit louder, and a third time. It hurt his throat and chest at the same time that it seemed to purge something from him.

Then he slumped back against the closest tree, a big one this time, and caught his breath. He scrubbed the tears from his face and just stayed there, head leaned back against the rough bark, eyes shut. The forest breathed around him. After a few minutes, he began to feel somewhat better, or at least less distraught. He scoffed, and blindly turned to go back up the deer trail, back to the Aerie. He was hungry and—

He ran right into something solid and unmoving, bounced back, lost his breath, and almost fell on his butt.

"What—?" he exclaimed.

And then he focused on what he'd hit, and his eyes and mouth got big and round.

"Oh," he stuttered, "oh, ah, um, excuse me?"

There was a unicorn on the deer trail.

He'd run right into its chest and shoulder, and he recognized it. It was the blue one that had saved him, Hawkwind, and the other children as they'd been escaping from Northnest castle, by fighting off a rainbow drake that had tracked them down. It was also the one he most often caught a glimpse of with Kassandra. He knew it was a male, and the little beard it bore under its chin further proclaimed that. Karo knew the females didn't have those, though they all had feathery hocks as far as he'd seen. The strong, dark blue of its hide was speckled with paler spots along its back, and transitioned to red rust at its extremities. Its mane and tail were dark grey near the roots and faded to silver at the ends. Its loosely spiraled horn was smoke grey.

It looked at Karo with a steady gaze, and made no move to flee. One thing was different than previous times he'd seen it. It seemed to glow a bit, or shine, as if the sunlight was particularly fond of it. He'd never noticed that before, and wondered if it was because he was turning into a mage that he could see it. It wasn't unpleasant at all. He supposed, something as magical as the unicorn should glow.

"I will glow more and more," said a masculine voice in his head, "every time you see me."

"What?" Karoland retorted.

The unicorn's mouth hadn't moved. It had talked in his head. It had known his thoughts.

"We normally do not enter the minds of others," the unicorn went on, dark gaze still as unmoving as a boulder, "except for good reason. You upset Sky."

Karo felt the blood drain from his face; he'd been caught, and called out—by a unicorn.

"It is good that you feel ashamed."

The blood that had just left his face rushed back, and he felt himself flush.

"Karolan Hawkrain Freyaliv," the unicorn said.

He gulped. It knew his name.

"You cannot have Sky."

His face twisted with confusion. "What?" he asked, yet again.

"You do not understand yet, what is happening to you," the unicorn said, a trifle more gently. "Your mantle of manhood is descending upon you."

Karo was perplexed. "My what?"

The unicorn finally moved. He seemed to sigh, and his head lowered a little. He took a few steps closer, and Karolan almost panicked, backing up a few steps of his own.

"Don't be afraid," the unicorn soothed. "I'll not hurt you. Here. Take some."

The unicorn stopped before him, turning its head, presenting its neck where its mane spilled down like a thousand fine icicles made molten.

"Take what, sir?" Karo asked, mouth gone dry.

"It won't help you with your magery," the unicorn went on. "Only time and practice will do that, but take some hairs from my mane, if it will make you feel better."

Karo's hand seemed to lift all by itself. Softly, he trailed his fingers among the strands that hung like thick threads of silk. He felt a power there, as though he'd reached into a pounding, icy waterfall, and he drew his hand back. His fingers seemed to

138

tingle for a few moments, and he rubbed them with his other hand.

He almost reached out again. He lifted his hand, but something held him back. Whether the tingling had been a warning or not, the power in this creature was not like his. It would not mix with his, and even if he could take some hairs, he had the strangest heavy sensation in his belly, that he shouldn't. The unicorn waited patiently.

"I can't, sir," he whispered finally.

It wasn't that he physically couldn't have pulled out a few hairs. Taking the hairs would be like cutting down that sapling Kassandra had hugged. It would violate something sacred, something he wasn't meant to touch or take, something much bigger than he was.

"Then you understand why Sky could not do as you asked."

Karo could only stand there, staring at the shimmering mane and the glowing coat of the unicorn. At last the unicorn moved, pivoting with such grace as should have been impossible for so large an animal, until it could face him again. Its large eyes, as liquidy and midnight-pool-like as Kassandra's, captured him.

"You will be an accomplished, powerful, and skilled mage, young son of the Hawk," the unicorn said, "in time, and you will be far greater for knowing there are some things you must not touch."

"What things?" Karo asked weakly, afraid he knew the answer.

"Things that, if you touch them at all, you will break them," the unicorn answered. "As difficult as it is to hold back, some things can only be appreciated from afar. You can love them only by letting them be."

Karo felt fresh tears slide down his cheeks, but wasn't sure why. He blinked, sending more down the same path. The unicorn bowed its head down, so its face almost touched his, and he felt its horn brush at his rumpled hair.

"Take heart, Hawkchild," the strange beast murmured into his mind. "There will be many loves, of many kinds, in your life.

There will be many pains as well, but, you humans, you cannot have one without the other."

Without another word, the unicorn lifted his head, and silently slipped past Karolan, heading down the deer trail, toward the little stream. After a few moments, Karo twitched about to call after him—but the trail was empty.

The End

Giri's Tale

These events take place when Giri is seventeen years old, approximately one year after the conclusion of the Northnest invasion and Hawkwind's escape with the four children. This same year, in Northborn, Altare takes Vor as his apprentice, but this story takes place in Weldom.

"No."

Pain: it ached. It throbbed in his chest with every beat of his heart.

"No, Giri."

His eyes hurt from weeping, his nose, too. His head had joined in, aching along with them. His throat was sore and knotted from sobs.

"No, Giri. I can never marry you."

He felt like something deep inside had been ripped open, like he bled within. Nothing had ever hurt so badly. He knew it would never end. Happiness, love, would never be his again. He could barely sleep, barely eat. Now and forever he would bear these scars until—

"Giri!"

His master's voice snapped out like a whip. Giri flinched a little, but didn't lift his head. He continued tromping with heavy feet towards the teleportation circle.

"Would you stir yourself to hurry along just a little?"

Colby Srawn, his wizardly master, was rarely sharp with him. He rarely needed to be. Giri was a fast learner, attentive, focused, eagerly obedient, almost frighteningly bright, and possessed of more and more magical power with every day that passed. Until his powers settled, around age twenty, they would keep growing. At the rate his were growing, he was bound to be one of the more powerful wizards of his generation. If he had the dedication and dexterity to go along with them, so he could utilize them fully, he would one day be a force to be reckoned with.

Currently, however, he wondered if it would be less painful to die.

Master Srawn sent more than just sharp words next. A harmless but pinching spark snapped Giri in the butt, making him hop and swat at his backside. He aimed a sullen glare at his master. Milsa, Colby's other apprentice and Giri's first and former lover, stood obediently at their master's side. She didn't look at Giri, and her expression was cool and composed under the large wine-colored birthmark that covered a large portion of her face.

Colby never snarled, but his "obey me now" face was leveled at Giri.

"Get in the circle," he ordered, voice as cold and hard as ice.

Giri shuffled a little faster and joined his master, opposite Milsa. It was only the second time Giri had been teleported. His master had taken him along once before, to show him what it was like, but had merely moved the pair of them from one teleportation platform to another. Teleportation was a terrifyingly difficult skill considering the many, many errors most wizards made while learning it. Done wrong, it would result in the death of anything living being teleported. Inanimate objects could also be split, burned, and deformed in a botched attempt.

Colby, however, was a pro.

"Thank you," he said blandly as Giri joined them. "Hands."

Colby took one of Giri's hands, and Milsa took the other, but the latter dropped it immediately with a faint sound of disgust.

"Giri," his master ordered softly, "tamp down your emotions. I can't focus with you shoving them at me like that."

"I'm not shoving anything," Giri gritted out.

"If you are this incapacitated, I will leave you here," Colby threatened. "You'll be a danger to yourself and of no use to anyone like this."

"I'll never be of any use to anyone ever again," Giri declared, feeling his sore throat start to choke up.

Colby didn't sigh, but nor did he release Giri's hand. "Milsa, a moment?"

The lady wizard pivoted and stepped away, out of the circle and to the edge of the platform, back turned. The wind tugged and snapped at her snug mage robes.

"I understand you're hurt, Giri," Colby said.

"You have no idea," he retorted. "I loved her. I loved her and she didn't love me."

Colby took a few breaths before replying. "Giri, you're very young—"

"Do you have any idea how incredibly not useful that is?" he spat, snatching his hand out of his master's grip.

"Giri, have you ever seen a little child fall down and skin its knee?" Colby demanded. "Have you?"

Giri almost glared at his master, but his better sense made him glare at the floor instead. "Yes," he muttered. "My little sister."

"And did she wail and cry like she was dying?"

Giri's head snapped up. "I know I won't die, alright? I know. It just feels like I'm dying."

"To your little sister, who had never been injured so badly," Colby went on relentlessly, "that skinned knee was a horrible wound, but to you, who had already endured your first skinned knee sometime in the past, it seemed not so very terrible. You knew she'd be fine. If you had asked her to run about after the fall, after the scrape was cleaned and the bandage put on, she would insist she couldn't. Is that right?"

"Yes," he grumbled.

"Even though it was just some skin scraped off, and her bones and muscles were all perfectly functional," Colby said mildly.

"It's not the same," Giri argued, clutching at his chest. "I'm broken inside."

"You are hurt; there is no doubt," his master nodded. "It has been a shock."

"It has," he agreed reluctantly.

"For you have never been hurt like this before. You didn't fall in love with Milsa, did you?"

Giri felt a blush burn his ears. "That was different. We weren't like that."

"So as your intimacy with her dissolved, there was no heartbreak, but you've allowed yourself to throw your whole heart in for Lanisala Salasis. You risked it all and lost. This is something most people go through in one way or another. It hurts now, but Giri," his master grabbed his shoulders, forcing him to stand up straight and face him, "there are people losing their homes, livelihoods, and lives right now in the south. I've been assigned to go there and do what I can to help them. You're my apprentice, so you're coming along to help, unless you tell me you cannot fulfill this duty."

Giri glowered and sulked, holding the pain tightly to him. It was all that he had left of his love for Lanisala.

But—

He was a wizard. His other love was magic. Perhaps going into danger, flinging some magic about, and getting lost in the rush of power would take his mind off the hurt.

"I'll come," he told Colby.

"Then straighten up and act like a wizard," his master ordered. "Milsa, we're going."

The lady apprentice came dutifully back over. Milsa was petite and fierce and passionate. Giri was already more powerful than she when it came to pure strength, but Milsa was much more skilled. Her control and ingenuity far outweighed Giri's. She also had years more experience than he, as she was more than a decade older than he was, and therefore knew more spells and magical techniques.

Colby in turn was around a decade and a half older than her. It was uncommon for a master and apprentice to be so close in age, but Milsa's first master had died unexpectedly, and she'd needed a new one. Colby had been available, and had taken her on. Then he'd taken Giri on, too, mainly because Giri had such potential he needed a powerful and competent master. That Milsa was also a skilled wizard was an extra safeguard when it came to the possibility of Giri losing control and blowing something up.

Giri took a breath and tried to wall away his emotional pain, and this time when Milsa took his hand she did not drop it like a prickly spider.

"Center yourselves," Colby directed, "and provide me what power you can spare. On three."

Colby counted down. Giri shut his eyes, opened his power wells to his master, and vanished from the teleportation platform.

The trio arrived in a courtyard in front of one of the Noble Houses in the south: House Patakara, he thought he remembered Colby saying it was named. Giri took a deep breath after the warp—and nearly coughed his lungs out. The air was stained with smoke. The sky was a thick, low grey-orange. It wasn't from some nearby campfire or outdoor cooking grill. A massive wildfire had taken hold of a portion of south Weldom and the smoke plume stretched for miles and miles, pushed ahead of the fire by the wind. Giri had never experienced anything like it. It even changed the quality of the light to something murky and dim.

Members of Patakara House, a few servants led by a tall man in finer clothing, came running out, scarves tied over their mouths and noses.

"Summon an air sprite," Colby ordered softly. "Keep your lungs clear."

Giri staggered from the power drain. Teleportation was wonderfully convenient for travelling long distances in the blink of an eye, but it took gobs of energy. The larger the object getting moved, and the farther it went, the harder it was. Colby had taken the brunt of the energy cost, but he'd pulled some from Giri and Milsa, too, to spread the burden so they all came out more or less functional on the other side.

The thought of giving energy to an air sprite filled Giri with reluctance, but Colby was right; this air was profoundly unhealthy. Wearily, he closed his eyes, softly sang the cantrip without coughing—air sprites always required a sung summoning—and while their host greeted them, Giri managed to coax over a small air elemental to his plane of reality. He opened his eyes to see it hovering in front of his face. It was white, nearly translucent, with rapidly beating insect-like wings that all but obscured a vaguely humanoid body the length of his thumb.

He offered it some of his own energy in payment for freshening the air around his face. It took it eagerly, and he got the sense that it regarded the polluted air with personal affront. Maybe that meant it would give him a discounted rate on its services. Giri invited it to ride on his head, and it settled on the braid that wrapped his upper forehead. Now all he had to do was remember to feed it some energy every now and then, to retain its assistance. Within moments his lungs stopped burning and the taste of smoke vanished from his mouth. He took an easier breath.

"Come along," Colby said, and Giri refocused on the situation.

He followed beside Milsa, who also had a sprite riding her head, into the house. The air inside was slightly better according to the sense of magical communication Giri detected from the sprite. Sprites—in fact all minor elementals—did not speak in a way Giri's ears could hear, but he could sense meaning and intention from it through his magical senses, and convey directions to it the same way.

The three wizards went with their host into a dining room where a meal was laid. It was plain food and slightly contaminated with the taste of smoke, but Giri tucked in eagerly, needing the energy the food would give him. Colby continued speaking with their hosts, which seemed to be only a couple nobles of Patakara House and a few servants. However, the house didn't feel empty. Giri assumed everyone else had evacuated to the Capital, or some other friendly House, rather than stay in the path of the monstrous wildfire. Why then was there so much human life energy around?

His answer came when a little girl in black braids stuck her head into the open doorway across from him, her big eyes scared and curious. She was dressed in a simple smock, feet bare, and a moment later an old woman in equally plain clothes came hobbling into view and chivvied her away. That explained it, Giri thought. The children and old folks from the nearby village were sheltering in the noble estate while the able-bodied stayed behind to fight the fires. It was a generous act of the nobility, but it was also exactly what they existed for. In peacetime the village supported the nobles. In times of trouble, the nobility flexed their influence and resources, and protected the peasantry.

After the wizards had cleaned their plates, Colby stood. Giri and Milsa copied him, and he turned to them.

"Are you ready?" he asked, and received two nods in reply.

There was no time to waste.

They were given horses and directed down into the nearby town. It was there that the local basecamp for fighting the fire had been set up. Giri knew that there were fires stretched over many miles of land, and by now had been burning their way across it for nearly a month. Several years of increasing drought had been ruining crops and turning the scrubby forests into tinderboxes. Something had touched off the fires, and they'd spread rapidly, merging into each other until much of the south was ablaze. Those who could evacuate had done so, but most of the common people had nowhere else to go. The local guard had of course stepped up to help everywhere, but a wildfire was not something to be fought with swords and spears.

Wizards had been dispatched to help protect the people and work with the local crews who were trying to cut firelines around the towns and villages. The three wizards reached the town, turned over the borrowed horses, and sought the command tent. For this part, Giri and Milsa had only to stand behind Colby, watching, listening, and then obey his orders. Giri had never been involved in fighting a wildfire before, but Colby had, so he claimed, and he knew where to go. Inside the command tent they found a large map of the surrounding area spread out on a table, drawn with features of the land as well as human habitations. A few people stood around planning defenses and looked up when the mages came in.

"Wizards, welcome. Indeed you are well come. We're expecting the fire to reach us tonight," an old grizzled man with a smoke-roughed voice said. He pointed a thickly calloused hand at the map.

"What's the situation and how can we help?" Colby invited.

"Unless the winds change, the fire should approach first here at the southern end of the village. We already have crews out cutting firelines, and the fields should form a natural break on the southeastern edge. The southwestern edge, though, the forest comes much closer to the houses. We'll need someone to watch for spot fires and help put them out, and any assistance in tamping down the head of the fire would be welcome."

"That can be done," Colby said. "What else?"

"If we can stop the head from eating us here, then we worry about our flanks, as the fire burns northward to each side of the town and tries to surround us. The road, here, along with what's left of the river, makes a good line already to the east. The fire should just pass by along it without too much trouble, but then the road curves out eastward as it wraps the hillside going up to the nobles."

"And the fire will be inclined to jump it," Colby nodded.

"That's right, again assuming the wind doesn't change. It's grass and scrub there, mostly. Grass burns easy and fast, and since the villagers here have reduced their herds due to the drought, there hasn't been as much grazing, so the fuels are thick and dry. We're thinking of trying a controlled burn to get rid of the grass ahead of the fire. A wizard might be useful there, to make sure our burn doesn't get out of hand."

"Done," Colby nodded.

The commander nodded in reply.

"What about this?" Colby tapped a small square on the map. It was positioned atop the eastern river, right by the road as it traveled north.

"That's the mill," another man said. He grimaced. "It's on the other side of the road, right next to the trees. We've tried to cut some clearance, but we're expecting to lose it. It's unfortunate, but we think the battle for it will just be too hard."

"Sometimes sacrifices must be made for the survival of all," Colby concurred.

The grizzled commander resumed his instructions. "Of course, we'll be moving our crews from the head as we go, as the fire burns down to the black. We can shift them along, keep pace with the front. If we see a chance to save the mill, we'll take it, but it's not likely. The curve is more important to defend. If the fire jumps the road here at the curve, it could burn back to the town. It could also burn upslope and take our nobles. They've got that wall—should help keep the fire out—and we've already done a burn around the estate, but the fire could still spot over the wall, especially since the winds are higher up on top of the hill."

His already gruff visage darkened. "All the young and old are sheltering there. We can't let it burn. The wizard helping us on the east flank will need to move north with us, to help guide the fire away from the estate."

Colby nodded again. "I see. What about your western flank?"

The old man grunted. "We're cutting fireline, but it's all forest. There is a river in there, but it's not much of one, and it's parallel to the fire's course, so it won't act as a break. Again, the wind should push the fire right past the town, heading north, but if it jumps the fireline, it'll still eat in towards the town and up to the nobles. The town has been gathering wood from the west lately, which has reduced fuels, but it's still a danger."

Colby nodded again. "I will be with your crews at the head

of the fire where it meets your southern line, until it burns down to black, putting out any spot fires in the town."

"Thank you, sir," the man bowed his head.

"Milsa, I want you in the west. Help them with their fireline. Some earth magic should do the trick to get them down to bare dirt. Then as the fire moves along it, watch for spotting across the line and put them out. Since you're dealing with forest, if the fire is in the canopy, it could get rather intense. Be cautious."

"Yes, Master," Milsa murmured.

"Giri, you'll be in the east. If they're doing a controlled burn, I want you there to make sure it doesn't get away. Summon a salamander or two to monitor the fire and tamp it down as needed. Keep it calm."

"Yes, Master," Giri echoed Milsa.

He could summon salamanders, just as he could summon sylphs, or air sprites. Usually salamanders were summoned to set fires, but they could also put fires out, or pull and push fires where the summoner wanted them to be.

"Once the fire comes your way," Colby said to Giri, "the road, the river, and the burn should provide a large safe area. Hopefully, you won't have to deal with many spot fires." Now he glanced between Milsa and Giri. "All three of us will move north with the fire as the head passes. Just keep it from jumping towards the town or estate. I will check in with you when I can, and will go to where I'm needed most. Listen to what the crews tell you."

"Lots of my lads and ladies have been fighting this fire all the way up from the south," the old veteran rasped. "Some towns have been saved and some haven't. The folks from those that haven't, myself included, they've been running afore the fire, trying to help as they go. They know this fire, the wind, the fuels. They know what it's likely to do."

"So listen to them," Colby repeated.

"You should take a waterskin and some rations. You'll be out there all day and into the night, and this is heavy work."

Their commander led them to a pile of supplies and they

took water and some pressed fruit and grain bars. They were also given a heavy, coarse cloak. It was too warm for this late summer weather, but it had a different purpose than to keep them warm.

"If the fire comes for you and you're cut off from your escape routes," the old man went on, "find a clearing with bare dirt and hunker down with the cloak tucked over you. Lay on your belly and dig a pit for your mouth. Dig into the ground as much as you can. Put your feet towards the fire. If you can't do that, run into the black. Don't soak your clothes, though. That will just steam-cook you. Be careful of cinder pits. You fall into one of those and you'll burn. The fire will run with the wind and uphill. I wish I could give you more teaching, but there's no time for it. Do what the crews tell you."

"Understood," Colby said. "Milsa, Giri, let's get going."

They stepped out of the command tent and Colby sent Milsa off at once, but he held Giri back. He walked him over to a quiet corner between a building and a tree where no one was about.

"Giri, you be careful out there," he instructed.

"I will, Master," Giri replied.

"I mean it. Your family would never forgive me if I led you into hurt."

Giri nodded, feeling a bit numb. The threat of the fire coming was real. He knew that. Somehow, it didn't feel as dangerous as he knew it should. He still ached inside too much.

"Listen to the crews," Colby went on. "They've done this before. You're just there to help, as some extra security."

"I understand," Giri said dutifully.

"If you get in trouble, if you need me, call. You're plenty strong enough to reach me, and we've shared enough magic that you should be able to direct the call properly."

"Yes, Master," he repeated. "I've done it before."

"Yes. You have. You are a skilled and talented mage."

Giri couldn't quite meet his master's gaze, but Colby gripped his arms in a bracing sort of manner and gave him a little nudge.

"Get going then. This should be a good exercise for you."

"Yes, Master," Giri said again, bowed his head, and turned to walk back to the road they'd come in on.

He found the fire crew up where the road curved. There were about a dozen men and a couple sturdy women walking along the road, talking, pointing, and considering. Giri stopped to look over the situation. The road curved out to the east to take a gentler approach up the high hill to where the local noble family had their estate. It would be a good hour's hike up the road from there to reach the estate.

Inside the curve was mostly grass, with a few clusters of short trees and shrubs growing along grooves where water ran down during the wet season. The trees looked pale and sparse. A few were clearly dead. On the outside of the curve there were more trees, much denser, especially to the south of the curve. The river ran along the outside, and though it was running so low it was nearly dry, it was enough to make the trees thicker and healthier year round.

This part of Weldom was always rather dry, but normally had a wet season for half the year with light but frequent rain showers. The other half of the year was hot and cloudless. Lately, the wet season had been starting later and ending sooner, with less rain overall. It meant the trees couldn't store up enough water to last them through the extended dry season. They'd started dying. The rivers and wells, too, had started drying up.

Or at least, that's what people were saying. Giri's geography and history lessons had indicated that droughts in this area were not uncommon, but there hadn't been one for a while, so a lot of tree cover had grown up while the rains were plentiful. Now it seemed, it would all be burned down. His ecology class had taught that this was normal; it was how the climate in this region worked and after the fire the forest would grow back up healthier, renewed. Some of the fauna even benefited from the periodic scouring of the forests. For the humans, however, it could mean death, starvation, and poverty — especially if their town burned down.

Giri reached the crew and introduced himself. Everybody was older than he was, and he figured he must look like a kid, especially since he wasn't very tall. Neither of his parents were all that tall, and he'd already gotten a growth spurt—that had petered out. He didn't like looking like he was still a child, and hoped he might get a few more inches in the next few years, if he was lucky.

After another hour or so of wandering and looking, while Giri followed them around, listening and feeling superfluous, the crew began to gather. One man waved Giri over to join them.

"The wind is calming," the man who seemed to be the leader said. "We're going to try a burn before the fire gets here. That'll widen this break, so hopefully the fire won't jump it. Shovels, twenty paces in and make some dirt."

Most of the crew made grunts of acknowledgement and began traipsing off into the scrub, shovels in hand. The leader, a tall man with worn brown skin and some grey in his hair turned to Giri.

"So what can you do for us, young wizard?" he asked.

"I can try to keep the fire calm as you're burning, so it doesn't get away from you," Giri said. "If there are spot fires, I may be able to put them out before they spread, or at least make them spread more slowly."

The man nodded. "That sounds useful. How are you with a shovel?"

"Oh, uh. I can use a shovel," Giri agreed.

The leader handed him one from a small pile beside the road and patted him on the back. "Come with me then."

Giri spent the afternoon digging up and turning over dirt, burying the grasses below it, to make a gap a few feet wide between the section of grassy hill they were going to burn and the rest. He supposed he could have asked an earth elemental for help, as Milsa was no doubt doing over in the forested area to the west. Earth was not his best element, however, and the human labor seemed like enough to do the job. He husbanded his magical energy instead. It wasn't especially hard work at first, but as the hours wore on, his arms and back began to ache.

The ache in his chest was still the greater, though. The manual labor occupied his body, but gave his mind plenty of time to go over and over his final conversation with Lanisala. He'd asked to wed her. She was about his age, they were both wizards, and they'd been sharing each other's beds for months. She was witty, and powerful, passionate in bed, and so lovely. How could it not have been a good match? Especially compared to most noble marriages, it was ideal. Salasis and Holstor were about equal in rank. Maybe Salasis was a bit higher, and there would have been negotiations about who would take the other's name—but Giri hadn't cared about that.

He'd asked her. Her reply had been clear and final, and she'd immediately gotten up, gathered her clothes, and left. He hadn't seen her since. At least she hadn't laughed at him, but still, his dreams had shattered, and likewise his heart. He knew he would never be the same. He would never care for someone again. As the hours passed, his thoughts got heavier, his resolve firmer.

The sky also got darker.

When they'd finished the line all the way from the inside edge of one part of the road curve to the other, they backed off into the part that was to be unburned, shovels in hand, ready to battle the fire if it tried to cross the gap. The leader walked down the line, and when he got to Giri he took his shovel and motioned for him to follow. They walked down to the southernmost point of the planned burn area.

"I'm going to start it now," he said. "It'll burn from here, with the wind. If there's anything you need to do to be ready to help control it, do it now."

Giri stepped back and began the cantrip for a lesser salamander. The crew leader knelt down and got some steel and flint from his pocket. Just as Giri's salamander popped into view, the first sparks landed in the dry grass and caught immediately.

"Off we go," the leader said.

Giri stood and watched with him as the fire began to spread. The leader pointed.

"See, it's heading that way, upslope, with the wind. It'll reach the fireline over there first."

"I think I'll walk the fireline," Giri offered, "as the fire reaches it."

"Good idea."

The fire spread rapidly once it got going, and it cast up additional smoke, darkening the day even further. The smoke also blew right towards where the fire crew was waiting on the other side of the fireline, in case the fire jumped it. They tightened their face scarves, crouched down, and did their best to stay out of the smoke, but it couldn't have been pleasant. Giri's air sprite continued cleansing the air around his face, so he never had to breathe the smoke in. If he'd had the energy, he would have summoned air sprites for everyone in the village, but he'd have to pay all those sprites, and it would exhaust him.

He sent the salamander ahead to patrol the line, magically telling it what could and must not burn. A few times the fire did jump the line, but either the salamander caught it, and put it out, or members of the crew converged on the spot fire and extinguished it with shovels full of dirt and stamping feet.

It seemed like the burn was working perfectly, but then the day darkened as if storm clouds had suddenly rolled in. It wasn't storm clouds; it was the main smoke of the fire. Giri turned to look and saw the smoke rising in banks of sooty darkness to the south, blocking out the sky completely.

A sudden burst of wind shook the trees and kicked up the dregs of their controlled burn. Several new spot fires started, but between the crew and the salamander, they were all smothered. The crew walked the burn as it ran out of fuel, making sure it was dead, as the black and grey smoke clouds loomed closer and closer. The light turned purple and orange. Ash began falling like snow.

The crew gathered, with the leader again waving Giri over.

"We're done here," the man said. "Good work everyone on the burn. Now we head back down the road. The head of the fire will be hitting the southern firelines we cut this morning. It'll come up beside the road. We let it burn. We just watch for spot fires and put them out. We move with the front, up the road. It'll burn up the hill and when we get there we keep it away from our nobles."

Giri followed as they began walking back down the road. As they did, the smoke cut off the sky and the falling ash got thicker. Fragments of charred leaves began falling from the sky, too. Darkness fell except for the daylight behind them, towards the north, and even that began to fade, until it seemed like nighttime. The wind picked up, too.

"Fires like this," the leader said, leaned a bit toward Giri, "they make their own weather. That's the wind you're feeling. You'll see the flames soon. What you see may be fearsome, boy. Try to stay calm, and stay with the crew. If it all goes bad, run back to the burn we just made and shelter under your cloak."

"Yes, sir," Giri answered, trepidation making his voice break.

They reached the town again, and Giri saw the first flames rising above the treetops to the south.

"It's in the canopy," the leader announced calmly. "It's what we expected. Our firelines are wide. They'll hold. Eyes open now for spot fires."

The fields at the southeastern edge of the town were already fallow, having been harvested recently. The dead plant material had been turned under, so although Giri began to see embers landing, none of them found much to burn. The thatched houses to the southwest, however, were another story. That wasn't Giri's area of responsibility—it was his master's—so he didn't run off to help. He did see a half a dozen lesser salamanders darting through the air, and when embers did land on the roofs and started to burn, the salamanders extinguished the fires by dancing and twirling above them and sucking the flames right up into their own bodies with apparent relish.

Thanks to Colby's elementals, the town might still have a

little damage, but their houses would survive, as long as the wildfire itself didn't cross the firelines and take hold. On Giri's side, the fire began chewing its way past the agricultural fields, staying to the east of the road and the river, and moved north through the trees. A few embers did fly across the road to land in the scrub, but the shovel wielding villagers and Giri's salamander put them out before they could burn more than a few feet.

It was surreal. The sky had darkened nearly to the black of night—but without stars or moon—as the fire rolled around them and the smoke blocked the sun. They could still see somewhat, partly thanks to the light from the forest fire, and Giri's salamander provided him with light as needed. They walked along the road, keeping pace with the head of the fire, though a few crew members lagged, making sure the still-burning forest wouldn't shed embers across the road. Giri watched the trees burn, and looked ahead to the as yet untouched trees, which he had no power to save. His eyes lit on the only structure still in the path of the fire.

"Are you sure we can't save the mill?" Giri asked as they watched the fire approach it.

The all wooden building had a finely built waterwheel, which was no longer turning due to the low volume of water in the river. A small wooden bridge, also nicely crafted, crossed the river from the road to give access. The trees grew almost up to the eaves of the mill, though the grass and brush around the building had been cut down.

"That would be a hard fight, young wizard," the leader of the crew shook his head, and spat some ash from his mouth. "There's very little clearance. If we'd had more time, we could have felled some trees, made a gap, but we had to get our priorities straight. Saving the town, people's homes and shops, is more important. The mill can be rebuilt. The millstones at least will survive."

"Maybe I could hold the fire off," Giri offered.

The man eyed him from his position of superior height. "We've only got a handful of minutes before the fire gets there."

"Will you let me try?" Giri asked.

The leader shook his head. "What would your master say if I got you hurt?"

"I'll take responsibility. Please?" he begged.

The crew leader frowned down at him, but Giri had been on the receiving end of both Colby's and Milsa's frowns, and they were experts. He didn't back down.

"I need to do this," Giri said. "I can do this. I can save the mill."

And if he did die? Well, so what? If he got burned and disfigured? So what? Could burns really hurt more than his heart hurt now? The leader was looking at him dubiously; he didn't believe him.

"I'm going to try," Giri declared, and strode off towards the mill without waiting for permission.

"Wizard!" the crew leader called. "Boy, come back!"

Giri called his salamander closer, using it to shield him from the heat as he approached the edge of the road. The heat drove back the crew leader as he tried to follow. Giri was ahead of the fire, but not by much. Embers and sparks were blowing towards him, but most of the smoke was going up. With his air elemental still clinging to his head, and the salamander between him and the fire, he was able to cross the bridge with near immunity.

His feet made plonking sounds as he strode across the bridge, and then gritty sounds on the path beyond it. He walked around to the side of the mill facing the approaching fire, and planted his feet, preparing to defend the structure. The first thing he could do was draw in power. The fire was pure energy, likewise the heat around him. In the few minutes he had, he drew and drew, trying to charge himself up, while he thought about a plan.

Giri looked up. The trees around the mill did indeed stretch their limbs out to brush at the walls and roof, but they were still higher than Giri could reach. If the fire climbed the trees, it could use the limbs as bridges to reach the mill. The salamander would have to stop it. He'd only have to keep the mill from burning until those branches were burned up. Then, no more bridges.

He could see the fire through the trees now. It was burning the brush along the ground and through the canopy of the forest above. The brush was cleared away from the mill, so that part at least wouldn't be a problem. The air pressed against Giri like wind, but the air elemental on his head kept his breathing free from smoke and the salamander kept him from feeling the heat. The fire came closer and the nearest trees began to catch.

The fire ran along the branches, crackling and hissing through dry leaves and twigs with surprising speed. With a gesture, Giri sent the salamander up to guard the roof. Immediately, the heat hit him like a physical blow and he flinched back, throwing up his arms in front of his face. He staggered back into the wall of the mill, and sensed the distress of his air elemental. It could clean the air, yes, but it couldn't handle this kind of heat anymore than Giri could.

"Boy!" he heard the crew leader yelling. "Get out of there!"

The light of the fire must have made him clearly visible. He'd have to walk back around the mill to get to the bridge, if he wanted to retreat, but if he just held out a little longer he could defend the mill while the head of the fire burned all the flashy fuel from the trees, and then the mill would be safer.

Giri gathered his energies and started to build a shield. His master had been drilling him on shields lately. Keeping out physical objects was the hardest type, but there were other types meant to keep out various forms of energy. Heat was one of them. If he worked it right, he could use the heat energy absorbed by the shield to power the shield, once he converted it.

He started small, building a protective layer of energy in front of his face, so he could lift his arms away. He expanded it, spreading it wider as he spread his hands out to both sides. The air elemental indicated its relief, and Giri, too, felt considerably safer with the shield in place. Some heat was still slipping around the sides, since he hadn't made the shield a complete bubble, but the main heat hitting his front was baffled.

Giri allowed himself a small smile. He'd done it. The shield took energy to run, but with so much heat around he could easily gather more. He glanced up. The salamander was still doing its work, keeping the roof of the mill from burning. It even seemed that most of the branches within range of the roof had suffered the fire now, and all the leaves and smaller twigs were burned off. The branches were still on fire, but not especially close to the mill.

He'd saved the mill.

The pain in his chest lessened a little. He was still worth something. He could still do good work. Perhaps he would be eternally alone, but there was still magic. Magic was worth living for. Giri took an easier breath of hot air.

Then a tree between him and the river let out a sharp popping. Embers and sparks flew, and before Giri could react, fully a quarter of the tree, comprising a few thick, burning branches and what was left of their canopy, split off and toppled towards him. Giri tried to dance back, but slammed into the wall of the mill. He turned to dash away, losing his concentration on his shield so that it collapsed like water.

It wouldn't have stopped the tangle of fiery limbs anyway. They crashed down, showering Giri in sparks as they hit the wall, slid down it, and trapped him in their scalding embrace. He ducked down instinctively. The rough cloak hood fell over his head, shielding him temporarily from the fire, and Giri called back his salamander — but he had to choose. The salamander was not powerful enough to protect him and the mill from burning. In fact, there were so many burning branches against the mill wall now, that it probably couldn't have stopped them all even if he'd told it to.

He called the salamander to protect him, and began batting at branches, trying to get himself out of the tree's grip before he roasted. His air sprite, however, had had enough. It vanished, taking with it the protection it had granted to Giri's breathing. Smoke choked his lungs and he coughed. It was hot, too, scorching on the way down.

Giri struggled out of the branches, swatting at his cloak and started rebuilding his shield. He sent the salamander back to the mill, but flames were already climbing the wall where the branches had fallen. A lesser salamander could not put out that much fire, and Giri called the salamander back.

He'd failed, and he was so hot. The heat was incredible, so far beyond a burn on a finger from a hot pan, or the radiant warmth from a fireplace. This was an oven, and he was the raw meat. It was time to escape.

Giri rounded the mill and came to a stunned stop. The bridge was on fire. A tree grew right near where the bridge landed on this side of the river. Either the fire had jumped from tree to bridge or some embers had landed on the bridge and it had caught. It was fully engulfed; there was no escape that way. There was a narrow gap between bridge and mill. Giri might be able to squeeze through it and cross the river. The flow was low, but the water would still soak his feet, and it was a good three yards across. Plus, the banks and bed were rocky and steep: dangerous footing in the dark. Still, there were few options.

"No time like the present," he muttered to himself.

But before he could make for the gap, the burning railing on the bridge fell outward, fetching up against the nearest corner of the mill, while the center section dropped into the dregs of the river, sending up a hiss and a cloud of steam.

"Wizard!" cried the crew leader from across the river. "Get away!"

Giri figured he could kick away the burning railing and still get through the gap—

And then the world blazed with light, heat, and the massive whump of an explosion. Shattered boards went flying from the walls of the mill. Luckily, Giri wasn't facing the mill directly, and a chunk of board hit his shoulder, not his face. Between the flying wreckage and the impact of the explosion itself, he was dashed to the smoldering ground, his shield in tatters, as burning wood fragments rained on him. The explosion had shaken the trees, so burning branches dropped down on him from above. The heat stole the air from his lungs and his skin tightened painfully.

Giri managed to push himself partway up, and reached down to smother the smoldering of his cloak. He struggled to his feet, smoke still clogging his lungs and making his eyes water. The mill was crumpled and ablaze, and blocking his access to the river. He had only a small slice of land free of immediate fire — the path around the mill — between the inferno that used to be the mill, and the trees still burning like torches. He gathered his will and power to try to make a shield again, but it was terribly hot, and he had to shield around himself in all directions.

His salamander flickered about uncertainly. There was so much fire now, the little elemental could do practically nothing to protect Giri from it, but he asked it to try to keep the heat off his face. Struggling after his breath, Giri tried to assess his options. With so much burning wreckage, getting to the river would hurt, probably set his clothing alight, and it was so, so hot. Many times the heat of a campfire, for the mill contained many times the amount of wood burned in a campfire, only Giri's unsteady shield was keeping it from cooking him at such close range.

He would get burned, possibly seriously, but if he stayed where he was, the heat would cook him and the smoke would choke him.

He looked around, squinting against the firelight and smoke. There was no black to run to. All the trees around him were still on fire, and the brush below them was burning, too, leaving pieces of burning wood all over the forest floor. Walking through that would burn his feet. How far would he have to go? Even if he ran — and didn't fall — his boots could catch on fire. His feet would cook inside them.

He had a slip of bare earth. He could hunker down in his cloak, try to hold a shield over himself, until it was safe to emerge. How long would that be? Another tree cracked just as he started thinking it, and more branches fell across the path, some of them landing in the blazing wreckage of the mill. One wall of the mill still stood more or less upright, but it began to shift and lean. When it fell, it would cover yet more of the path.

He was trapped.

Fear gripped his heart. His breathing sped up. Adrenaline began pumping, making him think a wild run through the forest might be his best bet. Maybe he could get out between the trees and get to the river. He could douse any fire in the water—provided he didn't break his ankles getting down the rocky shore.

But he looked into the oven that was the burning forest, and was afraid: terribly afraid. He feared the pain of burning, and death. His head felt light. His throat and chest were sharply painful from the smoke. His legs shook. His shield wavered. Giri fell to his knees, gasping after his breath, coughing and choking.

He needed help. Giri tried to reach for Colby. He should have been able to do it. He tried to extend his senses, his magic, but he couldn't seem to reach. It was like his magical call dissolved: as impossible to hold as smoke. Then it hit him. He was surrounded by fire. Fire cleansed. Fire unworked magic. It was eating his attempt to reach through it to his master.

He shook, but not with cold: definitely not with cold.

He was going to die.

He was going to burn.

"No," he choked.

If Colby couldn't help, something else could. Giri's brain obediently offered up the memorized cantrip. Almost breathlessly, he began the chant. He'd never done it before, but even though his words barely made sound, he controlled his coughing, kept it smooth, and spoke with intention.

His call was answered.

The greater salamander came crawling out of the blazing ruins of the mill. It looked much like a large lizard, fully as long as Giri was tall from nose to tail tip. Its black skin was crackled, showing white hot fire glowing from within, as though it were a conglomeration of animate lava rocks, solid on the outside, and molten on the inside. It crawled its way to Giri, its head on a level with his where he knelt, and waited.

"Save me," Giri croaked. "Save me from the fire."

He could tell it would. It made no sound or movement, but he sensed its agreement. He had read of the cost. It had to be paid before it would do as he asked. Hands shaking, Giri jerked up the left sleeve of the cloak and his mage robes below. He knew what would happen. He knew it would hurt. It was the price he would pay for his life. He would rather bear the greater salamander's payment, than risk the wild run through the burning trees.

Giri extended his arm towards the elemental, watching its yellow eyes. It opened its mouth, revealing rows of short, sharp teeth, all glowing pink-red like metal heated in a fire, and with a snap bit down on Giri's forearm. He jerked in reaction, and clamped down on a scream. It burned like acid and fire and a hundred spikes.

At the same moment, the heat of the forest fire vanished. The smoke cleared from his lungs and eyes. He was able to take a sweet breath, and coughed out the dregs of ash. Except for the nearly unbearable searing pain of the salamander's bite, he was at ease in the middle of the conflagration.

The salamander took from him his energy. He could feel it draining him, but it would not take it all. It would not kill him. He would survive this night.

He would survive his stupidity.

Colby would be furious.

Giri put his free hand to his forehead and almost laughed. Then the salamander resettled its bite, a bit higher up his arm, and that drove all mirth from him. He gasped and a whine of pain slipped out as his body quivered in reaction. It seemed, however, that the salamander had gotten all the payment it needed, for a moment later it let go.

Giri curled his wounded arm against his chest. The salamander's burning bite had mostly cauterized the wounds, but a little blood leaked from a few of the punctures. Its teeth were short. The damage was mostly superficial. He wouldn't lose any use of his arm or hand, but he'd carry the scars forever.

It would be a good reminder not to be reckless.

The salamander turned, a surprisingly rapid movement, but akin to how any lizard could sling itself swiftly about. It headed towards what had been the gap between bridge and mill, and waded into the wreckage. It tossed aside burning planks and wall studs, beams and braces. Its nose and tail both swept left, right, left, and right, sending the fiery wood flying. In just a few minutes, it had scoured down to bare earth, a path a good ten feet wide between Giri and the river.

At the same time, it had held on him whatever magic it used to keep him from cooking in his clothes and keep the smoke away from him. Now it stood at the edge of its handiwork and looked back at him, clearly expecting him to walk to the river. Giri got himself up to his feet, legs still shaking. He made the walk, staggering a little. He reached the top edge of the bank, and looked back at the greater salamander.

"Thank you," he told it.

It bowed its head, just a little. It hadn't done him any favors; it had been paid for its work. It jerked its chin a little, pointing towards the river, the road, and safety. Giri nodded, and began his careful descent down the rocky bank. His lesser salamander, which he'd never dismissed, came to hover in front of him. He asked it to go down by his feet and give him a clear view of the rocks by its light. With that help, he made it into the river itself, and sloshed his way across. The salamander helped him climb the other side, too.

On the bank, Colby was waiting, arms folded, just watching him struggle. Giri made it up the bank, and onto his knees in front of his master. He looked up, embarrassed and weary, but Colby wasn't looking at him now. He was looking across the river at the mill, or maybe at the greater salamander.

"They came and got me," Colby said flatly.

Giri didn't speak, just tried to catch his breath.

"You summoned a greater salamander to save your life, when your stupidity put it at risk."

Giri still didn't speak, just kept his head bowed.

"That's very impressive: the salamander, not the stupidity. If I were the type to strike my apprentices, I'd do it now. You could have killed yourself, and you didn't even save the mill."

Then the greater salamander's protection vanished, and Giri felt the heat on his back, even from across the river, and the stink of smoke in his lungs. He hacked and coughed. Colby tsked, muttering something swift and harmonious, and suddenly an air sprite—a different one this time—perched again on Giri's head, keeping his air clean. Giri sucked in an easier lungful.

"You're lucky the rest of the defense went well," Colby growled. "If I'd been caught up putting out spot fires, or if the fire had jumped Milsa's fireline where they couldn't put it out, I wouldn't have been able to come here and scold you."

A few of the fire crew Giri had worked with came running up with a stretcher.

"I can walk," Giri rasped.

"Get on it," his master ordered.

Giri got.

Giri thought he'd never get the smell of smoke out of his hair or off his skin. Repetitive baths were out of the question because of the drought, so he'd had to settle for a sponge bath to remove dirt, sweat, and soot, and then the services of a sylph to remove the scent. He'd been allowed to recover in one of the Patakara House's guest rooms, the villagers who'd been living there having gone back to their village now. Milsa and Colby, of course, hadn't gotten injured. In fact, Giri had been the only casualty out of the whole town except for one twisted ankle and several people who had gotten too much smoke.

The fire had done what fire did and blazed its way north, passing by the town and the noble estate. It had burned itself out on a rocky ridge some miles north—at least this part of the fire had. There were other parts of the south still burning. The rainy season was still weeks away. It was likely Colby and his apprentices would be dispatched somewhere else now. They would see more fire before it was done.

Giri stood by the window of his borrowed room, looking out at the blackened forest. It looked like a mess of charred sticks and spikes, rising out of a carpet of grey, with wisps of smoke still curling up in places from patches that still smoldered. Inside the curve of devastation, the town was all but untouched. The sky was still yellow or orange or grey in turns, but it was gradually clearing. It was a sight he'd not soon forget.

He looked down at his scarred arm. In time, the raw, red burns and punctures would fade to pale puckers. For now, it hurt like the blazes, as though it were still on fire, despite the cool compresses he'd put on it.

"I hope it hurts," Colby said as he came into the room without knocking.

"It does," Giri assured him.

"More than your broken heart?"

Giri's eyes flicked up, and he realized with some embarrassment that he'd forgotten about that.

"I guess so," Colby said, smiling a little. "In that case, I'll give you this." He pulled out a little jar from one of his pockets. "Burn cream: it will help."

A sense of profound gratitude washed over Giri. He bowed his head. "Thank you, Master."

Then Colby pulled him into a rough hug, making him twitch with surprise.

"Foolish boy," his master growled. "You could have killed yourself."

"I'm sorry, Master," Giri mumbled against Colby's chest.

Just as quickly, Colby let him go, gripping his shoulders to hold him at arm's length.

"Let me see that," he ordered, and Giri stuck out his arm. "Not as bad as it could be. I've seen greater salamanders do worse for lesser tasks. Sit down."

Giri sat, and Colby started smearing on the burn cream.

"I didn't expect the mill to explode," Giri confessed a minute later, as the pain began to fade.

"Flour," Colby said. "There must have been flour residue

in the mill, and all the wind and heat kicked it up: made it airborne. As soon as the fire reached it, it combusted rapidly, and caused the explosion. If you'd never heard of such a thing before, I doubt you could have guessed the danger."

"That makes me feel a little better," Giri said.

"Don't go feeling too good now," Colby smirked, wrapping his arm in fresh bandages. "I wouldn't want you to ruin your sulk and start feeling happy."

Giri shifted uncomfortably in his seat. "I'm sorry about my attitude, Master. I apologize."

"It happens to all of us who love and trust and give our hearts to another," he said gently. "You couldn't have known how much it would hurt the first time that trust is broken. The trick is not to stay broken, but to heal, and find the strength to love again."

"I don't know if I can," Giri told him, "or want to."

Colby finished tying off the bandage and set a hand on his apprentice's head. "You're young and resilient. You may not think it's possible, but you have the chance of finding deeper, stronger love than you had with Lanisala, unless you decide to never love again. It's your choice."

Colby stood up. "Now, we should get going. Come down for some food and then I'll contact the Citadel. They'll probably have another assignment for us."

Giri rose and followed his master, with his heart not exactly light, but mending.

The End

Juleena's Tale

This story takes place approximately eleven years before the invasion of Northnest, in the land of Weldom, which borders Northnest on the southern and western sides.

The child's shaking arm pointed out.

"There it is, Lady," the boy quavered. "There it is: the snake that bit Meggie. Oh, kill it. Kill it."

The young woman shushed him softly and drew, sighting on the red and brown banded, diamond-shaped head. Beside her, the child hiccupped into silence, hands clasped and trembling. The serpent was as thick as her thigh—what she could see of it. At least half of it vanished back into the yawning crevice behind it. She didn't recognize the species—she was hardly an expert—but had no doubt it could move quickly if it wanted to. She thought she and the boy would have time to escape if her shot didn't kill but angered it instead—

But she really didn't want to test that.

She held her breath, lining up the shot, gave a silent wish for the arrow to fly true, and then released it with her breath.

The arrow buried itself right where she'd wanted it: in the center of that angular head. The snake screamed. She hadn't expected that. She hadn't thought snakes could scream, and the volume of it seemed far more than such a beast could—

"Run," she gulped out as the body of the snake undulated, as she realized that it was not the snake's tail, but that the snake was the tail of something else: something huge, something enraged.

Her guide was already pelting away, back through the trees and bushes. When the beast emerged, a chill of horror rooted her to the ground. Taller at the shoulder than she was, the four legged creature lunged from its crevice lair. Its clawed forefeet spread wide and steady on the dirt, while its cloven-hoofed hind feet skidded a little, kicking up pebbles and dust.

Scorching eyes, one with a vertical slit like a cat and the other with the rectangular pupil of an ewe, swept over the brush the lady archer hid behind. She strangled a scream in her throat, turning it into just a whimper, but the beast's tufted, triangular ears homed in on the sound, and then its gaze followed.

Massive, carnivorous jaws gaped wide, and the young woman finally managed to get her legs moving. She staggered out of her crouch, nearly falling, and thrust herself up into a run, rapidly attaining a sprint. She ducked and dodged trunks and larger tree limbs while crashing right through bushes and less intimidating branches.

Behind her, the forest burst into flame.

This time, a wordless scream broke from her. The heat rushed up against her back, but she didn't feel any actual burning, so she kept running. It didn't matter where—anywhere—anywhere away, far away. With the primal need for flight pumping through her veins, all she could do was run as fast as possible.

She ran right into a troop of the local Guard. They were armed, swords and spears shining in the light, all of them roaring for battle—but they were humans. Even had they been sworn enemies, she would have thrown herself in among them. Any human was better to her than the horror that followed behind, and these recognized immediately that she was not a threat, but a victim.

They parted as they charged what chased her, allowing her to pass between them. The deep, primitive part of her brain registered that the danger was less now, and her feet faltered. A dozen more steps and she ran herself into the ground, nearly cracking her head on a tree trunk as she fell to hands and knees.

Distantly she heard the shouts of the Guard, and a roar of fury, but her heartbeat was pounding in her ears, and her ragged breath so gasping that it made the sounds of battle seem far away. Somehow, she hadn't lost her bow, and it slipped down off her shoulder to knock against her knuckles, but she didn't feel the impact. Her arms shook. Her vision began to spot with sparkles of black. Tears fell unheeded, oddly without sobbing. An inner voice told her she still wasn't safe, and she tried to start crawling.

How long she slogged through the leaf litter like a mewling babe, she didn't know. It couldn't have been more than a few minutes, but it felt like forever. Her vision darkened to her hands and the ground. Her bow fell behind. Then something grabbed her shoulders, pulling her up and back, and she shrieked, lashing out at what had her. Whatever it was grunted at the hit, but grasped her shoulders harder.

"Miss, you're safe. It's dead. You're alright," her captor declared, though he ears registered only every other word.

After a moment, her brain caught up with her eyes and resolved the face of the guardsman who held her. She saw the design of the rampant drake on his armor — the emblem of the Weldom Guard, picked out in the lemon yellow color of Trivale, the nearest town. Then the words he'd said began to make sense to her.

And then the shaking started. He seemed to see just what was happening, so as her gorge rose in her throat, he turned her and pushed her head down, so she vomited onto the dirt instead of onto him. Tears of shame scorched down her cheeks and the sobbing began.

A rough sleeve wiped her mouth.

"Here, here now," the guardsman muttered. "It's all safe now. The Captain's cutting off that thing's head right now."

A harsher sob gripped her.

"M-my fault," she stuttered.

"No, no, no," he assured her. "No one got hurt. Little Wensel got away, and pointed us right at you, not to mention that you ran right through us like a kitten with a dog after it."

She covered her face with her filthy hands, and felt the guardsman pat her back. Through her sobs she heard footsteps, and then something thumped onto the ground.

"Is this your bow, Miss?" another voice asked.

She managed to blink up. "Yes," she confessed, reaching out a hand for the bow the new arrival offered.

"And this your arrow?" The bow-offering guardsman kicked at the thing on the ground.

She sucked in a cry and recoiled, but the one who'd been comforting her put his arm around her shoulders and she huddled into it. The snake-head-tail of the beast lay utterly dead before her—her arrow between its eyes, blood coating its face.

"A good shot," the standing guardsman complimented. "Had it been just a snake, you'd have cleared the matter up for us."

"No one was going to come," she rasped out, eyes still fixed on the gory trophy. "No one believed Wensel."

"Take that away, will you Burken?" the guardsman holding her urged.

"Should show the weaponsmaster," so-called Burken grunted, and hefted the severed head again. "He'd have you teaching us how to shoot."

The young woman shut her eyes, turning and hiding them against the chest of her protector. He let her, while the barked commands and replies of the rest of the troop filtered through the trees. After a few minutes, her pulse calmed and she managed to stop crying, but her stomach was in a knot and her throat and face ached. By about the time she was lifting her head and wiping her nose on a handkerchief drawn from her sleeve, the rest of the troop came traipsing back, dragging the main head of the beast. Someone flopped the snake-head-tail across it, between its arching goat-like horns.

The man she recognized as the Captain of the troop by the spearhead sewn above the drake on his surcoat, led the group, and came up to where she still huddled under the arm of the kind guardsman.

"Are you hurt, Miss?" he asked.

"No," she confessed. "It just scared me."

"Scared me near out of my wits," the Captain smiled at her, "so I'm not surprised." He kicked the head. "It's well dead now: nothing more to be afraid of. Luckily, the fire it caused didn't take, and we put out anything still burning."

He cocked his hand by his mouth and stage-whispered, "a few of my younger men here wet themselves from fear, and a couple also lost their breakfast, so don't feel ashamed, Miss. Can we take you home now? What's your family name? I don't recall seeing you around the village."

"Oh," she uttered, feeling a bit calmer from the Captain's easy manner. "Yes. I just came down because I heard about the snakebites, and no one seemed to be taking it seriously. I'm Juleena Mrandis, from Lenali, not Trivale, of Mrandis House."

Every guardsman within hearing distance straightened, as if to attention. The smile vanished from the Captain's face.

"My Lady," he floundered. Then he flushed. "Hearthsraven, help Lady Mrandis to her feet at once. I beg your pardon, Lady, for not recognizing you. I'm new to Trivale, haven't been much to Lenali, and hardly expected to see nobility out here."

The guardsman who'd been gently cradling her got up from his knees and extended both hands down to her. She took them and he patiently provided support as she struggled to her own feet. The Captain was at her side by then, offering her his arm. With some reluctance she drew her hands away from Guard Hearthsraven's. Before she turned away to take the Captain's arm, she sought his gaze: truly looked to see the face of the man who'd so kindly cared for her in her fear and weakness.

His eyes were a rich red-brown, like the color the black maple leaves turn at the end, right before they fall. His face, though wide and coarse, showed not the slightest sign that he was a fighting man: no hint of anger, no sneer of bravado, not even any gruesome scars. There was only softness in his regard, and a slight bit of a smile on his lips, but then the expression slid away into neutrality, and he looked down with the usual servility of the commoner towards nobility. Juleena suddenly felt sad.

"This way, My Lady," the Captain said. "Watch your step."

The heads of the beast were dropped off in the center square of Trivale, the town where Juleena's guide Wensel lived, and where Meggie had lived. The girl had been bitten by the snake-head-tail when out playing near the crevice. Then a woodcutter had come in with a bite, too. Both had died. Snakes—much less, venomous snakes—being uncommon in their area of western Weldom, a message had been sent up to House Mrandis, the nearest Noble House and the one that oversaw Trivale, asking for advice and assistance in locating and eradicating the reptile or reptiles responsible. Juleena had witnessed her father and mother dismissing the message in favor of other, more pressing concerns.

"Please allow us to escort you home, Lady Mrandis," the Captain said to her once the story of the fight had been told to the gathered townspeople.

They'd cheered Juleena's attack more than the actions of the Guard, even though the Guard had apparently been sent by her father after all, and the Captain hadn't mentioned that Juleena hadn't been deliberately dispatched as a part of the troop, too.

"Hearthsraven, bring the snake's head," the Captain commanded.

A few other members of the troop had taken minor injuries or were covered in gore, and a couple others had lost control of their bladders from fright, so only Hearthsraven and another man were deemed by the Captain as suitable escort. Before they could depart, though, little Wensel ran over and threw his arms around Juleena's waist.

"Thank you, Lady," he declared into her belly. "My sister is at rest now."

Then he started sobbing, as Juleena petted his hair and assured him that she was, until his apologetic parents came over to pry him off her and take him home, their thanks given as well. It was a walk of a good twenty minutes from Trivale to the walls of Lenali. It wasn't one of the larger cities in Weldom, or even in western Weldom, but it was the largest on Mount Brasson.

Likewise House Mrandis was the most powerful House within it, but a minor House indeed in all of Weldom.

The Captain didn't speak as they walked, though Juleena had half expected him to chastise her for recklessness in going after an unknown danger in the woods with just a bow and a child guide, but it seemed he was leaving that privilege for her father. Thinking ahead, she figured that was exactly what she'd get, and she supposed she deserved it a bit, considering that the threat had turned out to be far more than a snake, and if the Guard troop hadn't shown up, she probably would have been killed.

Furtively, she glanced back. Hearthsraven and the other guardsman were walking behind her and the Captain. The snake's severed head was a gruesome burden in Hearthsraven's arms; he held it away from his body, though it had already stopped dripping blood. Her arrow was still imbedded in it. Hearthsraven had put on some thick leather gloves. She couldn't blame him for not wanting the feel of those dead scales against his skin, but found herself disappointed.

With a rush of blood to her cheeks she realized she'd wanted to see his hands. When he'd held hers to help her up off the forest floor, he hadn't been wearing gloves. His hands had felt strong, a little rough, and warm. He'd been careful to hold hers tightly enough to lift her up, but not so tightly as to hurt. Somehow beyond her control, her eyes flicked up to his. He was watching her, and their gazes met. His face had that soft, about-to-smile expression again, except there was also a shadow of sorrow now, and she whipped her head back to front, cheeks burning.

She completed the rest of the journey to Lenali with decorous obedience. The city was walled with stone, though not as impressively as many others. It had been dozens of generations since the area of Mount Brasson had been brought into the country of Weldom, and the city was newer than that. Bandits were rare, and monsters such as the one the Guard had just slain even rarer, and neither were likely to attack a city of any size. The walls were there instead for intimidation and control. The gates allowed the Guard to keep track of who went in and out. Though bandits were rare, criminals of other sorts still operated where they could, and the nobility of Lenali liked their city kept clean of such unpleasantness.

Juleena and her escort were allowed entry without a word, though there were raised eyebrows aplenty at Hearthsraven's grisly burden and the youngest daughter of Mrandis in the apparently custody of a Guard Captain. She passed through the gates with freedom a few times a week, for she often went down to Trivale or into the nearby forest by herself, so the wall guards knew her. It was an eccentricity her parents had allowed her once she had fifteen years, but she was always to leave word of where she was going and when she'd be back, and she was generally held to that schedule.

In addition, her great aunt had made her a magic stone that she could use to call for help — though Juleena was no mage herself. In the panic of flight from the monster, she hadn't been able to think of it. Even if she had, no one from Lenali could have reached her in time to prevent her from going down the monster's gullet. It made her wonder why she bothered carrying it.

The main roads of Lenali were paved with stone, and the group didn't have to leave them to reach Mrandis House. It was at the center of the city, at the end of the straight main road they'd entered on. They weren't alone on the road; citizens were out doing business and paused to stare as they passed, but none were bold enough to speak. Near the walls, the main road was lined with inns and shops, transitioning to the homes of richer people who weren't quite nobility, sprinkled with a few merchants and an inn or two that provided goods and services to the wealthy. Most of the buildings were made of fine, pale grey stone, the same as the walls and the road, some with wooden second floors.

House Mrandis had a wall, too, though it was much shorter and thinner than the city wall — the latter was wide enough for guardsmen to patrol along the top. The Mrandis wall was ringed with a strip of parkland, and enclosed an extensive garden and orchard with a few outbuildings, including stables, kennel, and a barracks for the half dozen guards assigned to the estate. The House itself — with two stories and two wings — was in the exact center of the grounds, and made of the same pale stone as the rest of the city. The main road circled the walls, resuming its arrow-straight course on the opposite side.

The buildings across the road all around the estate were also owned by House Mrandis. Servants lived in some, though most servants lived in House Mrandis itself. Artists, bards, or other craftspeople occupied others; a few of the elder Mrandises were firm patrons of the arts. Some buildings stood empty, ready to receive guests, and the rest were occupied by the Mrandis branch family. They were not in the main bloodline, but enjoyed the privilege of living off the fat of the House there, and some had their own gainful pursuits.

The guardsmen at the gate to the Mrandis estate recognized Juleena and the other guards immediately, and one left his post to walk with them the hundred yards to the mansion's main doors, along the smoothly paved drive. Juleena tried to keep her head high and not look like a brat that knows she's about to be whipped. She'd brushed off as much leaf litter and mud as she could, but it was still obvious she'd been crawling around on the forest floor. Her hair was tightly braided and hadn't come loose, at least. She hoped she didn't look too much like a hoyden.

One of the main doors opened before the Captain could knock. Hyldi, the head maidservant and Juleena's main keeper, stood there: arms crossed over her spotless white blouse and apron: equally white-haired head held imperiously tall, despite her five-foot height.

"Well," she pronounced in the tone of elders everywhere about to deliver a scolding.

"I'm not hurt, Mum Hyldi," Juleena tried to intercept. "No one got hurt."

The woman's well-practiced finger darted out accusatively. "What is that?"

The Captain bowed. "Mum, Lady Juleena assisted with

dispatching a dangerous creature in the woods, the very one Master Mrandis sent us out to destroy."

Hyldi showed her teeth. "And what were you doing there, Missy?"

"I was trying to help," Juleena protested, dropping the Captain's arm now.

"The Master and Mistress should hear this tale," Hyldi said, holding up her hands to declaim responsibility. She turned to shout over her shoulder. "Lori, bring a sack." She turned back to the guardsmen. "I won't have that foul head dripping on the floor."

An older boy appeared behind the housekeeper carrying a stained piece of sacking.

"Bring them to the blue room," Hyldi ordered him. "You," she narrowed at Juleena, "come with me."

The blue room was the main reception room where city business was done. Juleena's mother and father made the big decisions regarding Lenali and the handful of villages and hamlets within a day's ride—the largest and closest being Trivale. Her mother liked blue, and so had the room decorated in a dozen different shades of it. It wasn't a cheap dye in their region of Weldom, so it also showed off the relative wealth of the House. Juleena had always thought it would make more sense to have the room done in red and black, which were the House colors, but Mistress Mirassi got what she wanted.

As soon as Hyldi stepped in with Juleena in tow they had everyone's attention. Luckily, Juleena's parents were only sitting down with their son—Juleena's older brother and eldest child—for discussion of some thing or another. There were no supplicants or minor nobility to chase out before the dressing down could begin. Their surprise turned to alarm as the guardsmen arrived behind Juleena and Hyldi, bearing the severed snake's head.

"Juleena." Her mother stood. Mirassi was not a tall woman—only a half a foot taller than Hyldi—but she managed to tower even better than the housekeeper did. "Explain this."

"If Mistress Mrandis would allow me," the guard Captain cut in politely.

"No, I won't," Mirassi cut right back. "I'll hear from my daughter."

Juleena was acutely aware of the guardsmen around her, especially Hearthsraven. She didn't fear them, but rather disliked being humiliated in front of them. She tried to keep her chin and eyes both up.

"I went to see if I could help stop the snake bites down in Trivale," she began.

"I sent the Guard to handle that," her father intoned.

"I didn't know," she said. "I wanted to help."

She did not say that she thought her father was ignoring the incidents of bites. She knew enough that showing she doubted his leadership could start rumors flying: better to admit she was ignorant.

"I thought it was just a snake," she went on. "I didn't know it was a," she tried to pick a word, "a monster."

"A monster?" her father echoed with concern.

Now he stood. Considerably taller than his wife, Rodreric Mrandis had managed to pass his great height on only to his son. He was lean and lanky, with long dull brown hair he kept back in a tail, only a shade darker than his skin.

The Captain made bold to step forward again. "A chimera, Master Mrandis: the tail only was a snake. Your daughter, seeing only the snake, shot it with remarkable skill." He gestured and Hearthsraven angled the remains for optimum viewing. "She realized her error and made a run for it. Luckily, we arrived in time to head off the beast and slay it."

All three of Juleena's family members stared, brows universally furrowed.

"I thought it best to escort her home," the Captain concluded. "It was my impression that the experience was a difficult one, and I wished to make my report in any case. I have men scouting the area for additional chimeras but they are ordinarily solitary creatures and I don't expect any further problems."

"I thank you for the report, Captain," Rodreric said, "and for pulling my daughter out of trouble." He slanted a glare at his son. "I hadn't expected that when my son asked if he could teach her to shoot, that it would end in her employing her skill to try to slay chimeras."

"It won't happen again," Mirassi proclaimed. "There will be no more running about in the forest with bows and arrows. It is time you took an adult role in this family."

Juleena firmed her jaw. Her mother wasn't saying it explicitly, but she knew what she meant. She was eighteen now: the same age her older sister had been when she married. Her parents had been hinting broadly at it for the past year.

"But, I run errands for the House in Trivale," she protested. "I've established our relationship with the shopkeepers there. If I can't—"

"There are others who can run those errands, or if it must be you, you'll go escorted by the Guard, like a proper young lady," Mirassi said.

"I'll gladly detail any of my men to that service, Mistress," the Captain jumped back in.

Mirassi took only a pair of breaths to consider, and then pointed with her chin. "That one," she said, "the homely one with the snake's head."

Juleena felt a shock go through her.

"Are you certain, Mistress?" the Captain stuttered.

"You said any. Is this one of a disposition to abuse young women?" Rodreric challenged. "And you brought him into my House? What is he doing in the Guard in the first place?"

"No, no, Master Mrandis, not at all: the contrary," the Captain was quick to assure.

Her father set a fist on the table. "Done, then. Juleena, you will remain confined to the grounds unless escorted by a member of the family, staff, or this guardsman. Captain, kindly have him reassigned to the estate. His name?"

"Hearthsraven, Master Mrandis."

When the guards had been dismissed—Juleena didn't dare turn to watch them go—she stood alone in front of her family, with Hyldi back by the door to keep anyone else out. Everyone had sat back down again, and her father folded his hands on the table before him.

"Daughter Juleena of House Mrandis," he began, "you are a credit to us. Your tutors have always reported positively on your progress in your studies. You produce lovely embroidery admired by all. Your sewing is competent enough, if not particularly inspired: your singing and playing likewise. You treat the staff with kindness and firmness such that you have a mutual respect and they obey you."

Now he frowned a little and stirred a random bit of parchment with a fingertip.

"Your boyish habits of archery, wandering the woods and towns in mannish garb," his glance took in her stained trousers, "and cavorting about have been tolerated because of your youth, but you must now face your responsibilities as a woman of House Mrandis."

Her mother took over the lecture on filial responsibility. "We will begin negotiating for your marriage. As your brother and sister both have remained Mrandises, at some cost to us, and Cindra has already produced an heir, more benefit might be gained for the House by allowing you to take your husband's name."

A chill ran through Juleena. "You'd send me away?" she whispered.

Mirassi's expression darkened. "You understand that by accepting your husband's name you could gain a higher place in society, a finer standard of living, greater luxury than you know now? You might even gain the position to become mistress of a House. Of course you could still visit from time to time. Such an arrangement could help House Mrandis recoup the losses we suffered in acquiring your siblings' spouses. You do understand that you must do what is best for your House? Surely, you've considered before that this might become your duty, as is often the case for younger children? It cannot come as a complete shock."

She felt her jaw tightening and she tried not to grind her teeth together. "And I cause problems," she articulated. "I cavort, and have boyish habits."

"Your suitors need know none of your past, and you will present a mature face from now on," her mother said mildly.

Juleena nodded. "Yes, Mother."

Perhaps, if they wanted to be rid of her so much, she should be happy to go, but the life she knew was here. Hyldi, the one who'd been mainly responsible for raising her—far more than her mother or father—was here. Samira, the servant girl who had been her playmate all her life, since they were close in age, and was still her best friend, was here. The quaint village of Trivale—though her rank made it difficult for her to make friends there—was here. Even the more formal town of Lenali, which she'd lived in the center of her whole life, was here. The forests, the land she knew and loved, was here.

But if her husband, for it was inescapable that she had to have one, whether she wanted one or not, was brought here, she would never leave. When she had babies, they would be raised here, with those of her brother and sister, or she would be sent off to live in one of the branch houses encircling the mansion, outside the walls. Third and fourth children were often sent off, and their babies were then outside the direct bloodline of the House. Did that matter to her? If she were traded to a different House, it would probably be to a first or second son. Her children would potentially be in the line of succession.

Juleena closed her eyes and hid a wince. "Whatever you think is best, Mother, Father."

"That's a good girl," Mirassi smiled with quiet satisfaction.

"In the meantime, please do continue running the errands for us that you have been doing in Lenali and Trivale, just with a bit more decorum," Rodreric said. "In addition, you'll begin sitting in on our governing sessions, in case you ever do become the mistress of a House. It will be good for you to have some knowledge of what goes on."

"Your wanderings in the forest, however, are at an end," her mother directed.

"And then she said I can't go out in the forest anymore," Juleena complained to Samira, ever a willing listener.

"I'm so sorry Julee," she sympathized. "You knew this was coming, though."

"I did," she had to admit. "I just hadn't wanted to think about it."

Samira was about Juleena's height, though a bit leaner, with nearly white skin sprayed with plenty of red-brown freckles, and long red hair that she wore up under a scarf, as customary for servants. Her eyes were brilliant green, and she smiled often. Juleena and Samira had been raised side by side since they'd been babes in the nursery. Samira's mother had passed from a lung sickness several years ago, and her father was one of the gardeners. She had a little brother who was following in his father's trade.

"And did you really kill a chimera? At least you got to do that before having to get married and all."

"I didn't really kill a chimera," she sighed. "Is everyone saying that? Gossips. I shot its tail. Its tail is a snake, and I shot the end of it, the head. I didn't know it was connected to a chimera at the time. The guards killed the rest of it."

"It was still very brave, even if you did run away after."

Juleena turned to smile at Samira, now that her dress was laced up and tied by the maid's practiced hands. The two young women intertwined their fingers affectionately: dark and pale skin making a striking pattern.

"You're always so nice to me," Juleena murmured.

"Maybe they'll let me go with you to your new House," she said. "Sometimes a bride's maidservant goes, too."

Juleena shook her head. "No, no, Sami, your father and brother are here. Let's not both of us get ripped away from our loved ones."

Samira gazed mournfully at Juleena. A tear streaked down her freckled face.

"No, no, don't cry. I'm still here," Juleena soothed. She hugged her friend tight. "And maybe there will be some way I don't have to leave."

"You have to get married. All the nobles do," Samira mumbled into her shoulder before pulling away and smoothing her charge's ruffles. "Maybe I don't have to, and can be an old nurse like Mum Hyldi, but you have to."

Juleena winced and turned away. "I wish I didn't have to, but I do. They'll send me off to marry someone I don't even know. What if we can't stand each other?"

"Isn't that always the way noble marriages are?" Samira asked timidly.

Juleena shrugged. "I guess so. My brother got to meet his wife a few times first, and there was a lot more meeting and talking for my sister — you remember. If they're selling me, they'll be trying really hard, making me look good and taking me places. The sellers always work harder than the buyers."

Samira scoffed. "Noble children treated like horses, bought and sold: it's not fair. If I ever do marry, I can probably marry someone I like, maybe even someone I love, and there won't be any bargaining: just convincing my da he's good enough for me, like I'm some great catch."

"You're beautiful, Sami," Juleena declared, "especially when you smile."

The maid turned away, going to fetch one of Juleena's necklaces from the dresser. For reasons Juleena didn't understand, Samira never liked it when she complimented her looks. Other compliments she liked, but not that one. The maid carefully selected a necklace to complement the dress before turning back.

"Julee, have you thought about being in love, like in tales, like in the songs the bards sing?"

"I try not to," she replied shortly.

"I think it would be splendid," Samira breathed.

"You can dream of it, Sami. I daren't."

"Perhaps you'll love your husband?"

"Most of those tales of love end in tragedy, or didn't you notice?" Juleena pointed out. "What if I were married, but fell in love with someone else? My husband's brother? A manservant in the House? That would be nothing but suffering. No. It's better not to love."

Samira caught her eyes as she held up the necklace before her. "You know what old Hyldi would say. She'd say you would curse yourself into a corner, saying things like that."

Juleena just smiled. "Hyldi doesn't mean it."

"Doesn't she?" Samira fastened the necklace for her. "It's dinner time, my lady."

The next day Juleena sat through the four hours in which the elders of the House reviewed recent events, edicts, or issues that needed attention in their region. The High Ministers were the ones who truly ran the country, making large decisions that affected everyone, but they were all in the capital. In the rest of the country, the Noble Houses saw to it that the laws were followed, and dealt with any smaller problems that didn't fall under the wide-sweeping laws.

Juleena wasn't appealed to for her thoughts or opinions; she merely watched and listened. She found it rather dull—but knew that it was important. The common people relied on the nobility for guidance and assistance. The nobility had that responsibility, and answered to the High Ministers if anything went badly awry. The only part she really found interest in was the report from the guard Captain about the chimera hunt.

"And so," her brother was reading, "we conclude that this was an isolated incident, and the forests again are safe for entry, baring the usual possibility of wolves, wildcats, and wasp nests."

Her father nodded. "As expected," he said. "These forests are so tame I'm surprised one chimera showed up. It'd be blasted uncanny to have more than one. Juleena, take word down after we adjourn that we've judged the countryside to be safe again, or as safe as usual."

"Yes, Father," she replied.

"Remember you have to go with an escort. Guard Hearthsraven moved into the barracks here. Have the officer on duty fetch him for you."

She felt a strange and sudden pressure in her chest, just under her sternum, but tried to give no indication of it. "Yes, Father," she said again.

"What of the latest counts on the harvest?" her mother transitioned.

"Promising," her brother reported, "though still too early to know for sure how hard or easy the winter will be."

He moved on to reciting weights and volumes of various fruits, grains, fodder—Juleena failed to concentrate on it. His voice droned on as her eyes went out of focus, and she saw again eyes as red as maple leaves.

She looked into those eyes for real about half an hour later.

Hearthsraven had clearly made himself as presentable as possible to be the escort of a Noble Lady. He was so clean shaven his face was still pink. His hair was slicked back; as short as it was, and so close to his skin color, the effect was to make him look nearly bald. His uniform was impeccably clean and pressed. He even seemed to have cleaned under his neatly trimmed fingernails.

Juleena caught herself looking too long at his hands and tore her gaze away.

"I'm to pass a message to the Trivale council," she said evenly. "It seems I must bother you to escort me."

"It is no bother, My Lady," Hearthsraven bowed.

His voice was a little rough, but rich. That strange pressure in her chest redoubled.

"Let us go, then," she said, hoping her voice didn't sound rough, too.

She didn't take his arm, and he didn't offer, merely followed her like a shadow out the gate of the estate and down Lenali's main road. She'd been required to wear a walking skirt, bodice, blouse, and jacket—not her usual trousers, shirt, and vest. The layers of skirt fluffed and bunched about her legs as she walked, a sensation she disliked, but she'd managed to hide that she wore her usual sturdy pair of shoes below all that volume, not some slim, delicate set of slippers.

All the way through Lenali and down the road to Trivale, they said nothing. Juleena well knew the way to the council hall. There was always at least one member of the ten-member council on duty there, and the town used the hall as a gathering place for many activities so often there were usually several other adults and children of the town there, too.

School was held there during the winter, and small children too tiny for chores were sometimes dropped off at any time of year to be cared for by elders when their parents had some task that required all hands, leaving no one free to watch the babies. The old folks were almost always around, taking advantage of the fire that was kept burning in the hall on cold days, and sitting at ease with their peers to share gossip and talk about how much better things had been when they were younger. They'd be working on some task or other—knitting or carving or mending—if their hands were still good enough, and of course watching over the little children.

Sure enough, when Juleena walked in there were a half dozen of the town's eldest—two men, four women—sitting by the hearth sipping tea, with a trio of toddlers creating a masterpiece out of wooden blocks before them. A younger man, going grey but still able bodied, was sitting at a table at the far end of the room, chatting with another fellow. Everyone looked up as Juleena entered, and the two men at the back stood respectfully.

Even though elders had the right not to have to stand, a few were putting gnarled hands to the arm rests of their chairs, getting ready to lever themselves up, when Juleena took a few long strides over to them and bowed a little.

"How lovely to see you all," she greeted.

She made a subtle suppressive gesture with a hand, and knew their still-sharp eyes had caught it; no one tried any further to get up.

"And you, Lady Mrandis," one old granther winked.

"You're looking lovely, Lady Juleena," one of the women smiled, showing a nearly complete set of teeth. "Trying to look nice for someone special?"

"Pot calling kettle, Mum Bessany," Juleena replied smoothly. "You've had someone braid your hair up again." She nodded towards the two old men. "Watch out for these two knaves here; they look like the type that would endanger a woman's virtue."

They all grinned or chuckled, and she moved off before they could get any more momentum, stepping carefully around the remains of the toddlers' most recent attempt at a fortress—or something. The old folks would tease mercilessly; that was another privilege of age. Juleena only hoped she'd earn that right someday. She wouldn't turn tough and bitter like her mother. She vowed she'd be spunky and annoying and say all the uncomfortable truths she wanted, because old ladies had to be tolerated and couldn't be scolded into propriety anymore.

"Lady Mrandis," the older man at the back table greeted. "What brings you all this way to our little hall?"

"Councilman Thorred," she replied. "I bring word from House Mrandis. After a thorough investigation by the Guard, the countryside is declared free from Wild Ones."

"Only the usual critters again, then," he nodded agreeably. "Those, we can watch out for. Your news makes good hearing, what with the harvest getting started."

"Should you encounter any further dangers, don't hesitate to report them," she added.

"We shall, Lady, and we'll send word to the other towns, as well."

"My thanks. Have you any other word you'd like carried to the House?"

He shook his head. "None other today, Lady. We'll send a messenger if there should be aught."

She bowed her head slightly. "Good day then, Councilman."

He bowed more deeply. "Good day, Lady Mrandis."

Juleena turned to depart, giving a smile to the elders and the toddlers, one of which waved a wooden block at her. The little imp had curls of blonde hair and dimples. She didn't much want to marry some man she'd never met, or share a bed with him—certainly not right away—but if babies resulted, that she didn't think she'd mind. She only hoped she could raise at least the first one herself: that it wouldn't be taken away and given to nurses and a governess to tend.

Her smile faded. If her parents did wed her to a high ranking House, as they threatened, it was more likely she'd never really get to be mother to any children she might make. In that case, she wished she might be barren. She couldn't stand the thought of having to go through bedding a man she didn't care for, and carrying and bearing the babe, only to have it taken from her—and then being forced to do it again, and again.

"What are you doing, young pup, following Lady Mrandis around?" one of the old men barked as Juleena reached the door and her escort fell in behind her.

Hearthsraven pivoted. "Good sir, I have orders from House Mrandis and my Captain, sir, to provide escort for the Lady."

"Stratus, you rascal, I'll tell your pappy on you," the other old man threatened with a grin.

"My father is aware of my assignment, sir. Shall I inform him of your coming visit?"

One granther elbowed the other. "And why does Hearthsraven's son get to follow a pretty girl around while my grandson gets sent to muck out the stables?"

"Yours gets drunk on duty, you old gummer," Mum Bessany cackled, as Hearthsraven's cheeks colored. "Stratus minds his manners."

"Good day, elders," Juleena interjected, "but I have duties to attend to, and must take my guardsman with me."

She walked off, and Hearthsraven was forced to follow, leaving the chortling old folks behind. She didn't have any other duties, but she walked on into town as though she did, and made a circuit through the market before turning to head back home. Ordinarily she'd wander more slowly, looking at the goods, smiling and nodding and perhaps exchanging a few words with the merchants — but no longer. Servants had seen her leave, and everyone knew she wasn't to wander about idly anymore, so she had to return in a fairly prompt time.

Hearthsraven didn't speak until they were alone on the road between Trivale and Lenali.

"Thank you, Lady Mrandis," he said.

"I didn't give them a chance to do it to me, so they did it to you," she replied. "It was only fair for me to give you a bit of rescue."

"They tease you like that?"

She slowed her steps a bit, and he came up beside her. He was a good bit taller than her, and she had to glance up at him. "They tease everyone like that. Haven't you noticed?"

"Yes, My Lady, but you're noble; they shouldn't."

She smiled. "I'd be sad if they didn't. It shows their affection. No one else treats me with such kindness in Trivale, or in Lenali either."

He seemed to think that over for a minute. "You're treated with respect. It's important for you, and all nobility, to be treated with respect," he said at length.

She nodded. "Yes, but respect isn't the same as kindness, and I think everyone should be treated with respect and kindness, both, commoner or noble."

He thought that over, too. "I think I agree."

Juleena glanced up again, and found herself another smile. "Your name is Stratus?"

"Yes, Lady."

"I'm Juleena."

She could see him swallow, and he looked forward again, resuming a more military posture.

"I know," he muttered.

She stopped walking, so he had to stop, too. When she stuck

out her hand he looked alarmed.

"If you have to follow me around, we should at least introduce ourselves," she stated. "Juleena Mrandis. It's a pleasure to meet you."

She'd stuck her hand out like a man to a man, so he shook it that way, instead of bowing over it. Her hand almost seemed to vanish inside his: his were so much larger.

"Stratus Hearthsraven, Lenali Guard: my hand, my heart, my sword are ever in your service."

It was the pledge members of the Guard gave to the Houses they served, and not what Juleena had been hoping for. As his eyes moved over her face, she thought maybe he saw that, for after a moment, he added: "it is a pleasure to meet you, too."

A smile bloomed, unbidden, stretching her cheeks. Hearthsraven's face colored again, and he dropped her hand, and looked away. Her cheeks burned, too, then, and she also looked away, with the echo of his name in her ears: Stratus.

"Let's continue," Juleena murmured, and moved off.

Hearthsraven followed as before, and left her with a bow at the gate to the estate, without meeting her eyes again.

"There's a summer gathering in Firssan, in Croun," her father announced over dinner a couple days later.

Juleena looked up from her food in some dismay. Summer gatherings were basically parties that lasted around three days, hosted by large Noble Houses and attended by other nearby Houses. They were popular places for reaffirming alliances, or making new ones, by such methods as marriage.

"Mistress Mrandis will be attending, with Juleena, to introduce her to society, and hopefully find her a husband," he went on. "Ledren will go as my proxy."

Juleena's brother sat up to attention. "Father, may I bring Cindra?"

"Of course," Rodreric nodded graciously.

"Can I go, Father?" Juleena's sister Myra ventured.

"You will remain," he replied at once. "With your mother,

brother, Cindra, and Juleena gone, I'll need you and Camin here to assist with governing the House and region, and you have your wifely duties to consider."

The young woman nodded in acceptance, but was clearly disappointed. Juleena would have happily traded places with her. She'd never been to a summer gathering; children were not permitted. She knew there would be dancing, socializing, music, hunting, lots of food, games, and plentiful drinking. Everyone there will have been groomed to within an inch of their life in attempts to make their House look as good as possible. How each person performed in all the previously mentioned activities would be taken into account as well in how the Houses viewed each other and perceived their rankings.

Of course what really determined a House's ranking was how many family members it had, how many children, its wealth both in money and property, the luxury of its estates and grounds, how much political influence it could wield, and if any of its members past or present had distinguished themselves in a manner that brought national or regional attention. Rank was accumulated slowly, over generations. Disgrace, however, could happen much more quickly.

As a newly introduced daughter of Mrandis, every eye would be on Juleena. Her every movement, word, and expression would be scrutinized. Along with the ranking of her House, her performance would determine which parents would broach the possibility of pairing her with one of their sons. She wouldn't be a part of those discussions—her mother and brother would handle them—no more than any of the sons in question would get to join in on the negotiations. At most, the young people getting matched up could go to their parents privately and beg for their own preferences to be considered. Juleena already expected that she would have little say in the matter.

The table discussion had moved on to which horses to use, which carriages, what clothing to bring, and which servants. Juleena didn't contribute. Her opinion did not matter.

***

The carriage rolled on. Riding in comfort, together in the carriage, were Juleena, her mother, brother, and sister-in-law. It had been a journey of two days, stopping overnight at an inn halfway there. It had provided ample time for Juleena's mother to lecture her on the coming gathering, what to expect, and how to behave. Juleena had tried to listen to at least some of it, but more often than not, as she gazed out the carriage windows at the countryside, her mind had wandered, until she realized she hadn't been listening to a word her mother had said.

Three of their own guard—including Hearthsraven—rode in formation around the carriage, just in case, since bandits were uncommon but not unheard of, especially in the less patrolled areas between House domains. Occasionally, Hearthsraven would pass across Juleena's view as he circled the carriage, and her mind would be further distracted from her mother's words. He sat tall on his roan gelding. It was a big beast, for he was a big man. Juleena knew she spent far too much time examining the strength in his arms, shoulders, and legs. He stoutly did not look at her, but she knew he was completely aware that she was there, watching him. He straightened his posture whenever he rode on her side of the carriage.

A second, smaller and more modest carriage followed the first, carrying two maidservants and a manservant, the latter of which was driving it. A fourth servant who would tend to the horses and other more mundane tasks drove the noble carriage. If Juleena leaned out the carriage window a little—something her mother forbade her to do, so she only did it when her mother was napping—she could see the carriage behind and wave at its occupants.

Juleena could take some comfort that her own friend and servant, Samira, had been brought along. Hyldi of course was too important to the running of the House to be done without. Mirassi's maidservant, Kapri, had been brought instead. The two maidservants would be shared among the three noblewomen. Juleena had only gotten Samira because she was already so accustomed to serving Julee, tending her hair and skin, lacing her properly into gowns, and Julee had to be made to look her best. It could have caused problems to have someone else trying to learn how to do all that in a short time.

The daylight was fading as the carriage trundled its way into a town, leaving behind the jarring dirt road for the sudden smoothness of a paved one. Juleena snuck a look out of the windows before her mother jerked the curtains shut.

"Sit back, Juleena," she scolded. "It won't do to have the commoners gawking."

She obeyed, but was curious to see the town. They were in Croun now, headed to the House that was being kind enough to host them for the summer gathering. She'd never seen the area before. Firssan, the largest town in the region, was still a couple hours away by horse, but this House, House Holstor, was close enough, and Mrandis had a good enough relationship that they could stay there. One of Juleena's great aunts had married into the House, though not to a first or second son.

"Let us all be on our best behavior," Mirassi murmured. "Holster out-ranks us slightly, and we don't have any recent ties to them, so they are doing us a favor."

"A pity they don't have any available men," her brother Ledren muttered.

"A match with them would be ideal," Mirassi agreed, "but not possible. Not to worry, there will be other suitable matches at the gathering."

Juleena said nothing as the carriage passed through the town and then up a steep road. Her belly felt cold and heavy. At last the carriage slowed and stopped. There was some muffled talking from outside, and then it moved again, traveling for only another minute or two before stopping for disembarkment. The springs squeaked a little as the driver descended to open the door.

"Jedren," Mirassi prompted softly.

As proxy for Master Mrandis, Jedren exited first, and Juleena heard him greet whoever had emerged from Holster House to welcome them. Cindra went out next to join her husband, then

Mirassi, and finally Juleena. Her mother kept her close and their three guards took up positions close enough to be handy should something go wrong, but not close enough to look threatening to the Holstors, and Samira and Kapri came over to form a sort of guard around the unmarried woman, too.

A man and a woman were there to meet them, both looking to be in their fourth decade, with a phalanx of servants around them. The woman was comfortably smiling and seemed eager to meet the guests. The man, too, looked amiable, with a smile of his own half hiding under his mustache. Both had the dark skin and hair common to the most indigenous people of western Weldom, though the woman was considerably paler than her husband, possibly due to some parentage from central or even eastern Weldom. The country was a patchwork of acquired territories, encompassing a variety of physical types, and noble marriages sometimes spanned across vast distances, which did help refresh the blood and prevent inbreeding.

"Welcome to you all," the mustached man said. "We hope you will be comfortable here during your stay, and that you enjoy the gathering. House Tuma is a close friend of ours and will surely put on spectacular diversions."

"You must be fatigued from the long journey," the woman beside him picked right up. "Please allow us to show you to your rooms."

A half a dozen Holstor servants descended on the carriages, fetching baggage. Another went to take charge of the lesser carriage, and another to guide the Mrandis driver to the stables. Jedren's manservant came to his side, and together the group ascended the white stairs to the main doors of the house.

"These are the Master and Mistress of Holstor," Mirassi whispered to Juleena. "They honor us by greeting us themselves."

Juleena nodded, trying not to be too obvious about gazing around at the Holstor house. While Mount Brasson had expansive managed and wild forests, Croun was a region of wide, steep moors with only light and infrequent tree cover. There were two massive trees—oaks, Juleena thought—to either side of the main drive, but otherwise not many to be seen. Their house was made of stone, like the Mrandis House, but it featured different colors of stone in patterns and mosaics. It also stretched taller, more tower-like, while the Mrandis home was wider and squatter. Wind had played around them ever since they'd entered the region, and Juleena only hoped it wouldn't be chilly inside.

Her fears were unfounded, for the inside was plastered and tiled and softened with rugs and tapestries in abundance. Lamps and fires burned cheerfully. Together, they dispelled any impression of dank caves or dripping tunnels. Their hosts led them up a gracefully curving staircase wide enough for four to walk abreast, and around the hall that embraced the landing to a row of three rooms. Juleena's was placed between her mother's on one side, and her brother and sister-in-law's on the other, as was proper for the unmarried woman.

The room had a palatial bed, dressing table, wardrobe, a table and two chairs by the window, and a small lounge area with a couch, chair, and low table near the fireplace. Behind a folding screen was a divan for Samira to sleep on, but the bed was so big, Juleena thought she'd just invite Sami to share it, as they'd often done since childhood.

"A late supper has been laid in the small dining room," Mistress Holstor announced, "if you are not too fatigued to join us. Trays can easily be sent up, you'd prefer."

"You are too kind," Mirassi replied. "We would be delighted to join you."

"Please, take a few moments to refresh yourselves, and we will see you at your leisure."

Samira helped Juleena swiftly change from her traveling gown into one for dining, brushed out her hair and rebraided it, and then Juleena went with the others downstairs, where a servant was waiting to bring them into the dining room. The food was plentiful and hot, and she tried to be on her best manners as she ate. Conversing was not required of her; her mother and brother did all the talking with the master and mistress of

Holstor. No other Holstor family members were at the table.

By the time the meal finished, Juleena was perfectly ready for a bath and bed, and their hosts did not delay them. Though Ledren went with Master Holster to his study for drinks and some further talk, Mistress Holster pleaded weariness and everyone else retired to their rooms.

The next morning saw Mrandises and Holstors both getting ready for the ride to the first day of the summer gathering. Samira and Kapri descended on Juleena, lacing her into her finest gown, and pulling her braids so tight she feared they'd rip right off her head. Her mother supervised it all, with Cindra and Ledren looking in from time to time to add their own opinions.

After a hasty breakfast, they loaded back into their carriages—since Samira and Kapri would both be required as escorts for Juleena, both to help advertise her and remember and report every sign of interest or disinterest from the parents of unpaired young men. They'd been busy memorizing the House names and colors of everyone likely to be attending this gathering, so they could do their duty on that count, leaving Juleena free not to have to worry about it, but just be as charming as she could.

All the Mrandis women wore the colors of their House—red and black—somewhere on their person. In Juleena's case, her entire gown was in red and black, to let there be no confusion that she was Mrandis, and available for marriage. For Mirassi and Cindra, they just wore red and black ribbons woven into their braids, the way married women usually displayed their House colors. The Holstors wore their colors of dark blue and gold, as well, though they did not have any children of marriageable age to bring to the gathering. The married men had cravats striped with their colors. Unmarried men would wear long jackets in their House colors.

Juleena kept her gloved hands clasped in her lap, feeling nervous and wishing she weren't. The three guardsmen from House Mrandis rode along with them, too, along with three from House Holstor. They wouldn't be participating in the summer gathering itself, but providing security around the border of it, and being prepared to step in for the unlikely possibility that someone drank himself indecent.

When they arrived, the guards had closed in, and she felt Hearthsraven's—Stratus's—gaze on her. She forced herself not to look at him. Ahead of her was the main gate to the Tuma estate: tall wrought iron, with some kind of bird device topping each post. She could hear music and copious talking, laughing, and the clatter of dish ware, indicating dozens, maybe hundreds of people.

"Relax," her mother hissed at her as they began to pass through the gate.

She tried to, but she didn't think she'd ever seen so many people at once. They wore every color of the rainbow, and stood in groups or moved about beneath striped and checkered tents and awnings, since the Tuma grounds had few trees. Tables for sitting and dining and others holding food were scattered all about. She could see three different groups of people playing lawn games with balls, bats, or rackets. An elevated gazebo held a band of musicians.

Mirassi kept a snug hold of her arm.

"This way," she murmured. "Our Tuma hosts will welcome us."

There was indeed a large open-sided tent directly ahead, checked in the Tuma colors of soft orange and rich brown, where several people stood chatting, while an older bespectacled man-servant sat at the back with a book and quill. The Holstors led the way, and were greeted first, with the warmth of old friends. When it was the Mrandises turn, Ledren introduced everyone. Juleena saw that the servant with the book was checking off names. The Tuma Master and Mistress were elderly but not infirm, and welcomed them with every politeness.

Their driver had stepped down from the carriage and brought forward a chest of black maple wood. Within it were the finest of goods produced in the region the Mrandis House oversaw. Ledren presented it to the hosts with a deep bow, and they accepted it graciously, to add to the pile of other gifts they'd received so far that day. Gifts from the visiting Houses were traditional, and offset the expense of putting on the lavish gathering festivities. That ritual complete, Mirassi led Juleena away with Samira and Kapri following. Ledren and Cindra walked arm in arm in a different direction.

"Here now," Mirassi whispered as they paused in the shadow of a pink tent dyed in a pattern of roses. "You three will stay together. As I've told you, unwed women do not wander about alone. Stay within my view if you can, so I can point you out, but you mustn't cling to me."

Juleena's trepidation must have shown in her face, for Mirassi's expression hardened.

"No one wants a cowardly wife," she hissed. "Demure, yes, obedient, yes, modest, always, but if you shrink and shy and cower you'll be looked on as weak. Hold your head up and smile. You have a pleasant face if you'll just make an attempt to put a pleasant expression on it. Kapri will help with crowd control if you start to feel overwhelmed, or make your excuses to seek a place to rest."

"Yes, Mother," Juleena managed to assent.

"Ledren or I will fetch you when we need you. Otherwise, enjoy yourself, but don't overindulge in food or drink."

"Yes, Mother," she said again.

"Kapri, keep her out of trouble."

"Yes, Mistress," the maidservant nodded.

Kapri was tall and bony, almost as old as her mistress, and forthright enough to complement Mirassi's blunt personality. Juleena knew that Kapri would indeed keep anyone from hassling her—not that such rudeness would be tolerated at a summer gathering, and among the nobility, who were supposed to demonstrate said nobility in their behavior.

"Lady Juleena," Kapri said firmly, "let us take a slow walk around the vicinity. You need not engage in gaming or conversation just yet. Just see, and let yourself be seen. Samira and I will be with you the whole time, and you can talk with us freely.

Come now, my lady, be brave. The more confident you appear, the more interest you will excite, the more Houses will consider you for their sons, and the more options your mother and brother will have in making a match for you, so the more likely they will be able to make an optimum match. Do you understand?"

She nodded. It did make sense; her mother had been lecturing her similarly for a few days. Juleena took a deep breath and lifted her chin, settled her shoulders, and felt Samira tidying her hair, sweeping disarrayed strands off her neck so it all fell smoothly down her back. This was unavoidable; sulking or trying to pretend it wasn't happening would not improve the situation. Making an effort might get her better results.

"You look lovely," Sami assured her. "If you do see an eligible man you like, perhaps consider smiling at him."

The trio began to walk off, with Juleena leading and the two maidservants slightly trailing her on either side.

"Samira makes a good point," Kapri concurred, keeping her voice low enough that only they three would hear. "A young man who is charmed by you might make his interest known to his parents. It is always a benefit if there if some appeal between the matched pair, as well as a successful negotiation."

Juleena let her gaze wander lightly across the crowds. Here and there she spotted a young man in the full jacket of his House colors, but there weren't many. After a half an hour of moving at a sedate pace around the dining and gaming areas, she'd counted only seven, though it was possible she'd missed some or some hadn't arrived yet. Samira and Kapri murmured softly to each other behind her the whole time. Even though she wasn't actively listening, their voices were soothing.

"Would you like to stop for some food?" Kapri offered. "You are allowed to eat, you know, my lady."

Juleena nodded, continuing her pace but directing them now to the nearest table. Samira decorated a plate for her with bits of fruit and a little bread and cheese. Kapri guided her to a table under an awning with a touch on her elbow. Juleena sat. Sami set the plate and a fork before her. With as much decorum as she could manage she nibbled at the food, but it sat in her stomach like pebbles.

She succeeded in letting another half an hour pass as she cleaned the plate. During that time, she saw a few other young women pass by in the colors of their Houses—also husband hunting. They'd been among the crowds, too, and though some people had nodded at Juleena or even smiled, these other young women firmly avoided her gaze. They were her competition.

"They're all prettier than me," she muttered to Samira and Kapri.

"They're not," Kapri said flatly, "and even if they were, it wouldn't matter, at least not much. Your House status is far more important. This isn't the first summer gathering I've been to. I've seen it multiple times: everyone will be negotiating for an advantage, for the best results they can get. The physical appearance of the children being paired is of least importance, as long as they look healthy. You should demonstrate your physical sturdiness in a game or two, when you're ready, my lady."

Juleena nodded and finished her food. She stood and orbited the gathering again, paying closer attention to the games in progress. She knew all of them; they were mostly adult versions of games children played.

"You needn't test your skill against other unwed women," Kapri whispered. "It's better to avoid inciting jealousy. Find a game where the married adults are, and play graciously. You needn't win. You just have to look good."

All the formal clothing meant excessively vigorous games involving lots of running weren't possible. Juleena located a stick-ball game—which was just what its name said, a game involving knocking heavy colored balls about on the lawn with paddles—and added herself to the spectators, since a round of the game was already underway.

There was one other unwed woman currently playing, and two unwed men, but that was fewer than other games in progress, and Juleena felt comfortable with the rules and had played it herself many times with her family and the Mrandis servants.

There were ten people playing and twenty balls, two of each color for the ten players. A Tuma servant was keeping score. When the game concluded, everyone clapped and the top scorers took bows. As they cleared the field, they offered their paddles to audience members.

"My lady Mrandis?" one older gentleman queried with a little bow, extending the handle of his paddle in her direction.

"Master Lorinan," Kapri breathed behind her.

"Thank you, Master Lorinan," Juleena bowed back. "I'm sure a paddle used by you will give me luck."

"I can only hope it shall be so," he smiled.

Juleena accepted it, and the man moved past her into the audience. Kapri stepped up close behind her to tie her loose hair and braids into a gentle tail with a bit of ribbon, like that of the other women gaming.

"He doesn't have any eligible sons," Kapri whispered at her ear, "but he's closely allied with House Salasis, and they have two. That young man in blue and yellow is one of them."

"Thank you, Kapri," Juleena said politely when the maidservant had finished tying back her hair.

Samira and Kapri stepped back, allowing nobility to be the front rows of the audience, and Juleena stepped into the play area. The band on the handle of her paddle was purple, so the two purple balls were hers. The young Salasis man was playing yellow. There were three other women, and five other men, but no others were unwed.

Play began, and Juleena did her best, while also trying to be polite, amiable, and keep perfect posture, but she naturally wanted to win and it was hard to remember to do all those other things when she was calculating angles and guessing where her competitors might strike next. She didn't bother trying to keep track of everyone's exact points, but she knew who was scoring high and who low, and she adjusted her shots accordingly. Sometimes her plays brought applause and impressed murmurs from the crowd.

At one point, she struck a great blow against yellow—who

was scoring very well—prompting chuckles, and looked up with a satisfied smile only to see young Lord Salasis frowning at her. Her smile faltered. Within a few more strikes, the game was finished and the score keeping servant read the rankings. Juleena had finished third, right in front of young Lord Salasis, who finished fourth.

The audience applauded the group as a whole, and Juleena made a little bow. She congratulated the others on a game well played, but Lord Salasis walked off without acknowledging her. She rejoined Samira and Kapri after she handed her paddle to an older woman who took it without a word.

"You scored well, my lady," Samira said.

"In the game, yes," Kapri countered, "but not in the game of finding a husband. Lord Salasis did not like being beaten by you."

"It's just a game," Juleena protested softly. "Sometimes you win, and sometimes you don't."

"Well played, Lady Mrandis," said a voice behind her, and Juleena turned to see Master Lorinan smiling at her.

"Thank you, Master Lorinan," she said with a bow. "I did indeed have good luck."

"Skill," he corrected, his smile fading. "A pity."

Juleena was taken aback, but tried not to show it. "Your pardon?"

"It is not your skill that you're being graded on here," he went on, stepping closer and lowering his voice. "Is this your first summer gathering?"

"Yes, Master Lorinan," she admitted.

"Many Houses have difficulty when it comes to picking spouses for their children," he shrugged. "They focus entirely on what they can gain by the match, forgetting that the spouse they choose may someday be a Master or Mistress of their House, and that the House will flourish or falter because of their choice."

Juleena nodded politely.

"I could observe your strategic mind when you played, and

it does you credit. It might, however, complicate your House's selection of a husband for you."

Juleena bit her tongue.

Master Lorinan glanced back towards the game area. "You might also have excluded House Salasis from the running."

"I see," she replied. "Thank you, Master Lorinan."

He bowed. "May you enjoy the rest of the gathering."

She bowed back. "And you as well."

As soon as he turned, Juleena did, too, and strode off until she could find a place to sit in the shade, away from the bulk of the crowd. Samira and Kapri, of course, went with her. Without being asked, Kapri fetched a glass of juice. Without a word, Juleena accepted it and drank.

"Master Lorinan had a point, my lady," Kapri murmured.

"You're saying I should have thrown the game," Juleena gritted out.

"Not thrown it, exactly," the maidservant soothed, "just played with different objectives, for different goals."

"Like not beating an unwed man, a potential spouse," Juleena grunted.

"Sit up straighter, my lady, and smile," Kapri encouraged. "You mustn't appear to be dismayed."

"My mother looks dismayed all the time," she protested.

"Your mother is married with three adult children, secure in her position as Mistress of Mrandis. You are just beginning to build towards that goal. She can act as she wishes—within reason—with more benefits than costs. Your path is far narrower right now. Do put a more pleasant expression on your face."

"Is this how it will be for all three days of this?" Juleena asked.

"Yes, my lady."

Juleena fought to keep a smile on her face, instead of rubbing her face in her hands.

The mingling and gaming lasted until noon, when a proper lunch was served under rearranged tents and aligned tables.

Juleena sat with the rest of her family. Samira and Kapri joined the rest of the servants in tending their charges. Juleena's face was getting sore from keeping a happy expression. She hadn't engaged in any more games, but had watched several and applauded the participants—always being careful to be absent before she could be pressured to play.

She knew it wasn't the proper time to speak of the negotiations for her marriage, so she didn't say a word about it, and neither did any of her family. Her mother's expression was inscrutable. Her brother and sister-in-law seemed to be enjoying themselves. The food, at least, was good, but she reminded herself not to eat or drink heavily, no matter how good it was, per her mother's instructions.

Entertainment followed the lunch. Small stages were set around the estate grounds. On some were musicians. On others were orators or acrobats or jugglers. The most ominous stage, however, had been set aside for performers from the nobility. Juleena had been warned of this, and that she would be expected to perform something. This wasn't uncommon; noble children were trained from childhood to sing and play, girls and boys alike. Some even learned styles of solo dancing—all learned the styles of group dancing; that would happen in the evening after dinner.

Neither her playing nor singing was especially brilliant, but that wasn't the point. It would give everyone the chance to blatantly look at her, and demonstrate that she had the discipline to practice until competence had been reached. She'd had some time to think about what to do, and had chosen to play, not sing, since she feared nervousness would close her throat, but would not so strongly affect her fingers.

A piano was on the stage, and there were several handheld instruments to choose from on a table beside it. Juleena's instrument was the yaus, a large stringed type played with a bow, and so large that one end had to rest on the floor between her feet, and the upper part against her shoulders as she played. It wasn't common, but her paternal grandmother had given one to her as a birthday gift, and the old woman had been so kind to her that Juleena had taken it up once she got old enough.

Luckily, there was one here.

Much of the crowd settled down in front of the stage: only a few little groups or pairs wandering off to the other stages around the grounds. Juleena sat with her family, watching through a few different young people, as well as a few older, as they played or sang to accompaniment. After each performance, the audience would applaud politely, murmur a bit among themselves, and in a couple minutes some other person would get up to take a turn.

Juleena's anxiety twisted in her. She'd played in front of audiences before, but never any this large, and never in front of such a crowd of nobility, and for such high stakes. The current performer was another unmarried woman: singing along shrilly as a man in the same House colors as her played the piano behind her. It was impolite to wince, but Juleena could glance away with impunity, or even speak quietly to her companions, had she wished. She stifled a sigh and looked across the grounds to one of the few trees, hoping for courage.

There, she was surprised to see a set of tables had been placed. Some of the guardsmen, mixed together from the various Houses they'd accompanied, were taking their lunch. She recognized Stratus Hearthsraven immediately. He stood by himself, drinking something from a heavy mug. Up on stage, the singer mercifully concluded. Juleena clapped automatically, along with everyone else.

Stratus glanced over, and their eyes met.

Juleena pushed to her feet even as the last bit of applause was still fading, and threw her focus to the stage. No one else had stood up; she was able to walk to the tables of instruments without having to do the little oh-no-you-go-ahead no-really-take-your-turn dance with anyone. She hefted the yaus and its bow as though she were a peasant woman grabbing up a goose for butchering, and mounted the steps to the stage.

She swung the chair around, took a seat, and ran the bow

expertly across the strings to check the tuning. Of course, it had been perfectly prepared and the sound shivered on the air—deep and resonant. It was a beautiful instrument. Juleena settled herself and took a moment to breathe. She'd picked the piece she'd play during the carriage ride, and didn't change her mind now. The audience waited patiently. She took one glance up, but not at them; Stratus was still watching her.

Juleena put bow to strings and began: Firedrake's Revenge.

The song started sweetly enough, but the yaus was not an instrument for sweet songs. It's voice thrummed with power, and as the story of the song went, the firedrake—a mythical beast as far as she knew—was wronged, its babies killed, and when it had tracked down those responsible, it had its vengeance.

Juleena had never been a brilliant player, and she knew it, but this song was her favorite, and showed off the strength of the yaus. She put all her frustration of the day into the music, and didn't shy away from the more difficult notes, but rather seized them and wrestled them into submission. The yaus mourned with the firedrake, awakened with it to the stirring of rage, flew on its furious wings to find the killers, and frothed in the fight and victory, before subsiding into sorrow, into solitude.

When the last notes faded, Juleena lifted her bow, finding her arm trembling and fingers cramped. The audience was silent for a few long moments. Then somebody started clapping, and the rest followed: polite clapping, like that given to all the performers. Juleena stood and bowed. Of course: she couldn't expect anything different. After all, she was not that skilled of a player.

Juleena returned the yaus to the table and went back to her seat with a sense of relief; her duty was done. As she glanced at her mother, expecting to see approval, Mirassi's glare hit her instead like a slap. The Mistress of Mrandis hitched her neutral mask back into place at once, but Juleena knew the glare had been a message. She had done something wrong, and she would hear about it later.

Chilled despite the summer sun, her lunch now feeling like

a lump in her stomach, Juleena took a cautious glance over her shoulder. Stratus was still standing there. She met his eyes again. His mouth curved in a small smile and he lifted his mug as though it were a fine crystal goblet, toasting her.

Her own lips curled in reply. The lump in her belly melted, and the chill turned into a pleasant tingle in her back. Stratus smiled a bit wider, but then bowed and moved away. Juleena faced front again, now watching as a young man played a pretty bit of piano. Her mother sat stiffly beside her, but Juleena didn't fear her anger as much anymore.

Between the afternoon entertainment and dinner, the guests were given the freedom of the Tuma home, and most gathered separately in a variety of rooms. Juleena found herself shepherded into a small parlor at the back of the house. The Mrandis servants went along, bearing trays of drinks and light snacks. Juleena took a seat on a hard chair near the window, and Cindra, too, sat down, but Mirassi and Ledren remained standing.

Juleena's mother came and loomed over her.

"What possessed you to choose a song like that, girl?" she hissed.

Juleena frowned. "It's the song I'm best at," she protested.

"Didn't you hear what the other girls were playing?"

"Yes, mainly tinkly little songs inspired by flowers or romantic love—which they'll never get to experience themselves," she pointed out.

Mirassi sighed. "Do you know why they chose such songs? Because it creates a pleasant mood and memory of them: when the masters and mistresses think back on them, the pleasant mood will accompany the memory. When they think back on you they will remember a dark and violent feeling from that song you played."

"Firedrake's Revenge is not dark and violent," Juleena objected. "It's sad and righteous and sorrowful."

Mirassi planted her hands on her hips. "And that is how you want to be remembered?"

"Well." She twisted her fingers in her lap. "No, but it's my best song."

"You didn't have to play your best song," Ledren spoke up.

"And the posture to play the yaus does not flatter a young lady," Mirassi said.

"That's what I know how to play," Juleena pled.

"You can play the piano, too."

"Hardly," she argued.

"Or sing."

Juleena looked away, out the window.

"Don't sulk," Mirassi scolded. "It's not attractive."

"There's no one here to see."

"It's a bad habit. Sit up straight and smile."

Juleena complied, but when she forced her face into an approximation of a smile she knew it must look more like she was bearing her teeth in a snarl. Mirassi sighed again, almost a growl.

"Have some rest," she subsided. "We'll be called to dinner in an hour. After that will be dancing, and I expect you to be pleasant at least."

"Yes, Mother," Juleena said as politely as she could.

Samira offered her a glass of fruit tea, and she accepted it. Taking a sip, she found it quite flavorful, and it improved her mood a little.

"I shall be mingling," Mirassi huffed. "Ledren, you as well."

That improved Juleena's mood even more. The two went out, and Juleena sagged back in the chair.

"I'm going to take a nap," Cindra announced. "I'm quite fatigued from the day. Please don't mind me."

"Alright," Juleena nodded. "I hope you rest well."

There was a divan at the back of the room, and Cindra went to it, lay down, and shut her eyes. Kapri hurried over with a light blanket and covered her. Since no one was occupying the couch in the room, Juleena switched to it and patted the cushion beside her, so Samira came and sat beside her.

"Not everyone disliked your song," the maidservant said. "I thought it was the best I've ever heard you play it. You sounded inspired."

"Thank you, Sami."

Kapri sat down across from them. "Some of the guardsmen were watching, and they seemed to appreciate it, too."

"Did they?" Juleena muttered.

"I also think you performed well, but your mother has a point."

"I wish I didn't have to get married," Juleena mumbled on.

"But you do," Kapri reiterated. "If you play the game better, you'll get better results. The more Houses are interested in you, the higher your value goes, and the more your mother will have to work with when it comes to negotiating a good situation for you."

"But she's not looking for a good situation for me," Juleena grumbled. "She's looking for a good outcome for House Mrandis. She wants to turn a profit on me."

Kapri pursed her lips but did not reply.

"She's never cared about me," Juleena went on.

Samira put a comforting hand on hers.

"I'm sure that's not true," Kapri whispered, but not very emphatically.

"All she cares about is what she can get from me," Juleena added, warming to the subject. "The same as with the servants: wanting the most work possible. The same as with Cindra and Myra: wanting grandchildren from them. At least she won't care if I breed or not, once I'm married off to a different House, as long as they don't try to return me for being barren."

"Lady Juleena," Kapri broke in softly, but insistently. "We are in a strange House. You might be wise to save your strong feelings for expression at a different time. Also, I have heard your mother say that spouses don't get returned for being barren."

It was the closest Kapri could come to scolding her. She huffed and slumped against the back of the couch, crossing her arms. Kapri was right; this wasn't the place to be ranting; other Houses could possibly hear her. Samira put an arm around her.

"It can't be easy," she whispered. "You don't want to be married, but you're expected to do your best to make it happen as your mother wants. I'm sorry, Julee. How can I help?"

Juleena put her hands over her face. "Getting married isn't really the bad thing. I mean, it's not inherently bad. I just don't want to do it this way."

"Very few people marry for love, my lady," Kapri murmured.

She flopped her hands back down onto her thighs. "I know, and I'm not asking for that. I just wish I could be myself. Am I expected to keep up this charade even after I'm married? Won't my husband and his family find out what I'm really like eventually?"

Kapri looked away.

"It's like lying," Juleena concluded, "and it's not right."

Juleena ended up napping, too, curled up on the couch. She wasn't physically worn out—nowhere near it—but her mind was tired and swiftly embraced the opportunity to escape the situation. She slept until her mother and brother returned and awakened her.

"Prospects are not numerous," Mirassi announced, "but the few who are interested in you are Houses of quality. There are scarce Houses where a more interesting woman is welcomed, rather than one who is sweet and compliant. Competent, assertive women are usually kept by their Houses, since they are more difficult to marry off, and can be sure to help lead the House in the future."

"House Lupria seems to be the one with the most interest," Ledren said. "They have a second son who is also a bit different, and think the match would be good."

"Lupria's colors are black and yellow," Mirassi informed. "You should seek him out and dance with him tonight."

"Yes, Mother," Juleena consented.

"Salasis and Oberdon also both showed interest, as well," Mirassi went on.

"Salasis?" Juleena confirmed. "The son scowled at me because I bested him at a game."

"They have two sons," Ledren said. "They have interest in you for their first son, not the second, whom you met."

"He's a bit older, and has resisted settling down," Mirassi explained. "It was implied that he liked how you bested his brother, and his House Salasis is prepared to take any woman he wants, since it's so difficult to get him to agree to marry."

Juleena wasn't sure what to make of that. "What about Oberdon?"

Mirassi nodded. "Oberdon, as I hope you recall, is one of the largest Houses in south-west Weldom. A match with them would bring up your status considerably. They've married three daughters already, and this boy is their only son, their fourth child. Ordinarily, a fourth child would be married into another House, but two of their daughters—the first and second—they kept. The third married out. Their two daughters that remained with the House have had several years to produce heirs and have been unable to. Thus, they are keeping their fourth son, and need a wife for him. If his wife fails to breed, the House will pass to their branch."

She spread her hands and shrugged a little. "Such things happen, from time to time, but in order to avoid it, they are hoping for a sturdy, healthy, young woman. They admire your spirit."

Juleena couldn't help but sigh.

"Salasis's colors are light blue and yellow, and Oberdon light green and dark green," Mirassi said firmly. "Seek them out as well and dance with them tonight."

"Yes, Mother."

"I haven't seen the tables yet, or I could tell you if you'll be seated near any of them, but if you are, be pleasant."

"Yes, Mother," Juleena said again.

She sat quietly and listened as her mother spent the next half an hour detailing all that being pleasant entailed.

Finally, dinner was called and the rested and refreshed guests made their way back to the grounds where tables and tents had again been rearranged to seat them all. Fresh linens and place settings, an abundance of candles, and an array of servants were there to meet them. They passed by insect repelling lamps as they approached, spaced every few feet, and giving off a strong smoke, but within the ring they were free from summer bugs. Gauze curtains were lowered as well, to help keep insects out. The guardsmen were stationed around the tents, though they looked relaxed in the warm evening air; it was highly unlikely they'd be called to do anything.

"Welcome to our summer gathering," the Master of Tuma spoke once everyone had found their places and stood behind their chairs. "We are so pleased that you all could be here tonight. Together, we of the Noble Houses lead our country, and with our unity and cooperation a greater nation is born daily. A toast to all our members, young and old."

Everyone lifted their goblets, drank, and sat. The servants came forward with dishes of food, and the meal began. As was proper, Juleena was seated between her mother and sister-in-law. She took a glance around the table. Oberdon's green glimmered from the other end, much too far away for her to get an unobtrusive look. Salasis's blue and yellow was several seats down, on the same side of the table as the Mrandises—also difficult to look at. Lupria's black and yellow, however, was almost directly across.

Juleena took a covert look. There were four older adults. She guessed they were Master and Mistress, and the married older son with his wife. The fifth member of the family, in the full jacket of black and yellow, had to be the second son. He was studying his plate, eating slowly and methodically, without speaking, his shoulders slightly hunched. As Juleena paid quiet attention to him over several minutes, she noticed he never looked up, and never spoke to anyone. His family members—his father on one side and older brother on the other, never spoke to him.

In appearance he had medium brown skin and dark brown hair, but she couldn't see his eyes. With his face so lowered, she couldn't really see his face, either. He seemed a little soft in the arms and cheeks—not the athletic type. Different indeed: though being quiet and not liking crowds was something Juleena was familiar with, too. She wondered if perhaps in private he was more confident. Perhaps he was scholarly. She thought she remembered him playing the piano with great skill.

Well, with him so firmly ignoring everyone around him, there was no chance of catching his eye, but his family looked at her from time to time, and she made sure to have a smile for them when they did. They seemed to look happily on her. Well, perhaps it would be a match. Juleena found herself wondering if she really cared. She didn't want to love her husband—or anyone—anyway, so did it matter where she went as long as the man and House was tolerable? No Houses ever mistreated their incoming spouses. Such an offense would spread and lower the House's prestige.

The food was decent at least, and as guests finished, they rose and went out through the grounds along a candle-lined path, to where a wide, wooden dance floor had been prepared. Most House estates were too small to accommodate crowds of dancers indoors. Really, only the Houses in central Weldom were that big, thus the smaller ones set up outdoor dancing platforms. Musicians were ready to play at one end, and lamps hanging from poles circled the floor. Benches and chairs, too, were arrayed around the perimeter for those not dancing.

"Up you go," Mirassi whispered, giving Juleena a nudge in the small of her back.

Her sister-in-law Cindra went up with her, and they joined the growing group of women ready to dance the next dance. Across from them, men were gathering, and gradually the two groups strung themselves out into parallel lines, making sure there were equal numbers of the sexes. Juleena looked along the line of men and saw all three of her potential suitors.

Then the musicians struck up the first notes, and the dance was on. The lines moved towards each other, bowed, away again, and back in several times before shifting, and the two odd dancers at each end jigged down between the lines to circle each other and take center positions in the lines. It repeated, giving everyone the chance to dance with everyone else.

That brought Juleena into the center with each of the targeted men in turn. The Lupria man was first. Now she finally saw his face, since he wasn't looking at a plate of food anymore. He was bland, but unobjectionable, a bit shorter than her, slightly pudgy, and sluggish in the dance moves. He didn't smile, but many of the men didn't. His hand, when she took it, was cool and a bit clammy.

The second man was the Salasis older son. He was much taller than her, with a short black beard against rich bronze skin, broad in the shoulders, handsome, but also unsmiling. He gazed upon her with an expression of resignation, but his dance moves were firm and his grip on her hand commanding. Juleena found herself feeling a bit scared of him — or perhaps just intimidated.

The third man was the fourth son of Oberdon, the richest House in southwest Weldom and the one without any heirs. He was lean, paler of skin and hair than Juleena was used to seeing among the western nobility, and sweating with nerves. He looked upon her with an air of desperation. He fumbled her hand and blushed with embarrassment.

Juleena was relieved when the dance was over and she could go back to her family.

"Well?" Mirassi asked softly. "Any thoughts, my child?"

Juleena looked down at her lap. "They all seem to have their pluses and minuses," she muttered. "The Salasis son seems somewhat cold, but maybe that's because I don't know him yet. The Oberdon son seemed nice, but nervous, sort of like me. The Lupria son, I couldn't tell what he was thinking; he seemed so disinterested. I couldn't really say if I prefer any of them over the others."

"Good enough then," Mirassi nodded. "I'll continue negotiations with all of them, and see which gives the better arrangement."

"I might have a better idea later," Juleena felt she had to mention, "once I see them some more. Is it possible I might speak with any of them?"

Mirassi nodded tightly. "In the next couple days, there should be opportunities. Do inform me if you find one of them completely unacceptable."

One of them: so she had the chance to veto one, and one of the remaining two would be her husband. Juleena felt a sinking weight of dread go through her—she didn't want any of them. She tried to tell herself that it was just unfortunate first impressions, that getting to know them better would reveal their best qualities, and that her standards were too high. Yet, there were four other unwedded men she'd danced with, and two of them had been perfectly pleasant, smiling, nodding, and bowing to her with all politeness. Of course, they might have undesirable characteristics that weren't visible, too—and maybe she'd already lost any chance of being matched with them, because she had her own undesirable characteristics.

"Dance again," her mother prodded.

Juleena stood up, and obeyed.

The moon had risen and most of the young people had yielded the dance floor to older couples. Samira and Kapri stayed by Juleena at the benches. She was weary from the day, and eaten up with anxiety over the coming change in her life.

"Can we take a walk?" she asked Kapri.

"We can, my lady, if we stay in the lighted areas," the servant replied.

"Let's go then."

Juleena led them off. Some groups of guests had formed by the pools or under the trees, but she avoided them, walking instead through the heather gardens where tiny flowers sent up a subtle perfume.

Samira came up beside her. "Don't be dismayed, Julee," she murmured. "There is more to joining a new House than just your husband."

"Every one of those men has something about them I don't like," she muttered back. "Oberdon is the least objectionable, but what if I am barren? I don't want to be under that kind of pressure."

"You're surely not barren, my lady," Kapri contributed. "Your cycles are steady and regular, and have been for years. I'm sure you'll have no trouble kindling."

"And then your children would inherit the House," Samira encouraged. "Think of it, Oberdon House, the strongest House in the south-west, led by your children."

"But in a big House, I wouldn't get to raise them," Juleena objected. "Being a mother is about more than birthing babies, and they'd want me to birth a lot, since there are no others from the daughters of the House."

"Well, what about Salasis? You'd be wife to the first son, and it's not a huge House," Kapri suggested.

"I don't like him," she shook her head.

"I think he's very handsome," Samira offered.

"He scares me," Juleena confessed.

"Lupria then?"

"I don't think he cares at all what wife he has, or about anything," she explained.

The two servants fell silent and they walked that way for a while. Juleena was so deep in thought she failed to notice for a moment that they had passed the last of the candle lanterns that had been lighting the path. The moon was near full, and bright.

"Your pardon, ladies," a gentle voice said.

Juleena stopped, looking up, and saw a guardsman ahead of her.

"You've strayed from the path," he said.

He stepped aside to point, and the moonlight caught his face. Her breath hitched for a moment; it was Stratus. He recognized her then—she could tell by the way his posture softened slightly, and a hint of a smile graced his face. After a slight hesitation, he stepped closer and offered his arm.

"May I escort you back, my lady? The ground is uneven here," he said.

Without hesitation, Juleena set her hand on his forearm.

"I didn't realize how far I'd come," she mumbled. "If you would be so kind, Guardsman."

He began to walk slowly, and she paced him. Samira and Kapri followed.

"My lady is enjoying the gathering?" he said politely.

"Yes, of course," she replied, but as they moved into the light of the first lamp, she glanced at his face, quickly. He caught her eye just as briefly, and there passed between them a silent communication. He knew she wasn't enjoying it. She confessed it in her gaze. He was sorry for her, and wished it wasn't so.

Juleena felt a tightness in her chest as they walked back, closer to the dance floor. It was difficult to put a pleasant expression back on her face, and when she turned to thank him, taking her hand reluctantly off his arm, her mask slipped again, just for a flash of a second. So did his—and his look of such tenderness left a pinprick in her heart, and must have shown on her face.

He bowed quickly, perhaps to hide his face. "May you enjoy the rest of your evening, my lady."

Stratus marched back to his post. Samira and Kapri gave no indication that they'd noticed any of the silent conversation Juleena felt she'd just had with the man. In two glances she'd exchanged more with him than she had done dancing several times with her three suitors.

"I'm fatigued," she pled. "I wish to find a comfortable seat until it is time to leave."

Samira and Kapri went with her, and it was thankfully not long until the rest of the party joined them, and her mother announced their departure. Mirassi looked as weary as Juleena felt, so she hoped maybe she wouldn't have to endure much lecturing on the ride back to the Holstor House. They trailed along with other guests in going to the carriages and waited their turn. When their carriages pulled up, Stratus was there to help hand the women up the step and into their seats. When Juleena set her hand in his, she looked briefly at his eyes.

They were soft and gentle in the darkness.

She held his hand as long as she could.

***

The Mrandis party reached the Holstor estate before the Holstors did, but the Master and Mistress of the House didn't need to be there to greet them now; the servants knew them as guests and would welcome them in and help them get settled for the night. Juleena was well ready for it. Despite not doing anything particularly vigorous, weariness lay upon her like heavy winter clothing.

Stratus again helped the women down from the carriage, and she tried to thank him with a smile, but he wasn't looking at her, and when she followed the direction of his gaze, she saw why. The Holster House was lit up, far brighter than it should have been at such a late hour, and servants were bustling everywhere. There didn't seem to be any immediate danger, but Stratus and the other guards nonetheless surrounded the Mrandis party near the carriage, and soon enough a flustered manservant came over to them.

"Mistress Mrandis and family," he bowed, "I beg you please forgive this ruckus."

Juleena caught the scent of smoke, and then watched as a trio of men carried a large piece of furniture out the front doors. She couldn't tell what it was—because it was charred and blackened—maybe a couch.

"There has been a fire?" Mirassi asked, catching on as well.

Just then the Holstor carriage came clattering up behind them. Master Holstor burst from the door before the contraption had even skidded to a stop.

"Did he—?" the head of the family interrupted.

"Yes, Master," the manservant answered. "No injuries, and the fire is out."

"We should have been home. This wouldn't have happened."

The manservant bowed his head without comment, and the Master turned to Juleena's family.

"Please, Mistress and Lord Mrandis, forgive us this disarray. It is nothing you need concern yourselves with. Please go to your rest without upset or delay."

"I can escort you, Mistress," the manservant added.

Now more servants were dragging out a tarpaulin with wreckage piled on it—all partly burned and largely unidentifiable. Mirassi seemed to look around at the mess and decide that she wanted no part in it.

"If you would," she said shortly.

The manservant bowed again and pivoted. The Mrandis party followed, taking advantage of a chance when no one was dragging any other half-cooked furnishings through the doorway to pass inside. The smell of smoke was stronger in the house, all the windows were open in an attempt to clear it, and Juleena saw little bits of ash and smudges of soot on the rugs as they walked. Mistress Holstor hurried in behind them and snagged the nearest servant.

"Where is he?" she required.

Juleena found herself pausing in the hallway from curiosity. An older maidservant emerged then from a parlor to one side. She held a squirming, sobbing little boy in her arms. Her scarf was gone and her hair had half come down from its tidy arrangement. Ash smudged her cheeks and her face spoke of patience nearly worn out.

"He had a nightmare, Mistress," the woman panted, "at least we think so. We heard the screaming first."

The boy's head whipped around, identified his mother, and then he set up a squalling howl and began thrashing his way out of his nurse's grip. The woman—already tired from however long she'd been holding and comforting him—struggled to restrain him.

"It's alright, Bitta," Mistress Holstor encouraged. "Let him go."

The nurse bent down and got the boy to the floor without dropping him. The tyke found his feet and surged off down the hallway, face sticky with tears and the other fluids vigorous crying produced. Juleena took an uncertain step back as he raced towards her as fast as his little legs could go. He couldn't have been more than five years old: dark umber hair loose and disheveled, skin brown and rosy like cherry wood, halfway between his darker father and paler mother. His eyes were puffed up from sobbing, so Juleena couldn't see their color, and he careened into her like he couldn't see out of them.

The boy seized her skirts and looked up, squinting, seemed to identify her as not his mother or any other regular disciplinarian, and swept himself behind her, where he clung to her legs and hid his face, still howling.

"Giri," Mistress Holstor scolded. "Release our guest at once."

The little boy let out a fresh squall, and Mistress Holstor hurried closer, with Bitta the nurse following.

"I beg your forgiveness, Lady Mrandis," the woman pleaded, though Juleena could barely hear over the boy's tantrum.

Juleena knelt and reached for the boy. Surprisingly, he didn't fight her, but he kept his hands fisted in her skirts. She fished a handkerchief out of a pocket.

"Come now," she encouraged, as Mistress Mrandis and Bitta came up to them. "It can't be as bad as all that. You're not hurt, are you? I don't see any blood or anything."

She dabbed at the boy's face. His sobs hiccupped in his chest. His face was getting redder. He didn't seem able to stop crying.

"Your name is Giri?" Juleena asked.

He nodded but still couldn't catch his breath between his sobs. She put a hand on his chest, and the other on his shoulder.

"Look at me, Giri," Juleena instructed. "Just watch my eyes, alright? Will you breathe with me? I'm going to count. One, two, and we breathe in. One, two and we breathe out. Alright?"

Mistress Holstor and Betta stood over them, fidgeting with concern, but didn't interrupt.

"One, two," Juleena said. "One, two."

The boy almost managed it, so she did it again, and he did a bit better, so she added three, and then four. He had a few relapses, but soon enough the hitching in his chest had faded, and he just stood there, exhausted and leaking tears.

"Very good," she praised.

He folded up against her, almost upsetting her balance, and Juleena hugged him gently. Another cry escaped him, but Juleena shushed him.

"Do that and we'll have to do the counting again," she said. "Do you want that?"

He sobbed a bit, shuddered, and then quieted. Mistress Holstor knelt down beside them, smiling with gratitude leavened with concern. Bitta got to her knees, too, looking dreadfully ashamed.

"I'm sorry, Mistress, Lady," the nurse whispered. "I couldn't get him calmed down."

Mistress Holstor put a forgiving hand on her forearm. "Don't distress yourself, Bitta, all is well now. I think Giri just knows you well enough to want to misbehave. Is Andra alright?"

"Yalinda has her. She went back to sleep quickly enough."

"I suppose the nursery is ruined?"

"Quite completely, Mistress."

The mistress of the house gave a little sigh. "But no one was hurt, so I shan't weep."

Juleena petted the boy's head. He seemed to have dropped to sleep from utter emotional exhaustion. She sensed movement behind her and looked to see that her mother and Samira had approached. Everyone else had apparently gone on, following the manservant.

"Give Mistress Holstor back her son, Juleena," Mirassi said softly.

Juleena twitched self-consciously, and immediately began untangling the boy from her skirts.

"Oh, please worry not, Mistress Mrandis," Mistress Holstor smiled. "I am only thankful your daughter handled him so brilliantly. I do apologize for the trouble he's caused."

"My daughter has a knack for trouble, too," Mirassi grunted.

"She is so gentle and kind with children. Thank you, Lady Mrandis, for your generous assistance with our little wizardling."

"Wizardling?" Juleena echoed as she transferred the boy to Bitta's arms.

They all stood then, and Mistress Holstor smoothed back her son's silky hair affectionately.

"It's come on him earlier than is usual," she murmured. "We've been seeing the signs of it for a few weeks, and have sent for his grandfather, who is also talented with magery. He can't be appriced for some years yet, but with my father-in-law's guidance, he should be able to stop setting his bedding on fire when he has bad dreams."

"Gutted the whole nursery he did this time, Mistress," Bitta muttered. "But not a single burn on himself or Andra."

Master Holstor came striding up then. "All is well?" he greeted anxiously. "The little pyromancer has settled down?"

"Thanks to Lady Mrandis," Mistress Holstor smiled. "She soothed him when he was refusing to be soothed."

Master Holstor expelled a great gust of pent up breath, and bowed deeply. "I have never been so grateful to have such a guest. My thanks, Lady."

Juleena shook her head. "Of course. I just can't bear to see little ones crying."

Master and Mistress Holstor both smiled upon her.

"How much I wish we had a son your age," Master Holstor lamented, grinning at her.

"Dearest," Mistress Holstor scolded gently, but she, too, gave a little rueful shrug.

"You flatter me too much," Juleena bowed.

The boy stirred against Bitta's shoulder, and squinted open his tired eyes. "You're too old. Maybe I can marry your daughter," he suggested, with all manner of seriousness.

Everyone laughed or smiled a little—except of course Mirassi.

Juleena bent forward and petted the boy's cheek. "Dear little Lord Giri, if I have a daughter, I would be honored for you to be her husband."

"Alright," the boy nodded, still with the solemnity of someone making a very adult contract. "It's settled." Then he ruined his ceremonial mystique by yawning a yawn that hardly fit on his face.

"Stay with him, Bitta?" Mistress Holstor requested. "I'll come see you before we retire."

"Of course, Mistress." The nurse walked off with her burden of burgeoning wizardry.

"What terrible hosts we are," Master Holstor apologized, "keeping you from your rest."

"Lady Mrandis, is your gown ruined?" Mistress Holstor asked.

Samira knelt on cue and took a look at it. "No, Mistress. No damage is done. With a little cleaning it will be good as new."

"Leave it for our laundress, and she will fetch it directly."

"Thank you, Master and Mistress Holstor," Mirassi spoke up firmly. "We are keeping you from seeing to your household. Juleena, Samira, let us take ourselves out of the way."

The Holstors bowed. The Mrandises bowed. They separated in the hall, and went to the next tasks needing their attention.

"Get some rest," Mirassi ordered before leaving Juleena with Samira.

Kapri had come out of the room where Ledren and Cindra slept, waiting to attend to her mistress.

"Yes, Mother," Juleena consented.

Mirassi paused a moment longer, looking on her daughter with a complicated expression.

"You perplex me, child," she whispered at last. "You always have. Sleep well."

"And you, Mother," Juleena bowed.

Mirassi swept away, and Samira tugged Juleena into her bedroom.

"Your gown's a mess," the servant girl fussed.

"Don't worry over it. The Holstor's laundress will clean it. You don't have to."

Samira and Juleena got ready for bed, bathing and dressing in nightgowns, although Juleena's was silk, and Samira's cotton. They brushed out each other's hair, bound it all up into buns on the crown of their heads, and then flopped together on the big bed.

"That little boy was so cute," Juleena said, voice lowered to their usual nighttime discussion level.

"He was," Samira agreed.

"I want one like that someday."

"A little boy?"

Juleena smiled. "Well, apparently I have to have a girl now, to marry him. I did agree to that."

Samira laughed. "You can't make binding agreements with children."

"The Holstors would marry me into their family if they could," she recalled. "I wouldn't be surprised if they'd accept a daughter from me for Giri."

"You'd better do it soon then," Samira remarked. "That boy is already five or so."

Juleena hugged a pillow to her chest. "I like them. They're such genuine people. I wish they had a son old enough for me."

"You didn't like any of the choices at the gathering, did you? I could tell."

"They aren't choices," Juleena mumbled. "I don't get to have a choice."

"If you had to choose, which one?"

Juleena sighed into her pillow. "House Lupria, I guess. Salasis scares me, and Oberdon is too big, the House I mean. I wouldn't get to ever see my children."

"But he's so odd, Lupria," Samira commented.

"He is, but I think he doesn't really care who his wife is. In a way, that would give me some freedom maybe, and he's second son, so there wouldn't be so much pressure on me. Maybe I could raise my babies myself."

"But you don't like him."

"I don't like any of them. I told you, I don't want to be in love — or like."

Juleena closed her eyes and snuggled the pillow a bit tighter. She could say that to herself, that she didn't have a care for any man, nor want one, and yet why did that guardsman Stratus's face linger behind her closed eyelids? Why did she recall the warm strength of his hand holding hers? He was a far finer man than any of the three that might become her husband. So were other men at the gathering. Why did she have to choose from three such unpleasant ones?

"I'm sorry, Julee," Samira whispered. "I'm sorry you have to go through this. It's not fair."

"It's what I was born to," she breathed back. "Everyone has things they don't want to do, or don't like. We just all have different ones."

"Go to sleep, my lady." Samira petted her hair.

"You should sleep here, Sami," Juleena offered. "I'll bet it's softer and warmer than that divan."

"Thank you."

"Of course. Good night."

"Good night, Julee."

They were up early the next morning and dressed in riding clothes—at least, most of the nobility was. The old or infirm would be sitting it out. Samira and Kapri wore their usual utilitarian gowns, and Cindra had elected not to ride out for the morning hunt that would be the main activity for the second day of the gathering. Western Weldom had no prohibition against women wearing trousers when necessity dictated, and riding to hunt was one such situation. Juleena donned her riding gear with a sense of relative freedom.

Of course, the men would be doing most of the actual hunting. The women would just be following along, with the guardsmen around them in case of any danger. Juleena, however, had her bow, and hoped she might be able to get away enough to take a shot or two at some small game, if she was lucky.

For the journey to the Tuma estate, they still rode in the carriage however, since they might be too fatigued to want to ride home on horseback that night. Once they reached the Tuma estate the servants unharnessed the horses and made them ready for riding. All nobility learned to ride, and while some Houses were wealthy enough for each member to have his or her own horse, and to have particular horses for particular needs, the Mrandis House had only half a dozen horses in their stable, didn't breed them, and all had been trained to be versatile—able to be ridden as well as to pull conveyances.

Juleena milled around with the rest of the crowd while the mounts were readied, with Samira and Kapri at her side.

"You look more confident today, my lady," Kapri murmured to her.

"Riding and shooting I know how to do," Juleena explained, "and hopefully I won't have to mingle or anything."

"Just because you're not wearing the gown of an unwedded woman today, doesn't mean that everyone will forget who you are. The ribbons will help them remember, and they will still be watching you." Kapri gave her the firmest look a servant would ever give a noble. "Your mother's negotiations for your spouse are not yet concluded."

Juleena fought a huff of frustration, brushed a hand over her tightly woven braids bearing the aforementioned ribbons, and hitched a smile onto her face as the master and mistress of Lupria passed by, giving her a critical look in her riding gear, with a bow and quiver over her shoulder.

"You see?" Kapri whispered.

"Juleena," Ledren's voice summoned her. "Ivy is ready."

Ivy was the mare Juleena rode whenever she had the choice. She was older, but still strong and steady, if not especially fast. Juleena scratched at her crest in greeting, and Ivy hooked her head around to snuffle at her jacket, probably hoping for treats. Juleena buckled her quiver onto the saddle and checked the fit of the girth and other straps, but all seemed to be in order.

"Do try not to fall off, my lady," Kapri said from behind her. "Please dismount before trying to shoot."

Juleena half-frowned at her. "I only made that mistake once."

She wasn't skilled enough to keep control of Ivy without holding the reins, and she had to drop them in order to shoot.

That meant she had to get off and hand Ivy to someone else to hold while she shot, or tether Ivy somewhere. The one time she'd thought she could get away with shooting while astride, the snap-whoosh of the arrow had frightened her mount, and the horse—not Ivy, but a more inexperienced gelding—had put her on her rump in the grass, only to look back at her after a few strides in confusion, as if wondering why she wasn't on his back anymore. Ivy might be calmer than Maple, but Juleena didn't dare risk humiliating herself in front of anyone here.

The call came to mount up. Most of the women had a servant or guardsman beside them to assist, and though Juleena had hauled herself into the saddle a number of times by herself, it wouldn't be dignified to do so here. Just as she was looking around for help, a roan gelding came up beside her at a fast walk, and Stratus dismounted smoothly.

"Stand," he commanded his horse, and then: "My lady," he said, dropping to one knee and offering his interlaced hands for her foot.

"Thank you, Guardsman," she murmured, somehow too scared to call him by his name.

She set her foot in his hands, and he boosted her up—just enough to get her other leg over without sending her off Ivy's other side. He quickly got back to his own seat, and allowed her to precede him, following the leaders of the hunt. A dozen dogs ran off ahead, a few baying eagerly, but not yet with the tone that would mean they'd struck a scent.

Juleena nudged Ivy and she kept up with the vanguard easily. Most of the guard hung back, making a loose circle around the women. They rode for some time, heading to lower elevations where there was forest to be found. The hounds startled everything into flight or sent it to ground, but gradually, the dogs drew farther ahead, with only the most vigorous of the hunting men keeping pace.

Juleena knew her brother would be among them, watching how the sons of Salasis, Lupria, and Oberdon performed. A poor performance in the hunt would not exclude any of them from the running for Juleena's hand, but it was one more mark of status to be claimed. If they failed it, their value would be lower, meaning that Mirassi could ask more in exchange for Juleena.

She glanced behind her, at the main clump of women who had fallen back. They were walking their horses at a sedate pace now, chatting with each other. Her mother was among them. Ahead, the older men were pulling ahead, following the younger ones into the forest. Only Juleena and three other women were left in between those groups. Two guardsmen paced them, one of which was Stratus.

The nearest woman looked over at Juleena. She was quite a bit older — past her childbearing days certainly — but she sat her horse like she spent a lot of time there. She, too, carried a bow and quiver, and red and blue ribbons were woven into her slate gray braids. Her skin was warm and wrinkled like old parchment, especially from smile lines. The next woman over was in her prime, and didn't have a bow, but did have a sling, and also wore red and blue. Farthest from Juleena was another young woman: one she thought was also unwedded, who was marked in yellow and green. She was dark skinned and red haired, and didn't carry any weapon, but she and her mount moved beautifully together; it seemed that she was simply enjoying the ride.

"Thinking of shooting something?" the older woman called to Juleena.

Juleena bowed her head. "If there is a chance for it, yes madam."

The woman kneed her horse closer and stuck out a hand; Juleena leaned over and shook it.

"Sissilie," she introduced herself. "House Garanda, former Mistress, retired now." She hooked a thumb towards the next woman. "Gave the title to my daughter when I decided I'd had enough, name of Firella."

The next woman looked over, smiling, and bobbed her dark amber haired head.

"Juleena Mrandis," Juleena said with a seated bow.

"Indeed. We come from the frontier, as far west as Weldom

goes," Sissilie explained. "There are wild lands there, so we all learn to hunt. What say we get away from those noisy men and find us something small and tasty?"

Juleena bowed again. "I'd be delighted."

"Guardsmen, with us," Sissilie announced. "Go quietly."

Sissilie led them, with Stratus and the other guard following, and a third guard broke off at a gesture from a woman in the main pack, and joined them. They moved off at a steep angle to where the men had gone, and rode for a while, until all was quiet. They pulled their horses down to an amble, and moved through shrubbery and scattered trees.

"Good rabbit land," Sissilie whispered. "Let's dismount, go on foot."

They pulled up, but the girl in yellow and green stayed ahorse. Juleena slid easily down Ivy's side, and Stratus came up just in time to take the reins for her. She nodded at him in thanks, strung her bow, and strapped her quiver to her belt. Sissilie led Juleena and Firella into the brush, crouching low and moving as silently as possible, until they came to the top of a bank. In the meadow beyond, a few dozen rabbits were foraging.

Sissilie caught Juleena's and Firella's eyes, and went to one knee. Juleena did the same a few feet away, and Firella picked her own spot on her mother's other side. Juleena tried to gauge where her companions were shooting, and picked a target sure to be different. She drew.

"Three," Sissilie breathed. "Two."

Firella spun her sling, but the subtle noise of it didn't seem to alert the rabbits.

"One."

Juleena let fly, as did the other two, and three rabbits tumbled, kicking, at least one screaming. Sissilie drew again immediately, but all the remaining rabbits were sprinting for cover. Juleena never thought the matron would make another kill, but then a fourth rabbit was thrashing in its death throes, right at the mouth of a burrow.

"Well, done," Sissilie praised. "Let's fetch them."

Juleena had her rabbit dangling from her saddle as they ventured out a bit further.

"Good pheasant land that way," Sissilie had said.

"Better if we had a dog," Firella remarked.

"Toss some stones into the bushes."

"I can't shoot mounted," Juleena said. "Last time I tried, my horse shied."

"Here, have a guardsman hold her for you."

So Stratus rode his roan beside her, leading Ivy, as the group searched for pheasant. Juleena kept her arrow nocked, watching and waiting for birds to break cover. When three finally did, flying up together all of a sudden with a slapping of wings, two arrows and a stone went after them. One bird fell to earth, unmarked but for a bit of ruffled feathers, and Firella tied it at her saddle. The next time, four went up, and two came down, but the killing arrow was not Juleena's.

"A little further," Sissilie said. "Let's find Lady Juleena one more chance."

The sun was nearing its zenith, and they were supposed to be back by lunch, but they went on, and at last another bird broke cover. Only one this time, and Juleena aimed, steady, and let fly. The bird fell to the ground with a futile and final fluttering of wings.

"Well done, my lady," Stratus murmured.

"There," Sissilie grinned. "You're getting the hang of it. If only I had a grandson old enough for you, eh, Fiery?"

Firella smiled. "Alas, both my boys are too young yet, and no one really wants to marry into Garanda. We're far too low of rank: backwoods barbarians, really."

"If I might be so bold as to ask," Juleena said as she fetched her bird. "Where did Master Garanda come from?"

Sissilie chuckled. "There were a few prospects, but none good enough for my girl. She married the Captain of our Guard. He's given us four strong children and led our house to enough prestige to get an invitation here, though we thought it best he stay home with the babies, being a filthy commoner and all."

The mother and daughter laughed together at what must be a long-standing joke. Firella's eyes shone with joy.

"I couldn't have had a better husband," she confided. "Besides, the noble blood hereabouts is mixed and mixed again. I'd rather have some fresh for my babies."

Juleena tied her bird to dangle beside her rabbit. "It sounds like you made a perfect choice."

"Not many see it that way, Lady Mrandis," Sissilie said.

"Well," Juleena grinned as Stratus helped her to mount again. "I've already promised my firstborn daughter to little Lord Giri Holstor, but should I have more than one babe, I will certainly consider a match with Garanda, if you think it's a good one when the time comes."

Stratus passed Juleena back her reins, and she felt his gaze on her face like sunshine.

"We shall see what the future holds," Sissilie nodded. "Your mother has picked a husband for you?"

Juleena's mirth faded in an instant. "She's narrowed the field."

The group turned around and began taking the shortest route back to House Tuma.

"Do any of them strike your fancy?" Firella asked.

Juleena hesitated, not sure if she should speak of it. After all, the other unwedded woman in yellow and green was still with them, and within earshot. She'd keep the names to herself then, but she didn't see how expressing her feelings on the matter could hurt anything.

"Not particularly," she demurred, "but I've not had a chance to get to know any of them yet. No doubt they have their strengths and weaknesses, like all of us do."

"No doubt," Sissilie accepted. "And you Lalla?" She turned to look at the woman in yellow and green. "How goes your quest for a spouse?"

The young woman Lalla straightened. "Likewise," she said. "The possibilities are promising, but my parents have yet to settle on the best choice."

Sissilie nodded.

Firella shrugged. "That's as it usually is. Sometimes I wonder if it's the best way."

The hunting party of women was the last to return to the Tuma estate, and Juleena caught a glimmer of disapproval in Mirassi's eyes as she dismounted and unhooked her catch. A manservant was collecting the rabbits and pheasants from the women, and took hers with the assurance that they would be prepared for the evening meal.

"What did the men bring back?" Sissilie asked loudly.

"Two boar," the manservant answered.

Sissilie sniffed delicately as if that was the least she'd expected. "Not bad then. Lunch is ready?"

"Very soon mistresses, ladies."

He gestured behind him, to where the tables had been arranged. Servants were bringing out platters and trays. The delicious smell wafted around the area.

"Perhaps you wish to refresh yourselves before the meal?" he went on.

"Yes, of course," Mirassi said, grabbing Juleena's elbow. "You smell like horse," she went on under her breath.

Then, as if offended by that statement, Ivy threw up her head, nearly ripping the reins from Juleena's fist. The other horses danced, reared a little, and whinnied with apparent distress. Mirassi stepped back, out of the way of nervous hooves. Everyone had just enough time to start trying to calm the beasts before a stench rolled down over them. Bitter shrieks split the air, making the horses redouble their efforts at escape.

Shadows raced over the ground and everyone looked up. Women began to scream. Three creatures—far too big to be even the largest eagle—swept down over the estate, circling. Their wings screeched as they flapped, like metal twisting. Long, skinny scaled hind legs trailed down, below spread, fan-like tails. Their heads were small, borne on the ends of kinked back, naked necks. The nakedness continued down their undersides, where instead of fur or feathers, they had only wrinkled, loose grey skin.

The trio of creatures spiraled down upon the food tables, crushing them to the ground as they landed heavily, and scattering everyone nearby. They shrieked again, and any servant or noble that hadn't ran yet broke for the nearest shelter. Only the guardsmen and a few others stood their ground. The beasts plunged their faces—eerily humanlike except for a distended jaw full of sharp teeth—into the nearest platter of food. At the same time, they squirted their waste out their back ends.

"Festering harpies," exclaimed a guard Captain, calling to the guardsmen near him. "They'll not stop with the food. When they've finished, they'll kill anything they can catch. We must drive them off, or kill them, now, while they're distracted with eating."

All around came the sliding of steel from scabbards as the guards drew. The horses were frantic now, and Juleena couldn't blame them. The winged beasts were hideous, and their foul odor was making her nauseous. Combined with the fear streaking through her, she had to fight not to vomit.

"Tie the horses if you can," another guard ordered, "and stay behind these walls."

Juleena's group had stopped at the entrance to the estate, so there were solid walls to hide behind. The guards, including Stratus, advanced on the harpies in an orderly formation. Someone grabbed Juleena's shoulder.

"Snap out of it, girl." It was Sissilie. "You have a bow, use it."

Juleena glanced around. Mirassi had already hidden herself behind the nearest wall, and was gesturing frantically for Juleena to join her.

"I can take your horse." That was the girl, Lalla, her yellow and green ribbons trembling with the rest of her, but her gaze was firm.

Numbly, Juleena released the reins into her hands. Firella had already crouched by the gate, watching and waiting with a stone in her sling. Sissilie went to join her, standing up just behind her. Almost stumbling, Juleena went to the other side of the gate. She drew an arrow from her quiver. Her hand shook so she could hardly hold it.

Out at the food tables, the first harpy noticed the advance of the guards. They'd gotten quite close, and now Juleena could understand how large the beasts were. Standing on their taloned feet their shoulders hunched a good five feet taller than the tallest man's head, but they didn't seem very bulky. Their stomachs were getting swollen from all the food they'd been bolting, but otherwise they seemed to be mostly wing, leg, and neck.

The guards lunged and the harpy shrieked. Its wings slammed down, and Juleena realized now why the flapping sounded like twisting metal. The feathers were rigid and sharp—like blades. The first blow sent two guardsmen sprawling and bleeding, but others had dodged in, driving their swords, and the harpy screamed, her belly coated with blood. She danced back with another sweep of her silver wings stained crimson, stumbled, and went down. A dozen swords flashed down at her, and she bellowed her death cry.

It was to be the only easy victory the guards would have. Reinforcements came from the direction of the manor—both guards and armed noblemen—and the harpy nearest them, alerted by its sister's death, slashed its wings, felling three and making another dozen jump back. The other harpy leapt over its sister's corpse, shrieking at the killers. An arrow thunked into it, giving it a moment of pause.

Juleena looked over at Sissilie, who was nocking another. The harpy flashed and smashed its wings at the remaining guards, and two more fell, unable to get back in time. The others drew back, trying to pull their fallen companions away, and the harpy came on. Sissilie feathered it again, and again, but it didn't seem to notice. Firella's stones bounced off it, hardly making it flinch. The harpy struck again, and its bronze wings shone red as another guard fell. The beast darted its head down and bit the man's face. Bone crunched and he gave a gargled scream.

The guards tried to take the chance to strike, but it reacted fast—incredibly fast. Its wings slammed in, knocking three more guards off their feet and forcing the others back. It stepped forward, pinning one fallen man to the ground with its clawed foot. It drew back its head to strike.

Juleena realized that the man it had pinned was Stratus.

Her hands flew as she nocked her arrow. Her first shot went wide. She was aiming for the head or neck, since the harpy hadn't much cared about getting shot in the chest. She drew again, shot, and nicked its neck. The beast hesitated, hissing, as if confused how it had been hurt. Its moment of stillness was enough. Juleena put her next shot into its eye.

It screamed loud enough to make her drop her bow and cover her ears. The harpy staggered back, taking its foot off Stratus, and he surged to his feet with three more guards right behind him. Their swords stabbed in, again and again, as the harpy collapsed, wings flapping in a last desperate attempt at defense. The guards were too close to it now, inside its range, and the blade-like feathers missed them. Stratus swung again and severed its neck.

After a few more moments, the struggling ceased. The harpy lay still.

Juleena stumbled forward, forgetting her bow and quiver, and after a couple steps fell to her knees. She stared, watching as the bloody wings were pulled aside, until she identified Stratus standing up from the middle of the carnage. Relief flooded through her, and a sob burst from her throat. Tears blinded her vision as she bowed her head, shaking all over. Her gorge rose and she couldn't stop it, but at least her stomach was mostly empty, and she only retched up a little bitter acid. She fumbled at her pockets for her handkerchief.

"My lady."

She knew that voice.

"Are you hurt?"

Juleena managed to sit back onto her heels, shaking her head in the negative. Stratus touched a handkerchief to her trembling fingers. His hand was clean; he'd taken off his soiled gloves. She took the handkerchief and pressed it to her mouth.

"You're safe now. They're dead, all three," Stratus told her. He put a gentle hand on her shoulder. "Nothing can hurt you now." After another moment, he added, so softly she wasn't sure at first that she'd heard it: "I'm here."

She nodded and tried to take a steady breath. She counted to two silently, just as she'd done with little Giri the previous night, and then three, and then four, and managed to calm down a little. She wiped her face and looked at him.

"But it was you who kept me safe, wasn't it?" he murmured. "That was your arrow."

She nodded again.

He bowed his head. "Thank you, my lady. I owe you my life."

Somehow her hand had found his. She was clasping his calloused fingers. She wanted nothing more than to throw herself against his chest—covered with harpy blood or not—and cling. His eyes, red as the maple leaves in the fall, stared into hers, and she had the sudden feeling that he wanted her to do that, and that he'd catch her if she did, and hold on for a long time.

"Juleena," her mother's voice cried, almost as shrill as a harpy's.

"She is here, Mistress Mrandis," Stratus called out. "She's unharmed."

His hand was abruptly gone from her shoulder. His fingers slipped out from between hers. Cold despair bloomed like ice crystals inside her and she bowed her head, swallowing a moan. Desperately, before someone could take it away, she clenched his handkerchief in her fist. She heard running feet, and her brother was beside her, and Samira and Kapri coming up behind him. She reached out, but Stratus had stood up, and now Ledren on one side and Kapri on the other were urging her to her feet.

Hardly seeing, ignoring everything they said, she let them lead her to the house, around the carcasses of both harpies and humans. Women were wailing in every room they passed, until they reached the little parlor at the back of the house where they'd rested the previous day. Ledren and Kapri vanished, leaving her with Samira and Cindra.

Cindra sent off Samira immediately to fetch something or other, and helped Juleena to a seat. Her hands were still shaking and she stared fixedly at them. Stratus's white handkerchief peeked out between her fingers. The sudden fight with the harpies and what she'd done to save Stratus bounced through her head like broken glass. Her chest hurt but she wasn't sure why.

When Samira returned with towels and a basin of water, Juleena hardly noticed, and allowed the two women to remove her riding gear, give her a quick wash, and get her into a gown without a word or gesture of protest—except when they tried to get the handkerchief away. After a few attempts, they apparently decided to let her go on clutching it and Juleena eventually stuffed it in a pocket. Samira unbraided her hair and began brushing it out. Cindra knelt before her and took her hands.

"Juleena, are you well?" she asked intently. "Do you want to lie down and rest?"

Wordlessly she shook her head.

"You're not hurt?"

"No," she breathed.

"It was very shocking," Cindra murmured. "Of course we're all still frightened."

Fright was not what Juleena felt. The harpies were dead and held no more fear for her—only disgust.

Kapri came back into the room. "How is she?"

Cindra moved and sat beside Juleena. "Still a bit shaken, but she'll be fine," she said. "What news?"

"Three guardsmen have died," Kapri whispered, and Juleena looked up sharply.

"Who?" she blurted.

Kapri blinked. "Oh, one of Oberdon and two of Tuma," she said. "I don't know their names. Shall I find out for you?"

Juleena shook her head and relaxed. It couldn't have been

Stratus—she'd just seen him minutes ago, but he had taken blows. He might have been hurt and she just hadn't noticed it under all the harpy blood. She gripped the couch cushions, fighting the need to go check on him.

"Several more are injured," Kapri went on. "The surgeons are seeing to them. One horse got away and ran off, but it's being collected."

"The heads of the Houses are in conference?" Cindra confirmed.

"Yes, Lady Cindra. Do you wish to join them?"

"I could contribute little. It is as well I stay here."

She took Juleena's hand, having to tug a little to get her to let go of the cushion. Behind her, Samira finished braiding her hair back up. The maid came around and sat on Juleena's other side, taking her other hand. Kapri sat down across from them on another couch. Juleena stared at the rug, trying to get some shred of reason or logic through the pulsing concern for a guardsman she hardly knew that seemed to be taking up the majority of her mind.

"It's odd," Cindra commented. "We had a chimera not a month ago, and now an attack of harpies."

"Once, when I was a girl," Kapri offered, "there was a manticore sighting. When Juleena was little, a white wraith took over a tower ruin, far to the northwest. The guard went out and killed it. I don't know when chimeras or harpies were last seen."

"And now there have been two sightings in as many months." Cindra scoffed. "Sightings—these weren't sightings; they were battles. People died. I'm curious if other regions than Tuma and Mrandis have had similar trouble."

"If they have," Kapri murmured, "it could indicate something more serious than just a couple chance encounters."

"I fear you're right, Kapri."

Juleena hardly paid attention, and she was left with her thoughts and feelings for over an hour, before her mother and brother returned and announced that the afternoon and evening activities were cancelled. Everyone would be returning to wherever they were staying, to resume the gathering tomorrow, once the estate had been cleaned up.

On their way out, however, they were hailed by the cleanup crews.

"Mrandis?" the Tuma Guard Captain—not the one from House Mrandis—asked as he trotted up. "Mistress Mrandis?"

"Correct, sir," Mirassi said with a bit of a sigh. "We are about to depart."

"If I may beg a minute of your time?" He gestured over his shoulder towards the wreckage.

The mess of food and drink was being cleaned up, along with the tables and broken dishes. The three harpy corpses had been pulled aside, and guardsmen were stretching out the wings—and apparently plucking them.

"All the visiting Houses are receiving some feathers as compensation for the upset," the Tuma Captain continued. "All of your guardsmen joined in facing this threat and suffered injuries, and Lady Mrandis assisted directly by bringing down one of the harpies with her arrow. Master Tuma has decided you shall receive an additional allotment of feathers, and invites you to have your choice."

Mirassi gave the Captain a slightly suspicious look, but followed him as he bowed his way back to the corpses. The rest of the Mrandis party followed. As they got closer, Juleena saw that the men were using large pliers borrowed from a blacksmith to wrench the sharp feathers out of the wings at the base.

"You can see there are three colors to choose from: a darker pewter-like color, this silvery color, and the bronze," the Captain went on in a rush to please the Mistress. "They appear to be very similar to metal, and the edges are as sharp as a fine sword, but the blades you can make from these are more flexible, much lighter, and will retain their edge longer. The quill makes a fine tang, and needs only to be finished with a grip and any other accoutrements desired."

Several feathers had already been set aside in a pile, with an Oberdon ribbon stretched across them. It seemed Oberdon had gotten first choice since their guardsman had died in the attack.

"The quality of the feathers is the same regardless of color," the Captain continued. "Color is merely a personal choice. The longer feathers can be rather whippy, so perhaps are better for display than use as a weapon."

The Captain might have continued, but just then the Mrandis guardsmen approached. They all appeared to have changed their blood-soaked clothing for fresh. Juleena's gaze went right over the Mrandis Captain and the other man, and settled on Stratus, looking him over, head to toe, checking for signs of injury. He stopped at attention behind his Captain, and Juleena couldn't see any obvious damage. He was walking about, which suggested at least that he didn't need to be in an infirmary. A little tension left her, but she knew there were injuries that didn't result in bleeding or broken bones. He might still be in pain.

"Very well," Mirassi sniffed. "If these feathers are so valuable as you say, they can be put to acquiring the best possible spouse for my daughter." Her head snapped over to the Mrandis Captain. "Captain, please make the best selections based on your knowledge of weaponry, to the amount that our allotment allows."

"Yes, Mistress," he said.

"Perhaps," ventured the Tuma Captain, "Lady Mrandis would like to select one for herself, in reward for her valor on the field today?"

Mirassi's lip nearly curled and her eyes narrowed at Juleena. "What use has a woman for a sword? It is far better that these feathers be put towards her marriage."

Juleena wouldn't beg for it, since she knew it would do no good, and her mother was right—she didn't know how to use a sword, and would likely never be taught. Over her mother's shoulder, however, she saw Stratus lean forward and whisper something to his Captain.

"Mistress," the Mrandis Captain spoke up, and Mirassi turned back to him. "Might your two guardsmen have the boon of selecting a feather for themselves, as recognition of their bravery in facing such fearsome foes today? They both risked their lives in closing with the enemy, and Hearthsraven was nearly killed. He additionally struck the killing blow on the second harpy."

Juleena could see her mother's jaw tightening. Mrandis was not a powerful or particularly wealthy House. If these feathers were as valuable as the Tuma Captain was saying, giving any to her guardsmen instead of keeping them for the House was not a strategic move in increasing the House's prestige.

"Such generosity will inspire our guardsmen," Ledren muttered to his mother.

"Very well," she said with a modicum of grace. "I trust they will be sensible in their selections."

The Mrandis Captain bowed. "I only hire sensible men."

He nodded to the two men behind him, and Mirassi sighed audibly.

"You, too, of course, Captain," she said, "must make a selection as my thanks in leading our Guard to victory."

"My Mistress is too kind," the Captain bowed again.

Mirassi hesitated a moment as one of the other guardsmen was putting the pliers into Stratus's open hand. He looked up briefly and caught Juleena's eyes, before stepping over to the silver-feathered harpy. He bypassed the long primaries and wide secondaries entirely, going instead to the base of the nearest wing. In the center of the harpy's back there was again bare skin, like the neck, chest, and belly, though it was creased and weathered like old, thick leather.

Where the wing joined the body were a handful of slender feathers — scapulars — with vanes of nearly equal width. They weren't long enough for a sword, but a bit longer than an average dagger. Stratus used a wooden prod to sort among them: avoiding cutting up his hands. After a few moments, he made his choice, bent down, and carefully pulled the feather straight out. He took the quill end, and handed the pliers to his companion.

Mirassi nodded, apparently approving of his modest choice,

and turned to lead the Mrandis party away. Juleena got one more look at Stratus, as he wrapped the feather in a bit of old canvas, and then went where she was led, back to the carriage.

As an apology—and a means to dispose of the meals that had been planned for the day but would otherwise go to waste—baskets of food that hadn't been ruined by the harpies were sent back with all the departing groups of nobility. Included in the Mrandis ration was the bird and rabbit Juleena had shot. They had a late lunch when they returned to the Holstor estate. Everyone was quiet, but no one more so than Juleena.

The Mrandis guests had the run of the estate, with the exception of private bedchambers, so Juleena went out into the gardens to walk. Samira went with her. Movement seemed to help work out the constipation in her brain, and Sami let her devote herself to it without speaking. The maid seemed to have an instinct of when to talk, and when to give her mistress space. That was only one of the many brilliant qualities about her that Juleena liked so much. She was indeed such a dear friend, and Juleena thought again how lucky she was to have her—

Aghast, Juleena turned to her. "Sami, you're not hurt? I never asked. I'm so sorry. Will you forgive me? Where were you when the harpies came?"

A smile burst out on Samira's face. "I'm fine, Julee. I was in the manor, and when I saw what was happening, I stayed there the whole time, until it was safe to go out and get you."

Juleena took her hands. "I'm so glad. If you had been outside, or ran out because you thought you had to protect me, and gotten hurt, I would have been devastated."

"I'm just glad to hear you talking again, my lady," Samira teased. "For a while there, I feared you'd lost your voice."

"Let's go to the stables. I want to see that the horses are all right. I hadn't thought about them, either."

"They're fine, Julee," Samira tried to protest, but Juleena had her by the hand and towed her along.

She didn't let her skirts hinder her stride, and all but ran across the grounds to where the Holstors had their paddocks and stables. With the fine weather and extra horses brought by their guests, not many horses were actually in the stables. Juleena located Ivy and four other of the Mrandis horses turned out into a paddock together. After a few minutes watching them idling about together, Juleena was satisfied that they were none the worse for the scare, but two were missing.

She ambled over to the stable itself and found two Mrandis guardsmen grooming their steeds in the shade of the building. They both straightened up and bowed—along with a couple servants who were chatting with them—when Juleena came into view. One of them was Stratus. The other was his Captain.

The Captain came forward immediately.

"Lady Mrandis," he said formally. "I haven't had the opportunity to say so before, so allow me to say now that it seems I owe you the life of one of my best guardsmen, and I thank you for your valiant action."

She shook her head demurely, but her eyes were staring past the Captain's shoulder, at Stratus standing behind him. He stared back at her. He still didn't look hurt, and he was grooming his roan with no apparent stiffness or winces. Perhaps she could believe that he was really all right. She pulled her gaze to the Captain.

"I did only what any would do, who had the skill," she stuttered. "None of you were hurt?"

"Nothing my lady need concern herself over," the Captain said. "Let me thank you on behalf of my men for your kindness in coming to see for yourself that we are well. It is only because of you that we all emerged from that battle whole."

Her eyes had drifted back to Stratus. He didn't look away, and yet there was something mournful in his gaze; she knew it was in hers, too. Uneasiness began to stir in her belly. She resolutely turned her attention to the Captain again.

"I could not stand by," she babbled. "You may be my protectors, and I have nowhere near the skills of any of you, but who will protect me if my protectors fall?"

The Captain smiled a little. "Wisely said, my lady."

Juleena bowed her head a bit. "I am keeping you from your work."

"You are welcome any time." The Captain bowed more deeply, with Stratus copying him behind.

Juleena was reluctant to go, but she turned her feet away with Samira pacing her.

"I didn't see very well," the maid said after a few moments, "but I heard you shot a harpy dead—in its eye."

"I didn't kill it," Juleena corrected. "I think I just partly blinded it and shocked it enough that the guards could get close and kill it."

"I'm amazed. I would have been terrified. It was awful enough being in the house and watching through a window."

"The women of Garanda were shooting it, too," she explained. "I was too scared at first. I could hardly hold my bow, but then the harpy knocked Stratus down and stepped on him and I had to—"

"Who?"

"Stratus," she repeated. "Hearthsraven, I mean: that guardsman, the other one who was there with the Captain, with the roan horse."

"Oh," Samira subsided.

They walked leisurely for another minute, and now Juleena was suddenly feeling anxiety burning in her chest. She tugged a handkerchief out of her sleeve and fanned herself with it, only then realizing it was Strarus's handkerchief that he'd pressed on her after the harpy battle. It was plain and white, with a small letter H embroidered in one corner, nothing like the pastel-colored, heavily embroidered handkerchiefs she usually carried. Juleena supposed she should return it to him.

"You know his name?" Samira asked softly.

"He's the one assigned to guard me whenever I go into Trivale on errands," she explained quickly. "I asked his name; he told me."

"I see."

"Anyway, I had to shoot then. The harpy would have killed him."

"Of course."

"I was lucky to hit it."

Samira nodded. "You've always been good with the bow, ever since your brother started teaching you."

"The women of Garanda are much better."

"But you're the one that killed it, not them."

Juleena stopped walking. "I'm telling you, I didn't kill it; the guards did."

Samira halted beside her, but leaned close to whisper. "Because you shot it in the eye from a long way away, during a surprise battle, when you were already tired from shooting on the morning hunt, and while you were so frightened you couldn't hold your bow."

"Well," Juleena demurred, finding herself looking down at her skirts.

"To save Stratus," Samira concluded.

Juleena looked up and swallowed. "Of course. He's a Mrandis Guardsman."

Samira stared into her eyes long and steadily enough that Juleena had to fight not to flinch away.

"And you were looking at him," she went on. "When we stopped to get the feathers, and now when you were talking to the Captain, you were looking at Stratus more than at the Captain."

"I wanted to know that he was all right. He almost died," Juleena said, knowing she sounded defensive even as she tried to keep her voice even.

It didn't fool Samira.

"You like him," the maid breathed.

"What nonsense," Juleena huffed back, turning away now.

"Julee," Samira protested, turning to get in front of her again. "You do, don't you?"

"I told you, I'll never like any man," she insisted. "It just causes trouble."

"And you're right."

Sami grabbed her hand and held it pressed between her own palms. Only then did the maid appear to notice the plain white handkerchief. Juleena glanced down in a near panic and saw that the little H was plain to be seen. She whipped away the handkerchief and hid it in a pocket.

"Hearthsraven," Samira whispered, excitement and shock mixing in her voice. "That's his, isn't it? He gave it to you? And you're carrying it around? Oh, Julee, what a mess."

She snatched her hand back out of her friend's grasp. "There's no mess," she declared.

Juleena strode off at a brisk pace, making Samira hustle to catch up with her.

"What are you going to go?" the maid asked.

"Do? About what?"

"About Stratus," Samira hissed. "He likes you, too."

Juleena jerked to a halt. "What?"

"Can't you tell?"

"He does not," Juleena insisted.

"He was looking at you while you were looking at him," Samira babbled. "You two were looking at each other. I thought I was imagining things but you really—"

"Enough." She took off again.

"Your mother is going to marry you off," Samira lamented.

"And that'll be the end of it," Juleena agreed. "I'll get sent to some other House. I'll never see him again, so—so what?"

Samira hurried around in front of her, forcing Juleena to stop or run into her. She stopped. The maid put her hands on her lady's cheeks.

"Oh, but Julee, you two like each other," she whispered.

"So?" Juleena growled again, pulling down on Samira's wrists to get her hands off her face. "It doesn't matter."

"Why don't you talk to him?"

"Talk to him? When? Where?"

"The next time you get sent on an errand."

"And to what point?"

Sami blinked, thinking for a second, and her shoulders slumped. "I don't know," she admitted. "But, you're going off to marry someone you don't know, and don't like, and that's it. That's forever, but you're not married yet."

Juleena stared at her maid for a long moment. "What are you suggesting?"

Samira winced. "Nothing bad, just," she made a helpless gesture, "you have a chance to see what it's like, being with someone you," she swallowed, "love. Once you're married, you'll probably never have that again."

"And you think it would be better to indulge this, this, whatever it is, and then go on to live the rest of my life without it?"

"I don't know," Samira pled. "Just, it's like, what if you're offered some rare food, and you only get one chance to taste it? Do you take that chance, knowing you might like it, and then never get to have it again, or decline, and never know what it might have been like?"

Juleena walked away to take a seat under a lonely tree, on a bench in the shade. Samira went and joined her. Juleena leaned forward and put her face in her hands. Samira gently rubbed her back.

"I don't know what's wrong with me," she whispered. "I'm so confused."

"Don't be hard on yourself, Julee. This is probably the most difficult time of your life, getting paired up without a choice, about to get sent off to some stranger's House, and then add monsters and a handsome guardsman—of course you're upset."

Her voice came out muffled under her hands. "I can't stop thinking about him. Even when I'm not thinking about him, it's like I'm thinking about him."

Samira stayed silent, just passing her hand lightly over her lady's back.

"It's not the same as tasting some rare food," Juleena objected eventually. "The food doesn't have an opinion on whether it's tasted or not, and there are consequences to this kind of tasting. I know there are. Human feelings don't just go away after the meal. If I don't do anything, I know he won't; I'm nobility and he's common. So I could go to my marriage and leave without any," her voice faltered a little, "distress. But if I did something, what if, what if I never wanted to go to my marriage? What if I couldn't bear to?"

Samira's hand stilled. "You're right," she said. "I wasn't thinking like that. You're right. Maybe it's better to just stay away."

Juleena took a deep breath. "Either way, I will have regrets."

"Yes," Samira murmured. "I suppose you will."

She wiped her face with her hands and sat up. "Let's walk some more."

"Yes, my lady."

They got up, and resumed a leisurely stroll through the gardens, but Juleena's thoughts were anything but relaxed. She walked with one hand in her pocket, holding onto Stratus's handkerchief.

The third and final day of the gathering had a subtle frantic atmosphere to it. The second day had been cut short, and parents were still trying to finalize matches for their unwed offspring. Of course, firm agreements did not have to be made by sunset—negotiations could continue by post, and arrangements could even be made for the frontrunners to make personal visits through late autumn and even early winter. Marriages usually happened in late spring though, early summer at the very latest, so by midwinter's day bargains needed to be sealed, or shelved until the next summer.

If an agreement could be made on the third day, it could be announced during dinner, and that would get cheers and praise. Eligible children would be paired up and the options would narrow the closer the days got to midwinter. Of course, next year some new prospects would appear, as the next crop of youngsters were presented to society, and there was no lasting shame in not picking a spouse the first year a child was advertised.

However, Juleena could sense that her mother wanted her

situation settled. She was already a little older than most children were the first year they were brought to summer gatherings. Plus, her mother wanted her out of the Mrandis House before she did something else to embarrass the family.

The morning of the third day the womenfolk were asked to bring their embroidery, painting, or other art that could be done outside into the gardens of the Tuma estate. While they sat in clusters under the awnings, entertained by interspersed minstrels, the menfolk put on their sparring gear and got out their wooden swords and practiced genteel sword fighting under the sun.

Juleena brought her embroidery, which she was quite proud of, and sat with her family, with the womenfolk of Salasis, Oberdon, and Lupria not too far away. In response to whispered instructions from her mother, Juleena was sure to hold her hoop from time to time at an angle where the other mistresses could see her work. It was a small piece, a bolero, and already partly done. The fabric was fine grey wool, and she was embroidering owls on it in every shade between black and white. The representations were realistic; she'd done the first two based on a drawing in a book of birds, and was now doing additional ones based on the first two.

Of course, most of the other women were doing something flower-based. Juleena liked flowers, and had done several pieces featuring flowers, but her other current piece that had flowers on it was a kirtle, and it was just too big to drag outside and manage easily. She tried to compensate by smiling frequently, and conversing amiably with all who spoke to her. That seemed to work, and no one mentioned her unseemly behavior of the past two days—like winning at lawn games, riding off with a harridan and her daughter to shoot animals, or helping to slay a harpy. Mistress Holstor was sitting nearby, and talked up how good she was with children, which probably helped, too.

The menfolk meanwhile smacked at each other with practice blades. Juleena couldn't see much from where she sat, but she was certain her brother would find opportunities to test all three of her potential suitors with the blade. The guardsmen weren't participating, and Juleena found that fact to be enough to make her disinterested in trying to go watch. Some women did occasionally put down their work to wander over and observe, but Juleena never bothered. Embroidery was serious business; it was hard enough to concentrate on her stitches with women trying to talk to her, much less interrupting herself to go watch men she didn't care about beat on each other with sword-shaped sticks for mere amusement.

Lunch came and she put away her work to join everyone for food—this time without harpies. The men had all gone to bathe before eating, which she supposed would give her brother another chance to assess the physical qualities of her suitors. After lunch came the part of the day she was most worried about. It was time to mingle with the intent of getting to know her possible husband better. Every unwedded person was accompanied by a servant, and one by one set up to take a meander through the grounds with their suitors. The heads of the Houses organized it, making sure each potential couple got time to walk and presumably chat.

Juleena was paired up first with her suitor from Oberdon.

"May I present my son," Master Oberdon introduced, "Mikellan."

"May I present my daughter, Juleena," Mirassi replied smoothly.

"My lady," the son, Mikellan said, "would you care to walk with me?"

"I'd be delighted, sir," Juleena replied.

They moved off together, and Juleena let a soft breath escape. The introduction script had been followed perfectly, but now there was little dictation of what to say. Kapri—Samira being deemed to young to be a proper chaperone—followed a couple yards behind, beside the manservant that went with Mikellan Oberdon.

"You are enjoying the gathering?" he asked, rubbing his hands against the sides of his legs in a nervous gesture.

"It's been lovely," Juleena replied, deciding not to mention the harpies.

"Yes, lovely," he agreed, and then fell silent.

"This is your first gathering?" she asked.

"Second, actually, we went to one earlier in the summer, a small one, south of our House."

"I see."

"And yours?"

"Yes, my first," she answered.

He fell silent again, and so did she. They walked that way for a couple minutes.

"So, uh," he stuttered, "what do you like to do?"

"To do?" she echoed, not certain what he meant.

"I like reading," he blurted, "and I like composing. I write music for the lyre."

Juleena recalled back. "Did you play one of your own compositions two days ago? I didn't recognize it."

"Yes, yes it was," he confirmed quickly.

He then launched into an explanation of his theories of music composition and what he'd composed. By the time they completed the circuit of the garden and got back to where their parents waited, he was well into what sort of pieces he hoped to compose in the future, and had never returned to his question of what Juleena liked.

"Thank you for the walk," she said, back on the script.

"Your company made it all the more lovely," he replied by rote.

Master Oberdon and Mistress Mrandis exchanged a few more words, before Mikellan was led away.

"Well?" Mirassi asked.

"He likes to talk about composing music," Juleena reported.

"And?"

"That's mostly what he talked about the whole time."

Mirassi shrugged. "It is good he has something to occupy his time, and it is a respectable hobby."

The next suitor approached with his father — House Salasis.

"May I present my son," Master Salasis introduced, "Terkari."

"May I present my daughter, Juleena," Mirassi replied smoothly.

"My lady," the son, Terkari said, "would you care to walk with me?"

"I'd be delighted, sir," Juleena replied.

Terkari was tall, taller than his father, and rather than merely walking beside Juleena with a couple feet of space between them, he immediately took her hand and placed it on his arm, but he did not smile. She felt him purposefully flex his muscles under her fingers. She kept as much distance between them as she could, without having her arm completely straight.

"How old are you?" he asked as soon as they were away from the heads of their Houses.

"Seventeen," she answered, a bit taken aback at the blunt question. "And you, Terkari?"

"Twenty-three," he said.

"I've heard you don't want to marry," Juleena said, letting her irritation push her to be blunt back to him.

"I'd rather not," he confessed, "but my snotty little brother is about to, and I can't let his brats inherit what's rightfully mine."

Juleena raised her eyebrows, but said nothing.

"I will have to accept that my days of freedom are over."

"That is what we all accept, when we wed," Juleena commented, "but marriage need not be a prison in all ways."

He huffed a quiet laugh. "You have some spirit. So tell me, spirited girl, will you be good to your husband?"

"Of course," she said with a slight frown. "Husbands and wives should always be good to each other."

"Will you be bonny and bountiful?" he went on, now beginning to smile.

"As much as I may be," Juleena answered, starting to feel a bit uncomfortable.

"If I am to leave my wild ways behind, I hope to have a wife devoted and dutiful." He eyed her. "Have you known a man before?"

It took Juleena two full breaths before she realized what he meant.

"No," she gasped, and took her hand off his arm.

He frowned. "As most of the unwedded girls here. At least it means there shall be no bad habits to break, but inexperienced women are so uninspiring."

"I'm sure I don't know what you mean, sir," Juleena said firmly.

He took her hand and set it back on his arm.

"I still like your spirit," Terkari remarked, "and your innocence is even a little sweet."

Juleena focused back on the path ahead, wishing the trailing servants were close enough to hear. His words had been inappropriate, in her opinion, and her face heated with a blush. Beside her, Terkari chuckled.

"Look at you, all embarrassed. Wise enough to know of what I speak, if not the finer details, and warm enough for my words to affect you." He put his free hand atop hers on his arm, and tried to tug her closer. "I think I might like you."

"I'm not sure I can say the same," Juleena managed.

His smile broadened, and he winked. "You might change you mind, once you get to know me."

She pulled her hand off his arm, out from under his other hand. "And I might not."

In a few more steps they reached his father and her mother. The scripted pleasantries were exchanged, and Terkari smiled much more than Mikellan had.

"Well?" Mirassi asked on cue. "He seems most amiable."

"I don't like him," Juleena whispered, crossing her arms over her chest.

"Why not?"

"He made me uncomfortable."

Mirassi twisted up her mouth as though tasting something bitter. "He is much older than you, true. Matches with a big age difference can cause problems, but he does seem to like you.

254

Well, we'll see. Here comes Lupria."

"May I present my son," Master Lupria introduced, "Jerand."

"May I present my daughter, Juleena," Mirassi replied smoothly.

"My lady," the son, Jerand said, "would you care to walk with me?"

"I'd be delighted, sir," Juleena replied.

They moved off together, and she was relieved when he didn't try to touch her. Jerand stared at the path for a number of steps.

"How are you enjoying the gathering, Jerand?" she asked when the silence became too heavy.

"It's fine," he muttered, still not looking up.

"Is it your first gathering?"

"No, did this last year, too. It'll be just the same this year."

"Why?" she asked. "What happened last year?"

He heaved a sigh. "No one wanted me."

"That makes for sad hearing, although maybe lucky for me," she encouraged.

"You're trying to cheer me up," he grunted. "Everyone does that."

"Would you prefer to walk in silence?" Juleena asked.

"Yeah, actually. I hate being here."

Her brows lowered. "Perhaps, if you act like that, you will get exactly the outcome you predict. Is that what you want?"

He shrugged. "I don't know."

Juleena straightened her posture. Considering her own situation, she couldn't find much sympathy in herself for Jerand Lupria. He clearly wasn't putting in any effort, and though she didn't want to be picking a spouse either, she knew she had to do it, and would try to get the best one she could—out of the options she had. She grimaced.

"No one is happy to be here, you know," she told him.

"But everyone just accepts it," he grumbled.

"So do you."

"Yeah, I guess so, but I don't pretend to be happy."

He fell silent again, and Juleena gave up. They walked without speaking the rest of the way, performed the scripted parting ritual, and she turned to her mother.

"Mother, I don't like any of them," she whispered. "This one was absolutely despondent. Life is difficult, I know, but he's stubbornly negative."

Mirassi didn't give such a large tell as to plant her hands on her hips, but she fixed Juleena with a hard gaze.

"So tell me which would be easiest to tolerate," she ordered.

Juleena grit her teeth. "There are so many things to weigh. Oberdon might be the easiest to tolerate, personally, but what if I don't get to raise my own babies?"

"They won't be locked away in a tower somewhere. You'll get the chance to know them," Mirassi dismissed.

"But sing them to sleep every night? Read books to them? Teach them things? Take them outside to play?"

"Not every day, but sometimes, surely," she shrugged.

"I want to raise my babies myself," Juleena said.

"Then Lupria," Mirassi nodded, "though even there, it isn't the custom. You'll have more important duties—whatever House you go to."

"More important than raising my children?" Juleena retorted.

"Yes."

She sighed and turned partly away.

"Not to worry," her mother said. "I'll get a good arrangement for you."

Juleena nodded, but couldn't believe her. The arrangement her mother wanted was the one that was best for House Mrandis; Juleena was sure of it.

The young, eligible guests and the older ones not spouse-hunting for their children settled down for table games outside under the tents, while all the masters and mistresses who were looking to match up their children went into the Tuma manor. Kapri went, too, leaving Samira with Cindra and Juleena.

"Kapri will be carrying messages," Cindra confided under her breath. "The negotiations begin in earnest, and as they begin to sort out, the servants will be sent about with notes, notifying other Houses when they've been outbid."

"This is ridiculous," Juleena muttered. "I don't even get a say."

"Nor did I," Cindra told her.

Juleena pinched her brows together. "But you seem happy with Ledren."

"I am," she confirmed. "He is an agreeable man, and kind to me."

"Do you love him?" Juleena whispered.

Cindra didn't reply immediately. "In some ways, yes. He ensures I want for nothing he has the power to provide."

Juleena thought that meant no.

"Come let's play," Cindra encouraged.

The afternoon dragged on. Juleena played several games with various participants, but not with any of her three suitors. The unwedded were staying apart from each other now, especially the women from the men. There was nothing more they could do to determine the outcome of their parents' negotiations, and without knowing whom their chosen spouse would be, they weren't making moves in any direction.

Servants brought around drinks and snacks, but by the time the doors of the great house swung open, it was nearly dinner time. Juleena would have been hungry if her stomach hadn't been in knots. She hadn't been able to focus on the games, either, and had lost most of them. Cindra took her hand and urged her up.

"Let's find your mother," she suggested.

"I don't want to know," Juleena protested.

"All will be well. There may be challenges—there always are—but in time you will be content."

Content: that wasn't what she wanted. Or was it? Hadn't she said over and over that she didn't want to love her husband? Wasn't contentment then the result she desired? Her fingers and feet felt numb as she walked with Cindra, Samira following. They found her mother and brother, with Kapri, in the parlor they'd used the previous two days for rest. When Juleena stepped in, her mother smiled broadly at her, and her heart plummeted.

"Is it decided," Mirassi announced. "You shall wed in the spring."

Juleena found a seat on a couch, though she only made it there because Samira was firmly guiding her before her legs went too weak to hold her. She clasped her hands in her lap. The usual warm brown of her skin looked grey. She tried to speak, almost choked, and had to swallow twice before she managed it.

"Who?" she asked. "What House, Mother?"

"I'll announce it at dinner."

Juleena lowered her head into her palms. Samira put a comforting hand on her shoulder.

"Mistress Mrandis," the maid said politely, "may I go with my lady when she weds?"

"Well," Mirassi nodded. "We'll see. That might not be impossible. Compose yourself, Juleena. You shall smile when the match is announced."

"Yes, Mother," she murmured.

"I go to learn what order the announcements will be," Mirassi said. "I'll return and I expect you to be calm and collected by then."

The Mistress of Mrandis went out, and Cindra took a seat by Juleena.

"Don't be afraid," she encouraged. "I was frightened, too, but all for no reason. You will look back on this day with joy, and laugh at your fear."

Juleena closed her eyes, letting Samira rub her shoulders, and unable to share her sister-in-law's optimism. She slipped a hand into her pocket, feeling for Stratus's handkerchief. It was at first a comfort, but then she began to cry.

Juleena had at least started to learn to deal with the specter of her future by the time her mother returned. When dinner was called, she rose with all the composure she could manage, standing straight, with a neutral, if not happy, expression on her face. She could hardly eat, and drank a bit more wine than she knew she should—especially on an empty stomach—until Kapri took the wine away and replaced it with fruit tea only.

The announcements began with the most powerful Houses, and Juleena's anxiety jerked higher with each one. Several minutes were left between the announcements, giving her plenty of time to get more and more scared.

The Master of Oberdon stood up and Juleena caught her breath.

"I wish to announce the desire of my son, Mikellan, to wed Lady Tulavia of House Karimy."

The Mistress of Karimy stood. "Lady Tulavia accepts Lord Mikellan with pleasure."

Everyone applauded, and Juleena's heart was enclosed by a band of cold iron. Mikellan would have been the easiest of the three men to live with, she'd thought, but Oberdon had been a lofty House for a Mrandis to aspire to. The young woman who stood up as Mikellan stood was smiling and curvy, with curly dark hair and skin nearly the color of burnished copper. Their babies would be beautiful—but Tulavia would hardly know them.

Another announcement passed without Juleena or either of the two remaining possibilities being mentioned. Could her mother have suddenly negotiated with a fourth suitor? She hoped so, for neither Jerand nor Terkari interested her, but rather repelled her, each for a different reason. She didn't want to spend her life bound to either one.

Master Salasis stood up, and Juleena froze like a startled rabbit. It had to be the announcement for his older son, not the younger, provided an agreement had been made; the older one would definitely be announced before the younger.

"I wish to announce the desire of my son, Terkari," he began.

Juleena's heart beat painfully in her chest.

"To wed Lady Juleena of House Mrandis," he concluded.

Juleena's heart stopped for a moment, and then resumed beating, each pulse like the stab of a spear. Beside her, Mirassi stood up.

"Lady Juleena accepts Lord Terkari with pleasure."

Terkari stood up, smiling like he'd felled a dozen deer with a single arrow. Kapri pushed at Juleena.

"Stand, my lady," she hissed. "Stand."

Juleena got her feet under her somehow, and by bracing her hands on the table pushed herself upright. She lifted her chin, squared her shoulders, and tried not to cry.

"Smile, my lady," Kapri hissed again. "Smile."

She twisted her face into some approximation of a smile. The gathering applauded. Terkari stared down the table at her and licked his lips.

Juleena couldn't finish her meal. She thought she might be sick. She was only prevented from bolting by Kapri's hand on her shoulder the entire rest of the time, while further announcements were made. Lupria's Jerand found a match, too, with Lalla, the girl who had ridden with Dame Garanda, her daughter, and Juleena during the hunt. Lalla didn't look very happy about it. Salasis's second son got a match as well, with a woman Juleena didn't know: a timid-looking girl with purple and white ribbons.

"You'll have a chance to speak with your husband," Mirassi was saying as the dining ended and guests started moving about.

"He's not my husband yet," Juleena protested.

"It will still be chaperoned," her mother went on as though she hadn't spoken, "but you'll have more privacy. Kapri will be close enough to hear if you call, but you can otherwise speak without being overheard. Do be nice to him. His House has paid grandly for you."

Juleena ached inside. Of all the men—Lupria would have been better; at least Jerand hadn't scared her, or said those things. Some people were sitting down to more board games, or going off into parlors for drinks and conversation. Other guests were leaving already. Shortly, a manservant in blue and yellow approached Kapri. They spoke for a moment, and then he departed.

Kapri came to Juleena. "Your husband would meet you in the garden."

"He's not my husband," Juleena protested again.

"He will be," Mirassi scolded. "You had best get used to the idea. You could do far worse, girl. You will be Mistress of Salasis in your turn. Your children will inherit a House. That is a far step up from third born. Salasis is a House in good standing, slightly higher in rank than Mrandis. I've done well by you."

Juleena closed her eyes and turned her head away.

"Look at me, Daughter," her mother ordered, and Juleena reluctantly obeyed. "Don't ruin this. You will be pleasant and agreeable with him. Do you understand?"

"Yes, Mother," Juleena whispered, her throat dry.

"Ungrateful child," Mirassi shook her head.

Kapri led her to the gardens. The manservant and Terkari were waiting, and the latter looked up, smiling, as soon as Juleena came into view. He strode to her, reaching out both arms, and she compliantly put her hands in his. His hands were hot, making her think hers must be quite cold, but she didn't feel cold, just numb.

"My bride," he endeared. "Walk with me."

He placed her hand on his arm again, and Juleena let him lead her into the garden. Other couples were walking there, so they were hardly alone, but no one was close enough to hear conversation, and with the fall of night, only the lamps gave infrequent light.

"I hope you are pleased," Terkari said. "I am: very pleased, much more than I'd hoped to be."

"Yes, my lord," Juleena whispered.

"You do not seem so pleased, and I do wish to please my wife."

Befuddled, Juleena looked up at him. "I don't understand you," she confessed.

"Do you think I mean to mistreat you?"

"No, my lord."

Some hardness invaded around his eyes. "Don't lie to me. That's exactly what you think, isn't it?"

"I hardly know you. I don't know what to think," she explained.

He grunted. "Well, that's fair enough. Honest, at least."

They walked in silence for a time.

"I wish for a pleasant marriage," he said eventually. "I want no upset between us. Do you understand?"

"I want a pleasant marriage, too," Juleena said.

"Then we agree. Let us be husband and wife and do right by each other. We both have duties and must fulfill them. I expect you to be a good wife to me, and in turn I shall be a good husband to you."

"Yes, my lord," Juleena nodded. "That is only correct."

He stopped them in the shadow of a tree and turned towards her, stepping close.

"Then give your husband a kiss," he commanded.

She stiffened. "You are not yet my husband, sir."

"It is settled," he countered. "I shall be. There is no harm in it. Many such kisses will be exchanged between the newly betrothed tonight: more than that in some cases. Everyone knows that is what happens on these evening betrothal walks. That is why the chaperones hang back."

He leaned in. Juleena turned her head and stepped away, but he pursued.

"Wife," he murmured, a hint of warning in his tone.

His hand came up, catching her head, fingers hooked around the back of it, but still she tried to retreat.

"No," Juleena protested weakly.

She hit against the trunk of the tree and Terkari pinned her there.

"Just a kiss," he said. "There will be many between us over the years. Don't be afraid. I'll show you how it's done. You'll like it."

He leaned down again, but she kept her head stubbornly turned away. His mouth pressed against her cheek.

"Give me your lips," he breathed into her ear. "I will have all of you soon enough. I don't want to force you. Come to me willingly. Turn your head. Look at me."

She kept her face turned away, skin crawling with revulsion and heart pounding with distress.

"Juleena, Wife," he whispered on. "Come now. Keep your eyes shut if you want. It won't hurt. Let me show you. I have much to show you."

He applied pressure, trying to turn her head.

"Do not fight me."

His voice had turned hard. Swallowing down a whimper, Juleena complied, letting him turn her face towards him.

"That's right," he praised. "This will feel good."

She braced herself—and then a clarion shout rang out.

"Monster!" came the cry. "I saw it move, a shadow there by that copse."

Terkari jerked up, and Juleena gasped, opening her eyes. She could see little beyond the light of the nearest lamp, but shouts and screams pattered all around the grounds. The guardsmen started calling to one another and running towards the one who had yelled first. Kapri and Terkari's manservant came pelting over to drag them back into the manor, to safety.

Juleena experienced it all only as a jumble of sights and sounds. She realized Terkari was gone from her side. Kapri was herding her back into the parlor at the rear of the house. Cindra was there with Samira. The four women sat and huddled on the couches as the manor buzzed like a disturbed beehive. Juleena simply sat and stared into space. After a moment, she recovered enough presence of mind to rub her cheek where Terkari had kissed it, as if she could undo what he'd done.

"Are you alright, Julee?" Samira whispered to her.

She nodded mutely.

A half an hour passed. Cindra napped on the opposite couch, but the servants had to stay awake, and Juleena knew she could not sleep. Finally, Mirassi came striding in.

"A false alarm," she announced, making Cindra stir. "At least, the guards cannot find whatever was seen. We are being sent back to our lodging, all the guests are. The gathering is over."

Juleena did not get even another glance at her intended husband as they hustled to the carriages. Their guardsmen were wary and kept in tight formation as they rode back to the Holstor House. Juleena sat silently the whole ride, staring into the empty middle distance.

"Do perk up, Daughter," Mirassi said at one point. "You've made an ideal match."

Juleena did not reply, and her mother just sighed instead of pressing. At last, the carriages came to a halt. The Holstors exited their carriage first, making a quick retreat into their home. The manor was dark, as it should be on a night with no surprise fires in the nursery. Only one lantern was hanging by the main door.

"Do you think there's something out there?" Cindra asked softly.

Mirassi scoffed. "The guards are on edge because of the harpies. Someone imagined something in the dark. Let's go in."

"I want a moment alone," Juleena uttered. "Go ahead on in and leave me for a bit."

Mirassi opened her mouth to object.

"If there's nothing out there it's perfectly safe," Juleena cut her off.

"Very well," she grunted. "A moment, little more. The guards and servants need their rest, too, and the horses, and none of them can go to that rest until you go in the house."

"Yes, Mother," Juleena consented. "A moment, just to gather

myself, before seeing the Holstor household."

Mirassi lifted her head in what seemed to be approval. Juleena had used the right words to appeal to her mother's sense of propriety.

"Go on then, Cindra, Ledren," she said.

Juleena was left alone in the carriage. She heard her mother say something to the driver, and felt the carriage shift as he got down from the seat. There was a little more conversation between her and the guards, and the sound of men dismounting, and horses walking off, their hooves clacking on the paving stones.

Silence, darkness: at last Juleena took a breath, another, deeper, and a sob caught in her throat. She forced it down and tried to breathe past it. Crying would accomplish nothing. There came a soft tap at the carriage door beside her—the one on the side away from the manor, opposite the one her family had used to exit.

"Yes?" she said, her voice breaking.

The handle of the door turned with hardly a squeak, and the door opened slowly.

"Lady Mrandis?"

She shut her eyes. She knew that voice.

"You called the alert," she accused softly.

"Yes," Stratus admitted. "I thought you were in distress."

"I was," she confessed. "I thank you."

The guardsman hesitated for a few breaths before speaking further, and his voice was even softer. "I could not run over and strike him down. I had to think of something else."

Juleena's skin prickled. Her heart pounded. "I see."

"He is to be your husband?"

A rock lodged in her throat and she couldn't say it.

"You don't seem to like him."

"Are you married?" she was finally able to gasp out.

"No, my lady. Guardsmen are not allowed to marry until we have served five years."

"And when will that be?"

"I have a few months left."

"So you've begun to think of picking your bride?"

He was quiet for a few breaths. "My father's house is full, and I haven't the money for my own. I shall have to wait a while longer yet."

"But you'll get to pick whoever you want?"

"Whoever will have me," he said mildly.

"Who wouldn't?" Juleena blurted.

Outside, a horse stamped and harness jingled. She reminded herself to keep her voice down. She looked up and saw Stratus rest one knee on the step used for getting in and out. He half sat on the floor of the carriage, other leg folded below him, right before her. In the full moonlight their eyes met, and suddenly her hand was in his, and she didn't know how it had gotten there. His fingers were warm, and obviously strong, but he seemed to know his own strength and didn't crush her fingers with them.

"Stratus," she breathed.

He flinched, just the slightest bit. "My lady, I wish to see you happy."

Eyes fixed on his: she shook her head a fragment left and right.

"Did he hurt you?"

Now her eyes closed and a tear streaked down one cheek. "No," she rasped.

Stratus didn't respond and after a moment she managed to open her eyes again. He reached up, and with the lightest touch brushed the residue of the tear off her skin. Juleena's heart lurched into a flurry of beats and a surge of heat flushed her.

"He wanted to kiss me," she murmured.

"Did he?"

"No. Well, yes, on the cheek, but not," she struggled to swallow, "not on the," she couldn't say it.

Stratus's gaze darted down to her mouth and then away. "Good."

A calm, strong certainty filled her, and Juleena acted without thinking about it. Her free hand went swiftly and surely to his cheek. His jaw was a little rough; he hadn't shaved since the morning. Without hesitation she bent over from where she sat and found his lips with hers.

She felt an immediate pulse of consent from him, as his whole body responded, beginning to press towards her. His hand tightened on hers and his lips moved to kiss her back—but then he was reversing course: pulling away just as urgently. She tried to follow, to continue the contact, but Stratus took her wrists firmly and held her away.

"No, my lady, you mustn't do that," he said hoarsely.

"Stratus," she whispered, and was surprised at the note of pleading in her voice.

"I can't," he replied, and she heard an echo of her own pleading in his voice.

The heat cracked and pain seeped out through the gaps. Juleena clamped her jaws against a cry. He seemed to see it.

"Please, my lady, this," he stuttered. "We can't."

She took a shaky breath. "But I want to."

Now he was holding back words of his own.

"You want to, too," she accused. "Say it."

He looked down, as if ashamed. "Yes, but you're not for me."

She ached and couldn't talk as the pain paralyzed her throat. Stratus stood up and released her wrists.

"You should go inside, my lady."

Juleena stood, too, and he got out of the way as she descended through the door he'd opened. He was taller than her, but not as tall as—as that man she didn't want to think of. She lifted her chin to stare at him and tried to clamp down on the pain of thwarted need. Finally, she was able to swallow.

"Then I should give this back to you," she rasped, holding out his handkerchief.

Stratus stared at it, started to reach out to take it, but seemed to get stuck halfway there. "Keep it?" he quavered.

"I can't," Juleena breathed back.

Their fingers brushed as he reluctantly took it from her.

"I can't have you: the man I want," she whispered. "Instead

I have to have the man who'll force me on my wedding night and expect me to enjoy it, and no one will be there to save me."

He flinched as if struck and his face crumpled like he was about to cry.

"Good night, Stratus," she said.

Juleena turned and made her stately way to the door of the Holstor manor. She saw no one but a few servants taking care of final evening duties as she found her room, where Samira was waiting for her.

Juleena collapsed into a seat on the bed and started sobbing. Samira's arms went around her, and she rocked her, crooning comfort. Between the sobs, Juleena babbled her distress over her destined spouse—unintelligible and ungrammatical besides. Samira just soothed her, petting her hair and shoulders, until she got Juleena to stand up long enough to get her outer gown, shoes, and stockings off. Then she lay down, huddled up with Samira like when they were little girls, and finally her stream of blubbering objections slowed and faded into sniffles.

"I'm so sorry, Julee," Samira said at last.

She lay quietly: nose and eyes sore from weeping, but finally thinking again, as if all the crying had purged something out of her. Her face ached, except for her lips. They tingled pleasantly. Idly, she touched them with a fingertip.

"I kissed him," she mumbled.

"Terkari?" Samira gasped.

"No," Juleena corrected, "Stratus."

"What?" Samira goggled, jolting halfway up to sitting.

"It was nice," Juleena muttered on, now closing her eyes with the weight of sleep starting to steal over her.

"He kissed you back?" Samira hissed as quietly as she could. "He didn't stop you?"

"Yes, and yes—err, no. I mean, yes, he stopped me, after a moment."

Samira shook her shoulder. "Julee? Are you serious? You could get in so much trouble. Him, too."

"Mm-hm," she hummed. "Stop that."

Samira lay back down.

"I like him," Juleena sighed as sleep took her. "I want to marry him instead."

"You can't, Julee," Samira sympathized.

She made an inarticulate grunt. "I want to; I like him."

If Samira had a reply, she didn't hear it. Juleena had floated down into soft, dark dreams, where gentle arms held her, and she had no fear.

After breakfast the next morning with the Holstors, the Mrandis party packed up and prepared to return to their own estate. Juleena felt drained and empty like the skin shucked off a rabbit. Whenever her thoughts strayed onto her future husband she jerked them back and thought instead of that one happy moment with Stratus—when he'd been kissing her back, before he pulled away. She wouldn't think of his rejection. Instead, she drew out the happy memory-moment as long as she could, extending it.

The Holstors seemed to recognize that she was upset, especially Mistress Holstor. She found a moment as they were loading up and drew her aside.

"Juleena," the Mistress whispered, "a poor match is a difficult thing to live with, but there may be other compensations in your new home that you will find pleasant. Do not decide that it will be horrible and live these last months in your birth home as though you were already in Salasis House. You are not there yet so don't send your heart ahead of you to that dark place. Do you understand what I'm saying?"

Juleena blinked at her and tried to hear her. Mistress Holstor took her limp hand with both of hers.

"And the agreement you made with Giri, we'll hold to it. I give you my word. Your firstborn daughter will have first choice of him, when she's old enough, and we can let it be a bit younger than usual, if you'd like, to get her out of Salasis, if that's what you want. As long as they like each other, it will be a match, and we will pay Salasis to have her come here, whatever it takes."

Juleena jerked with a sob, and Mistress Holster suddenly hugged her as though she were her own daughter.

"We'll see if you can come visit sometimes," the Mistress went on. "Salasis is not so very far. Oh, Juleena, I'm sorry for you. Holstor will always be a friend to you. We cannot solve everything, but if you need help, send word, and we'll do what we can."

"Thank you," Juleena squeaked, but she couldn't get anything else out.

Mistress Holstor released her, and Juleena turned blindly towards the carriage. Someone handed her in, but she knew it wasn't Stratus by the feel of his fingers. She sat down beside her mother, across from Cindra. The driver chivvied the horses, and the carriage rolled out. No one spoke, so Juleena had plenty of time to get her emotions back under control, and after a while she recognized some truth to Mistress Holstor's words.

She wasn't in Salasis House yet. She had a reprieve: a little more than half a year. She would prepare for the wedding, true, but she wouldn't have to see her future husband until the actual day. He might send correspondence or even gifts, and she'd be expected to reply in kind, but that she could handle.

And she'd have half a year around Stratus. He'd rejected her, but not because he didn't like her. Of course it would be wrong to pressure him—she knew that—but she could still talk to him, still be near him. They didn't have to touch, but if he would just look at her, smile at her, speak to her, that would be enough to warm her. Perhaps that one brief little kiss would be enough even once she went to her husband's House, to give her some comfort through all that would come.

Despite her hopes, Stratus seemed to be avoiding everywhere she might go for the next week after the return to Mount Brasson and the Mrandis estate. Her parents were keeping her firmly home, as well, not sending her on errands to Trivale. She finished her owl embroidery on the bolero, and the flowers on the kirtle, and started planning her wedding dress.

The wedding would be bitter, but the dress didn't have to be. Of course, her mother had opinions—and dictates—but Juleena managed to stand her ground on a few points and achieve compromises. There were traditions to be adhered to as well. The outer gown had to be red and black, Mrandis colors, but wedding gowns had an inner layer, too, to be done in the colors of the House she'd be going to: Salasis's blue and yellow. The outer layer would be shed after the ceremony. When men switched Houses—which happened as often as women switching—the outer jacket was removed, revealing the colors of the man's new House below.

Of course, Juleena would embroider the whole thing. Many of the next months would be spent on it. She had to settle the designs first with Mirassi's approval, while seamstresses worked on constructing the actual garment with many measurements and fittings. Weddings always took place at the House that would be gaining the spouse, so Juleena and her family and the dress would travel to House Salasis.

Once Juleena had fabric samples, she required an outing: to pick the embroidery floss in proper colors. Trivale had the shop she liked to visit the most. Lenali had a shop, too, and though it was bigger and had more extensive stock, the floss was all imported from elsewhere. The little shop in Trivale was run by a wrinkled old couple and their daughter and her husband. They bought the undyed floss from a local who spun it from wool raised on the slopes of Mount Brasson, and dyed it themselves with their own recipes.

"You want to go to Trivale?" her mother protested.

"I always get my floss from the Betchals," Juleena reminded her. "They have better colors, and if there isn't something exactly right, they can make it for me."

"They're more expensive," Mirassi sniffed.

Juleena snapped to her full height. "If I am going to be wed, and wed to Salasis, I will have a dress as fine as I wish, or would you have me look inferior?"

Her mother twitched, as if surprised at her daughter's sudden vehemence, but subsided. "Very well. Take an escort and go."

Juleena grit her teeth and hid a smile. She would go, and she'd take Stratus.

With her fabric samples in her pockets, Juleena walked the road between Lenali and Trivale. Stratus walked beside her. He'd obeyed his Captain when the order came, without a glimmer of distress or protest, but he was icily quiet and composed.

"I apologize for what I did," Juleena said once they were away from the walls of Lenali. "I shouldn't have kissed you. I needed comfort, and I like you. I don't regret it, but I upset you, and I'm sorry for that."

He didn't say anything, but a glance at his face showed his perfectly smooth neutrality had shifted towards something more troubled. He cleared his throat.

"I liked it," he confessed huskily, and a thrill of joy went through her. "The kiss isn't the problem."

"The difference in our ranks," Juleena provided.

He nodded shortly. "I cannot marry you, and that is the only way I would be close to a woman, the only right way."

Juleena felt her throat pinch, and she smiled sadly. "You will make a good husband to someone someday. I'm jealous of her, whoever she is."

His face tensed. "Oh, my lady," he whispered, "how I wish you would have a good husband, too. That is all I wish for you, to be with someone who will honor and respect you, and show you kindness."

She had to look away, back at the road. The winter rains hadn't started yet, so it was still packed hard and smooth: easy walking. She had to blink to clear away tears so she wouldn't trip over nothing.

"Perhaps I will come to love my husband," she said. "Many noble women do, although they are paired with a man they've never met."

Stratus shook his head. "During the gathering, I had drinks one evening with a guardsman of Salasis. He told me the first-born son is a wencher, and even has a bastard from one of the servant girls. The second-born is not much better, though he hasn't yet lived up to his brother's example."

Juleena felt numbness creeping over her again, and a flutter of fear in her belly.

"Of course, it's all kept quiet," Stratus rumbled. "Houses keep their secrets. I doubt your mother or brother knew when they made the match."

She sensed Stratus's gaze on her, but didn't return it.

"My feelings towards him are not charitable, when I think of you going to him," he confided.

"He said he's leaving his wild life behind," she managed to say. "Perhaps he is trying to be more honorable."

"I hope that is true." Stratus walked for a few moments without speaking, but then said, "I'm still young, not much older than you, and I haven't seen everything, but I meet a lot of different men in the Guard, and I've been in it since I was thirteen, when I started by scrubbing out the stables and mending armor. Most men are decent, with only a few small flaws, such as we all have, but the ones I've met who tend to wenching do not change their ways. They only become better at hiding their indiscretions."

He stared at her again. "I worry for you, my lady."

Her heart hurt. She lifted her arm out toward him, bumped her hand against his forearm and slid it down to find his gloved hand, slipping her fingers among his. He squeezed for a breath and then let go, gently nudging her hand away.

"Someone could see," he apologized.

She nodded. "I'd get in trouble, and you'd lose your position."

"Demotion, at least," he confirmed, "if not discharge completely. I'm third son, and my father doesn't need another apprentice. If I lost my position, I don't know what I'd do."

Juleena nodded, tried to straighten her posture and clear

away gloomy thoughts. "What does your father do?" she asked lightly.

"He works with wood, cabinetry in particular," Stratus said, his voice also sounding less burdened. "My grandfather did much of the cabinetry at your house, the last time the kitchens were renovated. I don't remember it; I was but a babe at the time."

"He works with black maple?" she asked, referring to Mount Brasson's signature tree.

"Often," Stratus confirmed.

"And you're not following in his trade?"

"I would," he said, "but there is not enough work for three cabinetmakers in Trivale, much less four. The eldest son will inherit. The second son might stay and make a partnership, but might have to move to find enough business. As for me, cabinetry isn't an option. I'm healthy and sturdy though, and I want to protect people, so I went for the Guard. It seems a good fit for me."

"Yes, I think it is," Juleena agreed. "Your brothers are married?"

"They are, with children, too. I can sleep in the barracks, and often do, for my family's house is full to bursting, and another babe is on the way."

Juleena found herself smiling. "It sounds wonderful."

Stratus glanced at her and smiled a bit, too. "Does it?"

"Whether I love my husband or not, I will love my children," she said.

But that put a sobering note back on the mood, and they walked again in silence into the walls of Trivale. Juleena knew the way to the dyers, and Stratus followed. He waited outside while she went into the little shop to speak with the Betchals. The old father was there with his daughter, behind the counter, and they greeted her warmly, congratulating her on her wedding. She maintained enough composure not to disabuse them of the notion that it was a joyful thing.

They consulted with her, as she'd known they would, over

the best colors, listening to her plan and showing her samples. At last she arrived at a consensus for the colors needed for her black and red outer gown and left her order with them. For the blue and yellow they didn't have exactly the right colors and bade her return in a week to see what they could invent and to pick up the floss for the outer gown, which they had to make in the quantity she'd require.

Stratus was waiting for her outside, and bowed when she emerged.

"Where to next, my lady?" he asked.

"Unfortunately, that was my only business in Trivale," she said. "I shall have to return home."

"Allow me to escort you."

"Gladly," she said with a bit of a smile.

They began to retrace their steps back through town and to the road to Lenali.

"The Betchals had what you need?" he asked.

"Half of it," she answered, and decided not to tell him it was for her wedding gown. "They're working on the rest, and I'll need to come see them about it next week."

She glanced at him, and he glanced back, sharing a conspiratorial grin.

"Excellent, my lady. I'll be happy to escort you."

After that errand, for the rest of the week, Stratus didn't try to avoid her, but she had little reason to come into contact with him, and knew better than to try to manufacture something or sneak off to see him. Though her heart still ached in thinking of her future with Terkari, not Stratus, having the latter as a friend at least, and knowing he cared, gave her some comfort to hold onto in her darkest moments.

The day for the errand to return to the dyers couldn't come quickly enough. She was nearly skipping as she fetched the bag she'd carry her goods in and sought her walking shoes.

"Shall I send Samira with you to carry your purchase?" Housekeeper Hyldi asked as she buckled on her charge's shoes.

"It is only floss," Juleena said, "and I could make the guardsman carry it."

She decided to gamble on a bit of obfuscation.

"Must he come with me? I went for years on my own to Trivale," she begged.

"It is your mother's order, Lady," Hyldi refused—as Juleena had known she must. "Don't sulk now."

Juleena didn't play it any deeper. "Very well," she said in her best imitation of her mother.

"Since you are going," Hyldi said, "would you run an errand for me as well?"

"Of course," Juleena agreed.

"Just a message," she said. "The leaves are starting to turn and—"

"The autumn outing?" Juleena guessed.

"As you say. Deliver this order to Sammerman. Two of our baskets are beyond hope; we'll need some new ones."

"I'd love to, Mum Hyldi," Juleena said, taking the folded order. "Thank you."

"Don't linger playing with the cats," Hyldi scolded.

"I won't," she promised with a grin, and turned to head out the door.

"You're lying to me, Julee," Hyldi called after her.

It almost scared her, until she rationalized that Hyldi was talking about her true intention to dawdle playing with the cats at Sammerman's, not her secret affection for Stratus.

Stratus was ready as soon as Juleena came walking up to the guard post. The main barracks for the Guard was in Lenali itself, where they slept, ate, and trained. There was a small building inside the Mrandis walls, however, where half a dozen guards could live. It was finer living than the general barracks in the city, but still on par with what servants had. Juleena had never seen inside the guard post, but had heard that here each man had his own cubby of a room, whereas in the city barracks, they slept on bunks in open halls, with little privacy.

She nodded at Stratus, face carefully blank, and he bowed back, equally blank. They turned and headed out the gate.

"I have two errands today, Guardsman," she said, trying for impersonal but polite. "The first will be to the Betchals' as last week. After that, I must visit Sammerman, the weaver, to place an order."

"As you wish, my lady. I shall happily accompany you."

They walked in silence for a while, and Juleena had to resist snatching glances at him — but failed at that mission a few times. She felt her cheeks warm a little as she pondered how handsome she found him, even though he wasn't as classically handsome as many other men. His tanned skin that nearly matched his hair in coloration gave him a bland look, and his jaw was a little heavy, his nose a bit big, his brows noticeably pronounced, and his fingers were thick and blunt — but the soft kindness of his gaze, his smile, and the gentle strength of his hands: those were what she liked: what she found so compelling.

"My lady is lost in thought," he murmured, and when Juleena looked over she saw that his careful neutrality had fallen away. His cheeks bunched in a smile and she couldn't help but return it. "Will you share your thoughts with me?"

Now her face got hot. "Not these ones. Your pardon, good sir?"

"Gladly granted," he said. "I have been much in thought, myself."

"And would you share your thoughts?"

"I think I had best keep them as well."

"That's alright," she said. "I need not have conversation to enjoy your company."

His cheeks turned a bit pink.

"Or if you like, tell me about your nieces and nephews," Juleena suggested. "You said you have some?"

"I do," he replied readily. "My brothers have both married fine women I hardly think they deserve, sometimes. I am biased though, since I spent much of my youth being bothered by my brothers, as is often the way with siblings. My oldest brother is

Magnus, and his wife Alaurie. My other brother is Tamarus, and his wife Ona. Mag and 'Laurie have two children, a girl first and a boy second, and Alaurie is expecting her third in spring. Tam and Ona have only one so far, a boy."

"How old are they?" Juleena asked.

She let Stratus talk, and he didn't seem reluctant to do so. By the time they'd reached the walls of Trivale, she'd come to learn that he liked his niece and nephews, but she again got the impression that his parents' house was too full for him. She thought he'd probably better enjoy spending time with the little ones if he could do so someplace with less crowding. Still, as he described their childish antics, Juleena found herself smiling along with him.

"I wish I could meet them," she said.

Stratus paused. "I wish you could, too."

"I don't suppose that would really be possible," Juleena subsided.

"It would be a little odd," he agreed, voice low. "A guardsman wouldn't bring a noble lady to visit his family."

"I know."

The look they exchanged was tinged with sorrow and mutual, unspoken understanding. They walked the last bit of the way to the Betchals' in silence. Stratus took up a relaxed guard position in front of the store, and Juleena went inside. The Betchals had her order of floss for the red and black portion of her gown—on which she would embroider autumn leaves from Mount Brasson's signature black maples—and new samples for the blue and yellow portion.

She spent a few minutes talking over her options with advice from the Betchals, and settled on her order, to be picked up next week, once they'd made the volume of floss she'd need for the blue and yellow inner layer. Juleena passed over payment for the first portion, and bagged her purchase. With a farewell to the Betchals, she rejoined Stratus outside.

"Shall I carry your goods?" Stratus offered.

"They are of hardly any weight," Juleena said, "and perhaps

you should leave your hands free, should you need to defend me."

He smiled. "My lady makes an excellent point."

"To Sammerman's now," she said. "I have to place an order."

Sammerman the weaver did not have a shop in either town. He risked living between Trivale and Lenali—outside the walls—in the midst of the area where he gathered all the materials for his weaving. Or rather, his children gathered the materials, and he and his wife weaved. They had deliveries of materials that didn't grow for the picking on Mount Brasson, but most of what he produced was made from the reeds, grasses, and other plants his family harvested, or from wool, hide, or animal hair bought from villagers that raised it. Since most of the plant materials were gathered during summer and fall, and then had to last the rest of the year, Sammerman had a storage building a bit smaller than a barn, and a collection of cats to keep rodents away from his goods.

Juleena turned down the cart path that led to the Sammerman house, fishing Mum Hyldi's order from her pocket. Missus Sammerman must have seen her coming, for she met her at the door.

"Lady Mrandis," the stocky woman greeted, "will you come inside and tell us what we can do for you?"

"Yes, gladly," Juleena nodded.

"And is that little Stratus with you? I'd heard you were being shepherded around by an escort these days."

"My mother's command," Juleena confirmed, while Stratus gave the missus a bow.

"How big you've gotten. You come in, too. I can't have you looming about in front of the house and scaring off customers."

Juleena and Stratus followed the missus into the front parlor that was used as a business office. Juleena sat, Stratus stood behind her against the wall, and the missus bustled to serve them tea before sitting down herself.

"Do sit down, Stratus," the missus scolded. "What did I say about looming? Now, what can we do for you, Lady Mrandis?"

Juleena explained, showing her Mum Hyldi's order, and politely sipped tea. Stratus came and sat down at the table, too, and also drank, but remained silent while the women conferred. It took a little time to agree on exactly what they'd make for the Mrandises, but once it was settled, and the tea gone, Juleena thanked the missus and rose to go.

"Will you be wanting to visit the garner?" Missus Sammerman lured as she led the way to the front door. "There're kittens."

Juleena halted and bit her lip. "I have been admonished not to linger."

Missus Sammerman smiled broadly. "You'd be doing me a favor. Those kittens need some human handling to gentle them. My own children do what they can, of course, but they've been quite busy lately with harvesting. You know the way. I'll just get to planning your order."

She pivoted and disappeared down the house's hallway.

"I really shouldn't," Juleena muttered.

"Why not?" Stratus asked.

"Hyldi told me not to."

"You always do as she says?"

Juleena's eyebrows flew up. "You're suggesting I disobey?"

He shrugged. "What harm is there in spending a few minutes with some kittens? Are you needed back at the house immediately?"

"No," she answered.

He smiled a little. "You want to go see them, don't you?"

Her expression turned sheepish. "I adore cats."

"Me, too. Let's go see them."

Stratus touched her elbow, just lightly, as he headed for the door, and she responded, going along with his encouragement.

"No one will know but us," he assured her.

As they exited, Juleena took the lead again, going around the house on a well-worn path to the storage structure attached by a covered walkway. The sliding door that was the main entrance, rattled as it always did when Juleena slid it open. She stepped into the warm, earthy dimness inside, and Stratus followed her, shutting the rumbling door behind them.

The building was a single room, with shelving around almost the entire perimeter, and a few freestanding shelves running most of the several yard length of it. Light came in through the open windows up under the overhanging roof, allowing in some indirect light while shielding the place from wind and rain. The crisp scent of freshly cut reeds and grass flooded Juleena's nose, along with the musty scent of dried bundles of the same. There were balls of wool and piles of hides, too, adding faint animal odors to the mix. Completed baskets of a hundred shapes and sizes sat on shelves and hung from hooks.

Through it all crept and bounded furry little felines.

"This is Merry," Juleena introduced as a grey and black striped cat came trotting over. "She always greets everyone at the door. Some of the others are shyer."

Juleena gave Merry a welcome pet, and the cat switched to greeting Stratus, who stroked her, too. Then Juleena moved deeper into the room, calling out to the cats she knew by name. There was only a handful that lived in the garner, now with the apparent addition of a litter of kittens.

"The Sammermans keep only female cats," Juleena explained as she moved to the back. "They keep them inside, and keep males out, to avoid kittens, and to keep them from getting eaten in the forest. One of these ladies must have made an escape."

She sat at the place she always sat when she visited, on the edge of a bin built into a back corner of the garner, where the Sammermans tossed all the waste from their materials. It was all clean waste—woody ends of reeds, bits of grass roots, the hard edges of hides, and anything else unsuitable or accidentally ruined—and they emptied it regularly, so it didn't smell bad. The edge of the bin was wide enough to make a narrow bench.

Juleena sat, and soon enough the cats came to investigate. Merry was there almost at once, and then the braver of the others. There were two who almost never came close enough to touch. One cat, a tortoiseshell, came sauntering up with three kittens bounding around her.

"Jelly, it was you," Juleena mock-scolded. "You were a naughty girl."

Stratus joined her, sitting down on the other edge of the bin and shucking off his gloves. "She must have heard a tom she couldn't resist," he remarked. "I don't know if I'd call that naughty; she was just following her instincts."

Juleena smiled wryly, and pulled a long bent reed out of the reject pile. She purposefully avoided Stratus's eye.

"I guess you're right," she allowed. "I can't fault a girl for following her instincts."

She dangled the reed down at the kittens and there was an immediate rush to be the first one to slay it. One kitten, a white one with spots of tortoiseshell like her mother, made a tactical choice to climb up Stratus's legs and get closer to the bouncing reed. He ran his hand gently over its back, and it promptly reversed around to attempt to eat his fingers. Juleena laughed as he scooped it up.

"Easy, easy there little ice-lion," he cajoled.

Juleena watched, reed all but forgotten, as he cuddled the kitten's little furry body, until it calmed and snuggled into his hands. He lifted it up and touched his forehead to its stripey head, right between its enormous ears.

"You shall be a great hunter soon," he foresaw with a grin, "and catch many mice and rats. They shall all fear you."

It lifted its paws and put them on his cheeks, and mewed. As he lowered the kitten back down, he saw Juleena watching and ducked his head as if with embarrassment.

"I am not a strong enough man to resist kittens," he shrugged.

She stared at him with a sad smile perched on her lips. "If resisting kittens is a sign of strength, may it be I never meet a man stronger than you."

His gaze flicked up to hers, and stayed there. Freed, the kitten tumbled out of his hands, to his lap, and rejoined its fellows on the floor. The reed slipped from Juleena's fingers and the three kittens pounced on it with tiny ferocity as it landed among them. She inched her hand forward, reached out, and took Stratus's. He let her, and he didn't let go.

"Juleena," he began raspily.

Her heart leapt at hearing her name on his lips.

"You're in my thoughts," he went on. "All the time, you're there. I don't know what to do about it."

"You want me out of your thoughts?" she whispered.

"Yes, and no. If only," he swallowed, "if only you were a girl in the village, but you're not."

She tightened her hand on his. "Stratus, I don't know what to do, either. It's not fair."

"It's not," he agreed.

"Your company makes me happy," she told him. "If I can at least have that, I am content."

"Are you truly?"

His eyes requested an honest answer, and she braced herself to give him one. "I can't have any more, so I must be content."

"But you want more."

"Yes," she confessed, unable to hold his gaze any longer.

"So do I."

Juleena rotated, turning her knees away from him, but not letting go of his hand. Some hot kind of hunger was in her: getting stronger the longer she looked at him and spoke with him and held his hand.

"Why you: I don't know," she apologized. "Maybe because you saved me from the chimera."

"I didn't save you. The other guards killed it, and you'd already escaped."

"But you comforted me when I was scared. That's when this started. Maybe this is just because I'm scared and looking for protection."

"But you killed the harpy," he countered. "You didn't need protecting then."

"I didn't kill it, you did," she interjected.

"I needed saving then, and you saved me."

She couldn't argue with that. "I suppose I did."

"You have plenty of people protecting you from ordinary dangers," Stratus said, "and no one can protect you from Salasis: not me, not anyone, since your House has offered you up to him."

That name made her take a sharp breath. "I know." Juleena looked up defiantly. "If I must be wed to him, before that happens, I want to know what Salasis can never give me."

Stratus didn't look away, but nor did he speak, or act. He just blinked, slowly, pondering her face. Juleena turned back towards him and eased closer. He didn't retreat, but she still saw doubt in his eyes. She put her free hand boldly on his knee and leaned in a little.

"No one will know," she breathed.

"I will know," he countered.

Juleena nodded. "Yes. I want you to know."

Inside she was trembling, but her hands were steady, and she didn't drop her gaze. Stratus's autumn leaf eyes stayed firmly on hers. He lifted his hand and laid it against her cheek. Juleena's held breath escaped her, and she pressed into his palm.

"My hands are rough," he murmured apologetically.

"I love them," she declared.

She rubbed her face against his hand like a kitten, and felt his fingertips encourage, just the tiniest bit. She complied without hesitation, leaning in as he did, reaching for him, and their mouths met a little clumsily, and a little too hard, but that mattered to Juleena not at all. Her inner trembling broke out all over her.

How much time passed there between them, she didn't know. Nor did any thought that someone might come in through the rattling door and surprise them, or any worry about their relative ranks in society concern her. It was the brush of Stratus's sword-calloused thumb across her cheekbone, the soft rumble in his throat, the smell of the soap he must use when shaving, the taste of his mouth, and the glorious satisfaction of victory in her own heart that occupied her every concern.

A little sound almost like a whimper escaped her as Stratus began to draw the kiss to a close—so he pressed back in, prolonging it a bit more, and waited until Juleena finally forced herself to let him go. He didn't go far, keeping his face close to hers, and she bit down on every foolish thing she knew she might say. Perhaps because of that, he said one for her.

"We're in a lot of trouble."

A laugh that was not born of amusement bubbled from her throat, and she nodded, already feeling the prickle of tears. He stroked her face.

"How can I ever let you go to him?"

"I'll marry you," she blurted. "If they won't take you in, I'll leave them."

"And live as a simple guardsman's wife? No, that is not the life for you."

Juleena pulled back a little, tossing her head like a mare fighting a bridle, and Stratus let her go.

"Why can I not choose my life?" she demanded. "Why does everyone else think they get to choose for me? I would rather live in poverty with you, than in a golden cage with Salasis."

"No. No, I will not marry you, Juleena. You deserve better."

She stared at him for a long moment. "Do you listen to yourself? You can't bear to let me go to Salasis, but think you're not good enough for me instead? What is this lofty perfection you think I deserve? And can it be found anywhere in this world?"

Stratus shook his head. "Forgive me, please. I am speaking without thinking."

"You'll kiss me like that, but you won't marry me," she whispered. "I thought you said you wouldn't be close to a woman unless she were your wife."

"This," he stuttered, "it wasn't, I mean. Perhaps I spoke in error."

"So," Juleena swallowed, "you're not serious about us."

"I have never been more serious," he replied at once, voice gone from unsteady to unequivocal. "But," he faltered again, "I haven't thought ahead. I can't see how we could ever be together. It's just that I just can't stay away from you. I can't think about the spring, and what will happen when you have to go. If I let myself think of it, I feel like I can't breathe."

Juleena put her hands in her lap. A kitten climbed along the edge of the bin and timidly ventured onto her thighs. She picked it up and held it close, its soft baby fur against her throat and its little claws pricking at her skin.

"So we will pretend that spring isn't coming?" she quavered.

"Did you really think," Stratus asked softly, "that you'd marry me?"

She shut her eyes and a tear slipped from each. "That's all I want." She turned to him shamelessly. "Is that not what you want?"

He wiped her tears. "If only I could, I would do so in an instant."

Juleena managed to swallow and take a breath. The kitten mewed. She kissed its little head and set it back down on her lap.

"Perhaps something will work out," she mumbled. "Spring is a long way away."

Stratus just stared at her in silence for a few moments. At last he nodded.

"It is."

They left the Sammermans' barn and walked without speaking back to Lenali. Juleena had never known such painful, bittersweet happiness. She couldn't begin to understand or unravel it. Every time she glanced at Stratus beside her, she wanted nothing more than to jump into his arms, and for him to carry her away from everything: Mrandis, Salasis, and all the obligations and requirements her mother put on her.

But he wouldn't.

She knew it wasn't because he wanted her to suffer; it was because he didn't agree with that solution. He wanted a better one. She couldn't fault him for that; she wished there were a better solution, too. Lacking one, she thought it would do, but this was one command she could not force him to obey, and she wouldn't try to.

There was time. Something would work out. If she didn't believe that, she too felt like she couldn't breathe. So she wouldn't think ahead. She'd be in the moment with Stratus. She'd have faith that her destiny was not to be Juleena Salasis. When she thought of it that way, that there was a chance she could cheat what her mother had ordained, she felt stronger.

They parted at the gates of the Mrandis estate, bowing to each other without a word: cold and impassive masks back in place. Juleena pivoted and stalked back to the house. She delivered word to Mum Hyldi that the Sammermans had taken her order, and then sought her room, hoping to avoid seeing anyone else on the way.

Luck was with her, and once there she shut her door and went to the chair by her window, but despite the all the walking she'd just done, she had no wish to sit. She stood leaning forward with her hands braced on the frame, and stared out at the sky. Mount Brasson was not the only mountain around, only the biggest, and even it was not all that large. Its altitude did not even extend above the tree line, though snow did fall on it. Stabbing up at the early autumn sky were several other peaks, all smaller, but lovely nonetheless. The maple trees that carpeted them were beginning to turn. The hills would soon be golden, and then amber, and then scarlet at last.

Juleena heard the door open, and recognized Samira by the sound of her footfalls.

"One more season," she said as the maid came up behind her.

"I'd say two, my lady. You have most of autumn yet, all of winter, and some of spring at least," Samira said with forced cheer.

"You shouldn't come with me to Salasis," Juleena told her.

"Why not? You're my friend, and I'm your personal maid. I should go with you."

"The men there mistreat the women in the house."

Samira stepped past her, into her peripheral vision. "How do you know?"

"Someone told me," she said.

"Julee, have you been crying?"

She turned her head away, but caught her denial on the tip of her tongue. "Just a little," she confessed.

Samira was quiet for a while, and when at last she spoke again, it was in a bare whisper. "Julee, you've gone out on errands twice now, with Stratus. Did anything happen?"

Her hands tensed on the window frame. "What kind of thing are you talking about?"

"I won't tell anyone. I promise."

Juleena swung her head back to eye her, and kept her words all but silent. "You're my closest friend in the world, Sami. I love you like a sister, more than my real sister. We should have a fight, and you should get reassigned somewhere else in the house. You can't come with me to Salasis, and you can't know anything about what is or isn't happening with me and Stratus. If you don't know, my mother can't dismiss you, or blame you."

Samira seized her wrist with both hands. "Julee, I'll help you. I will do anything to help you be happy."

"And what about your happiness?" Juleena countered. "What about your future? What about your safety? I can't be happy if your life is ruined."

"Oh, Julee." Samira threw her arms around her, hugging her desperately. "Just tell me. Tell me what happened with Stratus," she breathed into her ear.

Juleena resisted both the hug and speaking for two or three breaths, but then gave in to both, and put her arms around her friend. "We kissed again," she admitted. "This time we both wanted to. I mean, he wanted to last time, too, but he stopped it. This time," she shivered, "neither of us stopped it."

"How was it?" Samira asked.

"It's," Juleena found herself blushing. "Kissing is strange, you know? Why do people show affection like that? And it was awkward at first, and we didn't know what we were doing, and it felt odd, and you taste the other person when you do it, which is sort of gross if you think too much about it, but it's also really, really nice, and warm, and," she trailed off for a moment. "Stratus is so gentle. I like him."

"That was all you did?" Samira muttered.

"That was enough," Juleena retorted. "That was more than enough. It was wonderful."

"I see," Samira said, and drew away to lean against the wall beside the window. "Are you going to do it again?"

Juleena turned back to staring out at the mountains. "I don't know. I hope so."

"Are you going to bed him?"

Juleena whipped her head back over at Sami. The maid spread her hands in pacification.

"I'm just asking," she said.

Juleena nearly choked as she tried to talk. "I don't know how I could possibly do that."

"Because you don't want to?"

She tried to collect her disarrayed wits. She turned away, and turned back, eyed Samira, and tugged on her skirt to straighten it when it didn't need straightening.

"I haven't thought about that," she muttered at last. "It's not practical, for one thing. How could something like that be hidden? Where could we find to — to — ?"

"Do it?" Samira provided. "You're much more innocent than me, Julee. There's some among the servants who find time and place to do it in secret. It's a risk, but it can be managed."

"Do you do that?" Julee gaped at her.

Samira shrugged. "No. I'm as virgin as you," she said. "I just know a bit more. No one talks to you about what happens between men and women, but I overhear it among the servants all the time."

Juleena struggled to regain a measure of composure. "Even if there were a time and place where no one would discover us, it's too dangerous."

"How so?"

Juleena made a helpless gesture. "In a lot of ways. I'm sure you can think of them."

Samira frowned. "Because you might make a baby together?"

The burning streak of heat that shot through her, up her back to strike her heart and then down to burn in her belly and below, surprised her so much she had to catch her breath.

"You can avoid that," Samira went on, still in a whisper. "It's all about timing. I don't figure anyone knows why, but there are certain times during our cycles that it won't make a baby, and other times it will. I can find out more details for you."

"No," Juleena hissed. "No. There's no need for that."

"Why not?"

"I told you, it's too dangerous."

Samira frowned some more. "We can make it so no one will know, and so there's no baby—what else?"

"Salasis," Juleena snarled quietly. "He'd know, wouldn't he?"

Samira opened her mouth, and shut it again. "You've heard about that? Men can tell when it's your first time, and when it's not, and it's supposed to hurt, and bleed and all."

Juleena nodded without speaking.

"You said women are mistreated in House Salasis," Samira recalled. "Are you saying the lords bed the servants?"

She nodded again. "Terkari even has a child by a servant."

"Then it won't be his first time on your wedding night," Samira stated bluntly. "So what if it's not yours, either? He'd be a hypocrite to complain."

"I don't think that would stop him," Juleena muttered. "Then again, he said he doesn't like inexperienced women."

"He told you that?"

She nodded. "On the walk at Tuma, before Stratus called out that he saw a monster."

"That was Stratus?"

She nodded again. "He saw Terkari about to force me to kiss him. He couldn't run over and stab him, or punch him, but he could call out that there was a monster to make everyone run back inside."

Samira stared at her for several long moments. "Stratus is in love with you, isn't he?"

Juleena shrugged, even as those words set some fluttery bit of her to singing. "That's the other problem with thinking about bedding him. He says he won't do that with a woman he isn't married to, so there's no point in wondering about it."

"But he'll kiss you."

Juleena leaned against the wall on the other side of the window, mirroring Samira. "Yeah."

"You two," the maid murmured. "You have to be together."

She shook her head. "We can't."

"You'll really go to Salasis?"

Juleena shrugged.

"Stratus will really let you go?"

She shrugged again. "We're not thinking about that. We're just thinking about right now."

"I'll help you," Samira promised, and went again to hug her friend. "I'll help you every way I can."

Juleena had no occasion to see Stratus for the next few days. At most, she caught a glance of him grooming his roan gelding in the autumn sun one day, in front of the stables. It was from a distance, and she was inside, so there was no way to even catch his eye, much less anything else. Her third and final trip to the Betchals' was coming, though, and he would have to escort her to pick up her order. When she let herself think of it — which was difficult to prevent — various parts of her ached, throbbed, or tingled. It was disconcerting even as it felt good; she'd never felt such sensations before, at least not at such intensity.

A disturbance happened two days before her errand, based on the sudden coming and going of the guard, however, and her mother called her and all the family to the blue room. The topic distracted her entirely from idly romantic thoughts.

"Several," the Mrandis Guard Captain was reporting as Juleena came in with Cindra, Myra, and Camin. "Shorter than a man, and stockier, and grey of skin, and vicious. I've never seen such wild abandon in a fighting creature. It was like they had no care for their safety."

Rodreric was too composed to give outward sign of his dismay, but Juleena saw a drip of sweat making its was down the back of his neck, below his bundled up and braided hair.

"Do you have any idea what they might be called?" Ledren asked the group at large.

There were several guardsmen in the room. None of them were Stratus. One of them shifted uncomfortably and looked around as if embarrassed.

"Sounds like the tales my gran used to tell us," the man mumbled.

"Go on, Pirk," the Captain ordered.

"Goblins, sir," he said. "They looked like my gran's description of goblins."

Rodreric gave a slow nod. "That's what I was thinking, too." He sighed and looked over at Mirassi.

"We'll need messengers," the Mistress of Mrandis said. "A chimera, harpies at the Tuma House, and now goblins, all within a few months of each other. Something's happening, and we'll need to ask the other Houses what they've seen. It might mean a call to the capital. We might need some help, but this can't go on."

"Is the Guard sufficient to secure the walls of Trivale and Lenali night and day?" Rodreric asked.

There were other hamlets further away, but they had no walls. Juleena worried they'd be on their own—that her father was abandoning them.

"The watch can be increased, yes, Master," the Captain confirmed. "There are some trainees ready to join for full duty, or at least we'll put them on full duty, ready or not."

"I want the people to feel safe," Rodreric emphasized. "We must be cautious, yes, but we can't let this threat scare us into hiding in our homes. The harvest is on, at its peak now, and we can't let the crops rot in the fields or we'll all go hungry."

"The first rains will probably come next week, Father," Ledren added.

"Any spare guardsmen can join the farmers," the Captain suggested, "and get the crops in, especially at the smaller towns. It will mean a week of hard work for everyone, but we'll manage."

"I don't know how we could manage without you, Captain," Rodreric praised. "See to your men. I'll visit the battlefield shortly."

The guardsmen all bowed, and exited in a tidy formation.

"People were hurt?" Cindra spoke up before Juleena had to. "What happened?"

"A crowd of creatures," Rodreric recounted, "goblins perhaps, came out of the forest south of Trivale. The farmers in the fields there saw them in time and ran before them back to the town. The goblins seemed to lose interest when they couldn't catch any, or perhaps were scared of assaulting the walls of Trivale. They hesitated and started to turn back or regroup, but the Guard came out and ran them down. None of the creatures escaped. A few of the guards were hurt, but none seriously."

Juleena felt a sense of relief. Stratus was posted to the Mrandis estate. He couldn't have been among the first guards to respond to an attack south of Trivale. He couldn't be among the wounded.

"It almost sounded like," Ledren picked up, "the goblins were just wandering about and happened across our people. Perhaps they weren't an attacking force at all: not sent intentionally, I mean."

"If the farmers hadn't run, I'm sure they'd have been hurt or killed," Mirassi stated. "That was enough reason to retaliate. They threatened our people."

"Indeed," Rodreric nodded. He stood. "Ledren, Camin, you'll come with me to the battlefield. Mirassi, you can organize the messengers?"

"Of course," she answered.

"I wish we had a wizard among us," Myra spoke up.

"It's not as easy as you think for wizards to send messages whenever they want," Mirassi retorted. "My grandmother was a wizard, and she could do many things, but sending messages over distance was not that easy. Still," she grumbled, "it might have been quicker than sending human messengers who will have to ride for days to get anywhere, and far less dangerous."

The three men departed, leaving the womenfolk to speculate and chatter.

"Juleena," Mirassi summoned, and she twitched with nerves.

"Yes, Mother?"

"You're still taking an escort whenever you leave the grounds, like I told you?"

Juleena bowed her head. "Yes, Mother."

"Be sure you do. If there's any sign of trouble I'll confine you to the estate completely. We can't have you getting hurt or worse out there."

Cindra looked over from her conversation with Myra. "We'll still have the autumn outing?" she pled.

Mirassi frowned, but Juleena knew her mother enjoyed the viewing of the maple trees in all their glory, and the picnic in the last of the sun before the long dark days of winter, as much as they all did.

"We'll have the Guard sweep the area first," the Mistress of Mrandis said. "And we'll keep them on watch during it, as long as nothing more happens between now and then."

"What do you think will happen?" Myra asked. "Will the capital send the army and some drakes to help us?"

"They need something to attack first, and this foe is too sporadic," Mirassi replied. "The Wild Ones are coming forth like they haven't in ages. I'm concerned that something is sending them, or forcing them away from their homes. It is that something that must be dealt with. Once we know what it is, then the army can act. Until then, we must all be on our guard, and cautious."

***

Nothing more happened in the next two days except that Juleena reached the beginning of another monthly cycle and caught herself wondering about what Samira had said—that there were times in a woman's cycle that she could start a baby, and times she couldn't. She knew the bleeding meant she wasn't pregnant—and couldn't be anyway, for she'd never known a man—and thought that surely the time she was bleeding then, must be one of those times she couldn't become pregnant.

But she really didn't know how any of it worked. If she was going to soon be married—which she didn't want to think about—surely she should learn more about the business of making and birthing babies. Was no one going to talk to her about it? She wondered if she should ask her mother. Mirassi, after all, had birthed three children. Surely she would know. Surely it was her responsibility to make certain her daughter was prepared for both marriagebed and childbed, wasn't it?

The first day of her cycle was always a little difficult, but her errand was on the second, and she was prepared for the walk to Trivale: with Stratus. She couldn't help but think of him in relation to all her speculation about wedding and bedding and birthing, but she couldn't bring herself to seriously contemplate trying to get into bed with him—even as her body was starting to tell her that it wanted her to.

Stratus bowed to her when she met him at the gates, and she noticed he was wearing his sword, which he hadn't worn the last times he'd escorted her. He saw her looking and put a hand on the hilt as they walked off to the main road though Lenali.

"Just in case," he muttered. "Since the goblins, we're being more careful. Does it worry you? You look a little unwell."

Juleena shook her head. "No, I'm glad you have it."

"Are you ill, my lady?" He looked on her with true concern in his eyes.

She shook her head again, and lowered her voice. "No, just that time of the month."

His eyes widened with understanding even as his skin flushed red. "You're alright to walk to Trivale and back?"

"Women learn to endure these things, Stratus," she whispered. "I'd rather be out and walking than curled up in bed like an invalid."

His gaze glanced over her mouth, and then he looked back at the road before them. "I should know better than to coddle you."

She smiled. "I'll let you know if I'd like some coddling."

His skin flushed an even deeper crimson. "My lady," he whispered in admonition.

"I'm sorry," she apologized. "You're right. This is not a good place."

He nodded an increment and resumed a perfectly guard-like posture and expression, his blushes fading. They made their way in silence the rest of the way through Lenali and down onto the road to Trivale.

"You weren't in the fight?" Juleena asked once empty fields and scrub spread out around them.

"I only got to see the aftermath," he said. "The Captain had all the guards down to see the bodies, and then sent us back to our posts."

"They were goblins?"

"That's what we're calling them, and they match some drawings in our records. We had a lad who's good with a pen make new drawings from the bodies. Then we burned them."

"Do you think there will be more?" she asked.

He tipped his head a little. "It's difficult to say. They weren't that hard to defeat, I'm told, except that they fought viciously. Not very strong, not very fast, but furious nonetheless: like little cornered wildcats. If we had been outnumbered, it could have gone badly. Luckily, there were more guards than goblins, and we're bigger, faster, stronger, and better armed and organized."

"If any should appear," she prompted.

"Run as fast as you can for the nearest shelter, the walls of Trivale or Lenali if possible," he answered immediately. "I will stop them from catching you."

A lump rose in her throat. "Stratus," she whispered around

it. "I, I," and she couldn't go on.

She fell silent, and a moment later he murmured back. "I know. Me, too. We must both be strong."

Their hands sought each other, and for a moment they held tight, but then they let go, as they knew they must. Stratus nodded ahead towards the horizon beyond Trivale.

"Clouds are gathering," he said.

"The first rain isn't due yet," Juleena said.

"I'm not sure the weather will keep to your schedule," he remarked amiably.

"If it is going to rain, I hope it doesn't hit until we're back in Lenali."

"We'll see. We could take shelter if we had to."

The walls of Trivale came into view, and in another few minutes Stratus was nodding to the guard on duty. They made their way through the town to the Betchals, and Juleena went in for a third time to collect her purchase while Stratus waited outside. There was a delay while she waited for a previous customer to finish, but then the Betchals were quick in getting her bundles of floss to her and graciously accepting their well earned pay. When Juleena stepped back outside, Stratus was in the street, where he could get a look at a wider slice of the sky.

"We should get back, my lady," he said. "This is blowing in quickly."

As if to underscore his words, a breath of chill wind whipped down the street.

"Take my arm," he encouraged. "Let's get you home."

Under other circumstances, Juleena might have thought it too suggestive, but for fleeing before a rainstorm it was exactly what a guard would have done for a noble lady. She almost said they should hole up in the town hall and wait for the weather to pass, but if it truly was a rainstorm, it could last for hours, even overnight, and there was still a chance to outrun it.

The ground was still summer-hard and beaten down, so the footing was good as they hurried through Trivale and to the road up to Lenali. The cold wind bit at their backs, and Juleena leaned on Stratus's strength as the wind tugged at her skirts and threatened to pull her off balance. She was breathing hard as they approached the Lenali gates, but it was also exhilarating to feel her heart pounding in the chill, with Stratus beside her.

They rushed through the gates just as the first drops began falling.

"Shall we call a carriage?" one of the guards at the gate asked. "You can shelter here and wait."

Stratus looked almost like he might agree, so Juleena called out. "No need, Guardsman. We're almost there. Thank you."

She tugged, and Stratus complied.

"We might get wet," he muttered.

"A little rain won't hurt, and we are almost there," Juleena panted. "I won't have a team of horses hitched up and sent out just for a little walk through the town. They and the driver would both get drenched. We'll make it before the rain."

Perhaps the weather had been listening, and in a fit of pique chose to prove her wrong, for just then the sky opened up and dumped on Lenali.

"This way," Stratus ordered, pulling her towards the nearest buildings.

The streets had already been deserted because of the approaching storm. Now, doors, windows, and shutters slammed all around. They'd reached the residential area, and Juleena probably could have knocked on any door and demanded entry — and gotten it — but instead she let Stratus pull her into a narrow gap between two houses where the roofs overlapped, creating a mostly dry alley. Beyond their meager shelter, the rain poured in sheets, reducing visibility to a murky few feet.

"This can't last long," Juleena declared. "We still have the autumn outing next week, and too much rain will knock all the leaves off, and soak the ground besides."

"As you say, my lady," Stratus agreed beside her.

They stood quietly, listening to and watching the rain come down, but after only a minute or two, the novelty of it wore off, and Juleena became acutely aware of standing in what was suddenly privacy with Stratus.

He seemed to realize the same thing, and cleared his throat. "I have something for you."

She raised a curious eyebrow at him, and he reached into the front of his jacket. He drew out a long, narrow object about the length of his forearm, and Juleena recognized it as a sheath for a blade—with a blade in it apparently, as evidenced by the hilt at one end. He drew it just a few finger widths to show her the curious two-edged blade.

"It's the harpy feather I took," he explained. "I had it made into a dagger."

His hand found hers and he lifted it up to press the sheathed blade into her palm.

"It's yours," he said.

Juleena shook her head. "It's yours. It's your reward for killing the harpies."

"Which I couldn't have done without you," he said. "I have a perfectly good sword, passed down to me by my uncle. I don't need this, and your mother took away your reward to buy you something you don't want. Take it."

Reluctantly, her fingers curled around it. "I don't know how to use it."

"Put the pointy end in anything you want dead," he grinned. "Push hard. Even with a harpy blade, killing things isn't easy."

"I'm not sure I ever could," she said.

"You kill things with your bow."

"I do, but a blade is," she frowned, trying to think of how to describe it.

"More personal," Stratus provided with a nod. "It's face-to-face. I hope you don't ever have to use it, but I want you to have it. Tell your maid to put a slit in your pocket and shift, and then you strap it to your thigh, under your skirts, so you can hide it, but reach it if you need it."

Juleena tucked it into a pocket, but the hilt stuck out. Instead, she put it in her bag with the embroidery floss and looped the bag through her belt, leaving her hands free. She wasn't sure how to feel about Stratus telling her she might need to fight someday—or talking about her thigh and skirts. Well actually, she knew how that last made her feel. She lifted her head.

"Some people say the gift of a blade will cut the relationship between two people," she said, "so it can't be a gift. It has to be a trade."

"I have heard that," he allowed, "but—"

"So I should give you something in return," she pressed on.

He shook his head. "I cannot accept a gift from you, my lady."

"Not a gift," she corrected, "a trade."

Juleena slid both hands up Stratus's chest, over his shoulders, up his neck, to hold his face: fingers around the back of his head and thumbs stroking his cheeks. She tipped her face up as she pulled his down. He didn't resist until her breath brushed across his lips.

"Juleena," he uttered, and she wasn't sure if it was a protest or an endearment, or both.

He was taller than she, and she arched up onto her toes a little, leaning her body in against his. His hands landed on her waist, as if he might push her away.

"A trade," she repeated. "Take it."

If there had been any reluctance on his part in their previous kiss, it was gone in this one. His arms wrapped her and clasped her tight to his chest, which was a good thing since when he did, she lost her balance, and depended completely on him to hold her up. Juleena suddenly felt all control she might have had swept away from her. Stratus held her and didn't let her go.

And it didn't scare her at all. She knew implicitly that if she were to resist, or make the slightest sign of displeasure, that he would stop immediately, but she had no wish to make him stop. She wanted this to go on and on, for her body was singing with it. Her heart was thundering like a mare in a joyous full gallop. And other areas were purring like an ice-lioness with prey in sight—or with a handsome male ice-lion in sight.

And she knew he felt the same. When at last Stratus drew

the kiss to a close and loosened his arms, he was breathing heavily, eyes dark and hungry, and he turned away as if to keep himself from doing something he knew he shouldn't. Juleena leaned back against the building behind her, also trying to catch her breath. Without his arms around her and his body against hers she was suddenly cold.

They waited just like that for the several minutes it took for the cloudburst to pass. When at last Stratus turned back around, he seemed to have calmed himself. He didn't say anything, though Juleena thought he might. Something like: "we should stop this." Or: "never again."

But he didn't. Instead, after some time looking at her, he said, "the rain is letting up. I should get you home."

She nodded. "Thank you for the trade," she whispered.

His mouth twitched as if he might smile. "Likewise."

Juleena was in something of a daze as she got back to the house. Some servants made a fuss over her being out during the cloudburst, but she was mostly dry and assured them she'd sheltered from it. She escaped them as soon as she could and fled to her room. There she threw herself down on her bed and hugged a pillow to her chest.

Samira came in. Juleena figured her friend had probably been watching for her return, so it didn't surprise her. The maid sat down on the foot of the bed.

"Julee, are you alright? More cramps? Or—?"

"I want him," she whispered, eyes squeezed shut, jaw clenched. "I don't want my first time to be with Terkari. I want Stratus."

Samira seemed to take her lady's declaration in stride—as if she had expected it. "Do you think he will?"

"I think he wants to," Juleena said.

"Julee," Samira murmured patiently. "You can't force him. That's as bad as what Terkari might do to you."

"I know." She hugged the pillow tighter.

Samira patted her foot, the nearest bit of her. "But you can ask him. I'll help you."

"Help me?"

"I'll get more information on when it's safe to be with him. The older girls will tell me."

"Sami, you can't let them suspect—"

"Of course not," she cut her off. "I'll tell them it's for me. I've been flirting with one of the manservants anyway. They'll believe me."

Juleena opened her eyes. "There's someone you like, too?"

"A little," she shrugged, her pale skin reddening. "Not like you. I wasn't planning on doing anything, maybe, but they don't know that."

The two young women stared at each other for a moment.

"It's a bad idea," Juleena breathed. "I know it is. If we get caught, he'll get demoted, dismissed. My parents might even try to do something worse to him."

"We'll make sure," Samira emphasized.

Juleena stared at her for a few heartbeats longer before she nodded. "Alright. We'll make sure, and he still might say no."

"You have to brace yourself for that."

"It won't be because he doesn't want to. I can understand if he can't bear to take the risk. It'll be alright."

Samira petted her leg a little. "Yes, Julee. It will be alright."

Juleena closed her eyes and drifted, thinking of her moment with Stratus between the buildings, in the rain, and hoped that somehow everything would indeed be alright. She pulled the sheathed harpy blade from her bag of floss and clutched it to her chest.

"He gave me a dagger."

Juleena squinted one eye open to look, grinning, up at Samira. The servant girl fought a smile in reply.

"How romantic."

The storm blew over quickly, and though it had pounded parts of Mount Brasson, there were still plenty of trees left with their gowns of autumn leaves. Mirassi's messengers had been dispatched to nearby Houses, and now all there was to do was wait and prepare for the autumn outing.

It was really just a glorified picnic, and everyone knew it, but it was held under the best and brightest of the trees, in some of the last of the autumn sunshine, and the consensus was to turn it into a celebration. Everyone was invited — child to adult, including extended branches of the Mrandis family. Almost all of the servants would come, too, and this year the Guard would be very much in evidence, to protect the picnic from any Wild Ones that might want to crash it.

Juleena was dismayed that a servant was sent to fetch the new baskets from Sammerman. It meant she had no excuse to go out on another errand with Stratus. Days passed without any non-suspicious way for her to see him. The autumn outing was scheduled for a few days ahead, and she at least hoped she'd be able to look at him during the outing. The guardsmen were going to be there, and as a guard assigned to the Mrandis estate, she couldn't see how he would be excluded.

Samira, at least, brought her the details she'd promised, and laid out a calendar as they sat together by the window in Juleena's room.

"Here," the maid pointed. "Your last cycle started on this day, right?"

"Right."

Samira marked the day with a number one. "Now we count ahead. I should tell you, this doesn't always work, but it works better for women like you, who have regular cycles that are always the same length."

The maid had numbered the days, until she reached twenty-eight. "Your next cycle should start here. Now these are the days you have to be careful of."

She took a bit of charcoal and shaded the days of the calendar, leaving some blank, and others gradually darker until a few days around day fourteen were very dark.

"How do you know this?" Juleena mused. "I mean: I know the other servants told you, but how do people know this?"

"Women have kept track of when they get pregnant and when they don't," Samira explained. "It's passed down from mother to daughter, over the generations. By now, we're pretty sure this is how it works."

"But if a married couple is, um, being together all the time, how could a woman know which time was the one that started the baby?"

"Well, they wouldn't, necessarily, but they're not the only ones keeping track. We are benefitting from the work of hundreds, thousands of women over hundreds of years," Samira said. "It was passed to me, and I'll pass it to others."

"So I can trust this?" Juleena muttered.

The maid shrugged. "It's better than nothing."

"There's no other way?"

"To prevent a baby? There are teas that might stop it, but I don't see how I could get them to you. People would notice."

"Could you say they're for you?" Juleena asked.

Samira winced. "But I'm not bedding anyone. Mum Hyldi would figure that out. This calendar is just good information for any woman, but to actually get the teas would make Mum Hyldi ask questions. She watches the tea supply."

"I know she does," Juleena accepted. She huffed out a breath. "Fine. Did you have any ideas about a safe place and time for us to meet and talk at least?"

"I'm sorry, Julee, I can't really think of a safe way. Going out to his room in the guard post is too risky."

"Incredibly risky," she agreed. "Someone would hear us or walk in on us, or see me coming or going."

"You can't bring him up here to your room."

"I guess not," she shrugged. "The guardsmen almost never come in the house. He'd be noticed and questioned."

"And you can't go renting a room in an inn in town. You'd be recognized," Samira shrugged.

"How do the servants get away with it?" Juleena asked.

"They go to each other's rooms late at night when everyone is asleep, using the servants' back halls."

"Why can't Stratus come in that way?"

Samira shook her head. "The back halls don't connect to your room."

"But they connect to your room, and your room connects to mine."

"Yes," the maid agreed cautiously.

"If he wore a cloak, and came in very late, he could come up the back halls to your room, and into mine."

Samira winced. "It's dangerous to have him in your room."

"Then," Juleena ventured, "what about yours? Could we borrow it? And you stay in here, in my bed, and pretend to be me, asleep?"

The two young women stared at each other across the table and fertility calendar.

"It's still risky," Samira said. "Someone might still notice."

"But they will think some unknown person is going to you, not me, if they see where he's going, so they'll just think you have a lover. You're allowed to have a lover."

Samira nibbled at her lower lip, and Juleena reached out to grab her hand where it lay on the table.

"This is getting you really involved," she said. "I didn't want that. You can say no. I don't want you to get in trouble with me."

"It won't be very often, will it?" Samira asked. "Not like every night?"

"No, no," Juleena assured her. "It might only be once, I don't know. He might refuse. Even if he doesn't, I might not be brave enough."

"But if you do, if you both like it," Samira murmured, "you might want to meet a lot."

Juleena sat back, blushing. "Maybe we'll have to think of something safer, if that happens."

Samira stared at her quietly.

"Besides," Juleena grunted, turning her head away. "It's only until I get married. What is that, five months now?"

"Something like that."

"But just for us to talk about it, can we borrow your room?"

Samira heaved a great sigh. "Fine, but not my bed."

"Alright," Juleena agreed. "That would have felt uncomfortable anyway." She looked down at the calendar. "Definitely not this week."

"No, this week would be bad. Wait until next week."

"This week is the autumn outing anyway."

"Yeah, so don't let him take you off into the trees."

"I," Juleena stuttered, "I don't think that will happen."

"Good then," Samira said.

The day of the autumn outing dawned sunny and as warm as mid-autumn ever got. The kitchens loaded the baskets—old and new both—to bursting with food and dishes and flatware. The baskets, ground covers, cushions, and blankets were loaded into sturdy one-horse carts able to handle the off-road terrain. The nobility mounted up, Juleena riding Ivy again, and the guards formed ranks around them. The able-bodied servants walked, while the very old caught a ride on the supply carts. Juleena had offered to let Samira ride double with her on Ivy, but the maid had elected to walk as well.

In an unhurried pace they moved off through Lenali and took a road other than the one that led through Trivale, heading for a particularly stunning stand of old maples near the river. The journey itself was a part of the outing, not just the destination and the picnic. Everyone gazed around, appreciating the trees in their blazing fall foliage beneath the crisp sky midway in color between summer's bold blue and winter's white. Children ran about, chasing each other or collecting the fallen leaves. Cindra and Ledren's daughter was too young yet to join the frolickers, but rode with her mother, with her nurse walking at the stirrup.

Juleena saw Stratus. He was in formation with the other guards—not just the six from the Mrandis estate, but another dozen from Lenali. He didn't glance her way except when he swept his eyes over the whole crowd, regularly checking that all was well. She tried not to glance his way, but the memory of their kiss in the rain was with her, beating in her blood, entangled with her decision to meet him alone again—in secret, at night—and it was difficult to keep her gaze from wandering to him.

The caravan reached the bank above the river and the servants set about preparing the picnic area: removing dead branches, putting down ground covers, and then layering blankets and tossing down cushions atop them. Others set out the baskets, while the guards created a perimeter both to watch for anything nasty trying to get in, and to keep picnickers—such as children who couldn't imagine that something bad would happen to them—from wandering out.

Juleena dismounted and let a manservant take Ivy to hobble and turn loose with the other horses in a clearing a little ways away where there was plenty of grass not yet sere. The children were indeed forming roaming packs likely to let their adventures carry them beyond the border of guards, and the adults began finding places to sit. Samira dutifully followed Juleena, who managed to avoid sitting next to her mother or father or most of her other relatives. She ended up sitting on the same blanket with her sister Myra and some of the Mrandis branch family: her mother's younger brother and his wife and daughter.

"So you're to be married at last," her uncle, Damarin, smiled. "House Salasis, I hear?"

"Do tell us about your husband," her aunt-in-law, Maresta, prodded.

"Is he handsome?" her cousin, Yusani, who was just about old enough to begin the husband-hunt herself added.

Juleena steeled herself and tried to pretend that she was at least content with the match, berating herself that she should have known that wherever she sat the topic would be her coming wedding. Avoiding her parents wouldn't avoid that.

"Quite handsome, actually," she began.

Samira gave her an encouraging smile, and Juleena tried to keep up her positive responses. As far as she could tell, she seemed to be convincing them, and as soon as she could, she turned the conversation around on them.

"And how about you, Yusani?" she asked her cousin. "Do you have any promising prospects on the horizon?"

The girl ducked her head and looked shyly at her mother.

"Our own summer gathering," the woman began, "brought a few possibilities. I think there's a boy in the Lorinan branch that Yusani has become quite taken with."

"He's third born in the branch," Yusani picked up quickly, "so he might come to Mrandis."

"Nothing is for certain yet," Damarin put in softly.

"I know," Yusani agreed, but she turned hopeful eyes up at her father and he smiled and patted her head fondly.

Juleena felt a fierce stab of envy. Branch members of the family didn't normally inherit the House, and over time their offspring would marry lower and lower on the social hierarchy tree, until in generations they would be common, while new branch members—such as Juleena would have become, had she not matched up with a firstborn from another House—would take over the branch residences as the elderly passed away, their children and grandchildren gone into obscurity.

It was something of a sad fate for branch members, but because they didn't inherit, whom they married wasn't as important. Yusani could marry the boy she liked, who liked her, without negotiations that took days to settle in order to pay for him leaving his House and coming to Mrandis. Branch families lived off their House, but had few disposable resources. A token would be given in exchange for the boy from the Lorinan branch, but it would be modest, nothing near what Mrandis might gain in selling Juleena to Salasis.

"I wish you every happiness," she told Yusani. "Will you tell me what he's like?"

The girl needed no second invitation. She launched into a detailed description of his appearance, likes, dislikes, hobbies, and hopes. Yusani knew far more about him than Juleena knew about Terkari or Stratus, and yet the former she was already arranged to marry and the latter she wanted to tempt to her bed—

and Yusani hadn't even confirmed that she would wed this boy from Lorinan. From the indulgent looks her parents gave her, though, Juleena thought it was already the next thing to settled.

Her envy grew. When at last Yusani took a pause to breathe and swallow some wine, Juleena excused herself.

"I think I've eaten a bit too much," she smiled sheepishly. "I had better try a little walk."

"The leaves are best appreciated while walking," Damarin replied graciously.

His wife, too, nodded with complete acceptance of this excuse, but Juleena was surprised to see—just for a moment—a little flash of sympathy in her eyes.

"I'll go with you, my lady, if I may," Samira said.

"If you wouldn't mind," Juleena concurred.

They rose and moved slowly among the picnickers. Juleena took Samira's arm and made a show of looking up at the rust and gold leaves. They weren't the only ones walking about, though most people were still sitting and eating. The cooks had made so much food Juleena had no worry of missing out. There would still be vittles even if she and Samira walked for an hour before returning. They headed into the trees, beyond which, somewhere, the guards had made their perimeter.

"Do you think you'll get married, Sami?" Juleena asked once they'd left the others behind.

"I don't know," she replied. "A servant doesn't have to. If I go with you to Salasis, I could be one of the nurses to your babies, and never need to have my own."

Juleena seized her hand. "Would you? I can think of no one else I'd like more helping to raise them."

Samira smiled at her. "Of course, Julee. If I'm allowed to go, and allowed to be in the nursery, I would do it with joy."

But Juleena frowned. "No, I forgot for a moment. It's not safe for you to be there."

"It can't be all as bad as you've heard," Samira ventured.

"Stratus told me," she said. "He spoke with Salasis guardsmen at the gathering."

Now Samira frowned, too. "Perhaps the guardsmen were exaggerating for some reason?"

"Terkari's words and behavior support it. I should at least go first by myself, and if it's safe, once I see with my own eyes, I'll ask for you."

"Alright," the maid agreed.

"And if it's not safe, you stay at House Mrandis."

Samira nodded meekly. "Alright."

"My lady and miss," said a voice, and both women looked ahead.

A guardsman, but not Stratus, stood among the trees a few yards ahead.

"I beg your pardon, but this is the edge of our patrol," he went on with a bow.

"I understand, sir," Juleena replied. "We'll turn here. Thank you for your vigilance."

They pivoted, but not to completely retrace their steps; Juleena didn't want to go back just yet. They walked along in silence now, and Juleena did find herself able to appreciate the autumn colors. Though she'd lived among these trees all her life, she'd never forgotten that they were stunning. Through the trees they noticed another guard after a few minutes, but they were inside the border. They passed four more.

Then they came to Stratus.

Juleena recognized him even from behind; he was looking out into the trees, away from the direction of the picnic. She stopped walking, and Samira took her cue and stopped, too. The maid nudged her and let go of her hand.

"Go to him," she whispered. "I'll watch here."

Juleena glanced around and then back at her friend. "There's no one near, but there's almost no cover."

"Just for a moment then? Talk to him, about you-know."

Juleena looked again through the forest of black tree trunks. There was indeed little undergrowth, but there were a lot of trees. It wasn't the safest place for an assignation, but everything in her pulled her to him, and she nodded shortly.

310

"I'll be right back."

Stratus heard her coming and turned with surprise, then delight, and then dismay, but he caught her hands as she reached him.

"This isn't safe," he said.

"I know," she agreed. "My maid is keeping watch. It will be safe for a moment."

"Your maid?"

"She knows."

This clearly concerned him.

"I grew up with her," Juleena told him. "She's my closest friend in the world. She's helping us."

Stratus was still frowning, though only with a little worry, no longer with fear.

"Her name is Samira. She was with me when we saw you grooming your horse after the harpy attack."

"Ah. I've seen her around the estate. She seems like a respectable young lass."

Juleena took a step closer so their bodies almost touched. She had to tip her head up to look at him. "I'm not getting sent on errands anymore, and I don't know when the next one will be," she said. "I want to see you."

He winced and lifted her hand to his lips. "And I, you, but I daren't risk either of us."

"Meet Samira at the back servants' door, at midnight," Juleena rushed on. "Wear a cloak."

Now he was frowning again. "What are you suggesting?"

"She'll bring you up by the back halls, the servants' way, to her room. We can meet there in secret."

Stratus shook his head. "This is unacceptably risky."

"Will you come? Please? How else can we see each other, and talk?"

"And what else, Juleena? Are you expecting more from me?"

His eyes, as red and brown as the maple leaves, stared down into hers. She couldn't lie, and knew if she told the truth he'd likely refuse, but holding back the truth was as bad as a lie.

"Yes," she whispered, "but not expecting, just," she swallowed, "wondering."

Pained frustration infiltrated his frown. "I wonder, too, but—"

"Please just come, and we can at least talk," she rushed. "I think we can both respect each other's boundaries for anything more than talk?"

He winced again, shutting his eyes and half turning his head away. Juleena reached up and put a hand on his shoulder. She wished she knew what he was thinking, but could only guess he was arguing within himself. After another moment, she rose up on her toes and placed a kiss on his cheek. Stratus let out a great breath and turned back to her, shaking his head a little.

"Fine," he grunted. "Fine. I'll come. We can discuss this more then. You can't stand out here with me like this, and I'm on duty."

A smile burst out on her face, and he could only resist that for an instant. Affection defeated distress, while uneasiness lingered in the background, and he bent his head to plant a swift kiss on her mouth. He pulled away just as Juleena began to reach for him.

"Save it," he teased ruefully. "You had better go, my lady."

Juleena protested with a huff, but knew her eyes must be twinkling.

"I'm not promising anything," Stratus warned. "I will come, and we'll talk."

"Not tonight. I'll prop up a book on my windowsill on the right day: that night, at midnight. You can see my window from the grounds?"

"I can," he acquiesced.

"Alright," she agreed.

Juleena stepped back, putting a prudent distance between them and bowed. Stratus bowed more deeply, and turned back to his surveillance of the forest. She walked swiftly back to where Samira was waiting, only partly visible behind a tree.

"What happened?" the maid asked as soon as Juleena joined

her.

"He'll come," she whispered. "I said for him to meet you at the back servants' door at midnight, and to wear a cloak, and you'd bring him up, but not tonight. I'll signal by putting a book on my windowsill."

"It is risky," Samira mumbled.

"He said that, too, but he agreed in the end."

Samira eyed her. "Did you talk about what you'd do at this meeting?"

"Not really," Juleena answered. "I said we'd talk. He agreed to talk."

"I suppose you will do some of that," she remarked.

"And we'll see what else, if anything."

"From what little I know of him, he seems like an honorable man," Samira observed. "I wouldn't get your hopes up, if I were you."

Juleena nodded. "I know. I shall try not to."

After a few more minutes of walking, they rejoined the picnic and as she'd expected, there was plenty of food left. They sat to eat some more, and Juleena found herself in a much more cheerful mood, with the prospect of seeing Stratus in privacy ahead in her mind. Even if they did only talk, that was better than nothing. The thought drifted by that she was quite fixated on him, and when she did have to leave for Salasis, no matter what their attraction had grown into, it would hurt terribly.

She knew it, but she could pretend otherwise. She could pretend that day would never come, and look only as far ahead as the night when Samira would help bring him to her.

The perfect night came a few days later.

"We will both depart for the local meeting, and then I will go on to Kedikan with our findings," Rodreric Mrandis pronounced in the blue room.

"Father, may I come?" Ledren asked.

"I will need you here in my absence. Tonight Lenali holds its city hall meeting. You will go in my stead."

Juleena stood with Myra and Cindra and Camin, and forcibly reigned in her rising interest.

"Cindra, you might wish to go, too," Mirassi suggested. "It will be valuable experience for you."

"Yes, Mistress," Cindra bowed.

"It will be a late night," Mirassi amended. "Get a nap beforehand."

The house would be emptied of the most dangerous people who might discover her infatuation with a certain guardsman. Myra and Camin had their rooms in the other wing of the house, distant from Juleena's—she still had her childhood room while they had a suite. Ledren and Cindra, too, had a suite, also somewhat distant from Juleena's room, surrounded by empty rooms where their children would eventually reside.

Juleena's parents' suite was the closest to hers, and they would both be gone. They would surely take a few servants with them, such as Kapri, who slept lightly. At the same time, the house would have distracting news to chew over, and everyone would be more relaxed because the Master and Mistress were away. With all the disruption to the usual routine, it would be easier for Stratus to slip inside.

Juleena had also entered the white days on the calendar. Tonight: she would send for Stratus tonight.

"How long will you be gone, Father, Mother?" Ledren asked.

Juleena was relieved that she hadn't needed to ask.

"I should return in a week, two at the most," Mirassi said.

"A trip to Kedikan is no quick jaunt," Rodreric said, referring to a major city in the west where a large portion of the army and several flights of drakes were stationed. "Don't expect me back for at least a month. Hopefully, I will return before the snows make the roads impassible."

Juleena nodded with the others and wished her parents safe journeys. All the while her anticipation was rising, but with it nervousness and even a little fear. She had no certainty as to how the night would end. She went directly up to her room and propped a book in her window.

It was shortly before midnight. Juleena hadn't been able to sleep.

"Stop pacing, Julee," Samira said. "And put on something else."

Juleena plucked at her shift. She'd put on a fresh one right after her extremely thorough bath. It was silk, not the linen or cotton a commoner would have worn, and clung to her skin. It smelled faintly of the lavender it had been folded with.

"You don't want him dropping unconscious at seeing you suddenly so unclothed," Samira went on.

The room was plentifully warm, despite the advance of autumn. Juleena had a fireplace in the wall that was shared by her and Samira's little room next door. The fire was burning low now, but it had heated up both rooms nicely. Samira handed her a quilted lounging robe in blue and violet, embroidered with silver leaves. Juleena relented enough to put it on.

Samira was still dressed, since she'd be going down through the servants' halls, but now she put on a cloak, lifting up the hood to hide her face. She picked up a candle lantern.

"It's time," she said.

Juleena nodded nervously.

"Wait here," Samira instructed. "I'll come get you. And you know it's possible he'll change his mind and won't come at all, or missed seeing your signal."

Juleena shrugged, but she felt certain he would come.

"I'll be back," the maid whispered. "Don't fret."

Samira went out through the door that connected their rooms and shut it behind her. Juleena strode over to the edge of her bed and sat. There was no point in looking out the window for him: it was dark on the grounds and her room didn't face the barracks besides.

An eternity passed, and then a second one. Juleena waited, trying not to fret — as instructed. Her stomach was in knots, and the rest of her burned, tingled, and chilled in turns. Her palms were sweating and she wiped them on her bedspread. The quilted robe was making her hot.

At last, she heard the door and looked up to see Samira stepping through. The maid shut the door as Juleena stood up, the latter almost shaking with anxiety.

"He's here," Samira breathed. "He looks nervous, too, so you two will be quite the pair."

"Oh, Sami," Juleena shuddered. "Should I really do this?"

"I'm no expert," the maid replied, "but I think that's something the two of you need to decide together, and if it doesn't feel right for either of you, don't do it."

Juleena nodded and took the candle lantern, trying to keep her hand steady.

"I'll get in your bed and be you, though I doubt anyone will check. They long ago stopped checking on you in the middle of the night," Samira muttered.

Juleena hardly heard. Her bare feet silent on the cool floor, she went to the connecting door, opened it, and stepped through.

Stratus had taken a seat on the room's only chair: a heavy, wooden piece that had been downgraded to servant quality when it became too worn. He had his hands braced on his knees, and his head a little bowed. The cloak he'd worn was hung by the door to the servants' hall, and he was dressed in simple trousers and shirt, unremarkable and nothing that would peg him as to occupation.

He looked up as Juleena came in and his lips parted with obvious surprise at her garb. She set down the candle lantern on the little night stand by Samira's narrow bed. The lamp at her desk was also lit, but low. Stratus started to stand.

"Please, no, good sir, sit," Juleena waved him down, and he settled back reluctantly.

She suddenly felt self conscious, and crossed her arms over her front. At the same time she wanted to go to him and be in his arms like that day in the rain. His warm eyes were steady on her and it made her blush and turn partly away.

"Won't you sit as well, my lady?" he invited, voice already

husky.

She shook her head, even though her legs felt unsteady. There was nowhere else to sit except the edge of the bed. She couldn't bear to look at the bed, much less sit on it. Besides, Samira had forbidden her use of it.

"I am here," Stratus went on after a brief silence. "Of what would you speak?"

The words jammed up in her throat. She even put her finger-tips there, but it didn't help her muscles relax.

"I confess I am nervous to be here," he went on when she was silent. "I am afraid of this being found out. No one saw me on my way, as far as I know, but it still concerns me. I know the Master and Mistress, and Lord Ledren and Lady Cindra, are away, but—"

"I know," Juleena managed to say. "So instead should we never see each other? Are you here to say we should stop this, and only look from afar, nevermore speak," her gaze went over to him, "or touch?"

"That day will come regardless," he said softly.

"But there is time. It is not this day."

"It is not," he allowed, and rubbed his forehead with a hand. "I could not stay away. Even if we agreed to stop, with all the best of intentions, I do not know that I could stay away from you now, no matter what I know to be the safer course."

"Nor I," Juleena admitted.

He stared at her, eyes somehow intense and kind at the same time. She couldn't bear it, and walked to him. As he would get up again, she put her hands on his shoulders, pushing him back to his seat, and he complied. Her jaw trembled, but she bent her head down and he tipped his up for a kiss, a long one that ended with his hands lightly holding her waist and her arms around his neck.

The sweetness of his mouth had drawn the fear out of her, heated her blood, and her focused certainty returned. She looked down into his eyes and he looked up at her—and she took a seat on his lap. Stratus's eyes widened at the move, but he didn't push her off. Instead, his expression grew hesitant.

"My lady?" he murmured.

Juleena inched her hips closer to him and his hands suddenly tightened on her waist, stopping her approach.

"Juleena," he revised, a hint of panic in his voice.

"Stratus," she breathed to him. "Please."

"I can't do this with you."

"Why not? I want you to."

He looked genuinely alarmed now. "There could be a child."

"I've taken care of that," she assured him.

He seemed to take her word for it, but had another argument. "I'm not your husband. He will—"

"He is no virgin," she interrupted. "You told me that yourself, and he told me he prefers experienced women. He asked if I had known a man and was disappointed I hadn't. He'll be glad."

"But we can't be married, and I am yet a virgin," Stratus asserted. His face pinched with concern. "I might disappoint you, and hurt you."

Juleena held his shoulders tightly. "I want to share this with you, not with him. I want to choose."

He closed his eyes. "You should get to choose."

"I choose you."

Stratus was silent and still.

"Do you choose me?" Juleena asked. "It is because we're not married? Does this wrong your unknown future wife?"

He shook his head. "It will take me years to get over you, no matter what we do or don't do. It's too late; you have my heart."

Juleena bowed her head and rested it atop his shoulder, and ventured the question she suspected was closest to the core of the matter. "Is it because I'm born to the nobility?"

Stratus was silent.

"Do you think I'm somehow better than you?"

Still he said nothing.

"I'm not," she whispered. "It's an accident of birth. You are the finest man I've ever known, far better than many noblemen, and the equal of the others. A man's measure is not to whom he's born, but how he lives his life."

He twitched. "And touching another man's promised bride is an honorable way to live my life?"

"He is the one who has sired bastards," Juleena countered.

"And that makes it acceptable for me to lower myself as well?"

She tucked her face against his neck. "Loving me is lowering yourself?"

"No, but you are promised to another," Stratus retorted. "No matter who that other is, you are promised."

She lifted her head and met his gaze. "I did not make that promise, and no one can decide my disposition but me."

He nodded. "And yet you will go."

Juleena stared at him. "Perhaps I will not."

Stratus stared back, and for several breaths they held still, perched like cormorants on a cliff side, watching the sea below until the waves calmed. Then at some unspoken signal, they dove.

When they came to stillness again, Stratus put his hands over hers where they were clenched in his shirt. "I'm sorry," he whispered. "I didn't please you."

Her throat ached. Her fists tightened. It was over too soon, and that which had been building began to subside, and she mourned its premature departure.

"I couldn't hold back any longer," he murmured on. "I'm sorry, Julee."

The endearment did some small measure to soften what was lacking, the emptiness that she hadn't known before was there. She forced herself to loosen her grip on his shirt.

"Please forgive me," he asked.

"Of course," she whispered. "I forgive you."

She untangled her legs from the chair, about to stand up.

"A moment," Stratus warned. "Here."

He managed to fish in a pocket and draw out a handkerchief. She took it, and stood with a wince.

"You're right," she muttered. "I didn't realize."

"You're bleeding," Stratus said. "Is it that time?"

"No, it's just," she sighed and turned her head away, embarrassed. "I hear it can happen the first time."

"I hurt you," Stratus regretted.

"No," Juleena declared. "I made you do this."

"I wanted to. You didn't make me," he refuted tightly.

She heard the rustle of cloth, and then Stratus came to her. "Juleena?"

She turned to him, but couldn't look him in the face. He put his hands on her shoulders and she leaned against him.

Voice low, he said, "Are you alright? We shouldn't have done this, should we?"

"We absolutely should have," she retorted, head snapping up to face him. "I don't regret it. Do you?"

Gently he stroked a strand of hair beside her face. "I only regret not pleasing you."

"You did please me."

"But not," now he looked embarrassed. "Not completely."

"Not completely," she had to, honestly, concur.

He kissed her, slowly and thoroughly, and tucked her close against him. Juleena didn't resist in the slightest, and though that building far-off pleasure did not return, a different heat spread through her and left her satisfied in heart, if not in body.

"Next time," he murmured to her as they parted.

Her hands tensed against him as hungry hope flared.

"I love you too much," he went on, almost a whimper. "Put the book in your window when you want me. I'll come. We'll get better at this, until I please you fully."

Ravenous victory flared in her and she clung to him. She wanted to shout it, tell everyone, and somehow mark him for all to see: he was hers. For some several more minutes they stood together, murmuring reassurances to each other, and the feeling faded to a firm, low pulse.

Finally, "good night," he whispered.

"Good night," Juleena replied. "And, thank you. I, I," but she couldn't go on.

He waited a few moments for her, until she dropped her forehead against his chest. He kissed the top of her head, and slipped from her arms, took up his cloak, and left with only one lingering backward glance.

Juleena felt she couldn't risk a trip to the house's shared bathing chamber, but there was an ewer, bowl, and cloth on the corner of her dressing table. She went to it, and tried to clean up. He might have seen some blood, but she really didn't detect much. As she finished, she found herself standing and staring into her mirror at her reflection in the near darkness. The lingering ache didn't much bother her. The hungry feeling of lacking something, some sensation, was more frustrating. Perhaps as Stratus said, they'd get better at it.

Mostly, she looked at herself and saw a different person, or someone significantly changed. As she'd told Stratus, she had no regrets, and looked forward to trying again. Nor did she feel like she'd abruptly gone from child to adult, but the mystery was gone, or at least dramatically reduced. It had been both more and less than she'd expected. More powerful because it was an experience she'd shared only with Stratus, and less physically significant than she'd imagined.

Samira seemed to be asleep in her bed, and Juleena didn't try to wake her. She just shed the robe and got in with her. They'd slept in the same bed often enough, ever since they were little girls who hadn't understood why Juleena got the huge comfy bed, and Samira the narrow hard one. Now Juleena had some understanding. She got the big comfy bed, and nice clothes, and fewer chores because she had to go marry a man she disliked and bear babies from him. Samira didn't get any of the nice things, but she could marry whomever she wanted, or not at all if she preferred.

"Julee?" the maid mumbled.

"Yeah."

Samira snuggled up close to her. "Did you do it?"

"Yeah."

"How was it?"

Juleena took a moment, unable to give an honest answer with just one word. "Wonderful, and difficult, and frustrating, and wonderful."

Samira made a grunt of acknowledgement. "I'm happy for you."

She felt the maid relax back into sleep, but Juleena couldn't be sure that happy was the right word. A crazy, painful joy fluttered in her chest, but it wasn't happiness. She thought it might be more like the feeling of getting a gasp of glorious air while something dark and deadly tried to pull her under the water, and she would hold that precious breath as long as she could.

Juleena didn't summon Stratus back the next night. She wanted to heal before another attempt. Instead she tried to distract herself by focusing on her embroidery, although it meant staring at her unwanted wedding gown for hours on end. She took a walk through the garden with Samira, though the weather was chilly, and saw Stratus at a distance as he sparred with two other guardsmen.

She didn't call him the next day, either, but she was counting days until her mother returned, and until her next monthly cycle would come. Finally, three days later she propped a book in her window.

"Do you think it's safe to bring him into my room?" she mused.

Samira winced a little. "Probably, but you can use mine again if you want. He'll still have to come in through my room, and go out again."

Juleena smiled. "Then you go ahead and sleep in my bed. We won't use yours, don't worry."

"Alright. I'll fetch him for you, like before."

"I'll ask if he knows his way now, so you don't have to next time, and can just sleep."

Night couldn't fall quickly enough. The hours to midnight crawled by at the speed of stubborn toddlers. At last, Samira went down the back stairway, and Juleena was pacing eagerly when she returned.

"Thank you, Sami," she whispered, pressing her friend's hand.

Stratus was waiting for her, and she slid into his arms without hesitation. He clasped her to him with equal nonexistent amounts of hesitation.

"How have you been?" he murmured to her.

"I'm fine. You?"

They mumbled nonsense at each other, asking about what the other had been doing, commenting on the weather, the advancing season, the absence of the Master and Mistress of the House and the possible attack at any moment of Wild Ones, but it was pretense, and they both knew it.

With only a moment of trepidation, he pulled his shirt off over his head, and looked shyly to Juleena. Very rare occasions had ever afforded her a glimpse of a man less than fully clothed, so she had little to compare him to, but she liked what she saw. Stratus had the body that came with a lot of sword swinging and shield toting. He was the type of man that would stand shoulder to shoulder with his brethren while the enemy broke like waves against their shield wall. He was still young yet, and not come into his full weight, but he was more than enough to lean fully against.

She had no hesitating in doing so, but he stopped her from rushing to the conclusion. It seemed he'd come with a plan, and Juleena let him execute it: surrendering to the sensations, and feeling already that heat begin to rise. She blushed as he drank her in with his eyes, and trembled at the sight of his tanned brown hands in such contrast against her darker skin.

For a moment an unwelcome thought asked her what she thought she was doing, giving herself to this man who wasn't her husband, a common guardsman, a muscle-bound fighter—but she squelched that inner whisper like she could a grape under her thumb. He was the one she'd chosen.

When Stratus finally encouraged her closer, her desire for him was a furious, demanding pulse. There was no pain, only pleasure, and it didn't take long. That building pressure crested and broke. He might have said something, but her ears weren't working very well and she heard it only as a rumble of satisfaction. The next moment Stratus was muffling his own cry against her sternum.

Juleena held him tightly, his ear over her heart where she was certain he'd hear it thundering, and that same voice she thought she'd squelched piped up again, whispering that now she'd never be able to let him go.

Juleena invited him again two days later, and this time he slipped like a shadow through Samira's room where the maid was sleeping, and warily into Juleena's.

"Are you sure this is safe?" he breathed to her.

"As safe as anything else we've done," she grinned back.

"I can't argue with that."

So she took him in her bed, with the curtains drawn around it, and only a candle on her headboard giving light. Juleena hadn't thought anything would ever supplant her memory of their second tryst, but here on a soft mattress, with Stratus's body pressing down on hers, she discovered a much more comfortable delight. And after, they were able to lie together and murmur their affection to each other.

She was able to call him twice more, each two days apart, but had to bring up an uncomfortable topic at that point.

"My cycle will start soon," she confessed as they lay in warm satisfaction. "And besides that, I'm expecting my mother back any day. She sleeps just down the hall, and her maid Kapri has the room beside Samira's."

"It will be too risky for me to come to you?" Stratus concluded.

"And even if you did, messy," she muttered.

"That doesn't concern me, but it makes things painful for

you?"

"I only have cramps the first day, usually, but I thought you might think it disgusting."

"It is something your body naturally does." He shrugged a shoulder from where he lay on his side, fingers wandering down her arm. "It doesn't bother me. Your mother and her servant, however, I can see could cause problems."

"They don't normally look in on me at night anymore," Juleena said, "not since I was much younger, but if they hear anything they might."

"So you might not be able to call me for a while?" he subsided.

She knew her face must be mirroring the distress she saw in his. "I don't want you to get in trouble."

"I appreciate your concern," he sighed. "To tell you true, I am amazed we haven't been caught yet." Stratus lifted her hand and kissed her fingertips. "We are living in stolen moments."

Her heart twisted painfully. "Indeed. I am alive when I'm with you, and I shall die when I must leave you."

His eyes closed and he clasped her hand. "Juleena. Saying so only makes it worse."

She needed to be against him, and squirmed closer until he'd taken her in his arms.

"You are sure you will have your cycle?" he muttered a minute later.

"Yes," she declared, although she couldn't be sure until it happened. "I took care of it."

His hands, though rough with sword callous, were ever gentle against her skin, and stroked down her back.

"I wish I could have a child with you," he whispered. "I wish we could live together and raise a family."

"I know," she whimpered around the sudden lump in her throat, and said back to him his own words. "Saying so only makes it worse."

"I'm sorry," he apologized.

"Me, too."

They lay there, and it was some time later that Juleena's eyes snapped open. The candle was burned down. She realized they'd fallen asleep, and twitched the curtain enough to get a glimpse towards her window. She shook Stratus's shoulder.

"It's pre-dawn," she said. "You need to go."

He rose with a resigned grunt and began fetching his clothes. She watched him from the comfort of her bed, pulling blankets around her as the chill of night came in through the open curtain.

"I'll signal again in a couple days if my mother doesn't return," she promised.

He smiled sleepily and bent over to kiss her. "I shall think of you with every breath until I see you again."

"And I you."

He turned to go, but she held his hand and resisted until he paused to look back.

"I haven't told you," she whispered, "though you told me our first time together."

His brows pinched with confusion. Juleena swallowed and licked her lips nervously, as her heart began pounding again.

"I love you, too," she breathed.

His expression transformed to something of equal measures of pain and joy, and he held her hand with both of his, and dropped to one knee before her.

"I know," he replied. "Sometimes I have wished you were just indulging a fancy with me, as nobility sometimes do, and that only I bore this burden, but I can see it in your eyes, and feel it in your touch, and hear it in your voice."

Stratus stretched in again to kiss her lightly.

"I can even taste it on your lips," he murmured.

Then his hands went to her face, and the joy in his expression was overcome by the pain. Tears streaked down his cheeks, prompting Juleena to the verge of crying, too.

"I'm so sorry," he rasped.

"Never apologize," she countered. "You are the greatest part of my life. You have given me more than I ever thought I could have, or existed to be had. I will treasure our time, and love you forever."

He rested his forehead against hers, shoulders shaking. She petted his hair and soothed the back of his neck.

"Now dry your eyes and go," she urged, "before the sun rises. I will call you again as soon as I think it's safe."

He kissed her again, a bit rougher and more possessive than usual.

"I love you, Juleena," he breathed.

Then he got up and was gone. She heard the door to Samira's room open all but silently, and close again. Juleena flung herself back down on her bed and hugged a pillow, buried her face in it, and cried.

Mirassi returned that day.

"Oh, don't look so upset to see me, child," the Mistress scolded at dinner. "I'm sure you've had a grand time without me watching you. Back to gallivanting through the forest again, were you?"

"Juleena has been very well behaved, Mother," Ledren reported.

"Oh, really?" Mirassi sniffed. "How goes your progress on your gown?"

"Two panels are done," Juleena answered truthfully.

Mirassi nodded reluctantly. "Good progress for a week."

Juleena nodded. "Thank you. I'll be happy to show it to you later."

"I'll be happy to see it. Knowing your work, it is sure to be exquisite. "

"And what of the meeting, Mistress?" Camin asked diffidently. "Have there been other attacks?"

"Incursions," Mirassi growled. "Several throughout the west were reported. Rodreric took the news on to Kedikan. I think it likely there will be a military response, but no army likes to move in winter. We will no doubt be on our own until spring."

"Things have been quiet here," Ledren reported, "as I told you earlier. The guardsmen are keeping excellent watch."

"We shall have to hope for peace through the winter," Mirassi intoned.

"The harvest was good," Cindra contributed. "The people won't starve this year."

"That is something at least."

Juleena obediently showed her mother the gown, and Mirassi complimented her work.

"You will make a beautiful bride in this," she said softly.

"Yes, Mother."

"Juleena," Mirassi said, after a moment. "I understand you are not pleased with my selection of husband for you."

She didn't say anything, just continued methodically folding the gown along the seams, to avoid wrinkles until she came back to work on it again.

"This is difficult for everyone. I was not fond of your father when he came to live here, chosen by my parents, but in time we developed a mutual respect and even affection."

Juleena tried not to frown too deeply, and kept holding her tongue. She doubted Terkari Salasis would ever have respect for her—for her wishes, wants, or even needs.

"You must make the best of it," Mirassi went on. "Treasure the positives, whatever they may be, and try not to focus on the aspects you wish were different."

"Yes, Mother," Juleena said automatically.

Mirassi sighed. "Dear child, whatever can I do to get through to you? To help you learn to accept what is best for both Houses, Mrandis and Salasis?"

She held in a sigh. "I'll do what I must, Mother. Do not be concerned about that."

Mirassi patted her shoulder. "I know you will. You have always been obedient, if a bit rowdier than is normal for a girl child, but there is more to serving your House than obedience."

Juleena's gaze darted over to her mother's.

"You will be Mistress of Salasis," she said, "and that requires leadership, initiative, and engagement. You cannot stand passive and just do as you're told."

"And what are you asking of me right now, Mother?" Juleena enquired.

Mirassi flipped out her hands with frustration. "You must embrace this change, Juleena. It is more than making a perfect wedding gown. You should be studying the history of Salasis, their economy, environment, and lineage. There's no escaping this marriage, you know. You can rise to the occasion or go meekly with a whimper. What is it about it that makes you reluctant: that makes you afraid? You must face those aspects in order to enter it with intent and energy. Tell me, my child."

Juleena raised an eyebrow, but didn't speak at once. She couldn't say that she was worried about her husband mistreating her. She couldn't reveal her information source, and after all, she had no actual evidence of it—even though she trusted Stratus's word completely.

Mirassi came and clasped her hands with an impression of compassion. "Is it the wedding night? Are you nervous about being with a man for the first time?"

Juleena almost laughed in her face, but managed to get her expression under control. Mirassi went on blithely.

"I was nervous, of course, but Rodreric did not insist on taking me to bed until—"

"Mother," Juleena spluttered. "I don't need to hear this."

Mirassi seemed to regroup. "I'm sure you've heard rumors that the first time hurts, but that's not necessarily true. It's just startling."

"Mother," Juleena repeated firmly. "I'm not worried about that."

"Are you worried about pregnancy, and childbirth?" Mirassi tried then.

Now Juleena heaved a sigh. "I'm sure that will all be fine. I look forward to having babies of my own."

"You'll have the best midwives. The Houses always do well by their women. Of course there's always the chance of complications, but that is a danger all women must face with courage."

"Yes, I have no doubt that House Salasis will take care of my health to the best of their ability," Juleena affirmed.

Mirassi scrutinized her face for a few moments. "Then what is it? You've always been a bold girl. Why the reluctance now?"

"I don't want to go," she said simply, and that was nothing but the truth. Going meant leaving Stratus, as well as her home.

Mirassi put a hand on her cheek, still examining her face. "You seem different."

Juleena had a surge of fear. Could her mother tell just by looking at her that she'd been bedding a man—and not her husband? Did Mirassi have some extra sense, since she was so mature and experienced, that informed her of such things?

"Well," her mother subsided, "this situation is bound to have its effects. I hope you won't lose sleep over it, truly."

"No, Mother."

Indeed, what was making Juleena lose sleep had nothing to do with Salasis.

The blood of her cycle began the next day, and though she'd had faith in Samira's calendar, she'd still held a quiet anxiety that despite that, she might still kindle. She took to her bed with relief as she endured the first-day cramps, and also with a sense of eagerness. If the calendar worked, she could safely continue meeting Stratus as long as she did it on the white days. Samira brought her a hot water bottle and tea to ease the pain, with a conspiratorial smile. Juleena returned it.

Despite whatever Stratus had said about not finding a woman's monthly bleeding disgusting, it still unsettled Juleena to think of lying with him while it was going on, so she let the whole of her cycle pass without summoning him. She was also concerned about Mirassi and Kapri being so close to her room, and even after the bleeding stopped, was hesitant to put the book in her window.

So days passed without her seeing him, and the calendar days got darker, into the time when she knew she shouldn't see him. The first dusting of snow coated the estate in white, and then melted off in a couple days as the weather warmed again. She began to miss Stratus terribly, not just the bedding, but him, the man: his voice, his looks, his laugh.

"Oh, quit moping around," Mum Hyldi scolded as she caught Juleena again looking out the windows at breakfast — in the direction of the distant barracks.

"You have been rather despondent, Sister," Ledren agreed. "Why don't you go for a ride? The weather is fine today, for late autumn, if you bundle up a little."

"I thought I wasn't to go out," Juleena retorted, a bit too sharply.

"Tone, Juleena," her mother reminded. "A ride would be good for your spirits, I admit."

"What about the danger of Wild Ones?" she counted, more civilly.

"I wouldn't see it as a problem, as long as you stay near the city. Ride around the city walls for a few circuits."

There was a well-worn path around the city, just outside the walls, which was in sight of the wall sentries should anything menace her. It was nothing compared to a ride through the countryside, but it was at least outside of the estate. Juleena felt excitement building. Would they really send her out?

"Must I take an escort?" she asked, putting some disdain into her voice.

"Well," Mirassi muttered. "On horseback isn't quite so dangerous as on foot, and if you stay on the path, no; I will permit you to go alone."

Juleena tried to hide her disappointment. Now she would have no excuse to have Stratus go with her.

Mirassi nodded. "Wear a riding skirt, not trousers, since you won't be hunting. You're to be a married woman and have an image to preserve. Hyldi, send a boy to the stables and have Ivy tacked for Juleena, and then send him on to the gate to tell the guards to let Juleena out by herself, and to watch over her."

Juleena forced herself to nod as if gracious. "Thank you,

Mother. I daresay the fresh air will improve my spirits."

It was just as well, she supposed. She wasn't into the white days of the calendar yet, and riding within sight of the walls would have given her and Stratus no privacy for intimacy anyway—but she could have seen him and talked with him.

As soon as breakfast was done she went to change into warmer clothes for riding, choosing a split-skirted gown as instructed, instead of her preferred riding trousers. When she arrived at the stables, she saw some activity, more than was warranted for tacking up one mare.

"Your pardon, Lady Mrandis," the horsemaster, a tough and sturdy man in his middle years, said. "We're taking the opportunity to exercise all the horses that haven't been done yet, and got the note to ready Ivy for you right in the midst of it."

Teenage boys, and even a couple girls, were holding the House's six horses while others were strapping on saddles and bridles, filling up the center aisle of the stable and the yard in front of it.

"At least the Guard have most of their horses out," the man went on. "If you'll wait but another minute, we'll have Ivy ready for you."

Juleena stood aside. The late autumn sun was weak, but did heat the exposed skin of her face a little, and kept her from shivering. In a few minutes, one of the grooms led Ivy forward.

"The horsemaster says she was worked hard yesterday, so not to worry about giving her a good run," he said shyly.

"Thank you, young sir," Juleena replied, although the groom was probably about her age, if not older.

"May I assist you in mounting, my lady?"

She accepted, setting her foot into his interlaced hands, and he boosted her up. Juleena moved Ivy off at a walk. She wouldn't ask the mare to pick up her pace until they were outside the walls of Lenali. The guards at the gate to the Mrandis estate let her through without challenge, and then she was riding down the main road through the city, hooves clopping on the stone pavement.

Although she hadn't agreed with her mother at the time, getting out of the house and into the fresh air—and by herself—did improve her spirits. Already she felt a lightening, a sense of freedom. People were out doing deliveries and shopping, and some of them smiled or bowed to her, and she waved back pleasantly. She took a deep breath, let it go, and felt stress melt off her, sliding down to pitter-patter on the stone below Ivy's feet.

At the main gate of the city she assured the guards on duty that she would just be making a circuit of the walls, staying within view of the watching guardsmen, and they let her go with nods and little move-along gestures. Beyond the gates, the road to Trivale stretched away, dipping down out of view until it reappeared in the distance where it met the town. Little streamers of wood smoke rose over the distant houses, but Juleena wouldn't be travelling there today.

Instead, she turned Ivy to follow the path that circled Lenali. It was well worn and frequently used by both the guard and anyone with enough luxury to be able to exercise themselves or a horse for no good reason other than the sake of exercise. Trees were not allowed to grow close to the walls, so instead clumps of heather and dense bracken coated both sides of the path. It wove up and down a little, as Lenali was not built on perfectly flat ground, but only on a mostly flat section of mountainside. Ivy knew the path well enough, and Juleena hardly needed to direct her. They made their first circuit in peace.

As she started her second, Juleena's sense of freedom grew. Although she was generally left to her own devices at home since she'd finished her schooling, and left alone unless she sought company, she'd still been stuck inside. Here, the guards from the frequent watch posts tracked her movements, true, but she need answer to none of them, and none of them tried to talk to her. It was the next best thing to being alone and liberated. For a moment she wondered if, a year from now, she would be able to feel such a thing. By then she'd probably be pregnant with her first child from Terkari, and bound to the house.

The dark thoughts soured her sense of freedom and Juleena

berated herself against such nonsense. She urged Ivy into a bit of a trot over a flat section of path, and let the breeze of it blow away her momentary gloom, but didn't really want to hurry her return to the estate, so she let the mare move back into a walk after only a few minutes. Then she heard hoof beats ahead, and as soon as an opportunity presented itself, she pulled Ivy to a wide spot beside the path and waited. Within moments three men came riding along the path towards her.

Her breath caught when she recognized Stratus's roan among the horses, and him in the saddle.

"Your pardon, Lady Mrandis," the man in the lead, the guard Captain at the estate, called out. "We're just taking a few laps around the city."

"Thank you all for your service," Juleena replied clearly. "I will ride on confident in the safety of the path."

All three guards reined their horses down to a walk, and passed her with polite nods. Stratus was riding at the back, and his gaze fixed on her. He smiled, and she returned it. As the other two guardsmen weren't looking back, she extended her hand, and he mimicked it, and their gloved fingers brushed lightly. He gave her a little wave as he moved off, and she copied him, face blushing with more than just the chill in the air.

It wasn't much, but at least she'd gotten to see him.

At that point, she was much closer to the main gate back into the city than the guards were, so she reached it without encountering them again, and made her way back inside the walls. Without any other business, she rode Ivy right back to the estate, but found the stable deserted when she arrived.

"Makes sense," she told Ivy cheerfully. "They took out all the other horses for exercise. They're probably expecting another snow storm, and then what will they do?"

She dismounted and led Ivy back to her stall. Someone had cleaned it out recently and put down fresh straw. Juleena knew enough to get Ivy's tack off and lay it over a rail at the back of the aisle. It hadn't gotten dirty on her little ride, but the stable boys would probably still clean it.

Then she took a brush from the basket hung on the front of Ivy's stall and began brushing the mare down. Of course she didn't normally have to groom her own horses, but she knew a little how it went, and found herself extremely reluctant to go back in the house. It would get horsehair on her clothes, but Juleena accepted that as a price she was willing to pay for a few more minutes of solitude. A servant would be the one cleaning her clothes, maybe even Samira, and Julee hoped whoever it was wouldn't mind too much.

Ivy hadn't gotten sweaty on the brief ride. Her coat didn't especially need brushing, and the stable boys might do it again anyway, but Ivy liked being brushed, and leaned into every stroke, even the inexpert ones. Juleena rewarded her with pats and gentle words, and let her focus narrow to the hiss of her brush and Ivy's rumbling breaths of pleasure.

So she startled a little when she heard another horse ride up. Ivy's stall was at the end of the aisle, and it sounded like the rider of this new-come horse dismounted near the entrance. She heard footsteps, and wondered if a groom or stable boy was anywhere nearby. She didn't want to greet a guest—it ordinarily wouldn't be proper for a Lady of a House to be in a horse stall.

Then Stratus peeked into the stall through the window where Ivy would normally stick her head out.

"You're here," he said with obvious delight.

Juleena stared, happy to see him but slightly alarmed. There appeared to be no one else in the stable at the moment, but that could change rapidly. The walls of the stalls were high—floor to ceiling between the stalls—but anyone could still walk over and look in just as Stratus had done.

Ivy nickered at him, and he put out a hand for her to sniff. Then he slid the door open and stepped in, closing it behind him. Ivy nosed his chest, and he reached up to scratch vigorously along her crest. That apparently convinced her he could be in her stall as long as he wanted, and she began nosing in her nearly empty feed bucket with great indifference to him.

The brush fell from Juleena's suddenly nerveless hand as

Stratus stepped close.

"I haven't seen you for days," he whispered.

He leaned in and Juleena couldn't help but give in to kissing him.

"I'm all over horse," she pointed out when they paused.

"Me, too." He quirked a grin at her.

"Is your horse alright?"

"Jypsim can wait. He's used to standing. I told my Captain I thought he was favoring a foot and got sent back early, but there's nothing wrong with him."

"You lied?" she accused gently.

"I wanted to see you. I missed you. It didn't hurt anything."

Juleena didn't resist as he wrapped her in his arms.

"It's been so long," he went on, voice muffled into her hair.

"I had my cycle," she explained.

"Good," he said with a sigh of relief, "I suppose."

"And my mother is back."

"Of course. I understand."

But he was pushing her, ever so gently, back until she was against the dividing wall to the next stall. Ivy apparently thought that was too close to her rump, and moved to stand sideways between them and the door.

"Anyone could come in," Juleena protested as he pressed against her.

"Not yet," he murmured. "Everyone's away."

"But—"

"Please?"

"We shouldn't."

"Please, Julee?"

"But—"

She knew what he wanted. She wanted it, too—desperately—but she knew better. They could get caught. Plus, it was not a good calendar day: not the darkest, but still dark, and Samira had said they were only estimates anyway.

Still, his hands were gathering up her skirts—and she was helping him, even as she knew she shouldn't, for so many reasons. And then, with only a little fumbling, it was decided, and she put her head back against the wall and gave herself up.

She knew they couldn't hide in Ivy's stall for long, but she didn't want to leave, and yet at the same time fear was moving in as pleasure faded. Stratus was watching her face and seemed to notice something was wrong.

"I shouldn't have forced you," he murmured.

"You didn't force me, Stratus, not at all," she whispered back.

"This was improper, pushing you up against a horse stall, as though you were some light-skirted serving wench," he went on. "You're a lady."

She kissed him lightly. "I'm your lady," she breathed. "And I liked getting pushed up against a horse stall. I'm sorry I haven't called you sooner. I can, in a few days, but we have to be silent, so no one hears. We just have to be careful."

"I know," he sighed. "I let my desires get the better of me."

"It's alright," Juleena assured him, though she wasn't at all sure it was, "but I should go."

Stratus kissed her once more, and then they both slipped out of the stall, Juleena being sure to take the dropped brush and put it away. He went directly to his horse, to begin untacking it, and she marched herself back to the house.

"I smell like a horse," she said as the servants greeted her. "I'll be in the bath."

That triggered one to scamper ahead to stoke up the boiler and begin filling a tub for her. Another went to get her clean clothes. Fear ate at her belly, and she ordered all the servants out of the bathing chamber as soon as she got there. Samira came hurrying in as the others were bowing out.

"Julee?" the maid said with concern, no doubt noticing how Juleena was rapidly stripping out of her clothes.

"Stratus caught me in the stables," she muttered.

Samira's hands flew to her mouth. "Did he—he didn't force you?"

"No, no, no," Juleena denied emphatically.

"But, did you?"

"Yes."

Samira shook her head. "It's not a good time, Julee."

"I know. Help me with this."

She did. "Then why did you—?"

"I wanted to," Juleena pled. "So help me, I wanted to, and so did he, so we did, and it was great, but now—"

"You want to try to clean up," Samira mumbled.

"It was standing," Juleena whispered with a furious blush. "Everything ran out. It'll be fine."

She stepped into the waiting tub and Samira went to the taps to adjust the temperature if Juleena needed it, kneeling down on a cushion outside the tub, head level with her lady's. Juleena sank down to her chin and did what she could.

"I'm sure it will be fine," the maid mumbled, although to Juleena it sounded like she didn't believe her words. "It was just once, and like you say, it was standing. I'm sure it won't happen."

"I should have told him it was a bad time, or tried to explain the calendar thing," she regretted. "I tried to tell him we could get caught. Anyone could have looked in and seen us. He didn't think we'd get caught—and we didn't—but I thought maybe he would think I was giving excuses to avoid it if I kept—" she sighed. "I'm making excuses now, aren't I?"

"Let's wash your hair," Samira soothed, and moved to take down her braids.

"Sami," Juleena quavered. "What if it happens?"

"It won't," the maid asserted. "I'm sure it won't."

Juleena nodded, and let Samira get to work on her long mass of black hair, but she knew that until she got her next cycle—about two weeks from now—she would be wondering and waiting.

Though she knew it was risky, she summoned Stratus to her room three nights later, once her calendar days were white again. They were silent, and Juleena detected no hint that any-one had noticed anything amiss the next day. Still, she waited another three days, in case it took time for a servant to report to her mother, but Mirassi still gave no sign that she'd detected Juleena's nighttime visitor.

So Juleena summoned Stratus again, and again two nights later, and again, and again, up until the coming day that she knew she'd be getting her next cycle. The symptoms she usually had leading up to it were all there, so she began to relax and laugh at her nervousness. Of course just one time, standing up at that, wouldn't be enough.

The day she expected the bleeding to start came—but the blood did not. No need to worry, she thought. Sometimes it was a day or even two late: not commonly, but it did happen. The next day the blood did not come, nor the next day, but her symptoms of its imminent arrival did not go away.

"Juleena," Samira said softly as her lady sat, embroidery for-gotten in her lap, staring out at falling snow.

Juleena made no response.

"Julee," the maid tried again. "You haven't started your cycle?"

"It's a little late sometimes. That's all," she muttered back. "I'm sure it will come tomorrow."

Samira knelt beside her chair. "If it doesn't, you had better pretend it has. Your mother at least will notice if you don't do as usual and seek your bed until the cramps can be stopped. Mum Hyldi will notice, when I don't fetch the tea for you."

"Sami," Juleena smiled. "It's fine. Sometimes it's just a bit late. You know that."

"It's usually never four days late, is it?"

"When I was twelve it was once two weeks late."

"Yes, but you'd just started getting them. Mine were irregu-lar at first, too, but they shouldn't be so irregular now. Please, Julee, pretend. I'll help you."

Juleena took a breath too quickly. "You think I'm, that it's— no, it can't be."

Samira put a gentle hand over hers. "It could be, Julee."

"No, the bleeding will start tomorrow."

"Whether it does or not, pretend. Promise me you'll pretend, Julee."

"Fine, alright," she capitulated, "but I won't have to pretend. I feel like I always do before it starts: tender breasts, a little bloated, a little headache, tired. Everything is normal."

"Alright. Then there's nothing to worry about," Samira smiled. "How's your embroidery?"

"Fine," Juleena grunted, but her eyes never left the grey, snowy sky.

Samira waited a few moments, but her lady said nothing more, so she stood up. "Call me if you need aught."

The maid turned to go, when Juleena grabbed her hand, and Samira turned back.

"Sami," Juleena breathed, barely audible. "What if I am?"

She knelt back down. "If you are," she whispered, "we'll figure something out."

"What?"

"There's ways you could lose it—"

"No," Juleena declared, free hand going to her belly.

Finally, she turned her head to meet Samira's concerned gaze.

"Then something else will work out," the maid whispered. "Don't worry, Julee. I'll take care of you. I'll help you."

"I am so unworthy of you," Juleena breathed.

Samira threw her arms around her neck. "No, Julee. Don't say that."

And Juleena crumpled into sobs.

Her cycle didn't come the next day, but true to her promise, she pretended it had. She lay in bed with the hot water bottle under the covers, though she didn't curl around it like she usually did. When Samira brought her the tea, she let it cool and had the maid pour it out the window while no one was in view outside. That wasn't difficult; since the snow had apparently come down with the intention to stay, almost everyone was indoors, and more snow was falling, to cover up the spot where the tea hit.

Juleena lay in a stupor. She still had the symptoms as though about to start her cycle, but they weren't going away, and each day they got a little more intense. She couldn't think about what might be happening inside her. Part of her was laughing and turning cartwheels in thick summer grass, surrounded by butterflies, while another part sat in a dark corner and rocked, hands over ears, eyes shut, refusing to talk.

Samira didn't bring it up, and Juleena was grateful; she didn't know what she could say. The rest of the week when she should have been bleeding passed. Then one morning the scent of breakfast turned her stomach. She managed not to throw up, to act normally, but she knew from watching Cindra's pregnancy that the nausea was a sure sign, unless she'd gotten a stomach sickness—and combined with all her other symptoms and lack of cycle, she had to face the likely truth.

She and Stratus had started a baby.

She didn't mention it when she called him to her room the next time, but he had a different concern to voice.

"Tracks in the snow," he said. "There were no other tracks between the barracks and the back servant's door. I had to take a longer route to avoid leaving a trail."

"Alright," she replied. "Then I'll only call you if there's already a trail, or if the weather changes so you won't leave one."

It meant they saw less of each other through the winter. Juleena was somewhat grateful, for her cycle had never come, the nausea had continued—though she rarely vomited as long as she didn't eat anything that incited the nausea—and she was noting little changes in her body. Stratus hadn't commented, but they made love in near darkness and almost total silence, so she assumed he hadn't noticed.

She knew that eventually he would. Everyone would notice. Eventually, she wouldn't be able to hide it. So far, her belly hadn't started to swell, and the heavier winter clothes she wore concealed any slight changes to her figure. She faked the days when her cycles would have been due to start, and Samira continued to cover for her. She worked on her embroidery and tried not to think about it. By midwinter she'd finished the outer gown and started on the inner—but even as her fingers worked, her mind kept pointing out that there was no point. She was going to have a baby by a man other than her intended husband. She would never wear the gown.

Juleena didn't know what would happen, but she was certain now that there would be no wedding to Terkari. A huge part of her sighed in relief, but the other part that was still hiding in a dark corner shook its head, put its fingers in its ears and started humming. Juleena couldn't think of what would happen instead.

Her father Rodreric returned near midwinter, carrying the news that a force was being put together to scour the forests and eradicate any Wild Ones as soon as the snow melted. Juleena paid little attention; her mind was elsewhere. As spring began to shake winter's hold, Juleena began to notice more obvious changes to her body. The nausea went away, but her belly had started to change from her usual slim abdomen to a slight bump—just slight, but enough make her fear redouble. Soon. Soon she wouldn't be able to hide it any longer, especially as the weather warmed and clothing became thinner, lighter.

She also found herself feeling more tired, even dizzy, along with other symptoms she hadn't expected—like fits of hiccupping. Samira helped all she could: making up stories, deflecting interest, and picking clothing for her that would conceal her shape. Mirassi brought up the wedding every time she saw Juleena, and asked after the gown. Juleena had dutifully continued with the embroidery, and assured her mother it would be done in time. Luckily, Mirassi never asked her daughter to model it.

There were other preparations besides the dress, and Juleena was surprised when she was sent out on an errand to take care of one of them.

"You know that since you are leaving House Mrandis," her father lectured, "House Salasis is providing considerable compensation for you, but I hope you also recall that new-come spouses bring a wedding gift to their intended."

"In your case," Mirassi picked up, "it will be many of the harpy feathers we were awarded at the incident at Tuma." She glanced at her husband with a bit of a bitter taste on her lips. "In our discussions we have decided that they should be properly presented, not just bundled together with cord."

"Commission a case for them," Rodreric ordered, extending a roll of parchment towards her. "Here are the required measurements." He returned Mirassi's look with a displeased expression of his own. "It is short notice, but the case will need to be done by the wedding."

"Take it to the cabinetmaker in Trivale. His family holds a long line of skilled craftsmen. Have him make it of black maple, with rests inside for each of the feathers, as in the drawing."

Rodreric picked up the mandate again. "Be certain he understands the design, and select the finest wood."

"Yes, Father, Mother," Juleena bowed, throttling her excitement as hard as she possibly could.

"Take an escort," Mirassi concluded with a dismissive wave of her hand, "and try to stay out of the mud, unless you'd prefer a carriage."

"The walk will do her good," Rodreric grumbled.

"Yes, I know," Mirassi spat back.

"Yes, Mother, Father," Juleena bowed again and, taking the roll of parchment, left the room with as much decorum and speed as she could manage—before either of her parents changed their minds.

Juleena presented herself at the Mrandis Guardhouse in her best walking boots and warm clothes that would protect her from the lingering chill of winter. It took the guard on duty a few minutes to call Stratus, and Juleena stood, almost shivering, as she watched clouds roll across the sky, blotting out the sun.

"Lady Mrandis."

She turned, concealing most of her smile. A thought declared itself, as it often did when she saw him now: *the father of my child.* She should tell him. She knew she should. It was how he'd react that she didn't know, and it scared her to think of finding out.

"I have an errand," she announced, showing the parchment roll for evidence. "Escort me please, sir."

"Of course, my lady."

He bowed and they moved off through the gates. Rain had washed most of the snow away, but a few dirty piles still lingered along the sides of the main road through Lenali. The walk was easy, though, on the stone road. When they reached the Lenali gates, the road turned to packed dirt: now mud. Patches of snow still clung to the ground: especially on the north side of any ridges.

"Let us walk on the verge," Stratus suggested.

Juleena led the way, until she slipped on a muddy patch and he steadied her.

"Would you take my arm?" he asked.

"I suppose it's only logical," Juleena agreed, but a hint of a pleased smile touched her lips.

The ground was indeed soggy and they ended up supporting each other more than just him supporting her.

"Where are we going today?" he enquired eventually.

Now she let her smile bloom. "Ah, yes. We're going to your family house."

Stratus gaped at her, jaw actually hanging for a moment before he recovered it. "You're not serious."

"I have an order for a cabinet," she said triumphantly. "Your father and brothers are to make it, on the orders of my mother and father."

He'd managed to shut his mouth, but his jaw muscles clenched. "I'm not sure it's a good idea for us to go there."

"But I want to meet your family," she pointed out, "and this is a perfect chance, with a legitimate reason."

"You know your mother and father would not approve of our secret. What makes you think that my family would?"

Juleena blinked. "I hadn't thought of it that way," she admitted, some of her excitement fading.

"We'll have to pretend, if we go there." Stratus turned his head away. "I'll have to lie to them."

"You're already keeping this from them, aren't you?" Juleena murmured.

He turned back to her frowning. "You're right. I am."

They walked in silence for a few minutes as the walls of Trivale came into view.

"I've never lied to them before," Stratus sighed finally.

The gate guards waved them through and one pointed meaningfully at the sky. Both Juleena and Stratus looked up, noticing what had the guard's concern. The clouds that had rolled in grey had darkened near to black.

"It looks like a spring storm," Stratus said. "Let's hurry. For better or worse, we're going to my father's house now."

They went as quickly as they cloud, but the quagmire that was the streets of little Trivale did not make for easy going. Juleena nearly lost a boot twice, and had to pull strongly on Stratus's arm to keep from slipping and falling a half a dozen times. All the effort was making her chase her breath and leaving her face sweaty, but she'd rather struggle through with Stratus than have asked for a carriage.

"There," he said at last, pointing down to the end of the street. "That's the house."

It was larger than Juleena had imagined — having never seen it before — and a good step above the classification of hovel, or hut, or shack. It was a proper house of a surprising three stories, though the third looked to just be a large attic at the peak. As might be expected of a woodworker's house, it was tightly paneled with all the corners sharply square and in excellent repair. To one side was an extension only one story high, that Juleena guessed might be the workshop where the cabinets were made.

She had just a few breaths to realize this before the clouds opened and dumped a river's worth of water on her. Stratus scooped her up in his arms and ran—as best as he was able through the gummy mud and pounding rain—up to the front walk. It was paved with stones, so he made better progress there, and then set Juleena back on her feet in front of the door. There, it was under the overhang of the roof, and out of the rain at least. He turned the latch and pulled the door open.

"Da, Ma, it's me," he called.

Stratus urged Juleena in through the door, into a little room with hooks for coats and cloaks, and racks of shoes and boots. It was stone floored, and a step up from it through another door-way Juleena could see a large dining room and kitchen with a hefty wooden table that could seat a dozen easily. Two women, one old enough to probably be Stratus's mother, and a younger one Juleena guessed was one of his sisters-in-law, came hurry-ing around the table where they'd been peeling vegetables.

"Stratus," the older woman exclaimed, and then jerked up short. "And who is this?"

Juleena tried to stand up straight and smile, but her clothes were soaked most of the way through, and her hair was plas-tered to her head; she knew she hardly looked the part.

"I've come with an order for Mister Hearthsraven," she said, even as her jaw started shivering.

She pulled the roll of parchment from her pocket. It was damp, but not completely soggy. The older woman accepted it when Juleena held it out, and then passed it to the younger woman.

"Ona, open that and set it by the stove to dry, will you? I only hope it hasn't been ruined," she instructed.

The younger woman, Ona—Juleena recalled that was the second son's wife—complied, with only one curious glance back at Juleena. Stratus squared his shoulders.

"Mother, may I present Lady Mrandis," he said formally. "As you know, I was detailed to be her escort, and her business brought her here today. Unfortunately, the rain intercepted us."

"Of course, of course," Stratus's mother nodded, and then she bowed, a little awkwardly. "My lady, if I may say so, you're drenched, and cannot remain in those wet clothes. Please come with me and accept a substitute until yours can be dried, and then we'll discuss the purpose of your visit."

"Thank you," Juleena smiled sheepishly.

Stratus knelt without being asked, and helped her out of her boots, which were liberally coated with mud.

"I'll clean these before your departure, my lady," he said.

Footsteps announced another arrival, and Juleena looked up to see who could only be Stratus's father. She could detect Stratus in his nose and chin, and in the kindness in his eyes. His hair had gone grey and stood out from his head: light and fluffy. He went clean-shaven and walked with only the slightest hunch, probably from many years bending over a worktable. Stratus's mother immediately explained the situation as Juleena stepped up onto the dining room floor in her stocking feet.

"Lady Mrandis," the man said with a bow. "I welcome you to my modest home. Please, I'll not delay you as you refresh yourself. Let us speak again when you are ready."

"Thank you, good sir," Juleena nodded, still feeling embarrassed about her entrance.

She let Stratus's mother lead her away, back past the kitchen and its large central stove, to a short hallway and one of the doors that led off it.

"I do beg your forgiveness," Missus Hearthsraven said. "I have nothing suitable for a noblewoman to wear. I apologize, but you can't stay in those wet clothes. Let me at least find something clean and dry."

Juleena began shedding what clothes she could, but Missus Hearthsraven had to come help her with the lacing on the back of her dress. Her shift at least had not gotten wet except for a bit around the neck and bottom. Missus Hearthsraven provided clean wool stockings and then dug in her closet for a minute. She was an upright woman, only a bit shorter than her husband, with a little extra roundness that might have come from age and bearing children. She also had an air of great tidiness about her. Her home was scoured clean, her own clothing crisp—though there were some sooty marks on her apron, which was what an apron was for—with her long grey hair bundled up under a scarf, and her closet was well ordered and organized. She ventured deeply into it, however, and returned from it with a pale yellow gown embroidered with green leaves and blue flowers.

"It doesn't suit you at all, I'm afraid, but it might fit well enough," Missus Hearthsraven said. "I was leaner when I was younger."

Another quick glance at the closet revealed that most everything else hanging in it—which amounted to only a dozen or so items—was in natural, undyed fabrics, like what the lady of the house was currently wearing. Juleena realized that Missus Hearthsraven must have just pulled out her wedding dress.

"Please let me help you with this, my lady," she asked.

Juleena complied, too uncertain to know what to say, and so off balance by it that she didn't even think about what her snug silk shift might be revealing about her body: such as the little bump of her belly, incongruous with her otherwise slim limbs. When the dress was on, Missus Hearthsraven tied the laces gently, and put a knitted shawl around her shoulders.

"Let me get a towel for your hair, my lady," she said, ducking out for a moment.

Juleena sat on the chest at the end of the bed. It—like everything wooden in the house—was beautifully crafted. These people certainly weren't rich when compared to nobility, but by the skill of the men and the care-taking of the women, they lived in a clean and lovely home. Her hostess returned with a towel.

"Should we take down the braids, my lady?" she asked.

"Perhaps if I just wrap it around?" Juleena suggested.

"Of course."

They bundled up her wet hair with the towel.

"Now come sit by the stove and warm up," Missus Hearthsraven invited. "I'll hang your clothing so it dries."

Juleena was guided to the seat at the table nearest the big

stove, which seemed to be used both for cooking and heating. As she sat, the heat warmed her back, and she shuddered with relief. Ona put a mug of tea before her.

"It's peppermint, my lady," the woman said with a little smile. Ona had a sweet face, ruddy brown hair, and dark umber eyes that glinted with good nature.

"Thank you," Juleena replied, also offering a smile.

She wrapped her hands around the mug and felt the warmth seep into her cold fingers. Stratus was nowhere to be seen, but his father and mother both sat down at the table, each with a mug of tea, too. Ona seemed to have cleared away the vegetables.

"So," the master of the house began, "I hear the Lady Mrandis brings me a business proposition."

"Oh, yes," Juleena stuttered. She glanced around for the parchment she'd brought.

"Here," Ona provided. "It's mostly dry now."

"Please," Juleena gestured towards Mister Hearthsraven, and Ona gave it to her father-in-law, who spread it against the table.

He examined it silently for a few minutes, while Juleena sipped her tea, and Missus Hearthsraven stared into her own mug as if in deep contemplation. The heat from the stove and tea was quickly melting away the rain's chill, and Juleena found herself sinking more fully into her seat than she normally would. She had to fight her fatigue to look attentive and poised.

"I'd heard about the harpy fight, of course," the master craftsman said at last. "So you're wanting a case to display the feathers?"

"Yes," Juleena answered, and then found her mug as fascinating as Missus Hearthsraven did. "They're to be my wedding gift to my husband," she all but mumbled.

"I am flattered you bring this commission to me, my lady," he said without missing a beat. "I can certainly create what you need."

"Thank you, sir," Juleena bowed her head, and had to struggle a little to lift it back up. She suddenly wished for nothing more than to be able to lie down.

"These instructions are clear, well drawn, and the rain hasn't hurt them enough to impede the work," he went on. "Did you wish to select the wood?"

"My parents have specified black maple, and did bid me pick the pieces, the finest you have of course."

The front door opened and closed, and Stratus stepped into the entry room. He set down Juleena's boots, clean now, and then removed his own and came up to the dining room. With a nod to his parents, he took position behind Juleena's chair, in an alert pose, still in his role of escort. From there, he also got the full benefit of the stove, and his clothes were wet, too. With him near, Juleena was able to perk up a little, and felt some blood move into her cheeks, but she still felt weariness weighing her down.

"I'll bring in my finest pieces," Mister Hearthsraven said. "If you would please wait here. I'll be right back."

Missus Hearthsraven had looked up when Stratus came in, and once he took his position, looked back down at her tea again. She didn't look up now, except briefly, at Juleena, who managed to prod herself into a cheerful smile.

"More tea, my lady?" Ona asked.

"Thank you." Juleena let her fill her mug. "Won't you sit? You needn't stand about and wait on me like a servant."

"Lady Mrandis is too kind," Ona smiled, and did as bidden, taking a seat by her mother-in-law.

A thunder of little running feet came from the floor above, and then two children came clattering down the stairs to the right of the kitchen. First was a girl with wavy brown hair, perhaps five or six years old, and then a little boy with hair that matched the girl's, a couple years younger. They saw the stranger at the table and came to a quick halt. The boy hid behind who was likely his sister.

"Grandmummy," the girl demanded, "who's that?"

She pointed, and Missus Hearthsraven sprang to her feet.

"Glory," she scolded. "Have some manners in front of our

guest. This is Lady Mrandis, from Mrandis House. She has work for your Grandda."

The girl seemed to think about that, putting the reprimanded finger thoughtfully in her mouth. "Grandda sees customers in his workshop," she pointed out.

"Lady Mrandis is special, and she was caught in the storm, and don't suck on your fingers."

The girl, Glory, leaned to the side to get a look around her grandmother at Juleena, who lifted a hand and gave her a little wave. Glory grinned, showing a couple missing baby teeth, and waved back. Missus Hearthsraven chivvied the children back up the stairs. Then a parade of three men came back in through the door to the workshop, opposite the stairs. Stratus's father led them, and the other two could only be Stratus's older brothers. Neither was as solid with fighting muscle as he was, though one was taller. Both had hair of a similar color, though neither was as tanned as he was. They gave him nods and smiles, and then lined up with their father.

"Lady Mrandis," Mister Hearthsraven said. "Please indicate which pieces you prefer."

Each man had brought an arm-load of planks, and showed them to Juleena in turn. She eliminated pieces until she'd selected what she thought were the best half dozen. By then the concentrated heat of the fire had baked the last of the chill from her, and her fatigue was getting heavier and heavier. Had she been at home, she would have gone for a nap, but here—

"Thank you, my lady," Mister Hearthsraven bowed. "I shall have your order ready in two weeks."

Juleena tried to smile at him. "It is I who thank you, Master craftsman."

The brothers filed out, taking all the wood, both rejected and selected in separate piles. The master of the house stayed, and exchanged a look with his wife, in which some mysterious spousal communication must have been conveyed.

"Lady Mrandis," Missus Hearthsraven spoke up, "I beg your forgiveness for such forward speech, but you seem wearied by the journey and the storm. Would you wish to rest here a while, before returning to Lenali?"

"The rain continues," her husband contributed. "The return walk will not be comfortable. You could wait here while we send for your carriage."

Here, among Stratus's family, lie down to sleep? Juleena's vision swam and she put both hands flat on the table.

"My lady?" three voices asked with sharp concern.

"Perhaps," Juleena quavered. "I am weary."

She braced herself and managed to stand. Stratus pulled her chair back for her. Then her head went light and she staggered a little. Stratus's hands were immediately on her shoulders, steadying her.

"It was a long walk," she muttered. "Please, may I lie down?"

Even with Stratus's support, one knee buckled, and then she seemed to be flying into the air. The next thing she knew, Stratus had her up in his arms: one under her knees, one behind her back. The wrapped towel fell from her hair. She thoughtlessly leaned her head against his neck and shoulder, wanting only the comfort of his support, and closed her eyes. He leaned his head a little against hers. She reached up to grab lightly onto his damp jacket. His scent was a bit stronger since he was wet, but not unpleasant; she knew it so well.

She felt as he climbed the stairs, and heard the sound of the rain getting louder over the sound of his heartbeat. A minute or three later, she felt him lower her, and a bed was under her. He slid his arms out and stepped away to close a door. Then he came back and knelt beside the bed. Juleena looked up at the beams of the slanted ceiling.

"The attic?" she murmured.

"My room," Stratus whispered back.

She touched the quilt below her.

"My bed," he breathed.

Juleena found the energy to meet his gaze. "You put me on your bed."

"My ma and da know," he said tightly. "I can tell. There's no hiding it. We should have never come here."

She lifted a limp hand and touched his cheek. "I'm glad to have met them. They're wonderful."

Her fingers curled hopefully, and he bent down to kiss her. For a moment, he half lay across her, and his weight sent up sparks of desire despite her tiredness. She pulled him closer, but Stratus gently broke away.

"No," he sighed. "You need to rest."

"With the rain, no one would hear," she mumbled.

"You're so sleepy you've become reckless," he teased. "They know I went up here with you. If I don't come back soon, my father will barge in and smack me with a table leg."

Juleena's eyes closed, an amused little smile managing a partial victory on her lips.

"This is your mother's wedding dress, isn't it?"

"I don't know. I suppose it could be. I've never seen her wear it."

Sleep tugged at her, dragging on her mind. "She put it on me."

"She wanted to dress a lady as she deserves."

Juleena felt his hand brush across her forehead. "But," she muttered.

"Sleep, my love."

"Stratus."

Everyone had vacated the kitchen except his father, and he sat where Stratus couldn't miss him as he came down the stairs. He knew better than to try to deflect or avoid this conversation.

"Yes, sir," he answered.

"Join me on the porch."

The porch was a little platform at the back of the house, opposite the front door, at the end of the hallway that also led to his parents' bedroom and that of his eldest brother and his wife across from it. It had an overhang to keep off the rain, and benches for sitting. A railing enclosed it, and from it part of the family garden was in view, with a couple fruit trees just showing the first signs of spring buds.

His father sat on one bench. Stratus took the other. The master craftsman sipped at his mug of tea and looked for a while out into the rain.

"I've always taught you and your brothers to be honorable men," he said at last, "and though your brothers have at times disappointed me, you never have, Stratus." Then he let the blow fall. "Until now."

Stratus kept his head bowed, staring at the floor of the porch.

"What do you think you're doing?" his father asked. He didn't raise his voice, but there was steel as sharp as one of his chisels below it.

He knew exactly what his father meant, and didn't try to deny it. Stratus swallowed and had to clear his throat. "I was following my heart."

His father said something not to be expressed around small children or those of delicate sensibilities, and then went on. "At the expense of your mind, your good sense? At the expense of everything? Do you understand what this could cost you, and her, and us?"

"No one knows," he asserted.

"Why?" his father demanded. "Why would you let yourself become involved with a noblewoman, and not with some old widow who could be allowed to indulge herself, but with a young woman betrothed to another man?"

Stratus ran a hand into his hair. "I love her. She loves me. We love each other."

His father's breath left him in a great gust. "Yes, I can see that, and you're incredibly lucky no one else has."

A few bits of Stratus's anxiety flaked off him, and he risked speaking more strongly. "I didn't pressure her into it. I tried to resist." He placed a hand on his chest. "She wanted me. I couldn't," he almost choked, "I couldn't turn away from her."

"So you've doomed her and yourself, and maybe us as well."

Stratus looked up with some confusion. "No, not if no one else knows. She," now he did choke, "she'll be married soon, and sent away to House Salasis. I won't see her anymore."

His father just stared at him: stared so hard and long that soon the son was fidgeting with much elevated nerves.

"What?" he asked tightly. "I'll stop seeing her. We'll stop. No one will ever find out, and it will be over. We'll both do what we must, and move on with our lives, alone."

"You don't know," his father stated. "She hasn't told you."

"What?" he asked again, more heated this time.

But instead of an answer, his father hid his face in his strong, scarred hands.

"Da?" Stratus tried. "Father? What is it? Tell me."

He let out another great sigh and rubbed at his forehead. "Lady Mrandis is with child. Your mother saw the signs. She wouldn't be one to mistake them. I suspected something was amiss with the lady, too, and when your mother told me, it made perfect sense."

Stratus sat as if nailed to the bench, staring at nothing, having heard nothing of what his father had said after the first five words.

"No," he uttered finally. "It's impossible."

"Not if you've been bedding her it isn't," his father growled, spearing him now with a fierce glare.

"She said she took care of it," he swallowed, "that it was safe."

"She was wrong then, and it's never completely safe. Good earth, boy, did I teach you nothing? Your mother is saying she's about four months along. She's at the point where soon it will be impossible to hide. You didn't notice the changes in her body?"

Stratus shook his head mutely.

"Or you didn't want to see, so you didn't. You ignored what was in front of your face because it couldn't be true, and if it was it would ruin everything," his father said softly. "Stratus, this is a serious problem."

Tears pricked his eyes and he found his hands shaking. "I'm a," he gulped, "it's my, what do I do? What do I do, Da?"

His father's hand landed supportively on his shoulder. "The

first thing you do is go talk to her about it. We've sent for the carriage. You have maybe another half an hour."

"But what do I do?" Stratus pleaded.

He looked up for his father's expression, which held a mixture of affection and pain.

"We will support whatever you and she decide. If together you decide to make it go away, and hide all evidence of what has passed between you, and return to your separate lives, we will keep your secret. If you decide otherwise, if you lose your position in the Guard, you are always welcome in my house. We'll make space for you in the workshop somehow, and hopefully our custom will not suffer too badly from it. Hopefully, Mrandis House will be satisfied with that punishment for you."

Stratus didn't even pause to consider what other punishment there might be—imprisonment, beatings, exile, or worse. His mind went straight to what pulsed in him with his every heartbeat. "And her?"

"That will depend on what her House does with her," his father said darkly.

"But—"

"Of course, if she has nowhere else to go, she will come here, and the child as well."

Stratus bowed his head and the tears dripped like rain onto the floorboards.

"Thank you, Da," he choked out. "Thank you."

Juleena woke to the gentle touch she recognized so well, and that familiar murmured voice in her ears, somehow falling under the drumming of the heavy rain on the roof.

"I'm sorry to wake you," Stratus said. "You've had only a few minutes rest, but I must talk with you before the carriage gets here."

"Mmm?" she grunted, stretching a little.

"Juleena," he breathed. "Can you look at me?"

She rolled onto her side and got her eyes open. "What is it?"

Stratus had his hand resting lightly on her shoulder. Slowly, he slid it down her side, and then let it drop down, coming to rest on her belly.

"We made a baby," he whispered. "Why didn't you tell me?"

All the tension, all the times she'd forced herself not to think about it, all the times she'd pretended and prayed no one would notice, burst like an overripe mumfruit, and her tears spilled forth. His arms were around her at once, rocking her on the bed, even weeping with her.

"I'm so scared," she sobbed, "and so happy."

"Me, too," he said.

Juleena managed to articulate sounds that sounded vaguely like, "I'm sorry I didn't tell you."

They kept rocking gently for some few more minutes, until Juleena found the fortitude to get her crying under control. Then she lay in his arms—at some point Stratus having joined her on the bed. They didn't speak for a while. Stratus wiped the remains of the tears off her face; she brushed her fingers over the stubble on his.

"We're keeping it?" he whispered to her at last.

"We're keeping it," she confirmed.

The words came so easily—so rightly. Everything else was broken, everything in her whole world, but this was right, so right, and it was the only thing that needed to be right. Her child, hers and Stratus's, would come into the world, and they would raise it, and be a family.

"When are you going to tell them?" he asked.

"I can't think about that yet," she objected, hiding her face against the quilt.

"Alright," he subsided. "You tell them when you're ready."

"I will, but Stratus, I don't know what they'll say—no, I know what they'll say, I think, but I don't know what will happen."

"I don't know either," he murmured back. "But if it turns out to be the best choice, you come here."

Juleena's eyes flew back open. "Are you sure? We don't have to go away?"

"My father says you're welcome. It will work out."

She shuddered and tears rose again. Stratus held her again. She thought it was all that kept her from flying apart.

The rain was still pouring down when the carriage arrived. Juleena had gotten back downstairs and used the master bedroom to change again into her own clothes, which had been hung up behind the stove to dry.

"Thank you," she'd told Missus Hearthsraven, uneasy and uncertain now that Stratus had told her his parents knew their secret—and not just that they were affectionate, but had made a baby.

The tidy, upright woman—mistress of her own little house—stared back at Juleena with a complex blend of expressions on her face. Worry was topmost, but there was no loathing, no despair. Then suddenly, surprising Juleena profoundly, the woman pulled her into a quick hug.

"How I wish my little boy were a lord," she whispered.

Just as quickly, she let her go.

"Get plenty of rest when you need it, but exercise is good for you, too," Missus Hearthsraven confided in a rush. "Take care of your feet, put them up regularly, and you'll need to stop sleeping on your back, so start getting used to that. Drink only mild teas, like peppermint. Leave off beer and wine, if you drink them—they can sour the blood. Oh, there's so much I wish I had time to tell you. You should see a midwife."

"My family doesn't know," Juleena breathed, mouth gone dry.

"I didn't figure they would," Missus Hearthsraven frowned. "They will soon enough. Your belly isn't going to be getting smaller until that baby's out."

"I know."

For a long moment they stood staring at each other.

"If you need anything, you come here. Understand?" Missus Hearthsraven ordered kindly, but firmly.

"Yes, ma'am," Juleena nodded.

She huffed. "I can't imagine what you saw in my son."

A smile tugged at Juleena's mouth. "I think you know, Missus. He's the kindest, bravest man I have ever met."

She petted at Juleena's mussed hair. "Well, he's not a bad boy."

"I never meant for there to be a child," she confessed, smile fading. "I tried to prevent it, but now," she put her hands to her belly, "there's nothing I want more."

Missus Hearthsraven shook her head. "All will be well. I can't imagine how, but somehow, all will be well. Don't you worry. Worry isn't good for the baby, or for you."

She leaned in, and kissed Juleena on the forehead.

Juleena went out to the carriage. Stratus was not allowed to ride in it with her—there was no question of that and no one dared to suggest such a thing—but he clung to the back of it with the footman, in the rain, all the way back to the Mrandis estate.

Her mother didn't get around to scolding her about her adventure until that evening. Juleena was reclined on the divan in her bedroom, wrapped in a blanket for warmth, head tucked under a lit lamp where she could read before bed.

"Yes?" she called when she heard the knock, and Mirassi swept in.

"You're not ill are you?" the Mistress grumbled.

"No, Mother," Juleena assured her.

"They said you got soaked." She folded her arms.

"It was alright. I got dry quickly. Thank you for the carriage."

"Of course."

"And Mister Hearthsraven said he'd have the order ready in two weeks," Juleena went on. "I picked the prettiest wood he had."

Mirassi nodded pensively.

"Is anything wrong, Mother?"

She shook her head and waved a hand. "Your marriage is coming so soon. It's only two months away now—less than that, actually. I suppose you've had enough time by now to get used to the idea?"

Juleena cast her gaze down. "I suppose so," she lied.

"You still seem uneasy."

"Please, don't worry about me," she said.

Mirassi stood there staring at her, until Juleena started to feel nervous.

"Everything will be ready soon," her mother muttered. "The gown is nearly finished?"

"Nearly," she confirmed.

"Then we'll see you in it soon enough, and you can begin practicing for the ceremony and the first dance. Perhaps we'll wait until it's a little warmer."

But there would be no wedding, no need to practice. If she tried to put the dress on, it probably wouldn't fit anymore—it had been tailored close to her shape of four months ago. She had to admit it. She had to tell her mother. Suddenly her hands were shaking, and she set her book down.

"Juleena?" Mirassi queried. "Are you sure you haven't taken a chill?"

She came around to the side of the divan and knelt. Frowning, she touched her daughter's forehead, cheeks, and gripped her hands.

"Your hands are cold, but your face is warm," she pronounced. "You're upset, child. What is it?"

In her head, Juleena prepped the words. She'd try to do it gently, of course. She needed her mother's support, not antagonism. Ready, she met her mother's eyes, parted her lips to speak—and couldn't do it.

"What is it?" Mirassi repeated.

The woman's brows lowered with either concern or suspicion; Juleena had always had trouble telling which.

"Out with it," she commanded.

Juleena's jaw clamped shut. She couldn't. Her mother wouldn't be supportive—she knew it. She'd be angry. She couldn't tell her. It would be better to just run away—but then she'd have to hide out at the Hearthsraven house, unless Stratus took her to a different town, a distant town. A search would be mounted. She'd be found eventually. Juleena shook her head, bowing it in submission. After a few moments, Mirassi patted her hands.

"Nerves," she diagnosed. "Get some rest."

"Yes, Mother," Juleena whispered.

A few more days passed without Juleena finding the courage to speak. A detachment of the army arrived, making camp just beyond the walls of Lenali and bringing much excitement to the city, though they hadn't brought any drakes. There were two Wizards with them, though, who could send a message to request the drakes when a target worthy of them was found.

Rodreric and the other men of the House spent many hours with the military men, guiding them around the mountains as the commanders set up their plan for sweeping the land for Wild Ones. Stratus and the other guardsmen assigned to the Mrandis estate were not drawn upon for assistance, but with so much disruptive activity it was easy for him to slip up to Juleena's room late at night when she left a book in the window for him. They lay together in the light of a single candle, and Stratus traced spirals on her belly.

"You're getting bigger," he breathed.

Juleena watched him, eyes heavy with weariness but body sated with pleasure. She'd wondered if they could continue being intimate as the pregnancy progressed, or if it might start to hurt, but she'd been surprised to discover that it was as enjoyable as ever, maybe even more so.

"I'm feeling things," she whispered back. "Little sort of twitches, or quivering, I'm not sure."

His eyes widened and he lifted his gaze up to hers. Silently, he spread his hand against her tummy.

"Not right now," she smiled.

"You haven't said anything yet, I take it?" he murmured.

Juleena winced. "I've tried. I just can't say it."

Stratus didn't argue, just lowered his head and went back to stroking her.

"I know I have to. I know. I will."

"I know," he nodded.

Then he let go a great breath and looked up again, finding a quirky little smile for her. "If you were as eager to tell everyone as you are eager for other things—"

She blushed hotly and flicked a nearby blanket over his head. "Oh, hush, you."

Stratus grabbed the blanket like a cloak and crawled closer. Juleena had to smother a giggle as he descended onto her.

"You hush, wench," he teased.

"Brute."

"Glutton."

"Beast."

He growled and pretended to bite for her neck. Juleena swallowed a squeal and bit his ear back in return. When they surfaced from the mock battle he tucked her close against him, stroking the long, smooth lines of her shoulder and back.

"Marry me," he breathed.

"Yes."

The hunt for the Wild Ones went out the next day. There wasn't much to see from the estate. Birds occasionally rose in clouds as the men marched through, literally beating the bushes. The results of the day's hunt were brought to the courtyard, and there at least, everyone could see. Juleena came down in a warm cloak and stood in the light of the torches with the rest of her family.

A group of eight goblins had been chased down. There were also three creatures that looked something like drakes, except with only two legs and wings, and much smaller, and colored like the spring treetops.

"Tree wyverns," the commanding officer explained. "Venomous, quick, and very dangerous."

"And that beast?" Master Mrandis pointed.

"Krine," the commander said.

"It doesn't look very dangerous, just sort of like a deformed deer."

Juleena looked, and had to agree, at least partially. It was about the size of a doe, but less lean, with stubbier legs and a thicker neck and rounder head. It was dappled like a fawn all down its back, up its neck, and out onto its face, with a very pale underside. Its ears were shorter than a deer's, and its tail longer. From its brow ridges spiraled forward two golden horns, curving upward. Its eyes were open, and looked like they might have been sky blue in life, but now they were glassy in death.

The commander stepped forward and gripped the krine's jaw. "See? Fangs? They're vicious creatures."

But the wounds to the animal were to its haunches, as though the dogs had hamstrung it. A single puncture wound—from a sword or spear—had severed some big vessels in its neck. It didn't look to Juleena like the beast had been vicious enough to fight. It looked like it had been hunted down and killed as it tried to escape.

"Stake the heads along the walls," Rodreric commanded, and several soldiers began hacking at the corpses with axes. He nudged the krine's body with a foot. "Do these taste like venison?"

"No, Master Mrandis," the commander answered quickly. "We can't even give krine meat to the dogs. It's not poisonous exactly, but slows the heart and can put anything that eats it into a deep sleep. Some who have eaten it never awake from that sleep."

"Burn it then, with the others, but let me have my man take the hide off first. It's got a nice look to it."

"The horns though," the commander ventured, "are considered valuable, even magical, by some."

"Ah."

The two men looked at each other over the body of the krine, and Juleena could guess what was going on. A hide, even an unusual one, wasn't particularly valuable, but golden horns—whether made from actual gold or not—were another matter, especially if a known value existed for them, or if they were magical.

The military task force was commanded by the capital, but the Houses were hosting them, not paying them, but the Houses were also a form of government that supported the capital, which did pay the military men. Who could lay claim to the horns — a spoil of the military venture helping the Houses — was the question.

"Can any one soldier be credited with the kill?" Rodreric shrugged.

The commander's eyebrows rose. "Yes, actually. Incentive?"

Master Mrandis nodded slowly. "Perhaps he should receive one?"

"A generous notion," the commander bowed. "And the other should surely grace House Mrandis' trophy room."

Rodreric nodded again. The commander put his hand out for one of the axes, and then knelt by the krine's head. Juleena winced and looked away as he methodically lifted the axe for a short, controlled strike. There were two wet crunches, and she felt a chill streak through her. In fact, she saw Kapri, standing behind Mirassi, shiver as well, and the whole group shifted a little, like a field of wheat brushed by a breeze.

She grabbed Samira's hand. "Let's go in," she whispered.

The next day dawned unusually gloomy. Fog blanketed the sky, hanging low and clinging to the stonework of the house and walls. It was cold for early spring, though not cold enough to freeze. New leaves and early flowers dripped moisture from the budding fruit trees in the grounds.

The military went out regardless, sweeping farther into the forests this time, but everyone else huddled behind their walls, still and silent, like rabbits sensing an eagle fly by. Juleena, too, sat by her window alternating between playing her yaus and reading and staring out at the fog. It was while she was doing this latter activity that she saw the dark shape move behind the ceiling of drifting mist.

The fog swirled as what could only be massive wings stirred it. A tail dropped down: long and silvery dark. The end was flattened like a spade, and the spine sported curling spines for several yards up from the tip. Then the taloned hind feet dipped below the fog, too, with claws so sickle-like Juleena wondered if the beast could even walk.

It was then she realized she was on her feet. A whimpering noise was fighting its way out of her closed throat. The creature in the fog flapped its wings, and now she could start to hear the sound of it. Then it roared, and she screamed in reply, not meaning to, the utterance torn from her lungs as she slapped her hands over her ears.

Juleena was not the only one. Shrieks and cries erupted throughout the house and surrounding city: a chorus of terror. The creature dropped as suddenly as though it had pulled its wings in and fallen. A section of wall around the estate was knocked over by the beast's forelimb, almost negligently, the way a human might kick over a chair without noticing.

Now she saw its entirety, and her hands went to her throat as strangled cries bubbled up. It was longer, nose to tail tip, than the whole house. Somehow it did manage to stand on those sickle-clawed feet. Its tail made a lazy slash that dug up half the house garden, and scarred three trees so deeply they probably wouldn't survive it.

Its wings were bat-like and black, its legs shorter, and its body lean and long like a cat's. Dense reddish fur covered its dorsal side, and scales that glinted like fish bellies its underside. The exposed skin of its legs, neck, and tail — between the fur and scales — was dark pewter. Its neck was longer than a cat's, but not quite as long as a horse's, and thinner, more snakelike. Its head was broad, though, with several twisted grey horns arching back off it, towards its hulking shoulders and wide chest. It opened its mouth to reveal a set of teeth wolves and ice-lions only dreamed of.

Juleena's bedroom door slammed open, and she jumped, screaming again, though not as helplessly as the first time.

Samira staggered in and the two women clutched at each other, shaking.

"What is it?" the maid gasped. "Is it a dragon?"

Juleena couldn't speak. Her eyes were stuck on the beast, and where the six guardsmen assigned to the Mrandis estate were rushing out to face it.

"Bow," she croaked.

"What?" Samira uttered absently, wide eyes still fixed on the creature down on the grounds.

The beast's shoulders came up as high as the second story of the house. Its gaze remained pointed towards the gates of the estate. So far, it hadn't paid any attention to the six men running up behind it, and they were stalking it cautiously, forming up together, on their guard with the tension of the life-and-death fight.

"My bow," Juleena repeated, a hair stronger.

"What?" Samira panted again.

"My bow," she growled in the face of her friend's terrified stupor. "My bow. Bring me my bow."

The maid just whimpered, and Juleena grabbed her, forcing her to look at her.

"Samira," she summoned, until at last some sense drifted back into her eyes. "Go fetch me my bow. It's in the armory. Bring as many quivers of arrows as you can carry."

Juleena gave her a little shove to get her going and turned towards the windows. She grabbed one chair, tossed it away, and then the second.

"Julee?" Samira quavered.

She whirled on her and stabbed her arm out, pointing imperiously. "Fetch my bow," she snarled. "Now!"

Samira startled like a doe and fled. Juleena pushed the table out from in front of the window. Then she twisted the latch on the window and pushed it open. Clammy mist scented of rusted iron flooded into the room. Juleena stood and let it wreath around her. Down on the ground, the beast—she'd never seen a dragon; she'd always thought they were heftier, rounder, full of massive muscle; this creature was lean—had stepped up to the main gates.

It tilted its head down, as if peering at something. Then it lifted its head up, nose towards the fogged over sky, and keened. Juleena slapped her hands over her ears again. The sound was piercing like a thousand teakettles whistling at once, but from a living throat, flavored with anguish and fury. The cry went on and on; the beast had to be emptying its entire lungs to make such an extended sound.

When at last it stopped, Juleena felt tears on her face. She lowered her hands and heard stumbling feet behind her.

"Here, here," Samira blurted.

She'd brought the bow and a half a dozen quivers. Not all the arrows were the right length for Juleena to draw fully, while others were a bit too long, but she would manage. She took the bow and strung it while Samira dumped the quivers on the nearby table.

"You're going to shoot it?" the maid panted.

"If I have to," Juleena grunted back. "It hasn't hurt anything yet, other than the garden and trees and wall, and I think that part was by accident, but if it gets violent, I'll shoot it. Stratus is down there."

The dragon-like creature lowered its head from its mournful position, adjusted its stance, and reached out to the walls of the estate. It was a good distance away, and its body partly blocked Juleena's view of it.

"What's it doing?" Samira wondered breathlessly.

It appeared to make a plucking motion, several times in a row, as if gathering something off the walls.

"The heads," Juleena realized. "It's picking up the severed heads that my father ordered staked at the top of the wall."

Behind the creature and to one side, away from that powerful tail, the six guardsmen had assumed a v-shaped formation, with the guard Captain in front.

"Begone!" the Captain bellowed. "Creature of the Wild,

leave this place or we will drive you from it."

The winged beast gave no indication that it had heard, just continued with its plucking motions. Then it lifted a wing, and Juleena noticed for the first time a strap around its chest, with a few little pouches hanging from it, all dyed black so they blended in with its dark skin.

"Wild One," the Captain cried again. "This is your last warning. Depart!"

The dragon paid him no mind. Methodically—Juleena thought: reverently—the creature opened a pouch and began putting the severed heads inside. The guard Captain behind it was bouncing on his toes, sword glimmering weakly through the mist.

"Men," Juleena thought she heard him order, "form up tight behind me."

There was some more muttering, but she was too far away to discern it. Her hands clenched on her bow, but she did not draw—not yet.

"It's not here to fight," she whispered.

The guard Captain, however, apparently did not have the same opinion. With a roar of his own, he charged, the other guards close around him, and dug his sword into the back of the beast's foot.

It grunted and kicked back, as if in instinctive reaction. Casual it might have been, but the strike sent four of the guards flying. The Captain took most of the hit, getting tossed back several yards until he tumbled across the muddy grass, into some shrubbery, and then lay still. Three others took shorter flights, slapped down on their backs or butts, and rolled about a little, groaning and starting to get back up.

The two remaining guards were Stratus and one other, a younger man, recently promoted on the orders of the Master of Mrandis to help fill out the ranks. Stratus stood his ground. The young man cowered behind him. The dragon sniffed, lowered its head and turned it back to investigate.

Juleena couldn't see any blood from where the Captain had

stabbed it, but still the beast lifted its foot and rotated it, examining the injury. A rumble shook its body, and it set its foot back down, seemingly none the worse. Juleena found herself wondering if the rumble had been of anger or amusement, or a mixture of both. It cocked its head and looked at Stratus for a moment, and then gave a little nod.

He lowered his sword point and stood a bit straighter. "Great One," he said, just loudly enough that Juleena could hear it from her window.

Again came that beastly rumble.

"You come," he went on, "to retrieve your dead?"

This time the rumble was definitely more of the angry type.

"Your allies?" Stratus asked.

Less angry rumble.

"Your friends?"

The next rumble had a hint of a whine traced through it.

"Our peoples are not living in peace," Stratus said. It sounded like an apology. "But some of your people have hurt mine."

The dragon lifted its head again, stiffly, and after a breath or two, nodded.

"If you don't stop them from doing that," Stratus ventured, "this will keep happening. I can't stop it. I am not the lord of my people, only a servant."

Juleena set her bow to lean against the window. The dragon heaved what seemed to be a sigh. It turned back to the gates once more, picked up perhaps another head, and when it turned back towards Stratus it adjusted its position so it could open its hand towards him. Juleena squinted and thought it was the krine head the dragon held, looking as small in its hand as an apricot would look in hers.

The dragon's jaws parted slightly, and a voice as old as the stars and as beautiful emerged. "She did not hurt your people."

The words seemed to shake the air, making raindrops suddenly condense and fall out of the pervasive mist. Stratus staggered as if the words had shaken him, too.

"No," he said, "I didn't think she had. It was not my feet that pursued her, nor my hand that slew her, but I apologize for her death. Can any recompense be made?"

"Where are her horns?" Now the voice sounded more like shining blades than shining stars.

"In the kitchen," Samira gasped. "The cook was cleaning them last night."

Then the maid was gone again, bolting out of Juleena's room. Juleena remained standing at the window, rooted to the spot, watching her beloved parlay words with the dragon.

"They were taken," Stratus confessed, "by those with no right to them."

"Where?" the dragon asked again.

The boy behind Stratus cowered down further, and then broke and ran. Neither Stratus nor the dragon paid him any attention.

"I don't have them," Stratus said. "I don't know where they are."

Those wings began to lift. Muscles tightened all over the great beast's body. A hiss came from its throat. Just slightly, Stratus lifted the point of his sword. His shield, too, rose in readiness, though what he could do against such a creature Juleena didn't know. Her numb fingers reached for her bow. Her other hand found an arrow on the table.

Then the front door to the servants' entrance to the kitchen banged open, and Juleena saw Samira come stumbling out. She fell once, got up, managed a few more steps, and fell again, but she held up over her head the two golden horns. She was trembling violently, clearly terrified out of her wits.

Stratus's sword and shield relaxed again. The dragon tucked its wings back in and fell silent. With a glance up at the massive creature, Stratus set down his weapons. He walked to where Samira lay shuddering, knelt, and put a hand on her head. Juleena supposed he must have said something soft to her. He took the horns from her and she curled into a defensive ball.

The dragon waited in utter silence as Stratus stood and returned to where it still held out its hand, with the sad severed head of the krine in its palm. The dragon lowered its hand a little, and Stratus reached up, even going up onto his toes. He set the horns atop the head, approximately where they were formerly attached.

"May I return these to you, and to her," he said.

The dragon's fingers and claws closed slowly around the grisly remains. Just as reverently as before, if not more so, the beast put the head and horns into one of its pouches.

"I will see to it that no more wanderers come to your lands," the dragon murmured, "to the best of my ability."

Then it raised its voice nearly to the point of pain for Juleena and surely all those watching.

"You will cease the killing of those gentle ones that mean you no harm," it declared. "Or I shall return, not to fetch my dead, but to send you all to join them."

It didn't need to say anymore. Juleena could imagine the destruction it would bring if it truly wanted to. An idle kick had knocked out four guards. An accidental bump had collapsed a wall. A simple flick of its tail had undone days of garden work and killed three mature trees. If it returned with the will to massacre, there would be no stones left standing.

Juleena felt hopelessly foolish, standing there with her measly bow. Perhaps she could have stung it a bit, but she doubted even an eye shot would do more than annoy it, and it would squash her in revenge, with no more effort than she made to butter toast.

"We are done here," it said, voice again like starlight.

"Yes," Stratus agreed.

The beast eyed him a moment longer. "Your people are lucky to have a wise one among them."

It reared up, spreading its wings, but didn't lift into the air. Instead, it scratched its pale belly, as though it had an itch. Then it slammed back down onto all fours, making Stratus stagger for his stance. The dragon held out a hand, one finger extended, sickle claw held sharply back. Something shone on its fingertip.

"For you," the beast said. "Wisdom should be rewarded,

and I was about to shed it anyway."

Stratus lifted his hands and accepted what looked like a translucent, pearly dinner plate. Juleena realized a moment later that it was a scale: a scale from the dragon's belly. The creature said not another word, and swept its wings wide. Stratus hurriedly retreated, and not too soon, for the dragon leapt straight up, and the wings flashed down, driving it up into the fog like a spear, and sending a torrent of wind across the grounds.

It vanished without another flicker into the mist.

Servants swarmed through the house, ascertaining everyone's safety and the integrity of the walls. Some people were wailing with lingering fear, but Kapri came striding confidently into Juleena's room, perfectly composed and intent.

"My lady, are you well?" she asked.

Juleena was shutting her window, her hands shaking. She felt no need to wail, but now that the danger was past she felt suddenly light headed and faint. Her heart fluttered in her chest and she swayed on her feet. Kapri was at her side at once.

"Sami?" Juleena wondered.

"She's fine," Kapri assured her. "Mum Hyldi is tending her."

Juleena stumbled a little, and Kapri caught her.

"You should lie down, my lady. I'll bring you some strengthening tea."

"Just peppermint," Juleena mumbled. "Only peppermint."

"As you like, my lady."

Kapri guided her to the edge of her bed, sat her there, and after a moment, loosened the laces of her dress.

"Lie down, my lady."

Juleena obeyed, hand going instinctively to her belly, and she rolled to her side. Kapri removed her shoes and set her feet gently on the bed. She pulled a blanket across her.

"Rest easy, my lady. All is safe now," Kapri murmured.

Then the serving woman was gone. Juleena closed her eyes and shuddered. Inside her, she felt a small, sharp movement, and she petted her belly. She was safe. Her baby was safe.

Stratus was safe. Samira was safe. Adrenaline continued working its way out of her, leaving her to quiver a little, but after some time she drifted to sleep.

She heard vaguely the sound of people in her room, but didn't fully wake until she heard her mother's voice.

"Daughter."

Juleena blinked her eyes open. Sun was streaming in the window, and two servants were putting the table back in front of it. Her bow and the arrows were gone. Kapri was setting tea that smelled of peppermint on her little beside night stand. Kapri didn't meet her gaze, and fled the room as soon as her task was done. Mirassi stood at the side of the bed, looking down on her. The Mistress glanced over her shoulder, waiting until the furniture-moving servants left. Juleena heard the door shut.

Keeping the blanket around her, she sat up.

"Are you well, child?" Mirassi asked softly. "Kapri said you collapsed."

"Not really," Juleena said. "I mean: I didn't collapse. Kapri helped me to rest here. I was a little distraught, but I feel better now."

"It was quite a distressing event for all of us," Mirassi nodded. "I suppose you saw it all."

"I did."

"And your maid got an even closer look."

"Is she alright?"

"She's fine," Mirassi dismissed. "I worry about you."

"I'm fine, too," Juleena assured her.

Her mother's eyes pierced at her. "Are you cold?"

"A little," Juleena said.

"The day is turning warm. I had the fire stoked for you." She kept staring, not a hint of softness in her gaze. "Remove the blanket, Juleena."

Now she did feel a chill, and dread flowered in her. Obediently, she let the blanket fall from her shoulders, onto her lap, in piles of folds around her waist. Mirassi's eyes swept over her: as much of her as she could see. Her jaw tightened.

"Stand up," she ordered gently.

"I'm still weary, Mother. Might I not rest a while longer?" Juleena asked, mouth dry.

"Stand up," Mirassi repeated, only more softly, and more firmly.

Juleena's body felt numb, her head light, her hands cold. She did as ordered, clasping her hands in front of her and slouching her posture forward a little, trying to hide—

Mirassi grabbed her wrists and yanked them apart. Juleena gasped with shock. Just as quickly, her mother darted a hand to her belly, made a quick circuit, and learned the truth. Her eyes, dagger-sharp and hard, jabbed at Juleena's own.

"You're with child," she accused in a low, deadly voice.

Juleena couldn't breathe, much less speak, but the dread burst out onto her face in flowers of trembling fear. Mirassi's expression turned grim, as if Juleena's reaction had been all the confirmation she needed. Juleena didn't see it coming. Her mother's hand slapped with a crack of skin on skin across her face, and Juleena tumbled back onto the bed.

"Slut," Mirassi hissed. "You've ruined us."

Juleena heard her mother's footsteps, then the door opening, the door shutting, and the turning of a key in the lock. Juleena lay on her bed, so shocked she still couldn't get a breath. Her lungs drew but her throat closed, until both burned, but not with as much agony as the red brand across her cheek, or the panic in her mind. Her mother knew, and she did not approve— of course, Juleena had known she wouldn't. She had gotten exactly what, deep down, she'd known she'd get: her reward for bedding a man who was not her husband and letting him kindle a child in her.

Finally after what must have been more than a minute, she sucked a serrated breath and moaned. Raw sobs ripped through her, and she lay in her bed and muffled them into a pillow.

"Daughter."

Juleena had sunk into soundless, lightless waters, and took some time surfacing from them. Her eyes were gritty, the left one a little swollen, and her neck was stiff. She'd fallen back into a shocked sleep right where she'd been huddling and crying.

Her mother stood again in her room, in much the same posture as before. The sun was gone, leaving the faint blue light of evening to seep in through the window. Someone lit a lamp, and Juleena winced. A quick glance showed her a covered tray on her table. Kapri moved closer, having been the one who lit the lamp over by the table, and now lit the lamp beside Juleena's bed, where the cold peppermint tea still sat, untouched.

"I ask for your forgiveness, child," Mirassi said. "I reacted instinctively, without thought, but all is not lost. Mrandis need not be ruined by your foolishness."

Juleena pushed herself up to sitting, and her stomach grumbled audibly; she hadn't eaten all day.

"I apologize for striking you," Mirassi went on. "It was not an appropriate response."

Juleena felt like her tongue was stuck to the roof of her mouth, and turned to clay besides. She had to swallow a few times before she could speak.

"Thank you for apologizing," she croaked.

"Tell me, Juleena," Mirassi requested. "Were you taken against your will?"

She put her hands in her lap and squared her shoulders. Her mother had apologized for the slap, not what she'd said, and no matter what she was acting like now, Juleena knew that her initial reaction had been what she'd really felt. Any hope of an amicable settlement between them was a thin one, about as likely as the guard Captain beating the mist dragon in a rematch—unless she lied. If she said she'd been raped and too scared to speak of it, her mother might relent, but she was usually a truthful person, and she could not lie about this. She could not veil her love for Stratus or the unborn child with a lie.

"No," she answered evenly.

Mirassi didn't miss a beat. It was like she'd expected that

answer. "Who is he?"

"I'll tell you," Juleena promised, "if you let me marry him instead of Salasis. Let us live in one of the homes for the branch family. The child will never inherit."

Her mother's eyes narrowed. "What will he pay for you?"

Juleena clenched her jaw. "That's what it's all about, isn't it?" she whispered. "You want to see how much you can get for me. You don't care about seeing me happy, or with someone I love."

"That's how it works," Mirassi declared without a flinch. "You know it. I paid for your siblings' spouses and now someone else pays for you. This exchange goes on over the generations. Without it, Mrandis will have less chance of attracting suitable spouses for your nieces and nephews. We need the value that comes from you. How much can he offer?"

She tried to keep a sneer off her face. "Nothing," she hissed. "He's a commoner."

Horror bloomed on Mirassi's face and Juleena saw her arm twitch, as if she were about to lift it to deliver another slap. "You spread your legs for some stinking farmer's boy in a muddy field," she spluttered, voice rising, "or bent over a table for some penniless merchant's son in the back of his shop, or leaned against a tree for a dumb woodcutter in the forest? You, my daughter, pretty, smart, skilled—you lowered yourself to that?"

Juleena suddenly found herself on her feet. "You'd give me to Salasis, to Terkari? To a man who already has a bastard child on one of his servant girls, and who tried to touch me at the gathering against my will? He is worse than any of the options you just described."

Mirassi was unmoved. "Tell me who did this to you."

Juleena snarled. "Never."

The Mistress of Mrandis didn't even twitch. "You will lose the child. It is late for it, and will not be easy on you, but it can be done. Then you will go to Salasis as planned. None save us need ever know."

Juleena wrapped her arms across her belly, fighting the fear those words brought. "No."

Mirassi nodded at Kapri, who went and fetched a steaming mug of something from the table. "Drink that," she commanded. "It will help you."

"No," Juleena repeated, stronger.

"You will make me call for men to hold you down?" Mirassi whispered. "I'll do it. I will pinch your nose and pour it down your throat with my own hands. You will swallow or drown."

"No," she said again.

Mirassi gave Kapri another nod, and the servant returned the mug to the table and went for the door. "I will give you some time to think on this. Rest, eat, and refresh yourself. You must be troubled and confused after today's events. I can accept that you're not thinking clearly. I will return tomorrow morning. By then I will expect you to have calmed yourself and come to realize that this is the only path you have to take. Say your goodbye, if you must, to that half-formed bastard in your belly."

Kapri held the door for Mirassi, who swept out without a backward glance. Juleena heard them lock it. She went immediately to the narrow door to Samira's room, but it was locked, too. They'd already thought of that. There were no convenient vines growing up to her window, nor carts of fluffy hay parked below it; there would be no escape that way.

Her stomach grumbled, the baby moved a little, and Juleena went over to the tray on her table. She lifted the lid, discovering a large bowl of hot soup. She sniffed at it. It was heavily spiced, and she frowned. From her mother's words, the tea sitting beside it was a potion to make her miscarry. She could bet the same potion had been put in the soup. There would be no edible food here.

She felt another snarl building and had to resist the urge to throw the tray across the room; that wouldn't help anything. The potions, however, had to be removed. She opened her window and poured the tea out. She followed it with the soup. For good measure, she dumped the cold peppermint tea out also. Juleena knew this was only a temporary solution. Her mother would not relent, and she couldn't stay.

Meditatively, she took a few deep breaths, looking out the window at the fading light. Tears would do her no good; planning and cleverness, and maybe ruthlessness, was what was needed now. She couldn't expect help from Samira—and didn't want her friend getting any more involved anyway. Mirassi was probably detaining and questioning her already. Juleena could only hope that she was lying about knowing anything. Perhaps her courageous act in fetching the golden krine horns had given her some protection. If she was now hailed as a hero, she couldn't be punished in any public way.

Juleena was on her own. She had to get out and get to Trivale. The Hearthsravens would shelter her; she had to believe that. The obstacle would be escaping the house and grounds and eluding pursuit. Plus, she didn't want any threat coming to bear on the Hearthsravens. Somehow, she had to protect them.

Through the open window came faint sounds of merriment. There was music and laughter. Juleena leaned out and tried to see the other windows of the house. Near the front, the windows for the biggest hall glowed with light. It looked like there was a celebration going on. Could they be celebrating the end of the threat from the Wild Ones?

She frowned, thinking. Perhaps that would make it easier to escape, if everyone was distracted by the party. If she could slip out, no one would notice until the morning. Or perhaps she could announce in front of everyone that she was no longer a Mrandis. Maybe a public declaration could protect her. It would shame her family more than if she just vanished, but it might inhibit pursuit if she made it clear she did not want to be pursued.

Juleena shut her window and started digging into her closet. She selected her sturdiest, plainest clothing and boots. Methodically, she changed into the clothing, first strapping her harpy dagger to her thigh. She didn't touch any of her jewelry or try to take anything valuable with her: that way, they wouldn't have a monetary reason to come after her. She took a cloak and threw it over herself.

She stood and looked around her bedroom. She had so many memories here. So much of her life had happened in this room. Leaving it felt odd, hollow. It was difficult to convince herself that once she stepped out of it, she wouldn't be coming back. All this luxury, this life of ease, would be gone.

There was one more thing. She went to her sewing basket and took her little bundle of embroidery needles. She could do that much to earn her keep among the Hearthsravens; she could embroider and perhaps find a merchant who would sell the pieces. She had a little pouch of spending money, too: not much, but an allowance given to her that she hadn't spent yet. She took that, too. She could use it to buy some floss and some simple garment to begin work on. She could even embroider on scraps of fabric; common people knew techniques to add bits of finery—such as small embroidered pieces—to their existing garments. She would do what she could to support her new family.

There was nothing else. Juleena went to the door and knocked firmly. She had to knock a second time before she heard the shifting of a chair on the other side of the door.

"I wish to speak to my mother," she declared. "Please take me to her."

"I am not to open the door, Lady," a young voice replied. It sounded like one of the two pages—both sons of married servant couples—the house employed.

"Then fetch someone who can," she commanded.

There was quiet for a moment, and then running footsteps. Juleena waited, and slipped her hand into her pocket to grip the dagger hidden there. She didn't want to use it, but her first objective was to get out of her room, and she might need it for that. Footsteps returned, two pairs.

"My lady," called a different voice, and Juleena recognized Kapri.

"Kapri," she replied. "I want to go speak with my mother. Where is she?"

"She is at the feast. She will come to you in the morning."

"Let me speak to her now. Please, Kapri."

"My lady, I cannot."

"Please," Juleena pleaded again, letting her desperation into her voice. "I want to talk to her about this. She's my mother. I need to ask her forgiveness. I need her. Please, Kapri. I can't stay here all alone. I'm scared. Please let me go to her."

Kapri was silent for a handful of heartbeats.

"I can't be alone in here all night," Juleena begged, "not with this. This is too hard. I need my mother."

She thought maybe Kapri sighed. The key turned in the lock and the door opened.

"Come with me," the servant woman said, and Juleena thought she detected some real pain in her eyes. "You can wait in your mother's chambers. I'll go fetch her."

Juleena stepped into the hallway, but didn't follow as Kapri began to move off.

"Kapri, you never had children?" she asked gently.

She halted and turned. The woman's eyes widened a little. "My duty was to care for your mother, and by extension her children: you, and your siblings."

"Did you want your own children?"

Kapri made a slight gesture, enough to send the pageboy scampering away. After a short time of staring at Juleena, she answered. "I knew it wasn't something I'd have, so I never thought about it much."

"But you did," she whispered, "didn't you?"

"It is irrelevant, my lady."

"Kapri," Juleena said. "I want this baby. Let me go?"

She winced like Juleena had suggested getting together to drown kittens over a nice bottle of wine. "I can't," she gasped. "Your mother—you know I owe her everything?"

"I threatened you," Juleena suggested. "You tried to stop me. I hit you. I'm crazy with my need to protect my unborn child."

"You are," Kapri murmured. "You are crazy. Mirassi will never let you keep it."

"She doesn't get to decide that. I'm leaving."

Kapri shook her head. "She'll follow you."

"Not if I'm ruined," Juleena said. "Not if I declare my condition in front of that party downstairs, so everyone knows."

"She'll take revenge."

"I will face that, when it comes."

Kapri just stared at her. "You love this child, don't you?"

"And my husband."

"Husband?"

"Well, not yet, not officially, but I'm going to marry him, not Salasis."

Kapri stood for some long moments, tearful eyes looking over her.

"You didn't get to marry the one you loved, did you?" Juleena asked.

The servant woman blinked and dripped a tear. "It was long ago."

"My mother didn't marry for love, either, so she doesn't think anyone should," Juleena declared. "Is that what you think, too?"

"Hit me," Kapri ordered. "Hit me hard. Leave a mark."

At first, Juleena couldn't do it, and stood there for several breaths, while Kapri waited. Finally, she lifted a hand, imagining she was hitting her mother instead, in return for being hit by her. Kapri shut her eyes, and Juleena smacked her hard across the face. The woman staggered and fetched up against the wall.

"Good," she uttered. "Now go."

Juleena turned and rushed away, down the hall, to the stairs, and to the party. There were two men standing outside the door, casually chatting with each other. Juleena raced up on feet that were nearly silent, and by the time they noticed her, she was already shoving the double doors open. One grabbed for her arm, but she snatched it out of his grip, and charged into the hall.

Three tables had been set up in a three-sided square shape. At the head table sat her entire family with the addition of Samira and Stratus in places of honor on either side of the Mistress and Master. The maid and guardsman looked up sharply—along with everyone else—but true fear stamped their faces for a blink before they nervously composed themselves. Many of the city's most prosperous merchants and craftspeople, plus the Mrandis branch family and the commanders of the visiting military, and the two Wizards with the military, were seated at the tables. Every eye was on her.

"Juleena?" Rodreric said first as the merriment died. "You're feeling better?"

Mirassi's face had gone waxy, and it was her Juleena was fixed on.

"I've never been better," she declared in a ringing voice. "I am to be a mother."

She stood tall, doing nothing to hide the modest bump of her belly. It could have merely been evidence of an enormous meal, but with her statement still echoing around the room, no one would see it that way. Her father looked like he was choking on something. Mirassi's teeth were bared. She stood.

"You will be a mother," she nodded, "once you marry your husband and go to House Salasis. You're troubled from the day's upset. Return to your room until your mind calms."

"I am calm, and I am carrying a child now," Juleena emphasized.

"You are overwrought and confused," Mirassi corrected. "You will be better with the rest I assigned to you. Kapri will take care of you. Where is she?"

"She tried to stop me coming, so I hit her," Juleena answered. "She, too, is afraid to face your wrath now, Mother. She's upstairs crying. I left her outside my door after I tricked her into opening it."

Mirassi's gaze was darting around the room, touching on manservants and the guardsmen who were there for the celebration. Even the Captain was there, though his arm was in a sling and half his face was as purple as a mumfruit.

"I'm leaving," Juleena went on as defiantly as she could, "and none shall stop me. I renounce my place in House Mrandis. I go to be with the man, the common man, I love, who unknowingly gave me this child, the man you will not accept as my husband—a man far better than any nobleman you suggested I marry."

"You're raving," Mirassi accused.

"Yes, and so completely unsuitable for marriage to House Salasis," Juleena pounced. "Madwomen can't be married."

Her mother's face contorted in shocked rage. "Ungrateful slut," she snarled. "You willful changeling whelp!"

"Mirassi," her husband gasped, standing and trying to draw her behind him, into his arms, and away from view.

She did seem to get herself under some kind of control, but her hand stuck out imperiously from under her husband's arm.

"Take my daughter back to her room and tie her to her bed," she ordered.

Some of the guards and servants shifted, and a few edged in Juleena's direction, but she tossed her head back and stared at them. She put one hand over her belly.

"My mother would have me drink poison to kill a babe conceived in love," Juleena announced. "She'd suggest the same for any child of yours she deemed inconvenient to her."

They halted their approach, glancing at each other with indecision. Juleena went on.

"I've renounced my claim to House Mrandis. I take nothing with me but the clothes I am wearing. No other House will take me as a bride now. Say I have gone mad. Say you have sent me off to a quiet place to live out my days in the care of nurses, with others who have lost their wits."

Damarin, Mirassi's younger brother, and Juleena's uncle suddenly stood. All eyes switched to him. He betrayed a hint of nerves by tugging his jacket straight.

"This is," he began, "indeed a difficult and unfortunate situation, but these things do happen."

"These things do not happen to obedient daughters," Mirassi retorted.

"Certainly, Juleena has not acted as a child of a Noble House should," Damarin nodded. "Perhaps she is correct that she does not belong in one. I think she would only cause trouble were she forced to end the pregnancy and go to Salasis." He bowed around at the gathered guests. "And there is no keeping it a secret anymore. I would invite Juleena to join me in the branch house for this night. Perhaps in the morning, everyone will have a clearer head, and a resolution can be reached."

He stepped cautiously out from his seat. His wife Maresta and their daughter Yusani also stood up and followed him. Juleena eyed him like a nervous cat, not quite poised to run but starting to feel her muscles tense. He stopped a few feet away from her, not trying to touch her.

"Have you eaten today, my niece?" he asked gently. "I can have my cook prepare something for you. You can watch her make it, and see that there is nothing in it that would harm you or your child."

Juleena's stomach growled, and she suddenly felt faint again. With the sudden possibility of escape before her, of someone who could help her, her heart began to calm, her anxiety to release its grip on her, and she knew exhaustion would follow.

"Can you walk as far as the branch house?" Damarin asked.

Her aunt came forward with measured steps, and offered her arm. Juleena's heart was still pounding, but she knew this was some sort of partial rescue, at least. She dared not glance over at Stratus, but she wanted to. Instead, she placidly took her aunt's arm.

"Let's go, Juleena," Maresta whispered.

She let her branch relatives lead her out of the room, and no one tried to stop them. No one even said a word.

Juleena was in a fogged daze as they walked out of the doors of Mrandis House, down the steps, and along the carriage path to the gates. Damarin led the way. Juleena's aunt held her arm, and Yusani came up on her other side and took her other arm, too. They were like soldiers, Juleena thought, guiding their wounded companion off the battlefield, to safety.

Past the gates, they followed the circular road to the branch house that was theirs. A servant met them at the door and Juleena heard Damarin explain in a hushed voice. The branch houses were still luxurious, compared to a common farmer's home, but had far fewer servants, and Maresta and Yusani themselves continued steering Juleena into the kitchen. They sat her at the big table used for food preparation. It was scoured clean and empty now, but momentarily a hefty woman in dress and apron came bustling into the room, still tying on her scarf.

"Hungry, are we?" she chirped. "Well, there's some easy vittles just waiting to be eaten."

"Juleena's going to have a baby," Yusani piped up. "She needs something good for making her and the baby strong."

The cook's cheeks bulged with a smile. "Well, what a lucky one you are. Just give me a moment now."

"And she hasn't eaten all day," Yusani went on boldly. "Her mother locked her in her room and tried to make her take poison to kill the baby." Her head flicked over at Juleena for confirmation. "She did, didn't she?"

Juleena nodded. Then the tears came. They burst out with an undignified sob, and Juleena hid her face in her hands. Maresta rubbed her back and made soothing noises, and the cook tsked.

"It's not right, Mistress Mar," the cook muttered, "if you'll pardon my saying. Imagine a mother doing something like that when her own baby is to have a baby."

"I know Chari," Maresta soothed, "but let's not upset Lady Juleena by speaking of it now."

Yusani wrapped her arms around Juleena's shoulders in a side-hug.

"It'll be alright," she assured her with the naïve confidence of a child.

Maybe, Juleena agreed, she was right. Maybe she'd keep her baby. Maybe she'd even get to go live with Stratus. Maybe Mirassi would even be talked out of taking revenge. But her mother, her family, was gone from her now. Her mother had tried to take away her child, keep her from the man she loved, and those were acts she could never forgive. Her heart ached, and she vowed she would never do such a thing to the child she carried. She put her hand on her belly, and felt a little movement. Into the ache her mother had left behind came a balm of warmth for this new life.

"Here now," the cook encouraged, "something simple for you to start. I'll have to do a bit more work for the rest."

She set down a plate of fruit, mainly winter citrus, and all of it varieties Juleena recognized. She took a piece eagerly, and her mouth rejoiced at the fresh, tart taste.

"Now here's some leftovers from the meal we simple folks had tonight," the cook went on, pulling a pan out from the back of the low-banked oven, where it was staying warm. "Will this suit you?"

Juleena nodded, "that's fine."

"Give me just a minute or three to plate it for you."

It was a mixed soupy dish with lots of potatoes and other root vegetables, early peas, and some meat. The cook cut two slices of bread and arranged them on a wide, shallow bowl. Then she spooned a plentiful serving of the main dish onto the bread, topped it with gravy from another pan, added silverware, and delivered it to her. Beside it, Chari the cook set a mug of fruit tea.

"I know what's safe for a mum and babe," the cook murmured. "I had two of my own, now, didn't I? There's just fruit and a bit of ginger to calm your stomach in here. Don't you worry."

"I'll get a room ready for you," her aunt murmured, and departed.

Yusani stayed, however, taking a seat at the table with Juleena. The cook gave her a plate with a few bits of fruit, too. Yusani grinned and partook.

"Don't worry," the young lady echoed the cook. "No one can get you here. My dad won't let them."

"Not even my mother?"

"Especially not her," Yusani went on, kicking her feet under the table. "She's scared of him."

"My mother is?" Juleena repeated incredulously.

Yusani nodded and grinned with pride. "He might be second born, but he's never let her boss him around, you know? That's why he had to come live in the branch house, even though there's space in the big house for the second born's family. She can't order him around and she doesn't like that."

"My mother does like having her way," Juleena muttered.

The food filled her aching stomach, and after all the stresses of the day, that was enough to trigger the waiting weariness to sneak up and claim her. She cleaned her plate, but was just about to fall asleep on it when Maresta returned with a lamp. Juleena said good night to Yusani and the cook, and followed her aunt to their bathing chamber.

Maresta helped her bathe, and then led her up one flight of stairs to a room at the back of the house. It looked out at a small garden and then the next house back, and back into the city—not towards the Mrandis estate—though it was late enough now that it was too dark to see much. Maresta helped her to bed and despite the unfamiliar surroundings she was asleep almost at once.

"A message for our guest."

Juleena looked up from her breakfast at the man who acted as the general servant for everything a male servant usually did in a House. He answered the door, tended the male members of the family, helped in the kitchen, made repairs that didn't require a skilled craftsman, did any heavy lifting, and most of the more difficult cleaning. At this moment he'd apparently answered the door. He was tall, bronze-skinned with a bit of grey in his thick black hair, and quite discrete; Juleena had noticed how well he kept his mouth shut even as his quick darting eyes hinted that he missed nothing. He was currently carrying a small letter on a plate and wearing a perfectly bland expression.

"For Juleena?" Yusani blurted. "Is it from Mistress Mrandis?"

The manservant bowed slightly in the girl's direction. "The bearer of the message waits in the parlor for Lady Mrandis's reply. It is not Mistress Mrandis." And he said no more.

Juleena stood to accept the letter. "Thank you. I'll just be a moment."

She stepped out of the dining room, into the hall, with the eyes of everyone following her, but no one moved to stop her. Just beyond was a little study, and she went into it and shut the door. In privacy she opened the note. It said simply: "Do you need me?"

There was no name—a wise precaution—but Juleena's face slipped into a smile and warm comfort swelled in her chest and belly. She thought there was only one person it could be from, especially since it bore a crude drawing of a kitten on one corner. He was offering to come get her, to wave his sword or whatever else was needed, and carry her away to safety. Juleena went to the desk and borrowed ink and a quill. She wrote her reply on the same bit of paper: "Not yet." She drew a second kitten beside the first and folded it back up.

"My reply is ready," she announced, returning to the dining room. "May I see the messenger?"

The manservant bowed her forward to the parlor, where a peasant girl just young enough to still avoid the attention of boys was waiting. Juleena passed her the note, along with a coin from her precious store. The girl winked at her, tucked the note down the blouse of her dress, and scampered off, running with the happy abandon of youth.

Juleena had just enough time to return to the dining room and finish her breakfast before the manservant appeared again, his formerly bland expression now a shade more serious.

"Master Damarin, Mistress Maresta," he said. "The heads of House Mrandis are here."

Everyone looked at Juleena again. It was time.

Damarin stood up. "Make them comfortable in the parlor. We'll be there shortly."

Breakfast was cleaned up. Juleena stood by herself for a minute, looking out a window with a view into the city. The morning sun was gilding the roofs golden.

"Are you ready?" Maresta asked her gently. "We'll be there

with you."

"She'll throw me out," Juleena replied. "I know she will, and that's fine with me, but I'm afraid of her going after the father and his family."

"You haven't told anyone who it is yet?"

Juleena shook her head. "And I don't intend to, but it can't be hidden forever, not if I go live with him, which I suppose I shall end up doing."

"We would welcome you here," Maresta offered.

"I want to be a family with my husband and child," Juleena said. "My mother and father still command who lives in the branch houses. I don't think they will permit it."

Maresta gave her shoulder a gentle squeeze. "We'll see. Come along now, and be brave."

Not only her mother and father were waiting for her: Ledren and Cindra were there, too. Cindra's expression was distressed, but the other three just looked somber. The Master and Mistress of Mrandis had already claimed the two best chairs in the room. Ledren and Cindra stood slightly behind them. Maresta guided Juleena to a seat on a couch and sat beside her. Damarin remained standing. Yusani had been sent to her room with a maid for company to wait for news.

"So," Mirassi said into the silence. "Let us conclude this insanity."

Rodreric cleared his throat. "Certainly this situation has been a shock to all of us. Let me be sure I have the events clear. Juleena is with child. Sometime after the time she was promised to Salasis, she contracted this situation and now she wishes to carry the child to birth."

"And marry the father and live as a family," Juleena added pointedly.

Mirassi seemed about to speak, but Rodreric put a restraining hand on her arm, and to Juleena's surprise her mother remained silent.

"Who is the father?"

"I'll tell you what I've already told my mother," Juleena

said. "If you agree to let him join the family, let me marry him instead of Salasis, I'll tell you."

This time Mirassi would not be held back. "And he's common," she spat, "without a coin to his name."

That wasn't exactly true, Juleena knew. Stratus drew a salary as a guardsman, but she wasn't about to mention it. It wasn't enough for him to pay anything significant for her.

"Juleena would be welcome to stay here," Damarin spoke up. "Perhaps she and her unsuitable husband could join the branch family?"

"She is promised to Salasis," Mirassi declared. "An agreement was made. When that is broken, word will spread all among the Houses. Our status will be damaged considerably, not to mention the spouse-price we will lose. Ledren's children will have trouble finding spouses of any quality."

"Salasis is hardly a spouse of quality," Juleena interjected.

"Salasis is a House with good status, and wealth enough to pay well for you," Mirassi countered.

"The Salasis son I was to marry already has a child," Juleena announced, "a bastard he sired on one of the servants."

Everyone shifted uncomfortably except Mirassi who just sniffed. Rodreric winced.

"That's unfortunate," he nodded, "but it happens sometimes."

Juleena pointed at her belly. "It does, doesn't it?"

"Is the father a servant of our House?" Mirassi pounced.

"I'm not telling you anything," Juleena repeated.

"Juleena," Ledren tried, "if you won't work with us, how can we resolve this?"

"Resolve this? Work with you?" she retorted. "What our mother wants is to poison me until I lose the baby so I can still marry Salasis, and then punish the man who gave it to me all unknowing, whom I love. That is all she will accept. Isn't that right, Mother? I have two choices: defy or comply."

Mirassi's teeth were bared, her jaw clenched.

Rodreric rubbed his forehead. "He should have known better, whoever he is."

"He did," Juleena said. "I told him I'd taken care of it, that a babe couldn't happen."

"So you lied to him?" Ledren said.

"No. It was taken care of, but then I messed it up. It was," Juleena grunted, "sort of an accident."

"Juleena," Damarin cut in again. "Did you purposefully orchestrate this situation to bring shame to House Mrandis?"

"No," she asserted.

"You were with this unnamed man because of mutual affection, love?"

"Yes," she nodded. "I didn't mean for there to be a child. I dreaded going to Salasis, to a loveless marriage, but I liked this man, and he liked me, and I wished to know, before I went, what true affection felt like." She shrugged tightly. "I got more than I expected."

"It doesn't matter," Mirassi growled, "what you intended or expected. What matters is what is. Rumors are already spreading thanks to your shortsighted announcement at the celebration last night. At this point, I don't think we can stop word of it reaching Salasis."

Juleena put a hand over her belly. "Then there is no need to make me lose the child. Salasis will no longer take me."

"They might," Rodreric refuted. "We've dispatched a messenger."

Juleena shook her head as fear tightened her throat. "No. I won't go to him."

"You thought you could get out of it by bearing another man's bastard," Mirassi snarled. "If Salasis will still take you, they'll say whether they wish you cured of the bastard, or if they'll permit it born before you go to them. Of course, they'll probably reduce what they're giving for you, though perhaps they'll be happy to know for certain that you can bear."

Juleena suddenly found herself on her feet. "You won't take my child," she declared.

"It would stay here," Cindra piped up. She put a hand on

her own belly. "It could be a companion to your next niece or nephew, if the sexes are the same, or become a servant of House Mrandis. It would be raised in the nursery, the way Samira was for you. Juleena, I'd make sure it was treated kindly. I promise you."

"No." Words came unbidden, pouring from her with emotion that swelled up and overflowed. "I'll raise my baby. I'll take care of it forever, no one else. You aren't killing it, and you aren't taking it. It's your grandchild, Mother," she all but shouted. "It's my child, your own daughter's child."

Mirassi's arm shot out, pointing towards her belly. "That is a mistake that needs correcting."

Juleena clasped her arms over her belly. "I love this child and I love its father. I will go to him and live out my days with him, and we will have more children, made in love, and I will be ten times, a hundred times, happier than if I had gone to Salasis to be raped on my wedding night and every day after until it broke my heart and spirit."

Her voice had been rising with every word until she was yelling loud enough that no one in the house could have failed to hear her. Tears streamed down her cheeks and her jaw shook.

Mirassi jumped to her feet, too. "Rodreric," she ordered in a voice icy with fury, "control your daughter."

The Master of Mrandis grimaced and didn't rise. He turned a pained expression onto his wife. "Mira," he pled, "let her go."

Mirassi's face split into a snarl as vicious as any wolf's. Her head snapped to glare at Juleena. She rushed her, gurgling as she came: "I'll show you your place, filthy, worthless, ungrateful child—"

Her mother's hands closed on her neck. Juleena tried to jerk away, tripped over the foot of the couch and fell towards the wall. Mirassi kept coming as Juleena's eyes widened in unbelieving horror. She tugged at her mother's hands, but they were too strong. Panic drowned her mind, but one hand reached for her pocket. Everyone else in the room was shouting. Rodreric was coming for Mirassi. So was Ledren; so was everybody.

Juleena's blood roared in her ears.

Then Mirassi leapt back with a shriek, as though Juleena's neck had burned her hands like a fully fired oven, but her hands went to her breast, where a spot of blood was staining her dark blue gown black. Juleena slid down the wall at her back, trembling like a terrified puppy, with her harpy dagger clutched in both hands before her. The tip glimmered with a bit of Mirassi's blood.

"The slut," Mirassi screeched. "The little slut stabbed me!"

Maresta was immediately beside Juleena.

"Put that down, Julee," she begged. "It's alright. She won't touch you again."

But Juleena kept her dagger tight in her hands, so tight her dark knuckles were nearly white. Her arms shook. Her clenched jaw trembled. Cindra had drawn Mirassi aside, making a quick examination.

"There's not much bleeding," Cindra was reporting. "It's not very deep. It's not dangerous. It will just need a bandage I think, but of course the physician should look at it."

"She tried to kill me," Mirassi hissed, and then turned venomous eyes on Juleena. "I'll beat you 'til the baby falls. You won't need the tea."

"Enough," Rodreric proclaimed. He stepped firmly between Mirassi and Juleena. "Mirassi, this is over." He looked over his shoulder at his daughter. "Juleena, I wanted so much more for you. I am ashamed that I allowed this to come to pass."

"I have everything I want," Juleena wept, "except a mother that loves me."

Maresta put her arms around her, rocking her gently. "Put the dagger down, Juleena," she urged again. "Please."

"We're going now," Rodreric announced, his voice thick, and thickening more as he spoke his to his disgraced child. "Juleena, it pains me, but you can no longer be a part of this family. Your mother gave you options, but you have chosen your path. We cannot indulge a disobedient daughter and waste House resources on the raising of a bastard grandchild. Your actions have cost us status and your sorely needed spouse-price. Go to the man that put that child in you, and come never more to our House. You are no longer a Mrandis. Your name will be struck from the books as though you were dead and no more shall we speak of you."

A sob wrenched its way out of Juleena's throat. Her whole body shuddered. She didn't see the sorrowful eyes Ledren or Cindra turned on her. They didn't speak as they left. Juleena managed to look up as Rodreric shepherded Mirassi towards the door. Mirassi's expression was pure hate. Another sob racked Juleena's body, and at last she set the dagger down beside her so she could try to wipe her face.

Then just as the Master and Mistress of Mrandis were about to leave, a single word made Juleena freeze like a doe scenting an ice-lion.

"Him."

She looked up. Mirassi's gaze was fixed on the dagger, her face a mixture of disgust and glee. Her eyes went back to Juleena's.

"So," she hissed, voice like the slice of a sword. "The very one I put you in the care of: that ugly, stupid guardsman. Why didn't I see it before?"

"What?" Rodreric uttered.

"That's the oaf you spread your legs for, little slut?" Mirassi gloated on, grinning like a snake. "That's his bastard in your belly?"

Juleena, still almost totally paralyzed, managed to shake her head jerkily.

"Mirassi," Rodreric scolded.

Again, she pointed triumphantly. "That blade: it's a harpy feather. He took it as his reward for slaying one of them at Tuma, and he gave it to you, didn't he?"

"No," Juleena pleaded, fear overcoming her resistance to lying.

"He is gone," Mirassi grinned even wider. "His position, gone." She snapped her fingers. "His family, ruined. I will see to it."

"The one who killed a harpy was Hearthsraven," Rodreric said. "He is also the one that treated with the dragon yesterday." His voice became stronger. "He saved our home, possibly our city, and surely many lives, maybe even our own."

Mirassi's vindictive stare never wavered from Juleena's face. It was like she hadn't heard anything Rodreric had said.

The Master of Mrandis grabbed his wife's arm. "Mirassi, enough," he commanded again. "Juleena has been punished enough."

"But he hasn't," she yowled like an angry cat, turning on her husband. "That swine took your daughter like a flea-bitten mutt on a prize bitch and you'd leave him free to do it again?"

Rodreric frowned. "Perhaps reassignment is in order, but—"

"I made him," Juleena gasped out. "He tried to do the right thing. He turned me down, he kept me away as long as he could, but I couldn't help it, and—"

Mirassi's face flashed back to her. "You disgust me," she spat. "You are not my daughter."

The Mistress of Mrandis wrenched her arm free from her husband's grip and stormed out the door. Behind her, Juleena burst again into helpless, frail sobs. Rodreric sighed.

"I'm sorry, Juleena," he said. "I wish this had gone some other way."

He drew a small pouch from his belt, and set it on the floor beside the harpy dagger. It clinked with the sound of coins.

"I cannot give you more, or it would be noticed. I do hope you will find happiness with Hearthsraven. He seems to me to be a good man, from what little I know of him. It's best I have him reassigned, to take him out of your mother's view, but I won't let her ruin him or his family."

Juleena managed to stutter her thanks.

"I'm sorry," Rodreric said again.

"I'm sorry, too," she sobbed. "I wasn't a good daughter."

Her father sighed. "Goodbye, Juleena."

Then he was gone.

***

It took some time for Juleena to calm down and compose herself. Once she had, she asked her uncle to send a message to the Hearthsraven house in Trivale. An hour later came a knock at the door, and Juleena came out to see Missus Hearthsraven standing in the parlor with a smile not untouched by sorrow, but a smile nonetheless. She opened her arms and Juleena sailed into them. She leaked some more tears, but Missus Hearthsraven wiped them away.

"So the day has come, my new, brave daughter," she whispered merrily. "Let us get you and my grandchild home, and we will start planning your wedding to my poor, unworthy son."

Juleena answered her smile with one of her own, and turned away long enough to say her good byes to her uncle, aunt, cousin, and the servants of the branch house.

"Mirassi won't stand for much," Damarin warned, "but if ever you need help, I pledge to do what I can. Just send a message."

"Thank you," Juleena said, giving him a hug. "And thank you Maresta and Yusani, and everyone for taking care of me." She shared out hugs to all of them. "Yusani, you go marry that Lorinan boy you like so much."

Maresta chuckled a little. "After the example you've set, I think we'd better let her do whatever she wants."

"And it does look like that's the way it will work out," Damarin added, giving his daughter's shoulder a squeeze.

Yusani beamed. "And tell us when you've had the baby," she ordered, "and if it's a girl or a boy, and what you name it."

"Alright," Juleena agreed. "I'll send a message."

Damarin pressed another pouch into her hand. "It's not much," he said, much as her father had.

"Thank you," Juleena repeated, and hugged him again.

"Neither Juleena nor her child will starve," Missus Hearthsraven promised.

"I should go," she said at last.

"All the best of love and luck to you," Damarin bade.

Juleena left with Missus Hearthsraven, the Mrandis estate at her back, and the road through Lenali before her. Missus Hearthsraven took her hand and guided it to her arm.

"My name is Helena," she said. "I don't suppose my foolish son told you."

"He didn't," Juleena admitted, "though he told me the names of all his brothers and their wives and children."

"And my husband's name is Ruslin. Call me whatever you like," Helena instructed, "though Ona and Alaurie call me Helena, or Mum Helena."

"Will they be alright with me living together with them now?"

"They'll be fine. You know, Alaurie is going to have her third baby in a few weeks. You'll be arriving just in time to help out with the other children."

Juleena smiled. "A house full of babies."

"Yes, indeed," Helena nodded, also smiling. "The Hearthsraven house will indeed be blessed with babies."

Stratus wasn't home when Juleena arrived, and she spent the day helping with the children, and starting to learn to prepare food—which she'd never had to do before. When she tired she sat by a window in strong light and started working on some embroidery, on a lovely, soft shawl Alaurie gave her in welcome. She was just beginning to set the table, guided by Ona, when Stratus came through the door.

His troubled expression, heavy with storm clouds, lightened like the sun breaking through when he saw her. They all but raced at each other, and he swung her around in his arms when he caught her. Then they stood in the dining room, wrapped in each other's arms, amid the smiles of their family, serenaded by little Glory's giggles.

When at last they could let go, they sat down together for dinner. Alaurie and Ona set to planning the wedding, but Juleena and Stratus hardly listened. They sat next to each other, holding hands—which forced Stratus to use his non-dominant left hand for eating. After dinner, Alaurie and Juleena were banished to the couches opposite the kitchen counters, on the far side of the dinning room table, while the others cleaned up, which didn't take much time with six adults and Glory's eager assistance.

Glory's little brother, Dansen, and Ona's toddler Juris played with wooden toys in front of the couch, until the clean up was done and everyone else joined them. Stratus inserted himself as Juleena's backrest. Ona and Helena took up items to be mended. Magnus sat at the table, cleaning and oiling several sets of leather boots. Tamarus stretched out on the floor and built block castles with his son. The master of the house opened a heavy book to a worn satin bookmark midway through, and began to read of monsters and magic, griffins, dragons, unicorns, and all manner of Wild Ones.

The children listened eagerly, except for Juris who seemed not to have developed the attention span just yet, and dropped off to sleep one by one. Juleena leaned back against her soon-to-be husband, the father of her child, and for some time just basked in the unfamiliar but soothing gathering of family together, and tried to get herself to believe that this was her family now, that she was a part of this exquisite magic.

She, too, drifted off to sleep, lulled by Mister Hearthsraven's deep and melodious voice, the crackle of the fire, and the scent of leather and wood. She woke a little as Stratus was carrying her up the stairs, and more fully as he laid her on his bed.

"I need to get out of these clothes," she pointed out, starting to sit up.

Stratus pushed her back down with a kiss. "I'll help with that," he grinned.

Stratus had indeed lost his position among the guardsmen assigned to the Mrandis estate. He'd been relocated to the Trivale Guard. It was a pay cut and a demotion, but it kept him closer to home, making it easier for him to see his family every day and sleep at home instead of in the barracks. His Captain who'd witnessed his negotiation with the mist dragon, however, had sent a glowing recommendation to the Captain of the Trivale

Guard, and everyone knew of his fame both in the defeat of the harpy and the pacification of the dragon, and he was treated with respect.

The knowledge that he had somehow stolen the Lady of Mrandis away from her destiny of marrying into House Salasis couldn't be kept a secret, and soon everyone in both Trivale and Lenali knew that, too. The guardsmen had heard what Salasis was like, and most of them were decent men who at least held that Salasis was not behaving honorably. They knew what Stratus was like and all had admiration for him. Neither Juleena nor Stratus received taunts or sneers from any of them, but the two conducted themselves with civility and decorum as well, which surely helped.

The wedding was a quiet one. Juleena didn't even have a fancy dress, although she'd embroidered the shawl Alaurie had given her with kittens and dragons—not harpies, because they were so vile—and wore it around her shoulders. Ona and Alaurie had wanted to involve all of Trivale with the traditional banquet tables and music and dancing in the town hall, but Juleena had pointed out, and all had eventually agreed, that making a fuss would only make House Mrandis more disgraced and prone to further revenge. Instead, the book had been signed in a short, private ceremony, with only the Hearthsraven family and Stratus's new Captain present—and one more. Juleena's uncle Damarin had snuck down to Trivale under a cloak and was there to stand as her next-of-kin.

After the wedding, Helena had taken both Alaurie and Juleena to the village midwife for a check up. Alaurie was almost due, and it was the first time in her pregnancy that Juleena had been seen by any kind of healer. Both women were pronounced to be healthy, and their babies, too. The midwife gave Juleena lots of advice—and so did everyone else. Helena seemed supremely confident that she could manage Juleena's pregnancy. After all, she'd had children of her own, and overseen Alaurie's previous two and Ona's. Juleena followed along as if in a dream, too happy to worry about anything.

A few days later the whole Hearthsraven family was surprised by a carter pausing outside their house to deliver a pair of heavy sacks.

"No need, Hearthsraven," the carter grunted when Ruslin tried to pay him for the unexpected delivery. "I've been paid already." He lowered his voice. "By old Mum Hyldi of you-know-where."

The man drove off his cart without another word, and now consumed with curiosity, several pairs of hands went to open the sacks on the kitchen table. Juleena stared in amazement at what they contained.

"My clothes," she whispered, "almost all of them, even my," her breath hitched.

There in the bottom of one of the sacks, crumpled up like thrice-used palimpsest, was the gown she would have worn to marry Terkari: black and red, blue and yellow, covered with her months of jewel-bright embroidery.

"A note, Julee," Ona spoke up, handing over a folded bit or parchment.

Juleena opened it and read, and reported. "It's from Mum Hyldi, the head of our servants—of the servants of House Mrandis, I mean. She says my mother ordered my clothing burned, but she thought that was a senseless waste and had most of them secretly sent to me."

"But," Alaurie ventured, "you can't go about wearing them."

"No," Juleena agreed. "I can't. No one can."

"Perhaps some of the fabric could be repurposed," Mum Helena suggested. "Or the dresses just saved, until someday they're safe to wear."

"They should be sold," Juleena declared, "not here, but in another town."

"Well," Missus Hearthsraven soothed. "We'll see about it. There's no rush. The undergarments at least can be reused. I was just thinking our stockings were looking thin."

Juleena didn't argue as her mother-in-law and Ona took the sacks away upstairs. It didn't really matter what happened to the dresses, as long as she never saw them again, nor the inhabitants of Trivale or Lenali. Mirassi had to think them burned. If word ever got back to her that they hadn't been, Mum Hyldi would be in trouble.

"Are you alright, Julee?" Alaurie asked gently.

She shook her head a little. "My mother hates me."

"She loves you, as all mothers do," Alaurie murmured. "There are just a lot of other things getting in the way of her love. If she didn't care, she'd have just given your gowns to someone else, your sister, or saved them for when her granddaughter gets old enough. You say House Mrandis lost your spouse-price. She can't afford to destroy gowns like these on a whim, but she's so sad you're gone, she couldn't bear to see them anymore."

"Because she hates me," Juleena repeated stubbornly. "I didn't do what she wanted. I defied her, so she scrubbed me from her life."

Alaurie rubbed her back a little, nodding. "You might not be a Mrandis anymore, but now you have a family that loves you, and a husband, and soon a child, while she's lost her child. I think it's true she did wrong by you, but she can't hurt you now. You shouldn't be angry at her anymore, Julee. You should pity her. She's in pain, to do a thing like this."

Juleena furrowed her brow, trying to take in everything Alaurie was saying.

"I'm not saying you don't have the right to be angry," she went on. "But anger is heavy. Maybe you shouldn't carry it around forever. Let me get you some tea."

"No, I can do it," Juleena replied immediately. "You sit."

Alaurie smiled indulgently, a hand on her enormous abdomen, as Juleena—only half as big—set the water to boiling and began fetching mugs.

"And someday," Alaurie concluded, when Juleena at last set the tea mug into her hands, "you should think about who has really won this war between you and her, and then you should consider forgiving her."

Juleena sat with her own tea and let Alaurie's words settle

into her mind and eventually trickle down to her heart. She felt her spirit begin to lighten. Maybe Alaurie was right, that anger was heavy and she'd been carrying a lot of it around. She hadn't ever thought she would, but she did feel a hint of sympathy for her mother: not much, just a little. Maybe someday she indeed would be able to forgive her.

Juleena set tea for the midwife on the table. Ona was helping Alaurie pace around the room.

"Keep walking," the midwife, a sepia-skinned woman with long grey hair done in braids commanded idly. She accepted the tea in a wrinkled but strong hand and grinned at Juleena. "I don't even know why I'm here. This is Alaurie's third and her second took hardly an hour. This'll be over any minute."

Juleena sat down across from her with her own mug of tea.

"Yours now, it will be your first," the midwife said after a long drink. "Get ready to be up all night and a day."

"Mine didn't take that long, Ma'am Paneli," Ona commented.

The midwife Paneli shrugged. "Juris was a little early, sort of small. It still took you a good ten hours."

"Don't let her scare you, Julee," Helena scolded as she tended a pot on the stove, getting it to boil. "You'll be fine."

"You're doing those exercises?" Paneli asked Juleena.

"I am, ma'am," she replied with a nod.

"To think," Helena went on, "a midwife is supposed to comfort and support, not terrify first-time mothers."

"I'm the best in Trivale," Paneli slurped. "Maybe the best in Lenali, too, because I don't coddle the girls. Birthing a baby is the hardest thing you'll ever do, especially your first. It's so hard it can kill you." She slurped tea again. "Their mothers and sisters give them plenty of sympathy. I'm there to make them work, and keep them and their babies alive."

"Paneli," Alaurie called urgently.

"Let's do this then," the midwife grunted, setting down her tea hard enough that a few drips jumped out.

Juleena was there to learn. Paneli thought that sometime

around midsummer it would be her turn. She'd been kept away from her sister Cindra's childbed, but the Hearthsravens had completely different ideas about it. Tamarus had taken the children out to play, and Magnus was in the workshop with his father, both of them sweating over some project or other and waiting for news. Stratus was on duty, so didn't get to participate at all, but that couldn't be helped. Helena, Ona, and Juleena were gathered to help Alaurie, with the midwife of course.

So Juleena stood by and watched and listened, ready to help if any of them needed anything. Paneli's assessment seemed to be accurate, however. Alaurie squatted over a layer of old towels that had been boiled clean and sun-dried. Helena and Ona held her hands and helped her balance. It still took Alaurie a good half an hour, and much panting, grunting, and even a little screaming, but then Paneli was catching the baby—which was also screaming—and it was all but over.

"A girl," Paneli announced, "with a good set of lungs, and all the standard appendages."

It was quite messy. Juleena hadn't really known what to expect, and sat rather wide-eyed watching the rest of the procedure. A temporary pallet had been set up by the stove, and Alaurie was moved to it as soon as she had been cleaned up a bit. Ona made her as comfortable as possible and gave her tea and fruit. Helena began cleaning up the soiled towels, while Paneli tended to the baby for a few minutes, washed her, and then deposited her still fussing onto Alaurie's bare belly.

"She looks good," Paneli said. "I give her good chances, and the weather is warm and the general village health steady right now."

"We'll wait the month," Helena murmured, "as customary."

"I'll report the live birth to the town hall, and check in on mother and child tomorrow," Paneli nodded. "Send for me sooner if you have need."

"Will you take coin or trade?" Helena went on, drawing Paneli away from Alaurie and Ona.

Juleena didn't hear the midwife's reply, for she went over

closer to the stove and timidly looked down. Ona noticed her, smiled, and waved her in, so she approached and knelt. Alaurie had wrapped blankets around herself and the babe. The little girl was mostly quiet now. Her tiny hand was wrapped around Alaurie's finger, and her eyes were shut. Juleena didn't know what to say, but stared in fascination at the new little life.

"That wasn't too scary was it, Juleena?" Alaurie smiled softly. "Don't worry. It's all worth it."

"What will you call her?" she asked in a near whisper.

Alaurie shook her head. "Not yet. We wait the month."

Juleena was perplexed. "Wait the month?"

"In case she isn't meant to stay," Ona explained quietly.

Juleena gave her a pained frown.

"They don't all stay," Ona went on. The young woman glanced up at Missus Hearthsraven's turned back, where she stood near the door with Paneli, and lowered her voice further. "Mum Helena had two daughters who didn't stay. So far, Alaurie and I have been lucky."

"For a month she will just be 'little girl.' After that, we'll name her," Alaurie said confidently.

Juleena's confused frown hadn't gone away. She couldn't let herself believe what they were saying. Ona reached out and touched her hand where it rested on her knee.

"I'm sure she'll stay," Ona said. "Paneli herself said it: she's strong. I'm sure your baby will be strong, too. Just sometimes, it isn't meant to be. Sometimes, we hold our babies only for a while, so we don't name them for a month, because if they're going to leave us, it's most likely in the first month. It makes it a little easier. It's something all parents know could happen. Did your—did you never hear about it?"

"No one really told me," Juleena managed. "Of course, I've heard of it, sort of, but it was always, I mean, I never—"

"You always thought of it as something that happened to someone else," Alaurie guessed. "I suppose it happens less often in the Noble Houses."

"Mothers can die in the birth, too," Ona said.

"I know," Juleena nodded nervously.

Alaurie put her hand atop Ona's, atop Juleena's. "It is the risk we bear to bring our children into the world."

Paneli was gone, and it seemed Helena had summoned Magnus, for he was suddenly there, and Juleena scooted aside for him. Alaurie's face lit up with joy, and his likewise, and he huddled beside her on the floor, an arm around her, his other hand delicately stroking his new daughter's head. Mother and father clung to each other and cried happy tears. Ona and Juleena got out of their way and now that the excitement was over, set about making dinner.

The new baby was the celebrity for the next several days, with Glory especially spending a lot of time helping her mother with her baby sister. Paneli the midwife stopped by daily at first, and then a few times a week, but it quickly became apparent that both mother and child had recovered from the birth and had good prospects. When the month of waiting was past, Helena and Ona—with Juleena helping as much as she could—made enough food for a party.

They sat to partake, with the baby girl in her basket in a place of honor at the head of the table, though of course she couldn't eat any of the food yet and surely had no idea the party was for her. Everyone ate with good appetite, but the food was second to what they were all really looking forward to—the naming of the babe. When at last the plates had been cleaned and Missus Hearthsraven had put a platter of apple oat cookies on the table, all eyes turned expectantly to Magnus and Alaurie, sitting on either side of their baby.

They reached across to hold hands.

"What is it? What is it?" Glory bounced in her seat.

"Hush now," Helena admonished gently, but she, too, was clearly eager to hear.

Magnus smiled and nodded at his wife.

"Evalyn," she announced. "We're naming her Evalyn."

The gathering broke into grins, quiet applause—so as not

to upset the baby—and soft cries of "welcome Evalyn—Evalyn Hearthsraven."

Everyone gathered around the basket to give the tiny girl a pat on the head or kiss on the cheek. Juleena, too, got the chance to touch Evalyn's delicate little hand. The baby had her eyes open, and was giving everyone a good look-over. All this excitement had her frowning as though she questioned their motives in coming to say hello to her en masse.

"Hi, Evalyn," Juleena whispered to her. "Welcome to the family."

Then came a knock on the front door. Mister Hearthsraven got up to go answer it. Juleena wondered if it might be Paneli, or maybe some other elder of the town, come to give their congratulations. Mister Hearthsraven did not immediately return, however, and after a minute, Helena led the group in clearing away any lingering dish ware on the table, and anyone not so occupied fetched their usual evening chores—mending or cleaning or whatever else could be done by lamp light—or entertainment in the form of toys for the children or books for the adults.

"Juleena," her father-in-law called then, and she paused as she was about to select a book. "Will you come here? You have a visitor."

His face was not cheerful, but nor did he give the posture that would suggest he thought the visitor dangerous to her. Juleena went to him, passing Stratus, who glanced at her with concern, but did not join her when she patted him reassuringly on the shoulder.

"You can speak with her in the mud room," Mister Hearthsraven murmured, and held the door open for her.

Juleena stepped down into the little entry room. A figure in a dark cloak was waiting for her. Then the figure reached up with youthful feminine hands and lowered her hood, exposing a head of red hair and profuse freckles.

"Samira," Juleena gasped.

The two women embraced, clutching at each other with warm fervency.

"Are you alright?" Juleena asked.

"I'm fine," her former maid replied. "I don't know if I fooled your mother when I told her I knew nothing about your pregnancy, and she demoted me to kitchen girl, but the cook is good to me, and Mum Hyldi, too."

They parted but kept holding hands.

"Julee," Samira whispered. "I come with sad news. Mum Hyldi thought you should know before all the town knows, and had me come in secret."

Juleena stilled with apprehension. "What is it?"

Samira's expression was indeed somber, and now that Juleena looked, she thought the young woman might have been crying recently. Even now, her face pinched up and her chin quivered.

"Sami?" Juleena breathed.

"It's Cindra," she gulped out.

Juleena's heartbeat hitched and pounded with dread, but Cindra had been happy and healthy last time she'd seen her. She'd always been healthy, ever since she came to Mrandis House, even through her first pregnancy and birth. How could anything have happened to her?

"She was with child, did you know?" Samira asked tearfully.

"She said something like that, yes," Juleena replied, recalling her sister-in-law's comment about their children growing up together.

"It went bad. It happens sometimes."

"She lost the baby?" Juleena guessed, feeling some relief that a miscarriage was all it was. "It was still early, only a few months, right? It's sad, but it happens sometimes."

Samira shook her head vigorously, some strands of loose hair lashing about her face. "Julee, she died. She died."

And then the maid was sobbing aloud, and Juleena wrapped her up in her arms, her own thoughts and feelings shocked like a fish slapped on a stone. It took a minute to penetrate. Cindra, so alive, such a gentle mother to her little daughter, such a kind spouse to Ledren—was dead.

"The physician," Samira hiccupped, "he said it was the pregnancy. It killed her."

"How can that happen?" Juleena babbled.

"She bled inside, he says. He couldn't do anything."

Juleena clung to Samira, and by and by the lump rose in her throat, hard as stone, and then her own weeping began. They rocked each other and mourned together. Some minutes passed until they both managed to straighten and wipe their cheeks.

"Thank you for coming to tell me," Juleena rasped. "Will you come in for some tea? We just named Alaurie's new baby. She's the wife of Stratus's oldest brother—Alaurie I mean, not the baby, of course. The baby's his daughter, Evalyn."

Her words had been nowhere near sensical, but Samira nodded like she understood perfectly.

"I should get back. I don't want to be missed," Samira said regretfully.

Juleena could only nod in acceptance, still too heart-sore to push for anything more.

"How's your baby?" Samira asked.

That brought a little smile to Juleena's face. "Fine, moving more now. The midwife says midsummer."

"You'll send a message, tell me if it's a girl or a boy, and it's name?"

"I told my cousin Yusani I would."

"I'll ask her then," Samira nodded. "Safer."

They stood facing each other for a few more moments, brushing away straggling tears and sniffling a little.

"Be well, Julee," Samira whispered. "I miss you."

"I miss you, too."

They hugged again, and then the maid put up her hood, and turned to step out the door, into the dusk. Juleena took another few heartbeats to herself after the door shut, trying to calm her emotions. Cindra was gone, and her unborn baby with her. That left only her daughter for Ledren to raise alone—or rather, the servants would raise her; there was no chance of the girl being neglected. In fact, now she would be treasured and pampered and carefully kept from any chance of harm.

Myra hadn't had any babies yet. Juleena wondered if Ledren might remarry; he was still young enough to get another wife and have more babies—except no, there wouldn't be much money for it, since Juleena hadn't been sold to Salasis, and the status of House Mrandis had taken a major hit from Juleena's behavior and banishment. Finding him a new wife would be difficult unless he tried to find one among the branch families of other Houses, where little payment would be needed other than the elevation of status, but Juleena suspected her mother would never allow such a thing.

Juleena took a deep breath and squared her shoulders. Mrandis had thrown her out; what happened to them was none of her affair any longer. She was a Hearthsraven now: Juleena Hearthsraven. She had a new family, and they needed her, and she needed them. Her own baby would be a Hearthsraven, too. The sorrow of Cindra's death still ached, but distantly; Juleena wasn't a part of that world any longer.

She turned and went back inside to resume the celebration with her true family.

The months passed into the heat of summer, through the last of the spring storms, and Juleena's time drew closer and closer as her belly continued to swell. Paneli the midwife kept more frequent watch on her, but at each meeting declared that all was well. Juleena continued the exercises she'd been set—meant to strengthen her body for the birthing, for she knew it would come as surely as the sunrise.

Very near the longest day of the year, it did. Helena, Alaurie, and Ona had seen and done it all before. Ona was sent to fetch Paneli. Helena prepared the towels and water. Alaurie sat with Juleena to help keep her calm and focused. The pallet by the stove was ready, for Juleena hadn't made the trek up to the attic to sleep for about a week, sleeping instead by the stove—though it was summer and the stove now was used only for necessary cooking, not heating. Paneli arrived and the waiting began. Hours passed as Paneli directed Juleena to walk about, or rest, or drink.

"I told you it would take a day and a night," the midwife asserted. "Stratus is a big fellow, and you're not exactly tiny, but that's a good sized babe you're carrying, and it's your first. Oh, don't look like that, you'll be fine."

The three craftsmen of the family stayed out of the way, doing their work that not even a birthing could justify delaying. There was nothing they could do to help anyway. Stratus came home after his shift to find the womenfolk gathered as womenfolk have gathered since womenfolk first existed: in the ancient ritual of birth-watch.

"Take the little ones out for a bit, won't you?" Helena urged after he'd bathed and eaten.

So Stratus took Glory, Dansen, and Juris to the town hall for a while, and even the long day eventually gave over the sky to the sparkling of stars. When Stratus at last returned—Juris sleeping in his arms and Glory and Dansen hanging on his tunic tails—Juleena was up and beginning to brace herself for the main event. But Stratus was sent then to bathe the children with Tamarus's help, and when Juleena started screaming he was up to his elbows in soapy water.

"Take them up," Helena ordered the men when they emerged with the children from the house's little bathing room.

Juleena hardly noticed as the three children, crying with distress at all the groaning and yelling she was doing, were carried up the stairs to their rooms on the second floor of the house. Magnus had already taken little Evalyn up, and Mister Hearthsraven had gone with him. Alaurie held Juleena's arm on one side: Ona on the other. Paneli and Helena were waiting, on their knees before her with towels and twine and a knife and boiled water, now just warm.

"Now then," Panelie nodded.

Helena knotted Juleena's shift up by her hip, getting it out of the way now that the men were gone. Then the real work began. Later, Juleena would feel that she remembered little of it.

All was pain and strain and vision gone nearly red with effort. Everyone kept reminding her to breathe while she felt like she was being ripped apart. She would never forget Paneli's eyes. They were sort of orange-brown in color, bright and piercing, and Juleena stared into them for however many hours it took. It felt like it must have been the whole night, but it wasn't, for after the baby finally slid into Paneli's strong, wrinkled hands, the sky was still dark and the moon was still up.

Juleena nearly collapsed, and only Ona and Alaurie prevented her from planting her face into the floor. Then Juleena heard the most beautiful sound she could ever recall: the first cry of her child. Blindly she tried to reach out, seeking the source of that sound, but her arms were still held.

"Almost, Julee," Ona soothed. "Just another minute."

She managed to nod, somehow recalling that there was a little more business to be done: the afterbirth.

"A girl," Paneli announced, much as she had after the birth of Evalyn, "with good lungs, and all the standard appendages."

Her womenfolk cleaned her up, dressed her a little, and bundled her onto the pallet. Juleena again reached her arms out for the source of the ongoing crying. With half an eye she noticed Ona scampering up the stairs.

Then Paneli brought her daughter to her and laid her on her bare belly. Suddenly Stratus was running down the stairs and beside her, too. He lay half on his side, his arm around her shoulders. They rested their heads together and looked down on their little girl. Helena was talking with Paneli, but neither paid any attention.

The baby sprawled, belly to belly with Juleena. Its skin was lighter than hers, not as light as Stratus's, and on her back, right down the spine, were a few splotches and speckles of even lighter skin. She had hair, and it was as black as Juleena's, though it was thin, still damp, and might be lighter when it dried. Her eyes were a little murky still, but Juleena thought they showed a hint of red-brown, like her father's. She'd stopped crying, and gently Juleena and Stratus together lifted her closer to their faces, laying her on Juleena's chest. Stratus pulled a blanket—the softest one the family owned and saved for occasions just like this—up over her, leaving just her head and shoulders bare.

"She's beautiful," Stratus uttered, throat sounding choked with emotion. Tears streaked down his face. "She's the most beautiful thing I've ever seen."

He reached out, and the babe instinctively clutched his finger when he nudged it into her little palm. She made a slight little gurgle.

"What shall we call her?" Juleena whispered.

"We can't," Stratus breathed back, "not for a month."

"I know, but provided the month passes, did you have any thoughts?"

They hadn't talked about it, although Juleena had been thinking of names for both boys and girls ever since she'd embraced the reality that she would birth the baby. Nothing she'd thought of had seemed exactly right, and she'd supposed she wouldn't know the exactly right name until she met the baby face to face—and until she'd talked it over with Stratus.

"We'll talk about it," he murmured, "as the month passes. Do you mind? Let's just wait, just to be sure."

Juleena nodded. "Alright."

Juleena was given several days of rest, with Ona playing nursemaid to both her and her little girl. Alaurie had her hands full with her own baby, and Helena took on the majority of the housework, with Glory as the oldest child being introduced to more and more chores. Stratus had been granted a few days off, too, and Ona was rapidly educating him on how to care for his daughter—though he knew some already from helping care for his nieces and nephews.

Eventually of course, Juleena regained her feet and strength. She'd been learning as much as she could about baby care from Alaurie's infant, and applied all she knew to her own child. The baby thrived, and both she and Evalyn benefitted from having two mothers who could nurse either child at need. Though both were too tiny yet to do much interaction, they seemed to sleep best when they were put to bed together.

Days became weeks, and the one-month anniversary of the baby's birth came. The little one was strong and bright, with a smile for all who looked upon her, so another naming party was planned. This time it was Juleena and Stratus's baby in the basket at the head of the table. They had discussed the topic of names when it seemed that the child would indeed reach the one-month mark. Many had been considered. Often, girl babies were named after their mother's mother, or mother's grandmother. Juleena had considered that, but in the end had decided not to leave her child marked with any link to Mrandis House.

Stratus had given a different suggestion.

"My mother had two girl babies," he'd said as they cuddled, all three, in his bed up in the attic. "Neither of them survived. The first didn't live the month, and was never named. It was firstborn, before me or my brothers. The second was born after us. I remember her, just a little. She was healthy and hale for almost a year, but then she got sick. So did the rest of us, but we survived it. She didn't."

"It wouldn't be an ill omen?" Juleena checked, "to use an unlucky name?"

"It was also my mother's mother's name, and she lived to be near eighty."

That was old indeed, especially for commoners whose lives were much harder than those of the nobility.

"What's the name?" Juleena asked.

He told her.

"It wouldn't upset your mother, if we used the name of her daughter?"

"Her heart is healed," he said. "I think she would be pleased to see the name finally passed on, as she tried to do."

"Alright then," Juleena agreed. "So it shall be."

So when everyone had eaten and the cookies were again on the table, and Glory was again bouncing with excitement, Stratus reached his hand across the table for his wife's. Juleena looked around at the members of her family—one she was joined to now by blood. Mister and Missus Hearthsraven showed grey in their hair. Magnus and Tamarus were becoming well versed in their father's trade. Stratus had the strength and skill to protect them all. Five children now in the house, from three married couples, cared for fiercely by their trio of mothers, brought joy and chaos and the promise of the future.

Juleena squeezed Stratus's hand and smiled down at her daughter.

"Vorella," she said. "Vorella Hearthsraven."

The End

Thank you for reading!

Did you enjoy the journey?

Please leave a rating or review on
Goodreads, Amazon, or wherever
you talk about books.

Reviews help books get to readers
who might enjoy them.

You can find more information about me
and my books, and updates on future books,
at my website or on my Facebook page or
Goodreads page.

www.elucidationimages.com
Kasmith Art & Books

About the Author

Katherine grew up in Fort Bragg, California and has since lived in Ithaca, New York; Morioka and Yokosuka, Japan; and currently resides in the San Francisco Bay Area, California.

Katherine's lifelong love of fantasy inspires her stories, while she draws upon her education in zoology and scientific illustration to infuse her work with realism.

This is her eighth fantasy book, the first collection of short stories from her Northnest Saga series. She has also released two children's books. In addition to writing and art, she enjoys making theatre, dancing, reading, and bird watching.

To learn more about Katherine's creations, visit Goodreads or elucidationimages.com. Find Kasmith Art & Books on Facebook.

Thank you for reading, rating, and reviewing!

www.ingramcontent.com/pod-product-compliance
Lightning Source LLC
Chambersburg PA
CBHW011204190726
48288CB00013B/3322